FLAWS
AND
PASSION

INNOCENT
NLEWEDIM

L.R. Price Publications Ltd

INNOCENT NLEWEDIM

Flaws and Passion

First published in Great Britain by

L.R. Price Publications Ltd 2017
27 Old Gloucester Street,
London, WC1N 3AX
www.lrpricepublications.com

ISBN13 : 978-0-9929037-8-7

DEDICATION

"I want to thank my family who have endured so much over the years. It has been a difficult journey, but your support and encouragement has not only inspired me to do more and become a better writer, but also a better person.

Although I am absent, I would like everyone to know that this event brings nothing but happiness to my heart and I thank God for giving me a voice and the medium to reach out to you on this day. "

FLAWS
AND
PASSION

INNOCENT
NLEWEDIM

FLAWS AND PASSION

CHAPTER 1

The children ran at the sound of the woman's screams.

Seconds earlier they had been playing in the snow outside. Now they rushed to the safety of their parents.

A crowd gathered outside the home of Mrs Adriana Meredian. A 57 year old widow who'd lost her husband to cancer two years ago. They banged on her door and shouted for her. It was several minutes before she appeared with blood smeared all over her bath robe and hands. Then she collapsed.

The crowd became frantic. A few pulled back into their homes, others shrank against walls while those at the fore front of the calamity tried to resuscitate the woman laying unconscious on the floor.

"Somebody call 999", one of the men shouted. Two mothers ran into their homes to get to their phones. They knocked over kids as they ran, and hit a few others gathered in the crowd so hard they fell sprawling in the snow.

Minutes the sounds of sirens could be heard in the distance. As the police and ambulance cars approached the scene, neighbours were pointing them in the direction of the old ladies house where many were gathered. Two police men and three paramedics dashed out of their cars. running towards the scene of the incident.

Everyone was in disbelief as they saw the medics spring into action. Children were watching in horror as the police officers tried to diffuse the situation, urging them to return to their homes whilst making room for the paramedics to carry out their duties.

Seconds later, a body was being stretched out towards the ambulance. But it wasn't Adriana Meredian, it was her daughter Judith.

CHAPTER 2

Adriana embraced herself watching in silent terror as her daughter clung to life and the paramedics fought to stop the bleeding.

Judith had multiple deep cuts on both her wrist with a six inch blade stuck to her chest. she was turning grey and her blood was everywhere, the floor, the linen she was covered in, the green suits worn by the paramedics, the trolley, her mothers blanket, robe and hands.

Adriana had already lost her husband and her son Ben. she couldn't lose Judith – she was her life, all she had left.

" Please tell me she is going to be OK," Adriana said in a strangled voice.

Neither of the paramedics had an immediate answer for her. They couldn't answer because they did not know.

"We are doing all we can to stop the bleeding. she is loosing blood very fast and we need to get her into surgery immediately."

Adriana replied by sobbing even harder. she wished her husband was still alive now. she had no one to share this burden with.

The ambulance stopped outside the hospital and the paramedics raced out of the ambulance with Judith on the trolley.

she had bandages on both of her arms, an oxygen mask over her face and all Adriana was hopeful about was that her daughter was still breathing, but barely. she raced into the emergency room with the medics but was taken into a side room.

she continued asking the nurses what was going to

happen to her daughter. she asked what they were going to do to save her life. she needed reassurance that her daughter was going to be alright. she was increasingly getting agitated so one of the nurses led her to a little cluster of chairs in the corner of the emergency hall and sat her down.

" You need to settle yourself down madam", the nurse said bluntly.

" How can I , my daughter is dying for goodness sake".

" They are going to begin operating soon so there are a few things we must do immediately", The nurse said.

" Like What!"

" Once you sign this consent forms quickly they will have your permission to start operating".

she signed the consent form.

Moments later the nurse stormed off with the documents while another approached the distressed woman offering her some tablets and a cup of water.

" Here, drink this, it would help calm your nerves a little bit. Operations go on for hours, you need to relax". The nurse said.

Adriana could trust her for reasons unknown to her at that particular moment but she did as she was told. she swallowed the tablets and drank the water unable to stabilise the cup in her trembling fingers. The nurse assisted her as she was sat in the hallway, watching other nurses and doctors in hospital scrubs hurry towards the operating rooms to save the lives of other casualties.

she felt completely lost and terrified as she sat quietly tendered to by the young nurse who was just about her daughters age. The young nurse put one arm around her. she reassured her in gently voice.

" They are going to do everything to help her". The nurse said. she knew Judith was in a very critical condition and not likely to survive but she pressed on.

" We have some of the best doctors on call today. I am confident she will pull through. she is in very good hands". The nurse said.

" What are they going to do to save her?"Adriana asked.

" They are going to open her chest cavity to make sure she hasn't ruptured any vital internal organs. These things are tricky. Once they can stop the bleeding, they can repair her wound. she did loose a lot of blood before she arrived".

It was the best the nurse could say appreciating the condition the girl was in when she arrived. The nurse knew to keep her reassurances within a professional capacity and this is what she was doing.

" she did it to herself...she just cut herself very badly...And the blade to her chest...I couldn't believe my eyes when it happened. Nothing else matters now. If Judith dies, I'll have to die too because I have nothing else in the world to live for" Adriana said.

The nurse held the grieving mothers hands and let her cry on her shoulders. she felt the old ladies despair. There was nothing more she could do but console her.

The nurse could hear the PA system paging Dr Bernard Oakfield. He was the first in command in the trauma unit with a length of practice extending 15 years as a surgeon.

" That call out is for your daughters doctor. If any one can save her, He will. He has never lost a patient yet and we all call him the miracle worker. Mother luck must be on your daughters side today because it's actually his day off work"

But Mrs Adriana didn't feel so lucky.

A clock in the waiting area ticked away the minutes and the effect of the codeine phosphate she had consumed was starting to take its tow. The nurse gently removed her blanket and replaced it with another.

Adriana sat miserably in her chair and within

minutes she was fast asleep.

CHAPTER 3

Dr Bernard Oakfield entered the operating room and all of the nurses and other doctors turned to look at him. He was rapidly filled in by the residents who'd been tendering to Judith until he arrived.

This was his second patient of the day despite his emergency call to duty. He was known as the messiah of the trauma unit with a track record know for never loosing a patient in his entire length of practice. All the resident nurses aspired to be like him and he was only 35 years old. Even the much older surgeons looked up to him in so many ways believing that his command in the operating room was more than just his skill set. He was truly inspirational. Perhaps Judith had a chance of surviving this trauma. Just maybe. According to his prestigious record, it would be his first failure in this very same unit.

The six inch blade stuck in her chest had missed her heart by millimetres. Upon examination he was hopeful as the damage was manageable.

But time was running out.

He listened to the grim recital, despite its irregularities, Dr Bernard was not willing to give up all hopes yet.

He barked orders at the other residents as they fought to keep Judith alive.

she'd clearly lost too much blood so they had to repair very fast before she slipped into a coma. There were one or two moments when it seemed as though they were starting to loose her, but as much as they were fighting to save her, Judith Meredian herself was fighting to live.   One of the residents put forward a toxicology report before Dr Bernard, and for the first time it was clear that she was heavily induced by several controlled substances already heavily streaming in her blood. They were dealing with a very complex procedure as she was likely to die from the presence of these substances alone. An overdose case wasn't unusual for the doctors.

In the absence of the injuries currently been treated, a patient like Judith would have undergone a much less complex procedure to revive her. The toxicology analysis reported the presence of a combination of substances such as cocaine, amphetamine, LSD, Methadone and a host of other class B drugs. The effect of the combination was lethal and the quantity consumed hinted to the doctor what had led her to self harm.

He fought like a lion to keep her going despite the fact that the deck was stacked against them.

The damage was gradually coming under control after 2 hours of surgery.

The evil forces where no match for the doctors expertise and his scalpel.

The time was 4 o'clock pm and after 3 hours at the intensive care unit Judith Meredian was in stable condition.

Dr Bernard Oakfield let out a long sigh of relief.

The residents present did too.

They were all smiles now as he'd done the impossible again.

He got several hugs and the customary pat on the back as he walked away from the operating table, and pulled his surgical mask off his face with a look of accomplishment. He lived for moments like this. He loved saving lives, particularly when there was a mountain of doubt stacked against him. He loved saving the lives of his patients but something struck him differently about this particular patient.

It stood against his professional ethics to get involved with the private lives of his patients. The limitations of the law left those in his profession despondent in most cases but there was something here he found very intriguing.

Needless to say, he knew nothing about her. He saved her life, he knew how important it would be for her family to hear the good news. He again had made a real difference against the pointless destruction of human life. And now he has won yet another battle, as he always did, it all seemed worthwhile, he was a few steps closer to be called a god.

It didn't matter to him how much longer he had to practice, this was his calling, and so long as he continued saving lives, he was a very happy man on his way to achieving an illustrious career.

In the next room he disposed of his surgical gloves, washed his hands, and took off his cap. He looked into his eyes long and deep as he stood before the mirror. This had been his ritual for the last fifteen years. What he felt as he looked at himself was a sense of genuine fulfilment. His passion for his work was undeniable. Although the fatigue of the last few weeks was evident, that did not matter.

He was interrupted by his second in command at the trauma unit.

" You did it again! Come on now, you must be on cloud ten and beyond. I can imagine you are rubbing shoulders with the almighty himself now. Do tell me, how does it feel to pull another one of your tricks out the hat?". Dr Adam said, sounding more mesmerizes than elated.

" This is our profession Adam. It is what we are meant to do on duty". Dr Bernard replied.

" Save lives, I know, I know that much, but it's just how you make the impossible seems so easy every time. I was convinced we were going to loose that patient at some point during surgery". Dr. Adam said.

"Hmmm". Bernard responded as he changed into a

more appropriate attire.

" Doesn't it strike you as odd how it's turned out. I was almost certain that the blade grazed her heart to cause a rupture, I mean the excessive bleeding... the overdose...I don't get it. I just don't get it". Dr Adam said, slumping into the chair as he watched Dr Bernard put himself together.

" It is our decisions on the operating table. You know this better than anyone else in this unit," Dr Bernard said.

" And your decision was not to give up hope on your patient?"

" Exactly."

" The chief is happy you took the emergency call to come in today. I mean it is your day off today right?". Dr. Adam said couple steps behind the doctor as he tried to match his strides.

" Absolutely. I couldn't think of anything better to do. I guess it was the patients lucky day after all".

He thought silently of his admiration for Judith's fighting will. Little did his fellow surgeons know that it is the patients will to live that counts more, he's just there to keep them alive. That was the key. He fought for those who fought for themselves. He could sense these things on the operating table and his senses were strong with Judith.

Although she was unconscious, he felt like her soul communicated with him all the way through. He snapped out of his current frame of thought. It was moments like this that made him realize he has been on this road way too long.   He was on his way to tell the girls mother the good news.

A muscle tensed in his jaw as he walked through the hallway of the trauma unit. Even though he had good news, he always kept his game face on. He walked with a stride of confidence as he approached her. He knew she was dying to hear the outcome of the surgery. They all were at this point. He remembered

Judith's face again as he did with all his patient at a time like this. He remembered each case, the circumstances, the outcome, and most of all, the excitement on the faces of each patients family when he breaks the news.

This was his profession, every single detail mattered, because he cared for all his patients above all.

CHAPTER 4

" Good evening Adriana ", his voice was bold and very masculine.

" Oh Doctor",Adriana said, her voice still filled with despair. she tried to get up from her chair but he stopped her.

"NO, NO, NO, please remain seated". He said. He could see the fear in her eyes.

" I am Dr. Oakfield", he had been in this position many times, he loved this part. It was filled with suspense. This was something he did to boost his ego a little bit more. Dr Adam played along as this always made part of their lunch time banter. He knew he was the bearer of good news, so it was OK for him to approach the patients family how ever way he saw fit.

" Please tell me about my daughter doctor, I am mortified as it is".Adriana said.
There was a sharp intake of breath as she looked into the eyes of the man who was about to break the news that could alter her life for the rest of her living days.

" Your daughter is fine madam, she is in a stable condition now.". He gently touched her arm and flashed a champion smile, his perfect set of white teeth were immaculately blinding. For a moment she thought she'd never seen teeth so white. The words she'd just heard echoed in her head several time before she could respond.

" Oh doctor. I cannot believe my ears. Where is she, when can I see her. Oh my dear Judith. I thought I'd lost her forever.".Adriana said, tears of joy trickling down her wrinkled face.

" We did everything we could and we are happy with her current state. But you can't see her just yet.", he said, stroking her palm gently.

" But you would soon. Perhaps in the next few hours". He added. He'd landed his Oscar winning speech. For the first time since dawn, Adriana smiled.

" Oh Doctor. How can I ever thank you". she said reaching out to hug him.

" Please don't thank me. she had divine favour. she is very lucky to pull through". He said hugging her back.

" But I do advice you return home and get some rest yourself. one of the nurses will contact you with information about when to return. Your daughter need a lot of rest too. she lost so much blood", he said rising up form his seat.

" I am over the moon doctor", "I thank you very much". she added." I can't thank you enough".

" It is all well madam. The nurses will advice you from here on". He said as he looked into her once fearful eye which was now replaced with delight.

There was smiles all around the reception area where they were seated. All the nurses knew the good news besides Adriana . But they loved this moment of their work. Dr Bernard signalled for a nurse to attend to her before he made his infamous exit.

Adriana tried to absorb what she had just been told. she felt as though she was in a dream. But this was happening now. Her daughter was alive and well. she watched her savoir walk away escorted by another man who was constantly hoovering over his shoulder. It was easy to imagine how many wives and daughters and families at large who'd thrown themselves at his feet with gratitude and relief after he delivered such great news.

Dr Bernard was looking forward to his home time. Jazz music, red wine, TV dinners. He had cleared his desk because he knew, unless it was yet another emergency call, he would cherish the next seven days. As he heaved a long sigh, he reached for the phone to call his chauffeur. The phone rang once, and he spoke.

" I am on my way out". He said briefly then hung up.

It was Friday. He always looked forward to his days off work when it started on a Friday. He knew how busy he'd been the last few weeks, so he knew he deserved this break. However short it was going to be, he was happy he was finally going home.

CHAPTER 5

SIX MONTHS LATER...

Dr Bernard Oakfield continued his work at the hospital and he'd been in close communications with Judith Meredian.

she had labelled him her saviour and in every sense of the word he had turned out to be just that.

A lot of his other patients had maintained their constant gratitude to him by way of the occasional thank you cards and flowers, but it was almost impossible for him to keep Judith within that cordial category. she was back on her feet three months after her surgery and everyday since then, she spoke to Dr Bernard once and most times twice a day.

He'd learnt a lot about her within the last three months but every passing day was a new day for him to learn something different about her. He saw her for what she truly was, a witty, charismatic, passionate and endearing soul. He always imagined her to be an exact reflection of himself. He always considered himself to have a strange sense of humour that a lot of his ex-partners failed to understand, but Judith was his perfect match.

They spent the odd weekends together on his days off work and by now they had gotten considerably close.

He was in surgery for the last six hours and at nine-thirty he walked out of the operating room. It was his last day on duty after what appeared to have been the longest month on call. He walked to his office for the first time in hours. It was the best part of the night for him, usually he would sit in his office having one cup of coffee after the other chased with his favourite digestive biscuit while he sort through his patients case files, but today wasn't to be one of those days. He'd done that for the last four weeks. He was ready to go home.

As he walked into his office and sat behind the desk he looked at the time. It was almost quarter to ten. He sighed and reached for the phone. His first point of contact would usually be his chauffeur but there was someone else he had to speak to first. He knew she would still be up, they'd spoken briefly once in the morning before he went into surgery, and he knew she was expecting his call back. Twelve hours later was forgivable. she knew how busy he'd been for the last four weeks, and she respected his profession more after her time at the hospital. It was a life changing experience for her and she had him to always be thankful for her second chance at life.

He punched in her telephone number on his mobile phone and held it close to his ear. The phone rang once, and she answered.

Her voice sounded excited as she always was when they communicated with each other.   she had always matched his larger than life personality with her own special brand of enthused mannerism.

" Hi Ya! I've been expecting your call", she was in high spirit and her excitement forced a smile onto his face.

" This is why I've called. Just finished my last surgery for the day", he said.

"Let me guess, you've saved another innocent victims life", she said with a hint of sarcasm in her voice.

" You guessed right dear. You know me too well already.", he replied.

He was always engulfed with his work and very rarely did he have to communicate work related details with anyone besides his colleagues, but he felt at ease doing so with Judith. They spoke about anything and everything because she did love what he did as much as he did. For her in particular, he was interested in her aspiration as an actress. For each of them, it was an all consuming passion neither of them could conceal.

" It would be epic to expect anything less from you", she replied.
He sounded exhausted, but relieved to be honoured, humoured and appreciated by her.

" You know I do my very best, each patient presents their own set of challenges", he replied.

" You must be shattered after all that hard work", she said, sympathetic and concerned.

" I am, but this is something that comes with the territory". He laughed as he spoke trying to disguise the fact that he was beat after another day in the life of Dr Bernard Oakfield.

They hadn't seen each other for the last few weeks. They looked forward to any possibility of sharing their time together but it was always down to his availability.

He was used to his busy schedule at the office but she demanded more of his time than he'd cared to offer to anybody else outside of work. she was very aware of his commitment to work, but most of all, she knew his day off started after tonight.

" How's your script reading coming along?", he asked, trying to shift attention towards her besides himself.

For the last month she had been working on a manuscript of a new screen play that was intended to land her a major role in a film. It was hoped that this would be her big break into the movie industry. And as dedicated as Dr Bernard had been with work, she spent day and night memorizing and working on her role respectively.

It was a big deal for Judith. A break through project if you may and her dedication to this project fascinated him. This opportunity presented itself shortly after news got out that she'd attempted to take her own life.

" It is an intricate project. I've had the papers glued to my hands everyday". she said, sounding a little tired. she had been studying it until six AM the day before, and continued by noon on this current day. It was important for her to show utmost dedication as she feared it might be her only opportunity to break into the industry as a full-time actress. she had told him she was going to be playing a leading role for the project and he understood how important it was for her to get things right. This particular project required her to meet with the director of the movie in a couple of days, and he knew she'll be gone for some time. He was hoping they'd be able to spend sometime together before she left, and all he wanted to do was see her again.

" I am almost finished here, what are your plans for tonight henceforth?". he asked,

" Besides reading some more, nothing at all. Now you've mentioned it, I think I do need a little break from studying this manuscript. how about you?", she asked in return, expecting a more definitive response as to the reason he asked.

" The rest of my evening is pretty much open to myself and my sofa and whatever my wine rack holds", he said, forcing a smile to her face.

" Well, I made some spaghetti and meatballs an hour ago, but I haven't gotten around to sitting for dinner yet". she added.

" Well then, I might just have the perfect bottle of red wine to chase that dish of yours. Why don't we meet at my place", he said, pausing briefly for her to confirm her attendance.

" Sure thing. I'll love to. I know how terrible you are at cooking. And I know how much you love my cooking, so it'll be my pleasure". she said with laughter.

" Great. I'll have to pass on my planned visit to M&S then", He said, forcing a smile on both their faces." But despite my frailty with domestic chores, I'll compensate for that by being the best host, you just focus on getting your lovely self down to mine".he added

" Of course", she replied as they both laughed. There was an ease in communication between them. They were not married, neither had they contemplated speaking openly about being a couple, but if it was to be considered, they both ticked all the boxes that fit a matching pair. They had developed a constantly flourishing relationship and unconsciously, they were passionately becoming devoted to each other.

" Would you rather I picked you up on my way home?" he asked.

"Errm." No, don't trouble yourself. You head on home and ill catch a cab,"

He smiled at her confirmation. He was dying to see her. Making plans to be with her was an episode of his life that had been on hold for quite some time. Not because he didn't get the occasional dates with other female admirers, but primarily because he did not have the time to date properly. But with Judith, she brought a certain kind of calm to his life as it was now. she was a breath of fresh air and a new sense of purpose,she was someone he'd longed to be in a serious relationship with for the last few years.

" OK then, I guess we have a date. I'll see you very soon", he said.

" OK Doctor". she replied. He sensed the humour in her voice but it only made him envision how beautiful and sensuous she was.

As he hung up, his assistant entered the office giving him the all clear he needed to hear.

" I have forwarded all your reports to the chief resident. He is satisfied that there will be no further complications he can't handle in your absence. " she said.

" Brilliant", he said signing off the remaining paper work on his desk.

He was beyond exhausted but he had his special way of keeping collected. He needed the next few days to relax and he could hardly wait about leaving and the only thing on his mind was Judith.

He called his chauffeur from him office phone and was out of the hospital moments afterwards. He arrived home thirty minutes later and hurriedly he tried putting his house in order. He'd stopped his maid from cleaning up after him. He was meticulous with the way he wants things to be. Moments later he was in the shower listening to some loud music.

Shortly, Judith arrived. When she approached the door to his flat she realised it was unlocked. she tried knocking and using the bell a few times but got no response. she could hear loud music coming form inside his flat. she imagined that he had stormed into the flat not realizing he didn't lock the door.

"Dr Bernard. she called out to him as she walked slowly into his house. she called out to him again but the music suppressed her voice. They had shared a kiss once but that was as intimate as they'd been since they've been seeing each other. she didn't have the confidence to parade herself around his house without him present so she turned around to walk back to the door, then she heard his voice.

" Oh hello Judith", he said as the music stopped abruptly. she turned around and their eyes met. He was standing in nothing but his towel. Tall and lanky, his athletic body was chiselled and dripping with water. To her eye he was a perfect male form. Embarrassed by the awkwardness of the situation she hurriedly took her eyes of gazing at his well defined abs". He noticed she was shy at that point so he smiled broadly. Judith felt a tingle of excitement as she smiled faintly and lowered her face.

" I am sorry I had the music on too loud.". He said.

His face with an even more broadened smile, realising that she'd never seen him like this before.

"I got to the door and realized it was unlocked. I did call out for you a few times." she replied, returning her gaze at him but this time focusing on his face alone.

"Please come have a seat" he said, ushering her into the living room area. "Let me take this from you" He added, motioning toward the food items she had in her hands.

" Hmmm this smells delicious", he said, walking into the kitchen as Judith took a sit in the living room. His flat was a sleek New York style apartment with a 360 degrees view above the city from the inside. He placed the items in the kitchen then joined her in the living room.

" That could have been me getting mugged and ending up in my own operating table with gun shot wounds to the body for leaving my door unlocked". He spoke as he walked into the living room.

"You are right. Anything could have happened, you should be a lot more careful next time. Good thing it was just little lo' me then eh!

" You are right, but little lo' you came to my rescue instead," he said, sitting down next to her, placing his hands on her lap while he looked into her sexy blue warm eyes.

He leaned his face closer to hers and they kissed. He could see that despite of the gruelling sixteen hours he had just spent at the hospital, she was utterly smitten. He was instantly aroused by her. she had an intense effect on him. she placed her arms around his shoulders as they kissed. They both longed to hold each other. Her kisses were sensual, she made his senses rattle with pleasure and she could feel it so she moaned in delight.

"If only you knew how good it feels to be in your arms", he said, pausing briefly and looking into her eyes.

" I don't think you need words to explain what you mean doctor". she replied.
They both grinned at each other and then continued kissing passionately.

Moments later he opened up a bottle of wine, served her a drink and left to change into a more appropriate attire. It wasn't the first time she'd brought food to his home. she went into the kitchen and heated up the meal in the microwave. she loved her home made dishes so she learned to serve them correctly. As the microwave counted down, she sipped from her wine glass and imagined what all of this meant to her. she felt safe around him. What's more, he saved her life.

"I am beginning to feel like this is something we could both get used to". He said. His voice startled her, bringing her senses back to the present time.

" It does feel special", she replied, handing him a glass of wine.

" I'll be gone for a week or so in two days. Its a shame I can't be around for the rest of your days off".she said, but her eyes clouded as soon as she said it.

" I understand that you have to meet with this director person. I know it is very important for you to nail this role. He said, sounding considerate.

" Yes it is. I need to go over the details with Nicholas Wright", she said,"He is the head of the film corporation." He is setting up this meeting with the film director who has the final say on who to cast." she added.

" I understand. It'll plan out just the way you want it to, then you will be back in no time." He reached for the dishes to assist her with serving the meal. He was wearing a black cashmere robe. she could glimpse that he was naked underneath the bathrobe.
" Do you get to serve all your girlfriends dinner in just your bathrobe or am I an exception to the fact that you

are doing so now.?" she said, sipping from her glass and trying to disguise her amusement. He smiled at her, and then poured himself more wine. He took a sip first then spoke.

" You are exceptional that is a fact. But do I get to serve another girl in my bathrobe, or at all? the answer to that is NO".

she didn't say anything but she returned a much smile.

They gazed at each other with undeniable admiration while they sat down to have their meal on the table set in the middle of the kitchen. There was something very inviting about her smile that made her more appealing to him tonight than she'd ever been. He had a well groomed face and gorgeous body that exuded his success and accomplishments and this was an aphrodisiac for her. He looked younger than his years and she wondered how it is so that another woman hadn't made a husband and father out of him yet. At the moment it was easy for her to imagine him in a tutored waiting for her at the alter while she strolled down the aisle wearing her immaculate white wedding dress.

" So do you like it?' she asked, fishing for compliments now that she cared to admit it.

" It's lovely. Your cooking seems to be getting a lot more delightful, I can't say I wouldn't want to get used to this." He said.
she giggled,smiling at him as they savoured the meal on the table.

" You should make this for me again. You have the culinary skills of a master chef", he said, smiling at her.

she laughed.

" What!!! What is so funny?"he asked, wanting to know what part of his compliment to her was amusing to her. she continued laughing, and motioned to his teeth. He picked at it with his tongue and then washed it down with a gulp of wine.

"As I see you like it this much, you leave me no choice but to cook for you again".she said, as she filled their glasses with more wine. They both felt good been in each others company, just the two of them. No responsibility to anybody else but themselves. He couldn't wait to get her into his bed and make love to her, and then sleep the night away and waking up at what ever time suited them both. He rose up from his chair and began to clear out the dinner table,she watched in admiration of how well domesticated he was.

" Oh dear look what time it is" she said.

" It's pretty late, but as much as I can't advice you to journey back home this late,I can assure you that we can spend the remaining few hours until dawn properly entertained by me".He said,

" I guess if you put it that way, who are my to turn that down" she said, her eyes dancing with excitement as she spoke.

" You know that means you'll be sleeping on the sofa tonight", she said, making her way into the living room. He laughed in amusement but gave no immediate response to her remark about their sleeping arrangements.

" You don't say", he replied, as he walked to join her on the sofa. He opened another bottle of wine and refilled her glass. He couldn't stop looking into her eyes. she knew his intentions, she wanted him to feel that way, and yes, he did.

" So long as you'll be willing to spare a duvet,a pillow or a blanket, I wouldn't mind giving up my bed for you." He was like a little child on his birthday licking the cream from his birthday cake with his tongue.

" I'll have some time to reconsider", she said. she saw him for what he truly was. He was a nice guy, and absolutely charming. How ever way the night ended, she was convinced that he would have earned it. she was prepared to show him how fortunate he was, and how much she felt towards him for saving her life. They looked at each other admiringly. It was impossible not to notice how spectacular they both appeared to each other. They clearly did compliment each others desire. The thought of working those long hours the last few weeks was clear of his mind now. He was anxious to get her into bed and the thought of this ignited his desire even more.

She smiled at him faintly. AS they were both silent at the moment, it was undeniable what thought festered on their minds.

" I want to thank you for been here with me tonight." he said, placing his hands on hers as they sat next to each other. They were thankful to each other and this was all that mattered.

He finished the drink in his glass hurriedly and then rose to his feet. He stood in front of her, and reached out for her hand. Without question she gave her hands to him and he pulled her off the sofa. He grabbed the half full bottle of wine and ushered her into the bedroom. It was well past one AM now and they were past tipsy. He led her to his bed side and began to kiss her. she got onto his bed and he slipped into bed next to her, and she smiled as he took her in his arms and held her close.

" On second thoughts, I think you'll be much more useful to me in here that you would have been on the living room sofa." she said. This forced a break out of laughter between them.

" Well thanks for the reconsideration", he said, kissing her immeasurably until she let out a soft moan. He began to caress her, and within minutes nothing else in the world mattered. They were locked in each others arms. It was what they had dreamed and fantasises about since the first date when they had met. It was Saturday morning and Dr,Bernard woke up alone in bed. she'd woken up before he did to surprise him with one of the ways a lot of people would agree to be the best way to wake up to. she thought she could make him breakfast and serve it in bed before he woke up, but he was in his boxer shorts walking into the kitchen before she noticed him. she was preparing an all English breakfast.

" Hmmm, something smells nice in here", he said, startling her with his voice as he approached.

" I didn't expect you to be up just yet", she said with a smile. she was only wearing his white long sleeve shirt with half of the buttons undone..she walked towards him and planted a kiss on his lips. They both looked happy and relaxed. The night before was amazing, and the morning was off to a great start. Her first time love making experience with him was top shelf material and she was truly satisfied. she wanted more of what she'd shared with him because she had not felt this way in a long time about another man. she didn't choose to be in a relationship only because she hadn't found the most deserving guy.

" Wow there's a lot going on in here. First I get the pleasure of dinner, now breakfast, I must say you do know how to spoil a boy". He said, lifting his body to sit on the granite counter.

she smiled at him and reserved a response while she whisked the eggs in a grey ceramic bowl.

" Have I done anything in particular to deserve this treat?"he added, "because what so ever it is, every boy should do more to still keep a girl around after the first night like the one we had".

" Lets just say you've earned it", she said with a smile. she enjoyed pleasing him.

Her presence was a more soothing distraction from the usual gore he saw at work on a regular basis. she felt her efforts was the right thing to do so she did it wholeheartedly. she laid breakfast out on the kitchen table and they both sat down to eat. she looked sexy in his shirt with her erect nipples. It was a well deserving breakfast and moments later they found themselves cuddled up in bed. All that mattered just then was the private world that they shared now.

At around one PM they were out on the town. For the last few hours she had thought less about her work.

she had to get some more reading done, but she felt slightly guilty having to bring this up as a reason to break up this date. she convinced herself that could always do it later. He had made an emergency reservation at an Italian restaurant- his favourite cuisine. They walked hand in hand. The autumn breeze was soothing, and it was so calm they could hardly separate themselves from one another as they walked through the city centre.

They enjoyed each others company over lunch. She told him more about her aspirations and other things she wanted to work on in years to come.

He was patient to listen to all she had to say and she admired him more for that. He liked hearing all she had to say, he loved the fact that she was a passionate soul. she laid emphasis on every single detail when she spoke of any particular topic.

He loved that about her. she was amazingly witty and relentlessly focused when she was working on anything she genuinely had an interest in. It was part of what made her special. Added to the fact that she had extraordinary great taste. she was the typical feminist at times, in some cases, she felt she didn't get the same roles and acting opportunity most men did without trying hard for it.

She had been aspiring to land her first major role for the past five years, but more often than not, she did turn down roles that were offered to her which she didn't find challenging enough, or which did not match the sort of character she'd always imagined herself to be in a movie. It was something that had irked her for years.

But it was also the substance and high taste in her that had kept her going. she found herself pursuing a career in an industry where men kept the control of the power in their exclusive little world.

It was a very old fashioned way of looking at things but she knew not much had changed in the world, and to challenge all expectations, not expecting to be thanked for it. In fact, she was about to have a meeting with a prominent director in the British film industry and it was down to him to decide if she got the role or not.

she was annoyed that this was her preordained fate but it was something she was determined to overcome. At first, no one else had wanted to give her a leading role in a high budget movie, and now that she'd stumbled upon the opportunity to be that lead character she had always dreamt of, she felt she was prepared to do whatever it took to secure her chances. It was sort of a desperation, she admitted that much to herself, but at least she knew better that anybody else that she had championed this cause right from the beginning.

Judith and Dr Bernard talked about family life. He needed to understand better how she had ended up in his operating table close to the point of death. He had been the number one man in the trauma unit for a number of years but he only saw a rare case like Judith's once in a blue moon. He was itching to get the facts out of her, but at the same time, he didn't want to be pushy about it. He had tried to keep his distance from the entire situation but he seemed to be lured in despite his better judgement. His feelings were strong with her and moments like this which they shared would only make it impossible for him to tear himself away. He had to content himself with been her saviour and lover first, then someone she could trust, before she could open up well enough to talk to him about her childhood or any other circumstances that had built up until the point of self harming.

After lunch, Judith and Dr Bernard took a leisurely

stroll through the park, watching other couples enjoying special moments together in the gentle autumn breeze.

As they wandered along, they stopped by the pond to watch the swans swimming in pairs, they wandered if they were sharing a romantic stroll just like they both were, but all the same, there was romance in the air.

They talked about having children from time to time, but the prospect seemed to be wishful thought as he was at the heights of his career, and she was about to delve into one which would almost certainly keep them absent from home more than three weeks at a time.

They were bound to both get too busy with their careers, and having a child would require the ultimate sacrifice. Dr Bernard had always believed that a child would somehow keep him at home more than at the hospital. It was a life style choice he was comfortable with if he had to make that decision in comparison with chasing a career, but he wasn't convinced Judith was cut out to be the stay home type of woman. Judith vented her concerns of the thought that she believed a child would some how come between them, rather than keep them together, Dr Bernard begged to differ. The conversation of having children made Judith feel threatened, and he noticed this. He didn't want to scare her off so he seized all predispositions.

The autumn breeze was relaxing, and they were both tired when they got back to his flat. The sprawled out on the sofa speculating on the possibility of spending more time together as amazing as that which they'd shared the past twelve hours. They watched TV all day that afternoon, and after a few hours of indulging themselves with a few movies, he was surprised to realise that she'd brought some work with her. Without question he let her use one of his spare rooms. One of which he'd converted into a mini office. It was crammed with his medical books, an assortment of medical text, magazines and old newspapers. His computer was set up there, he used it on occasions when he found himself home alone with nothing to do but work from home.

she was intrigued by the degree of effort he put into his work. In a lot of ways their career paths were widely divergent, but she could relate to his field of practice. she was a pharmaceutical student and remembered how heavily she had to rely on medical text books to comprehend her subject of study. she was more intrigued of the fact that she knew virtually nothing about being a surgeon. she had a fair grasp of what it entailed but not considerably enough to declare her interest in it. But for the most part, she had a healthy respect for the fact that Dr Bernard earned a decent living. He earned a big salary as the head of the trauma unit, which was something she knew she would have to accomplish as an actress. and she chafed at the fact that she wasn't earning at all, and felt like she should be.

But she was happy she had the opportunity to turn matters around. she had lived in the same home for years since she was thirteen years old and was beginning to feel claustrophobic. Her decision not to pursue a career in pharmacy denied her the opportunity to be earning a big salary on a monthly basis. it was something she understood very well and accepted. she sat by the desk with the PC on it and she read until it was nearly mid-night. By the time she returned to the living room, Dr Bernard was asleep in front of the TV. He had drunk half a bottle of wine, and was feeling relaxed and content. Judith thought of returning home while he slept. she thought of leaving him a note so as not to wake him but she couldn't come to terms with the best possible decision to make. she sat next to him for a while and watched what was showing on TV. It was a repeat of what one of her favourite soaps. It was one o' clock by then, and he was woken up by the sound of a car crash form the TV. He sprung back to life.

" Oh my goodness, how long have I been out for?!" he said rhetorically with a tired voice, but Judith felt to respond nonetheless,

" You've been out of the count for at least over an hour. I found you snoozing away at about midnight", she said with a smile on her face.

" And you stayed", he replied. " How considerate of you", he added.

" It didn't seem appropriate to leave while you were asleep. Moreover, I didn't want to wake you up either", she said.

He kissed her for being ever so thoughtful.

" We should go to bed, I have to get up early in the morning. I've been in the same cloths for two days". she said softly. she didn't want to bring up her travel plans at this time. Her only excuse was that which she had just established and it seemed to work it's magic.
Dr Bernard followed her into the bedroom. It seemed ironic considering it was his house but he felt comforted by the fact that she felt at ease around him. He let her lead the way, and a few minutes later, they were in bed, with their arms comfortably wrapped around each other.

And ten minutes later, he was snoring. she watched him sleep for a while before she did too.

CHAPTER 6

Judith's phone rang. It was her mother.

she didn't know where she'd been. It was unlike Judith not to tell her mother where she was going or where she would be staying if she wasn't returning home. Judith didn't want to reveal her relationship with the doctor to anybody at the time, especially her mother. She didn't want to get into the habit of lying to her either. she imagined that she could just ignore the phone call and turn up at home whenever she does, but she knew her mother would be worried. she always was when ever she didn't hear from her. she answered the call and told her mother she would be home soon.
Her conversation with her mother had woken him up.

"I hate to leave you, but I have to go", Judith said as she climbed out of bed and into her dress. she got dressed and sat by the bed side as she slipped on her shoes.

" That's OK", he smiled sleepily at her, he was content that she had stayed with him this long to begin with.

" You know I'll be travelling tomorrow as well right?", she said, shooting him a quick look to make sure she wasn't talking to his sleepy body.

" Yes of course. You have to meet with the director of your project", he said.

" I'll be gone for a couple of weeks. I wish I could return sooner." she said. It was wishful thinking on her part. she knew there was an even greater chance she could be there longer, but this was her way of letting him know she'd jump at the chance of seeing him again sooner rather than later.

" Dr. Bernard knew the score as it was. He too probably wouldn't be home after the week ends. He loved his time off duty but he was a workaholic. He had stayed at the hospital for a week straight on several occasions so it wasn't unusual for him to comprehend Judith point. They accepted the fact that they wouldn't see each other for a while but struggled to admit this openly.

" I'll call you from Liverpool as soon as I'm settled in". she wasn't particularly sure where she'll be staying but it was promised that her accommodation and living expenses would be taken care of by the film company.

" Make sure you do. And if you need anything, I mean anything, do not hesitate to let me know", he said, with a hint of genuine concern on his face. she knew he cared about her dearly.

" You do not need to worry."

" I was hoping to make love to you before goodbye" he said, she knew how much she would love to share a moment of passion with him, but that would have only made it impossible for her to leave his arms.

"I feel the same way but hold the thought...." I'll be back into your arms before you know it. Ill tell you as soon as I know how the timing is all going to work out" she said.

They both smiled at each other as she got up to leave. He tried to get up to walk her to the front door.

" Oh No please don't. Don't get out of bed. You should rest some more.", she said. He smiled at her and laid back down.

" I can manage letting myself out", she said with a decent smile.

" Have a lovely trip and be sure to keep me informed all the way through", he said.

" I will", she replied, blowing him a kiss as she left the room. An instant later he heard the front door shut. he laid in his bed thinking about her before he fell into slumber.

His whole world had revolved around work but

now, she'd given him reason to look at things differently.

He was satisfied with the way things were but also wished it could be a lot more than it was.

He had never thought seriously about been in a new relationship. He was a novice in this arena. As a matter of fact his last meaningful relationship was five years ago, and before then, it was never more than a single night affair or a three months ordeal. He was convinced there was a lot to learn about properly dating a woman. He got comfortable with the on and off affairs. it was less stressful and suited his work shift pattern. In a way it made him feel less involved with whoever was available to share a brief moment of romance with him. Before he fell deep into sleep, he couldn't help thinking about their love making together. Their total involvement with each other. Where was the place for another girl if he could re-live these moments with Judith. she was good at what she did to get him to this point. He wondered if he'd regret putting things to an end if it became necessary. But why would it come to that. Who in their right mind would want something this incredible to end. he was happy he didn't have to think about patients at the hospital as they come in at the brink of death. That too traumatised him on occasions, but he was fully trained to deal with these issues. He liked to think of his relations with Judith as a source of escape. Dr Bernard had the absolute control and competence over everything that happened in the operating room, but with his feelings for Judith, he wanted it to overwhelm him. He thought about them together, the more unconscious he became. He accepted the fact that there was nothing he could do to change the way she made him feel. As for Judith, she was a necessary introduction to his life, and he knew he needed this experience with her.

Within a short few minutes, he was fast asleep.

CHAPTER 7

Marcus Billingham was a graduate student who studied business administration but now was an agent. He needed experiences to fit on his CV while he prepared for his own career. He took the opportunity to be Judith's PA. He had a photo graphic memory. He served his internship with Mr J Wright's company.

Mr James Wright was the founder of the film company interested in sponsoring Judith's role in the movie , But Nicholas Wright, his son was the predecessor. Marcus Billingham had played his role in landing the Wright's as he's worked for the family for a whole year. Introducing Judith to Nicholas Wright was a plus for his credibility, but it was Judith who had done all the initial work so far. The Wright's family had always wanted to screen her and she'd know about this for a very long time.

Judith read through her manuscript and other materials she had prepared for Nicholas Wright and Adam Shore the movie director.

Marcus Billingham chatted with her to go through some minor details ahead of their meeting. He was confident that he had laid all the relevant facts before the other side, positive that Judith's presence alone should be enough to land her this role. As always he knew she had all it took to impress the clients. He had been with other ladies seeking the same prospects, but Judith was in a league of her own.

Nicholas Wright was someone Judith had spoken to a few times, but she had never met him in person. He was a man who could pull all the necessary strings to make things happen.

INNOCENT NLEWEDIM

The train arrived at Liverpool station just on time, and Nicholas Wright had a Mercedes Benz waiting to pick them up. He had booked them into the Four seasons Hotel which was close to his private resort. Once they settled in, Marcus left her to get out on the town. The meeting wasn't until the following morning so he had a lot of leisurely time. Judith was happy to stay at the hotel, and compose her self for the all important meeting ahead of her. she anticipated some travelling, as it always was with the Wright's. They were in an exclusive way of life that saw them conducting meetings on private planes and yacht's. she had been told to bring her passport just in case, but this was something she was always prepared for. she loved travelling. It was something she enjoyed more about becoming an actress.
Her mobile phone rang an hour later and she was it was her mother.

" Hi, love,you alright," she said as she waited for a response from her mother.

" I was about to ring ya'", she added briefly.

" It was good mum. I just got into the hotel about an hour now, I am just getting my things in order." Her mothers voice on the other end was excited. It was a voice Judith recognized as one her mother spoken in when ever she witnessed her moving in the direction of her dreams.

" Aww thank you mum. I can't say I am not a little bit nervous." For once she admitted she was slightly off balance.

" I did get everything I need mum." she said

" And its a residential suit. I have an entire apartment inside this room." she sounded mesmerized.

" I am looking forward to meeting them yes." she said,

"I am sorry mum, I should have called you sooner.", Ill be up for a while tonight so I will ring you again later."

" I can hardly wait," she admitted to her mum. Besides all her ambition and sophistication and success as a well educated girl, she always sounded excited like a child at moments like this.

Her mum understood how important it was for her to be climbing up these social ladders so she'd vowed to give Judith all the support she needed. With her and her mother, there was always something to talk about.

" OK mum I will. Before bedtime" Judith said then added" I'm still having trouble sleeping but like the doctor said its a phase that will pass."

"OK mum I will," Judith said, taking in health pointers from her mother.

" Don't worry everything is under control." she said,

" I am alone at the moment yes, my assistant is out for a while.", she added. " I will ring room service soon as well. You make sure you have something to eat too OK"

" Fine, I'll speak to you soon", Judith said. Then got off her mobile.

she sat by the bed side as she collected her thoughts. she thought of her meeting in the morning which was the single most important thing on her mind. she thought of Nicholas Wright and tried to portray him based on her vivid imagination. He was still a young man. In his early forties. He was Forty-one to be exact this year. About five years older than Dr Bernard. Nicholas Wright was what everyone expected men to look like in England. Healthy, full-of life and ambitious, and running a successful business. But her only fascination with was with his families business, wealth and power. They have been responsible for the sustained careers of a lot of the mainstream actors/actresses she had watched on TV as a child. Nothing else she knew so far about him intrigued her. she called Dr Bernard afterwards to let him know how she was getting on.

" Hello doctor," she said, with a faint smile. He knew her to be sarcastic when ever she referred to him as just doctor. And he smiled too.
" Nice to hear from you.", How was your journey?" He asked, noticing she sounded tired.
" Not bad at all, I am just sitting by the bed side. I been on the phone to mum, I've unpacked the basics things and now I feel a bit sleepy." she replied.
"Yeah, you need to get as much rest as you can", he said,
" You are right that is exactly what I need to do. A long shower and some well deserved sleep" she yawned sleepily.
" I'm surprised they haven't called you back into the hospital." she said out of curiosity.
" Funny you say that, They actually did, A boy came in who'd taken a nasty fall. he broke four ribs doing back flips with his friends at the park."He said,
"I respectfully declined. The patient was in a lot of distress but his case wasn't critical. The surgeon on call got delayed on his flight back from America so he wasn't on duty early enough, but they found a replacement surgeon. Poor boy is going to be in a lot of pain for months, But I'll be back there a day before my days off finishes. There isn't much to do at home without you around. He added.
" You are the only doctor I know that every patient would want to be treated by, Hey, all thanks to you, I am still a part of the living.", she said. He'd gotten used to the praises he got following his work, but he accepted that this one came from a good place.
"SO what time is your actually meeting holding?" He asked.
"First thing tomorrow morning" she replied."And I am sure once I am well rested I'll be ready for it." she thought about their moments together. " I will be missing you, that much is true". she said, sounding slightly embarrassed.

" I will miss you too," He said. They both smiled, holding the phone, thinking of each other.

" I will let you know how it all goes tomorrow,". she said.

" I wish you all the luck in the world.", he said, his face gazed at the ceiling of his living room. she smiled at the thought of what he said. she needed all the luck she could get, as much as she knew she was on a preordained schedule, It was 50/50 for her at this point but she wanted the better half.

"Thanks a lot. That means so much to me", she replied.

" I can't imagine what your days would be like once this meeting is in the bag. You will be on the road for days at a time. And I'm usually trapped within the hospital walls. Do you ever think of how crazy our lives would be?" he inquired, staring at the ceiling as he spoke, expecting the roof to reveal to him a glimpse of the future.

" I know how you mean. It makes you think about other important things that makes you want to gain meaning perspective on life as it is now in comparison to how you'd like it to be." she replied.

" I was mulling it over today when I got up. I was thinking how possible it would all be to juggle our lives if we were to get serious. It would take a lot of dedication and time."

" I understand. It is a question of how ready we both are for all the changes yet to come". she said.
He was serious about the subject and she knew it. she doubted her self at this point. she wasn't sure if she was ready for the commitment needed to keep this feeling she had for him long lasting. she hadn't thought about it seriously until now. she imagined how she could make it all work out considering their already overburdened existence. The idea did appeal to her but the reality of what it was going to take was daunting. she knew how

much having a loving family meant to her. And she was open to this completely, but she felt it wasn't the right time. she hated to disappoint him. He on the other hand was expecting this to all materialize in a way where she completely accepted this but it was all in the hands of time.

" We can always talk things through when you return. Right now you need your mind clear of any distractions." He said.

she had never seen talking about settling down before now, but this was something she didn't want to keep absent from her present life. Gaining a secure career was all that was on her mind at the moment. she was on her way to securing the right source to bring that dream to a reality and now was a perfect time for her to think closely about her future.

" I'd better let you get some rest, Judith, or you'll be too exhausted to do anything in the morning.", he said. she laughed at the thought of what he meant, He knew she was a lady of leisure if it came down to her choice. but knowing her, he knew she wouldn't miss it for the world.

" Thanks for been understanding. I will call you tomorrow at my best available time:, she promised, stifling a yawn, hoping she'll get up later to study some more before the meeting.

" OK no worries. I will be expecting your call. And thanks for calling in, I do appreciate it." he said.

" OK I will, have a good evening." she said with another yawn.

" Take care," he replied. They hung up then, and it took her five minutes to fall asleep. she didn't manage to get herself into bed.

It was an hour later when the sound of her mobile phone ringing woke her up. It was Marcus Billingham. she spoke to him briefly, and he explained he was clubbing with some friends, and that she shouldn't wait up, but he promised he would be in on time to make the meeting in the morning. They confirmed the time and place of meeting had she was satisfied he would not disappoint.

It was 7am the following morning and she'd got up, showered and dressed. she remembered her last conversation with her mother before she retired to bed last night. she told her to give them a piece of her that the would never forget, and this was all she was ready to do this morning. she had brought an all black linen suit with her, and she looked sophisticated when she prepared herself and stood by the mirror. As she stepped out of the hotel rood, there was Marcus standing in the hallway outside his room. He observed her in her her black suit, high heels, gold jewellery and a smart bag that carried all her papers.

" Wow, you look ravishing." he said, " They would love you". He said, reassuring her she had a stunning appearance. she fitted the corporate look, and on the screen, or off screen, she was a head turner.

" Thanks Marcus" she said with a smile. They walked down the hallway into the elevator and made their way down to the lobby. They walked swiftly through the reception area and entered the waiting vehicle assigned to them for the day.

When they arrived at the agreed location, Judith took the lead and walked into the room with the elegance and purposeful stride she'd thought through days before now. she looked at the time and it was nine Am exactly. she surveyed the room, and within moments, she was waved over by the receptionist.

" Hello, are you Ms Meredian?" the receptionist said, her Scottish accent distinctive.

" Yes I am", Judith replied. " Your meeting has been arranged in room two. Please just follow the signs posted on the wall. You can't miss it, I believe you might already have someone waiting for you". The receptionist said, with a big smile across her face.

" That's lovely thanks". she said, looking around to find the leading sign. Marcus followed as they walked down the centres corridor and into the meeting room. Marcus was pleased with everything he'd done to set up the trip."

" I have no doubts you'll be the actress of choice on this project.", Marcus said as they approached the room.

" Why are you so optimistic?" she asked.

"Just my gut feelings if I'm honest. Besides, if I was the client, I'll cast you without a doubt." he replied.

She smiled entertaining his humour and optimism. It wasn't another But she said nothing so as not to appear too assuming. As she entered the room, she saw two men already seated. It was Nicholas Wright and Adam shore. she worked out the process of elimination in her head and instinctively, she was able to tell who was who. Both gentlemen rose to greet her as she approached the table. Nicholas spoke first.

" Pleasure to finally meet you Judith", He said with a firm gripped handshake and a smile.

" I too am pleased to meet you. In person" she added.

" please meet Adam shore, Your casting director" Nicholas said. He is going to be running the entire project. I am sure you are already aware of all of that bit of information." He said,

" Pleased to meet you Mr Shore. I have seen a lot of your work, truly Inspirational", she said with a smile as she shook hands with him. He was pleasant to the eyes but didn't give much away outwardly.

"Please have a seat" ,Nicholas said, As the waiter, served freshly dices fruits in a bowl, coffee and fresh baked croissants.

" How was your stay at the hotel. I'm hoping your were served properly", Nicholas said.

" Indeed so. Thanks for all that, It was a bit more than I expected. It was pleasant indeed. " she said.

" I imagined you had to feel relaxed enough so I spared no expense.", Nicholas said. He was all she imagined him to be, confident and arrogant in the same token, it was his charm and it worked just well for him.

" It was a treat. Especially considering it was just the first night," she said.

They all laughed in equal measure. she was aware of how to introduce the ice breakers when she was in these sort of environment, and it worked just right.

" I am pleased about everything I have come to knowledge of concerning your past work and future aspirations Ms Judith." Adam spoke gently.

" You should be, after all, I told you we had the real deal on our hands", Nicholas said. she didn't mind he had interrupted her response to what was said, but she just smiled.

" I am only going to say this out of professional courtesy. I know you've been going through something lately but I'll like to hear from you directly that you are fit and prepared to take on the role if it was offered to you. We are expecting this to be a lengthy project and we need to make sure you would be able to handle the pressure on the road." Adam said, with a concerned look on his face.

" I would be. I believe it's going to be worth all the hassle in the world. And I just say that going by my understanding of the lead characters role in the manuscript." Judith replied.

"I see you've taken a lot of time out to go through it all". Adam said, observing her response and attitude towards the questions he asked.

" Indeed I have. I mean, it's a phenomenal piece of writing." she said, " I am positive it is going to go very well through out its production." she added.

" I feel the same exact way, It is one of my favourite works so far, so all hands are on deck to ensure it is executed properly".

" I can confirm that personally. a lot is riding on this one Judith. We are really hoping for you to deliver, the only way we believe only you can", Nicholas said. she admired the vote of confidence coming from him, but again, he interrupted her. she saw Nicholas to be just as she imagined last night. He was tall, well built, and had an over powering air about him. He was in some ways frightening, but she imagined it was just the power streak. The preconceived idea she had about him was getting the best of her. But this was not her challenge. As far as challenges were at present,she needed to remain calm and composed. she understood this was his world and she wasn't about to get into a popularity contest with him.

"It is nice to know I am on the preferred list. I.e., if there is a list at all", she said. Diving into the deep end and seeking direct responses, wanting to know if this was just another show off meeting for Nicholas Wright.

" I can assure you that a few others had been considered, but neither of them have made it to this very meeting", Adam said, with an unassuming smile across his face as he grabbed his cup of coffee and sipped from it.

" We did have other choices Judith. But I can assure you, It's always a split decision thing with these sort of arrangements." Nicholas said, trying to take keep her on her toes. But he knew what he was after. It was her he wanted on set of this project playing the leading role. He had pulled all the necessary strings to make that much happen. He held all the cards as he always did and now his power over the table was really felt by Judith for the first time.

" I am sure it will be a very smart choice, and an informed one too when the final decision is made,". she said, while she drank her cup of coffee. They talked animatedly about the project and their plans, and by now, Judith calmed any fears she had. she did not fail to put forward her suggestions of the characters role as she thought following the notes she'd made over the last few weeks. They accepted her suggestions and made note of all that she had introduced.

" It's interesting how you've been able to premodify the role Judith. I think that is very impressive. It shows you've given it some real thought.". Adam said, for the first time, showing real excitement towards her involvement in the role.

As they conversed, They filled her in on the tour areas needed to be visited before the went into production. They had decided to start the tour in London, then Los Angeles before heading to New york where a lot of the final preparations where to be resolved. she was expected to spend the next three days in Liverpool because it was where all the flight arrangements were going straight from. And then the following week, they were off to America. And then, All the necessary details would be provided to her when filming was going to commence.

she was hoping this wasn't going to be a test run all the way through out the trips. It would be such a confidence breaker so she need foreclosure. As they chatted over the remaining details, she commented on the prospect of their their desired choice. It was obviously a source of serious agitation for her, Because of Nicholas' remark on split decision choices, she was determined to know her fate before the end of today's meeting.

" I've had so much time to engross myself with the role of the character, but if for any reason it is going to be offered to anybody else, I'll like to know right away, as I would not want to be seen wasting anyone's time. I'm sure you fine gentlemen have more pressing things to engage yourselves with.". Judith said, Her confident side wasn't going to be tamed by Nicholas's puzzling remarks. Nicholas smiled but remained silent momentarily as he glanced through the remaining papers before him. He was a good guy and incredibly witty. But he could also be unbelievably stubborn. He spoke resting the papers in his hand on the table.

" I have no reservations about offering you the role right here and now, but there still is a road tour ahead of US. You still have to make your impressions felt but the other parties relevant to this project. Then and only then will a final decision be made Ms Judith. But I can assure you, You do not have to worry about much from this point on.". Nicholas said. If you didn't know him well enough, you would misinterpret his way of going about things. a lot of people took his objections personally, but those who have had successes dealing with him, understood to be patient.

" Do not worry, Judith, I am happy to take you on the road. At least you'll be able to have a real taste of what it would be like when we finally get this project on the road." Adam shore said,

" Certainly", she said, but she wasn't entirely calm just yet. Nicholas was a very smart man. a lot of his approach he'd learnt from his father, and he always followed the same formula and vision to keep the company afloat.

She shot a quick look at Marcus, Who had been silent the entire time taking notes and nodding when necessary. she smiled at him and he returned one too. she trusted his better judgement and she needed to hear his thoughts on the meeting based on his opinion under observation. He hadn't come this far by being a poor judge of matters discussed over theses sort of meetings. And if he said there was still real hopes on landing this role, she knew he'll be the first to know it, besides both men sat before her.

" You have selected for yourself a brilliant agent Ms Judith. He spoke very highly of you. AS so he should, But I have respect for his aspiring statue." Adam said, as he'd notices they were both locked eyed.

Everyone smiled appreciating the truth about what was

said.

" We honestly cannot look into the future with these things, we take one step at a time until the very end. I hope you do understand". Adam said.

" I do", Judith replied, nodding in agreement as well.

" You will be hearing from me soon, but I must say it was delightful to meet you Ms Judith. I have a good feeling about you coming on board" He said, rising from his seat and shaking hands with everyone present. He walked out of the room, into the reception area and then into the parking lot where he had a car waiting.
Inside, Nicholas and Judith sat back and chatted more about other things. He was particular about her private life. He had told her he was single and she was surprised to hear him say this. It was difficult to believe what she was hearing but she listened all the same. she wondered how he was unattached, and more so, if he was, He Probably had his own family situated somewhere nice and peaceful abroad, away from the prying eyes and the media that took a keen interest in his families fortune. she wondered if he was perhaps divorced. It would take an endearing kind of woman to put up with the figure she saw before her very eyes but her senses led her to believe there was more to him than what met her eyes.

" I usually won't discuss these matters with just anyone, but it leads me to want to know more about you."' he said
" In due time Nicholas, or should I call you Mr Wright?" he asked

" Which ever sits better with you",he replied.
There seemed to be a lot of depth about Nicholas from what Judith could see, so far, he had doe exceptionally well for himself. she was very much impressed with the way he conducted his business affairs, and she thought such a man would be any girls dream to have.

" Well then Nicholas, what exactly would you like to know?", she asked.

" a lot by the look of things, but what's the hurry.." he said smiling." I am sure there is a lot of time for us to get to know each other much better."
Everything piece of information relating to the project was laid out impeccably and so they quickly reverted to the main reason they were both present. Judith was enormously impressed with his attentiveness, particularly when she expressed her desires to becoming a full time actress. she admired the way they ran the family business. she wished someday, she too could sit down to discuss an upcoming actor/actresses career over breakfast. As the day went along, he did mention that he was impressed that she did come out right with wanting to know if she got the role or not. But he made it so plain that he was going to do everything in his powers to secure the deal.

" I must thank you for sticking out for me the way you did. It was disruptive at times, but I see how your approach could have been effective". she said, Nicholas laughed before he responded.

" I didn't mean to interrupt you at any point. Judith. If you must appreciate, I have been doing this for a number of years, I know how the cookie crumbles." he said,
she didn't know his approach was calculated based on his experience, but she looked embarrassed for mentioning this now.

"I do apologise. It's just that I had prepared myself to respond to the most challenging question thrown at me during the course of today's meeting. And interestingly, I didn't think it was that difficult a sitting not to be able to deal with anything". she said.

" Point taken. But I can assure you, you wouldn't have to find yourself in any such difficulty if I was present. Its what I am here for, After all, you are my prospective client." He said.

she knew the project and all it entailed was going to be a pain in the neck, she knew this much, but she had just been convinced by him that she wasn't going to be alone. she could see that his intention were genuine, well at least with respect for the fact that his family's integrity was on the line, and he would so everything he could to keep things neat.

" Everything will be OK" He said. Optimistically. And the truth is, if you want anything in life, You need to stand up against all opposition to grab what's yours." He said,

"I am thankful for the sound advice. I wouldn't forget this in a hurry". she said firmly.
" I trust I will always have your full support", she said. Observing his mannerism as he responded.

" Look, I have dealt with all kinds of people in this business. Time wasters and down right, NO clue members. I can handle the occasional lot with lack of confidence, but I will not raise your hope just high enough to crush it. if I am sitting here now, it only means I am interested in seeing things materialize for all of us. but if I had any doubts, It will not get this far with me. Someone else would have been sitting in this very chair on my behalf."
" So you mean to tell me categorically that You have my best interest at heart?" she asked still digging for a more direct response.

"Yes I do". he said. His response suited her to perfection. she would have loved to hear the same from Adam shore, but he was long gone now. she was just as happy making this appointment to begin with, and somehow, she was looking forward to whatever else that followed.

" How is your health generally? I want you to know you can talk to me about this. it is eventually going to be our full responsibility when the contract stages approach." he said with a look of concern. she hadn't even thought of it until then. she had been advised to keep clear of any situation that would flare up her anxiety. she was extremely please to hear that he still asked about her health.

" I am doing much better now since the incident. The local press exaggerated the facts a little bit, but I guess that is what they are good for. Anything to get a headliner". she said. Her response forced a smile on Nicholas' face, He knew the game very well. it was always at the readers expense, whether it was good news or bad news.

" There are some remaining unanswered questions but in time, I produce a more detailed report from my physician, but for now, I am fine to get on with the things I enjoy doing?" she said

" I am pleased to hear this much form you. If I must say, You look very well to me", he said. " everything will be dealt with appropriately, especially with your health concerns at the forefront of everything we will be doing over the next couple weeks.".

" I would very much appreciate that". she said. He was reassuring and this meant the world to her.

"I do imagine we might have a lot more to talk about absent of the official formalities. Perhaps in a more conducive environment where you wouldn't have to feel pressured into answering any questions you didn't feel comfortable with". He said, his charming personality more radiant than she'd cared to notice earlier.

" What are you proposing Mr Nicholas?" she asked unassumingly, responding like she did not know what he was suggesting.

" I was thinking dinner, or lunch perhaps before we begin our tour." He said.

She did not want to decline, neither did she not want to accept. she was in a quandary. His piercing brown eyes where so lovely to look into and she's just had an amazing time talking to him. Nicholas had his way with everything. Even if it took sometime, he got what he wanted in the end. It was his gift, and one he knew to use to his advantage when it was necessary. He was aware she was caught by surprise with his offer, but it made him wonder why. Many girls would have jumped at the opportunity instantly, but she wasn't to be seen as others. she knew that any form of desperation could be picked on and explored and she wasn't ready to be taken on that ride. But he was the perfect eye candy. Certain qualities about him reminded her of the doctor. Nicholas had his suspicion that there could be someone else, but this did not deter him for this plight.

" Do you like Italian food?" He asked. she was amazed by his precise intuition. she shot Marcus an awkward stare believing he must have revealed to him things she would have rather confirmed herself, but Marcus returned a confused stare. It clearly wasn't his doing. Nicholas was on a roll here, and she was beyond impressed by his first guess been right. she nodded, still hesitating and perplexed by how he'd managed to ask about her interest in a cuisine she never says no to. But while she was trying to decline gracefully, he spoke.

" On second thoughts,Why don't we make it lunch", he said. I mean you must be famished after all this talking." he said.

As it turned out she was looking forward to a nice meal. Perhaps not her favourite cuisine, but seeing there was an offer on the table, she accepted.

" Lunch it is then." she replied.

"Brilliant I send for my driver to pick you up at 3pm. Is that OK with you?" He asked.

" 3pm is fine." she replied.

" See you soon then", Nicholas stood up and exited the conference room after shaking hands with Marcus, Judith and the manager of the establishment who stood in to make sure they were served distinguishably. Judith and Marcus returned to the hotel room, having light conversation about the meeting in general.

3pm came and past and it all turned out to be a very pleasant evening. After her second meeting with Nicholas, she seemed to be a lot more at ease with him. Even Nicholas himself was relaxed and appeared less intimidating. By the time she was dropped off at the hotel, she felt like she knew all she needed to know about him.

" I will see you in a couple days", he said with a broad smile as she got out of the car. she smiled in return as she nodded.

" You have my number you can call me directly if you need anything sorted while your hear." he added.

" I am already way too overwhelmed to begin to know what I could need sorting about besides the obvious but thanks nonetheless." she replied.

He laughed good-naturedly, and like Judith, he looked irresistible in his evening suit as she did her dinner dress.

They'd been out shopping for her just before they sat for late lunch. she was thrown off course when she realised where he was taking her to eat. she admitted she hadn't make provision for such an occasion, But as Nicholas was the perfect gentleman, He sorted it, like he always did.

They had the same kind of effortless style and high taste for exquisite things. it was a common ground for them and their evening out revealed this much to her.

Most of his friends had assumed he had finally summoned up the courage to have a lady by his arm in public, but after much speculation, he put them straight, introducing her as herself without the coupled title. she thought to herself how adorable he was to maintain that she was just a client on a trip to the city he practically controlled.

He was a nice guy, she said to herself as she watched his car disappear from sight. she went back to her room imagining how much longer she would have to keep up appearance like this.

She loved it all.

The glitz and glamour. Everyone around her was well dressed and polished. It was a great environment to be in and she knew she fitted it just well. she believed she would do just fine with all this new developments around her. After just one night, she could tell what difference it would make in the long run.

Until now she was convinced she had been living her life in the shadows of others. The world she walked into tonight seemed to accept her more than her day to day world. she knew the class difference was exponential, but she was convinced now she did not want anything else but to be part of the elite. The movers and shaker of the world responded to her like she was one of theirs and this filling was very fulfilling. she talked to her mother about it later on that evening. They were both flying high on the thrill of what had happened and what was yet to come. she did trying to contact Dr Bernard to fulfil her promise but she did not get through to him. she imagined the hospital had somehow managed to bend him against his will to attend work. So she left him a message on his voicemail.

As she laid on her bed and thought of her day, she could imagine herself living in hotel rooms like this one, been spoilt by the servants. It seemed like a life befitting for a girl of her calibre. she loved everything about it. she let her imagination run wild as she believed everything and anything was possible if you lived in a world like the Wright's daily. she laid on her bed lost in deep thoughts and saying to herself that this was the life she aspired for and everything she loved and wanted,and then with a satisfied smile, she let sleep consume her body.

CHAPTER 8

It had been an exhilarating week for Judith. she had been attending movie functions, meeting new partners to set up the production contract and every relevant publishing rights, so that all aspects of the current project would be handled by the Wright's company.

she spent days talking to several editors, potential corporate sponsors, independent agents, commercial filming agents, lawyers, accountants, health insurance sales men, Actors and actresses from every part of the country and abroad. The emerging faces only had to be in with the right crowd to gain recognition and acceptance into the next available movie role, but Judith wasn't in amongst that crowd. she was part of the reason the crowd gathered where ever they attended. Every one was interested to know who would play the lead role for this particular box office potential film. And the Wright's were at the forefront of this entire campaign. These sort of film gatherings was a culture in itself. One which Nicholas' great grand parents happened to be a part of since the Forties.

They had photographic memorabilia dating back the early days of the British film making industry. His grand father kept pictures of himself with renowned British film directors like Michael Powell, Carol Reed and David Lean. His family was raised on this culture and the public who knew almost too well of their family history respected their prominence. All movies that had been commissioned by the Wright's had been box office smash hits. This had been their play since the late 60's.

The British film industry recognised their worth, and now it was yet another rally for who would be selected to form the casting crew. The entire knowledge of this process was never thoroughly revealed to the public, it remains the case presently, but this was the anticipation such functions created within the industry itself. A-Listers could put them selves up for consideration but it usually is down to families like the Wright's to decide who gets cast.

Even though the wrights' were not openly campaigning at any one point, several smaller film companies assigned to such responsibility were usually sponsored directly by the wrights family. Despite their amassed wealth, anyone with large funds to invest had to be made aware of this project. And there were always public/private companies ready to make a contribution.

The wrights were hugely favoured because of the integrity they'd maintained over the years so Nicholas was confident that all the filming rights and binding agreements were going to be set up and handled by him successfully.

Over the next coming month, he was prepared to give the press all the answers they needed to justify why his family had decided to make this business decision. Judith was thinking about the final number of film to be sold, and the price, and how many countries were going to buy into it for their own market, there was so much intricate details that she always felt she ought to know about which was now readily available to her during these functions. This made her truly grateful for this opportunity which was sponsored by Nicholas Wright.

Nicholas Wright was immensely impressed by the efforts Judith had put into her role during the functions, and particularly so with the way she took command of interviews on the companies behalf, a tactics Nicholas was always reserved about and felt he was the only one suitable to address publishing agents. He was intrigued by everything she did, and couldn't believe the level of involvement she showed. They could be at opposite ends of the function area but they couldn't keep their eyes off each other. It was always as if they were in their own little world and no other person present existed. He was delighted to be working with her. It was the end of the second week since she left London and her mother was understandably nervous about it. she had been told her daughter had anxiety issues, so she feared for her well-being. Whenever they spoke over the telephone Judith would reassure her that everything was just fine, and that she didn't need to worry about things excessively.

Earlier in the week, she had promised her mother that if the campaign functions were going to extend longer than the end of the current week, she would return home for the weekend to spend some time with her.

By the end of the week, Nicholas had told her that all the loose ends were no where close to been tied up, and he felt that a lot more travelling was expected. Judith was prepared for all that was needed to make sure the Wrights family was satisfied. she had spoken to the doctor as regularly as time had afforded her, but she knew he needed them to be together again. she wanted this much but there was very little she could have done about it in the last two weeks. This made her think a lot more about what family life would be like if she was constantly on the road.

she thought about his career too, if he was to be her husband someday, how would he fit family life into his dedicated service to the hospital. He had been at the hospital on and off since his last break and was spending more time at home now than he had done in a few years. But they both knew these spells of freedom for a medical practitioner was always short lived. The hospital used to be undermanned but there seemed to be an improvement now as new staff had been reassigned to practice at the hospital. It did not take away the fact that he was still the head of the unit and his presence was in high demand, but it only meant that he had more people to train and have them do a lot more of the basic work he would have had to deal with himself.

The day had ended well for Judith and now she performed her evening rituals at the Hotel she way living in.

She had her dinner, soaked herself in the bath with lavender and scented oils, she applied her facial mask and pranced around the suit with a white towel over her chest and another wrapped over head. she watched a few of the televised functions she'd attended earlier on in the week on the entertainment channels. It was so surreal. she saw herself constantly on TV now mingling with Sophisticated personalities of the British   Film Industry. she was excited that everything was going on smoothly. it was all she expected it to be, and not the rare occasions where she found herself dissatisfied with the organisers she associated with forcing her to pull out at the last minute.

It had just been exhilarating for the last two weeks and she was beginning to enjoy herself. Before her last tragedy, she didn't think she would have been half as prepared for this experience as she was now if things didn't happen the way it did. she felt good about herself.

Stronger and more confident than she'd ever felt in years. she felt good not only because of her shot at the prospects of being the leading character in the movie, but also that somehow, she believed she was a part of history.

Even   Nicholas had told her, she was just as graceful in a room full of people like Marilyn Monroe was during her performing career. This was the only comment coming from Nicholas that made her understand how he and others saw her, not more how she saw herself. she could only dream of living her life in anyway comparable to the Hollywood superstar. But all the same it was always better to be classed amongst the greats. she spoke to her mother on the telephone while she pampered herself, and much more, they watched the same television stations, so whenever Judith appeared, they would both burst into laughter and have more chit chatter about the day that event was recorded. They spoke for hours and finally decided to call it a night.   When she got off the phone to her mother she decided to call Dr Oakfield. she looked at the clock on the wall, it was 1:30AM and she imagined he would be in surgery, but she picked her mobile phone and punched in his numbers to try her luck.

There had been a break in communication between them and she could tell that he would be upset. But there was very little she could have done to change the way things were the last couple weeks. she had promised him that she wouldn't let her busy schedule come in-between them, but the reality of things as it stood proved otherwise.

The phone rang several times and went into his voicemail. she was reluctant to leave him a message so she tried ringing again. After her third attempt without an answer, she gave in. she spoke into her phone sounding tired.

" Hello Doc, I've tried getting through to you, I can imagine you trying to save yet another life. This trip has turned out to be a lot more hectic than I thought it would be, but it gets all the more exciting every passing day. I can't say I wish You were here with me. But I do. I also feel like I owe you an apology, I have not fulfilled my promise to you, just so you know it's been due to circumstances beyond my control. it's just been crazy the last two weeks. I hope you understand". she said, Pausing briefly. she felt good about the sincerity in her message.

"I will be back in London by the weekend, it would be lovely to spend sometime with you before I leave for Los Angeles on Monday. Well, call me when you get some free time." she added and placed her mobile phone down by the bed side.

she had to admit it to herself, she missed him, and the nights she spent alone were her constant reminder. she longed to be touched. It had been an exhausting week for her and she felt she deserved to be pampered. she fought the desire she felt growing inside her, it was a feeling she knew very well. It would take a few more days if this urge was to be extinguished so she tried to cast her mind on other things. Although challenging, she was able to focus on her next days assignment. It was the distraction she needed to focus on other things besides her guilty pleasures. The coming days were over soon enough and she was back in London on Friday afternoon.

she returned home early on Friday morning and was glad to be with her mother. They spent the day together catching up on lost time, she loved to be with her mother. she felt now was the only time she had to learn all she needed to know about their family history. she asked all the vital questions and she was happy getting all the answers she needed. she saw her mother grieve over her fathers death. she knew they truly loved each other, she always thought it was rear to find such happy couples. she never could remember them having an argument as a child, there was always abundance of love to be shared amongst them as a family and it was painful to see her mother live out the rest of her life absent of husbands love. It had been a hellish experience for them so now they only had each other to care for one another.

They shared a special mother daughter bond and the night was sealed with an evening meal specially made for Judith. It was a celebration of her accomplishment this far appreciating her career and her mother went all the way to show her admiration. Before the night was over she had spoken to Doctor Oakfield and they'd agreed to meet the following day. He wasn't scheduled for his days off until the next weekend but considering she was going to be away for another three weeks, he felt duty bound to make himself available for her at least for a couple of days. He entrusted his work load to be handled by his second in command, and insisted that unless it was highly critical, he wasn't to be contacted until Monday morning.

It had been a very busy week for him, but as promised he left the hospital at 3.00pm on Saturday.

He was excited about his meeting with Judith but a part of him felt that their passion was wearing thin.

He arrived at his home just under an hour later and hurried himself into the bathroom to tidy up.

Judith was expected any moment now and he needed to be seen as the well groomed male figure she adored. He got himself dressed in his comfortable lounge attire and played some Jazz music to set the mood. As he helped himself to some wine and sprawled across the couch to catch a glimpse of what was showing on TV, he heard his door bell. That must be Judith, he thought to himself.

He approached the door with a grin and nothing short of the feeling of an excited child who was about to receive their fondness gift. He opened the door and their eyes met. she was wearing a long over all coat, and the kinkiest six inch heel shoes he'd ever seen.

And the scent of her perfume was divine. she noticed the hint of admiration on his face and she wondered if he knew she was here to fulfil her desire and promise to him.

" You look ravishing". Gazing at her as he held open the door and watched her walk into his living room. When he turned around he saw her standing without her coat. she looked like a goddess in her red and black laced underwear.

He smiled at her in admiration as he walked towards her. As their bodies met, they kissed passionately. It was an intense moment of fulfilment for them.

" It's always great to share moments like this with you Judith", He said, Gazing into her warm eyes. He ran a practised hand up her silky thigh, and then kissed her again.

"You make it worth my while doctor. I may be one of your patients who needs to be saved right now". He smiled at her, then kissed her harder again. He was beginning to unwind from the pressures of his manic work routine.

" I was beginning to think I wouldn't see you again. I've lost count of how many times I wished you'd turn up at my door step to surprise me". He said.

"Well you can say now that wishes do come true", she replied, leading her hands through his shirt and stroking his chest.

"I guess It does, perhaps after every two very long weeks". He said. Forcing a smile on to her face.

"You are so adorable", she said. she was thrilled that he felt her absence. it was an unusually good feeling for her considering that she hadn't dated very much in the past. "It hasn't been particularly easy for me either". she added.

" I understand how much this project means to you. I don't think I've met anyone as driven as yourself. I believe it will all be worth it in the end. You deserve your Big break.". He said. she felt good by the validity of his words. He had told her that she was an amazing actress, and the wrights would be foolish to pass on her role as the lead character.

" Its a shame I have to be gone for another three weeks, maybe longer depending on how things plan out". she said.

" I'll Have to cherish every minute with you then just in case it is my last." He said, the sarcasm in his voice was unmistakable.

" I hope you are not too tired because I have a Treat for you", she said, with a hint of seduction in her tone.

" For you I'm prepared to stay up for another 48hours If you know what I mean", he said, and she smiled. He was dead tired but couldn't let it show. He noticed how sexy and pretty she looked and couldn't help running his hands through her body.

she was a very beautiful woman, he couldn't imagine another man having her in the same ways he wanted. Although her career roles may prompt such indulgences, he tried to accept her professional expertise.

All the same, he was proud of her. He had never cared about how many other partners his past lovers kept. In his world, it was unimportant. He had met a few who had gone as far as openly admitting to him that they were seeing other people, so he always dealt with them on the surface. He didn't care then but he imagined why he did now.

He was a desirable man at the top of his professional status. Every girls dream of a perfect man to call their own. The financial disparity between them maybe be an issue for her, in truth, It would always be an allure for beauties like herself. Perhaps a distraction in most cases when she finds herself in amongst the rich and famous. This was a point of concern for him. He wasn't sure how she would handle the situation if it came down to it, but he let this thought pass.

"I need you to want me like your life depended on it" she said. He smiled at her lasciviously and she laughed. He already had a healthy appetite for her but what she said made him want her more. Even though he was worn out, he was never too tired to have sex with her.

" I think I can do that". He said.

They held each others hands and she let him take the lead as they walked into his bedroom. They spent hours in the bedroom exploring the endless depths of each others sexual desires. After that, they lay on his bed, relaxed and naked. After a few short conversations about the moment they'd just shared, he was fast asleep. she expected this to be the case. After all, he was only human.

He was handsome. she was genuinely attracted to him as she watched him sleeping. As challenging as their lives and career pursuits were going to become, she hoped that she would always have this yearning desire to be with him. she couldn't overlook the fact that there were a lot of admirers in the industry who would jump at any opportunity they found to bed her.

she also couldn't escape the fact that this much was also probable for him if they spent so much time apart. she knew that a lot of other men would discourage her from pursuing her dreams as an actress, but he never did. Instead he encouraged her.

He knew she loved what she did, and it was important that she did it to fulfil her own self worth.

Judith placed her head on his chest and listened to his heart beat as he lay sound asleep. Unable to sleep, she let her mind wonder into the coming weeks.

It was her first official trip to Los Angeles. It was a huge deal for her. It was part of what she always dreamt of, low and behold, the time was here. Unaware of how exhausted she was, she too drifted into a peaceful sleep and they slept through the night.

It was 9AM on Sunday and she was woken up by the sound of Dr Oakfield's voice. she could tell that his conversation was work related, he sounded frantic.

she got out of bed and walked slowly into the living room where he was taking his call.

Who ever it was on the other end of the phone and whatever it was they were talking about, there was no doubt that it was serious. she tried to make sense of it all by listening closely to his responses. she had never seen him so serious. she made him notice her presence and sat next to him on the sofa.

Shortly afterwards, he got off the mobile phone, looking disturbed. Ever so gently she touched his shoulder. He looked at her an instant later and with deep sadness in his face he spoke softly.

" There has been an accident." Dr Oakfield said.

He sighed deeply as he tried to compose himself. He had serve at the trauma unit for an extensive number of years and it always took a lot from him psychologically to process information like the one he had just received. his face looked blank for a short while before he was able to convey the news to Judith.

" A school tour bus took a tumble on the on its way back from Bradford. Fifty critical, nine pronounced dead. All children. That was the chairman of the hospital,he needs me back in surgery immediately".

He looked at Judith mournfully.

" When did this happen?" Judith asked.

Just about and hour ago. Apparently it is all over the news. He sat back in shock and turned on the TV. " They are calling in all surgeons and medical personnel to duty for this one. Any more deaths would raise national hell." He said.

There were bulletins about it on every local channel. The crash site looked horrific. He could see the ambulance services hastily trying to move bodies out of the bus which was practically up in flames, from what they could see, there was so much smoke surrounding the area, and the fire services where working hard to put the fire out. The cameras panned to the snarl of ambulances arriving at the scene. people where still been ushered away from the burning bus. Children where covered with blood and lacerations.

Dr Oakfield couldn't believe his eyes neither could Judith.

"What in God's name has brought this upon those

innocent children?" Dr Oakfield said, shooting up from the sofa and dashing into the bedroom to prepare himself.

In his absence Judith spoke in a choked voice.

" Oh My Goodness, God save them". she gazed at the television in shock. It was at moments like this that she felt the more sorry for medical personnels like Dr Oakfield.

They had to step into an already hopeless situation and try to restore hope. It made them less human than they really were. At least he had slept for a few hours, and had regained some strength to deal with the reality of this tragedy. it was going to be a very long haul for him, she knew this much evidently.

she rushed into the bedroom to find Dr Oakfield hurriedly putting on his medical attire. By the looks of it, he was going to be diving straight into action once he arrived at the hospital.

" This is awful, is there anything I can do to help?" she asked. feeling a sense of obligation as a medical professional herself. Her heart ached at what she had just seen on the news and it did remind her of why she took on pharmaceutical studies at university.

" I would say yes, but I don't think the time is suitable for you to make unscheduled plans. By my understanding, they are sending in as much support as is needed to handle the situation. You have to be out of the country in the morning to deal with an all important project that means the world to you. I would not want to be the one to encourage you to give that up."

" But this means the world to the families of those affected. I would love to help.". she said.

" I am sure you would, but trust me, this is not your call darling. Moreover, volunteers aren't much help in situations like this. it only bring about more confusion. Trust me, you are better off far away from the hospital, the site of most cases like this one isn't particularly easy to take in."

He kissed her on the forehead and minutes afterwards he was gone. she returned to the living room and she sat in horror as the broadcaster officially stated the number of deaths and injuries on the scene. it was such gruesome details been televised and she was in utter disbelief. she considered herself lucky to still be alive, and could only begin to imagine what the doctor would be going through within the next few days in attempts to save lives.

Twenty-four hours had past, and she'd been glued to the television watching the chaos unfold. she had been on the telephone to her mother on several occasions within that time and they shared their sympathy for the victims.

she stayed in his flat expecting his call, but all to no avail. Judith prepared herself for her flight which was scheduled for noon. she discussed all the necessary details with her agent for the purpose of leaving no loose ends. she wasn't expecting a call from him anytime soon which was understandable, but she left him a note and placed it by his bedside.

she wrote a note to the doctor expressed her disappointment about the turn of events. she made it clear that she would contact him when she arrived in America.

she did state however that she had concerns for the distance and time soon to be created between them and it was going to be difficult for her to cope. she knew he would be dealing with chaos for days so she wished him strength to see things through. It was a heart felt note and she believed he would read it, perhaps in a more relaxed state whenever he returned home.

she left the flat worrying about him and this made her feel helpless as she didn't know what to do about anything. Doctors were trained to deal with situations like this, but in reality, when major emergencies like this occurred, all limits and guidelines went right out the window. it was always down to the brave professionals to deal with the situation without loosing their balance on duty. she knew they would demand a lot of his time at the hospital until the situation was well under control.

she knew he loved the rush of moments like this, it kept him on his toes, and she knew he thrived on it. He had a soft spot for children, she knew he would give it his all to save the most lives he could, but knowing his track record, she feared this emergency was going to alter the record of his impeccable work history.

she arrived at the station and was going through her materials before her flight to Los Angeles. she was due to leave in six hours and couldn't board her flight without speaking to Doctor Oakfield.

she called him one more time and to her surprise, he answered. He told her it was absolute chaos. He said he hadn't stopped working since he left the flat.

They had lost quite a lot of deaths.

"It must be awful for the parents of those children," she said, sounding worried.

" It is. For the first time, I've lost my zeal to continue this profession. I just feel so sorry for the ones we lost. The entire situation was beyond our control." He replied sounding exhausted. But this was what she feared for the most. It was something she had long since expected. An uncontrollable situation that would affect his drive towards work. she knew he had a soft spot for children, and they happened to be the ones he had to cater for.

" I am very sure you saved the most you can." she said, trying to reinstate his confidence.

" I did. I saved all those assigned to me, only five passed. These five were critical who were left unattended to by other surgeons. I've instructed for a committee to sit for a hearing on this matter. We were all assigned a sizeable amount of patients, I can not for the life of me understand why those children were left unattended to. I just can't." He said.

" Don't worry about it. You've done your very best. Everyone knows you have maintained a high standard of practice at that hospital. It is not your fault that those children passed. No one is going to hold you responsible." she said.

" The poor sods died due to internal bleeding. And perhaps the shock of what had happened was a contributing factor. I am absolutely mortified." he replied.

" I wish I could stay around to welcome you back home but I leave for America in six hours. I am angered by the fact that I would be gone for quite a while." she said.

" It's OK. I understand. Your career is shaping up Just the way you always hoped for. I say Make the best of it. Do Call me when you settle in. But I've got to go now,I need to return to surgery." There were some more children in unstable conditions that he needed to see to.

" OK I will." she said, then she hung up. she knew he would be dealing with chaos for days, so she didn't bother ringing him before she left.

It was hard to believe it. she was off to America. Her trip was to be a life altering experience by comparison, and so shockingly unimportant in view of the tragedy faced by the families of those children who had died.   The accident had claimed the lives of so many children who had hopes and drams of becoming something significant to the society in the future.

At the hospital, there were hundreds of people scattered all across the halls. There were people on the trolleys been moved from one theatre room to the next.

The entire staff were working overtime to keep the situation under control and inevitably they were all exhausted. Those who couldn't be fed were put on Iv's.

There was an unlimited amount of food supplies to

sustain the patients and their families who had refused to leave the hospital until they saw their children in a more stable condition. It was a circus at the hospital, although ironic, it was more tears than any form of amusement.

As The day unfolded, Dr Oakfield worked tirelessly to sustain as much life as he could. It was a relief for him to see that a lot of the families of those children who had survived were beginning to panic less following the news that their children were in a more stable condition.

Judith sat in her hotel room, watching the news about the incident. I was reported that the accident was primarily due to tour companies negligence and matters were been investigated further.

she tried to focus on the trip ahead of her but the news was all too distracting. she felt like a kid going going to camp for the first time. she felt a combination of fear and excitement.

In between her preparations to leave, she had been on the phone to Nicholas Wright. They spoke at length about the Los Angeles campaign and particularly about the accident that had occurred in London.

" It is such a terrible news," He said, " I have been on the phone trying to send relief aid to the hospitals where these children are been attended to,"

" Yes it is. I happen to know someone very dear to me who happens to be at the forefront of the whole calamity." she said.

" Who is this person?" He asked, prying for more details.

" A doctor. A very special person in my life at the moment. He is the head surgeon at one of the trauma units." she said.

" Which hospital?" he asked inquisitively.

" St Helia." she replied.

" You don't say, That happens to be the only

hospital on top of the entire situation as it stands. My last request was for aid items to be sent to this particular hospital." He said.

" It is not particularly a good time for them at the hospital. He told me a few things about how things were been dealt with and he didn't sound too happy." Judith said.

" Well who would?" Nicholas Replied." Anyway, why don't we distract ourselves with more exciting matters. The big show in LA is in two days. Are you psyched up for it?" he asked with amusement in his voice.

"There is going to be a dinner party to announce all the associates and potential investors tomorrow night, there after, we are off the the heart of Hollywood where you get to have a real feel of what it is going to be like on set. We are going to be travelling back and forth London-Los Angeles when we get closer to the shoot, but for now, its gong to be hands on procurement. We need to make sure we have the right guys on call." He said. His elaborate description of what was to be accomplished made Judith realise that it was all going to be one hell of a journey before she could actually get cast.

she knew that this was all she longed for and by the end of it all, she was going to be familiar with the ins and outs of the movie industry. But for the moment, as it was all beginning to unravel, she was nervous. she was in on the big time she had worked for all her life and it was enough to make her anxious.

she was looking forward to meeting famous actors and actresses and embracing the experience with all her heart. she hoped that she would be well received, which means that there was guaranteed prospects of future castings. Her hearts ambition was to be loved and having so much followers on her social media websites, which would ensure her feet strongly secure in history. she imagines herself on the Hollywood walk of fame. If this particular project was oversold and hit number one on at the box office, she knew he It was highly desirable for her to be heading overseas on this project. If they were successful with taking on the project, this would be real victory for the Wright family. she was hoping for this much to be the case.

" I have to admit it Judith, I feel like we are on to something special here." Nicholas said sounding enthused by the whole prospects ahead of them.

" Well that depends on what you mean exactly." she replied sounding jittery.

" Come on what's impossible at this point? As much as I know your a virgin to this sort of events, you'll soon find that this is part of what would make you hunger for more each time there is a new project at hand". He said.

" Well I am not sure how to process this whirlwind of emotions." she said.

" Try hard to relax. By the time we get to LA, you'll be more excited to get things rolling than you are now just trying to imagine things. I promise you will love it." " Well we will have to wait and see how well I get on won't we?" she said.
" Sure thing Judith. I will be with you every step of the way. I believe in you. You moved like a real natural couple weeks ago, keep that up, and in no time you will be up and running with confidence."

" OK. If you say so". she replied.
They discussed more about specific details. He gave her the details of who would be attending the dinner and suggested a preferred style of attire an for her. she wouldn't have know how to approach any of these event if it wasn't for Nicholas and for that she had him to be thankful for this opportunity.

" I am glad to have you talk me through these things. there is so much detail to take in, truthfully, I'll be lost without your support."she said.

" That's why you have me on your team. I think we do need to get a move on though. If we miss our flight, we miss the dinner event, plus there isn't any other flight out of the country for another two days. " He said.

" Although I have made arrangements for a private Jet as an alternative,I hope we wouldn't have to use that option just yet." He added.

" Oh wow. really. I've never been on a private jet before." she said.

" Well that is the part of the perks you'll be getting as we progress. Having said that,If it does become necessary to visit New York, I guess you would be having your first time experience very soon."
she was excited about the sound of it all. she had imagined everything happening no other way, and to know it was all happening one way or another was truly exhilarating.

she wasn't used to this kind of lifestyle but she was eager to savour every moment. He briefed her on every last minute detail and she took notes.

" I had better get my self ready then." she said.

" Yes you better. I have made reservation for us shortly after you arrive. it's at my favourite Italian restaurant on Melrose. I think you'll love it. I thought we could see the town before dinner. Perhaps do some last minute shopping if need be. It's a shame we won't be on the same flight but I've double checked all your reservations. You'll have all the assistance you need when you arrive so do not worry too much." He said. " You don't mind I've gone ahead to make reservations do you?"

she hesitated. she had thought about his intentions momentarily and thought it would be unfair to Dr Oakfield if she was to make herself available to Nicholas Wright in the way he proposes, but she waved the thought.

" I am not sure I can have you cancel it if you've made the effort already. But I guess it would be a good way to go through any other details we haven't addressed yet. I do trust you still maintain your professional integrity." she said.

He laughed and promised to keep things neat between them.

" I'll be good. After all, we do need to begin to learn a great deal about each other if we are going to be working closely.". He added.

"You do have a fair point." she said.

" You are going to be very proud of this relationship with the family when this is all over." He said.

" I do hope so." she replied." I am grateful already as it is, anything more would be added value.". she said.

" I am prepared to go all the way with you, so long as you return the same.". He said.

" I would." she added, sounding sincere and very humble to have been granted this exposure.

" I am sure you would". He said sounding pleased. Their communication had been very straightforward, and so far, they both seemed pleased about moving things forward. she thought through things as she ended the conversation. she wanted everything to go well so she forced herself into an optimistic state of mind.

A few minutes later she called for her hired driver to meet her at the hotel lobby packed her things to leave. Less than forty-five minutes later she was at the airport, and on her flight.

As promised all reservations were in place when she arrived at LAX. Shortly after she settled in, she was contacted by the manager of the hotel she was checked into. He told her that a driver was waiting for her to take her to lunch whenever she was ready. Full of excitement, she prepared herself and went out to see the beautiful sunny city of Los Angeles. As promised they met at the Bottega Louie, Nicholas had been there at the opening of the restaurant and loved it. she arrived in a limo and Nicola Wright was waiting outside to receive her. He looked as handsome and well dressed as he always did. she was looking just as stunning and as always there was a warm sensation between the pair when ever they met each other. she always looked more like a model than an actress, as he did a male model than a business executive. she admired his sophisticated nature and quick witted sense of conducting business. They'd both had good times together and to date, she hasn't been able to fault him on any level.

They hugged and kissed each other twice on the cheek. They chatted as they approached the entrance of the restaurant. They were welcomed and shown to a quiet corner table. They ordered lobsters and then a steak meal as an alternative option chased with the best red wine on the menu. As they sat and chatted, conversation led to her love life. This was unexpected but she felt obliged to discuss the subject with him.

" You spoke warmly about this Dr Oakfield. Tell me about him." he said. "I mean it does sound to me like you two have a lot going on at the moment."
she smiled at him as she sipped from her glass. Then she spoke" He is a lovely gentle man from London. And we have been dating each other for a few months now. As I am sure you know of my health incident, believe it or not he saved my life."

" I took some time to look him up. He seems like quite the messiah at the hospital." Nicholas said trying to disguise his sarcasm and prior investigative measures.

" I can see how you'd come to that conclusion. The fact is he is. Perhaps the best in the region if you ask me," she said confidently.

" How do you aim to strike a balance with you new found pursuits and his busy work schedule. It must become exhausting keeping up with each others busy lives, especially when you begin this project." He said.

He noticed she was puzzled bout this line of questioning but he let her take her time to respond. she did feel uncomfortable discussing her private life but she indulged his inquisition.

" It isn't going to be easy. Nothing really is these days. There is always some level of difficult involved especially when it comes down to serious relationships. But we are keeping our options open for now. Marriage and having a family together has been discussed, and I do intend on giving that aspect of my life some serious thought and consideration."

The waiter arrived asking if they needed anything, and Nicholas waved him off.

" So you do plan on settling down and having a family. With this guy or are you keeping that open too? He asked with a grin on his face.

" He is my only interest as it stands. So yes." she said it in a surprisingly firm tone and he felt her defences were raised at this point.

" I hate to pry, but seeing that we are going to be spending a lot of time together, I hope you don't mind me asking you these questions.

" I don't mind the questions. it's the intent behind them that always seems to interest me more." she said, keeping a straight face and leaving no room for him to read her.

" He realised there way more to the depths of her feelings for the doctor but he wasn't sure how to confront her about it.

" As much as I would like to be in a meaningful relationship with someone. Having kids and settling down is very demanding. I have tried to convince myself it's not for me, perhaps it may never happen." she said.

" Are you not sure he is the one to fulfil that aspect of your life with?" He asked wanting to get to the depths of her feelings for the doctor.

" It would be disappointing for him if I was ever to admit to him that I was never going to be his significant other half. But the same time it doesn't change the way I feel about him. He is a very good man, and any woman would be lucky to claim him as hers." she replied. " in so many ways, it would actually be a relief to have that aspect of a girls life satisfied by someone she could trust. It would only take my unavailability and lack of interest to have any kind of doubts about him, but even at that, he deserves to be happy. He works too hard". she added.

" So you wouldn't be disappointed if he was to get involved with somebody else in your absence?" He asked, he seemed hungry to know exactly how she felt.

" He is a dazzling young man. After all, nothing has been set on stone for us. I know I do have strong feelings for him and it would be a shame to jeopardize that over something less meaningful". she said.

" Do you think he feels the same way about you then?" He asked.

" I know he has a keen interest in having a relationship with me that should lead to kids and a marital status, but it's too early to say. we have had this talk about it a lot lately."

" But you are not ready for that." He said not expecting a direct response from her.

" I do know I am ready to take this project on the road. That is all I seem to have on my mind at the moment. I just can't see the point of anything else stopping." she replied.

" How would you manage the situation if you were in my shoes? I mean you haven't particularly been out spoken about you private life." she asked.

" Well I was married once upon a time. she was a lot like you. Career minded,fiery, and a lot of the time brutally honest with her opinion and how she translated facts." He said as he paused to dig into his steak.

" So, What happened? that summary of a lady fits

my idea of a perfect match for Mr Nicholas high and mighty Wright", she said forcing a roar of laughter among them.

" she was actually based out here in LA. she was the reason I moved the business out here 5 years ago. It was all lovely to begin with. Believe it or not, I was prepared to settle down here in Hollywood. she was a TV presenter when I met her. she wasn't big on the idea of marriage as she had tried once and it didn't quite work out how she expected."

" But you managed to talk her into it right?" Judith asked leading him into more specifics details.

" Yes. Well it only seemed right at the time. We both had it all figured out. Well I thought we did." He said.

" But then Two kids and Three mansions later, she turned into a money monster. Nothing seemed enough to please her until I ended up in court with divorce proceedings against me."

" No prenuptial agreement?" Judith asked almost certain she knew the answer to her only question.

" Well there wasn't. It didn't seem necessary at the time. Money was never the issue for me. After one year of monthly court appearances, I paid her off. Plus the state gave her full custody of the children. I went through the entire process wanting to have my kids closer to me, but when it went pear shape, I let it as it was. Paid for alimony and maintained the courts directions to communicate with the children."

" That seemed a bit unfair." Judith said.

" You try telling that to the Judge whom I almost pushed off his high horse when he ruled In her favour. He ruled that he was convinced I lived such an extravagant lifestyle that It was difficult for him to believe that I would be available to give the kids the sort of attention and upbringing they deserved. Never have I heard such nonsense in my entire life. I provided for my kids. As a matter of fact, they had too much of everything to ever feel neglected." He said.

"And what happened?" she asked

" Put it this way, she landed herself just enough to never work another day of her miserable life". He said. Judith could only begin to imagine how much settlement he referred to by speaking of it in such manner. But she knew the Wrights families worth. it was probably a hand out to his ex-wife, but that alone was only left to ones imagination. Nicholas smiled at Judith as she remained silent allowing his to speak at his own accord.

" it was never quite the same after that. We were never quite comfortable being in the same place at the same time. Although I bought another home here in Hollywood, I began to find the entire experience distasteful. So I returned to England."

" How did you fair with the kids?" she asked.

" Well that aspect of the whole situation was the most unpleasant. I had to wait until they had a break from school to spend any meaningful type of time with them. But even at that, I had to deal with her as well. it was never fair on them, but the evil mother had her way of trying to turn them against me.

" I won't write her off entirely. she was OK for a while. But suddenly she turned malicious even towards the kids."

" How do you mean?" Judith fired on with her questioning. Applying just the same amount of intensity to exude her curiosity.

" she would leave them indoors for days without a nanny, and when she returned, she would abuse them physically. Eventually, she found a nanny to look after them but then, she came home to them less and less often."

It was a troubling story for Judith to listen to. she was raised in a happy home. It was impossible for her to understand how other children were raised without the abundance of love she experienced as a child. she wondered how they must feel now, and how damaged they must be psychologically as a result of their mothers bad behaviour. Judith pressed on wanting to know more about his ex-wife.

" Why didn't you press charges to reverse the courts decision?" she asked.

" That's another story. We got into all sorts of arguments over this issue, and for the sake of the kids emotionally stability, I tried to make less of a legal matter out of the whole situation."

" Poor kids" Judith said.

" I couldn't understand what it was that got her so distracted, so I hired a private detective to monitor her affairs. Now that's where it all blew out of the water. All along she was involved in a volatile relationship with another woman." Nicholas said.

" What do you mean?" Judith asked.

" I mean, she was romantically involved with another woman for several years. Perhaps way before we got involved. They had more ups and downs than the Thorpe Park roller coaster. The only way she could have kids was to form a loveless relationship wit a man, and after the issues arrived, she didn't need the man any more." He said.

" And the target was you." Judith said.

" Precisely." Nicholas replied." When I threaten to expose her scandalous affair, she gave me custody of the children without batting an eye. Afterwards she went missing for a couple of years. Needless to say, They both got got eloped in Vegas." he added.

" Did you hear from her or did she visit the kids?"

" Nope. Not once after she handed over custody." he said.

" You must have hated her for it." Judith said.

" I did." He said." With a passion" HE added.

" But I learnt to accept it. I didn't know much about married life until I realised this was a real possibility.

And to crown it all. There is a whole community of others these sort of things happen to." he said." I didn't feel so bad after I realized that." He added

They both laughed over it. she was pleased to see he had found a way to deal with situation after such heartbreaking events"

" Oh well. It did turn out OK after all. I love my kids and I learnt how to play mummy and daddy at the same time. plus they keep me pretty busy. At times like this when I'm on the road, they are happy spending time with my parents. I think they Love Grandpa, and grandma a lot more than they love me. But hey, as long as they are happy. Nothing else matters.

" It must have been difficult raising them all on your own." she said.

"It was hard at first. I must confess. I had zero patience, But you learn to adjust everyday." he replied. " the beauty of it is, you learn to make the best decisions on your own. It might not always seem that way, but with no one to undermine it, you build a stronger relationship with the kids as they learn to accept your authority as the law." He added.

"Sounding a bit like a control freak there Mr. Wright." she said with a smile. He smiled too and let the ambiance pass as they dug into their food.

" I must say, what did come as a shock was the news of her death." He said. His words startled Judith.

" she Was found dead in her Las Vegas Pent house Suit. Apparently she was basically living the life of a rock star. Doctors say she died of a possible heart attack. By my understanding she died penniless." He said.

" That must have been heart breaking news for you". Judith said.

" For me No, but for the Kids, I couldn't tell them. My parents had to do that in my absence. I couldn't bear the look on their face to deliver such a terrible news to them." He said.

" I was very bitter about it for a long time. My kids were going to remain motherless for the rest of their lives. To make matters worse, It was her supposed partner who instigated the whole break up with us. she led her to believe their relationship was genuine, but in reality, she was after the fortune. she trusted her with everything, until one day she returned to realize everything was gone." Nicholas said.

" Would you say she deserved it?" Judith asked.

" Truthfully, I couldn't care less about anything that had happened to her. I always felt there was something dishonest about her, so I wasn't entirely surprised about her misfortune. I still get angry about it sometimes as I never could believe how I let myself fall into the hands of such a creature. I've learnt to get through without letting it trouble me as much. I'm just not going to do anything that foolish again." He said.

He sounded bitten by his experience and it appeared to Judith that he wasn't prepared to be bitten twice. He had been betrayed by the one woman he had children with, and it was obvious he wasn't ready to jump the broom again. By the sounds of it, Judith directed the portion of blame to her. she wasn't who she appeared to be in the beginning of their relationship and he had to suffer for it putting together the pieces.   For the first time she could sense his vulnerability regardless of his tough exterior. It was easy to see that he was prepared to play it safer. It was a very intriguing background information about Nicholas and she was drawn to him in more ways than she did prior to this date.

she wondered how a man so dashing was still single regardless of his failed marriage. she pictured him as one of those men who, once bitten, was never open to having any serious relationship that allowed companions get too close. she considered the depths of what she had just heard, and thought, perhaps that wasn't the case. he was probably open to having another meaning relationship. One that would reconfigure all the trust issues his past marriage had created. she thought he might be willing to entertain a committed relationship with someone worthy. Either ways, she thought he'd had a valuable experience in life.

" There is a lot about you than what meets the eye Nick", Judith said, smiling at him.

He smiled at her in return. Particularly hearing her refer to him as Nic.
" Well it depends on what your looking at Judith" He replied. Flashing his perfect set of teeth.

" I think your experience with your ex-wife has made you a much better man". she said.
" Well thank you. Ill accept that compliment. I think I deserve it." He replied.

" I am not sure how I would cope if I were in your schools, but your story sure is a valuable lesson for anyone considering to get into the world of marriage." she said.

" But don't get me wrong. Marriage can be a beautiful thing. but people who don't get to have same experiences do know that such experiences exist, so they are safer leading a loving life in a household with a flock of kids." he said.

" It is a shame what your ex-wife did. It does take men like you to speak up about it to create a general awareness about these sort of things." she said.

" Can you imagine a man of my statue on a TV talk show talking about this stuff. How embarrassing." He said, laughing out loud despise himself. Judith saw sense in what he meant.

" It wouldn't be embarrassing, it would just be more of a statement about your thoughts on the issue and your level of concern for other men in your position who get exploited by the re-occurrence of such practice." she said.

" I think it is a smart concept to air, but I'll hate been the one to spill. Men in my position Pay out to get these sort of issues behind them, not to have a televised programme serve as a constant reminder." He said.   she shook her head in agreement. she hoped there would never be an issue of such in her life. she was happy to carry on without any real commitment if it means that she avoids this experience completely. But reality was always something different. It presents it own set of moments that distorts the possibility of that ever becoming the case until it actually happens.

" Well let us save that thought for now. Just consider your self lucky to have been granted forewarning." He said.

" Well thanks you Nic." she replied.

At a glance there, he saw that there was a spark between them. Seeing that the subject matter painted her gender in such negative light gave him an edge to gain her trust. But in-spite of the warmer reception he received from her now , he was most delighted that she'd spent the afternoon with him. When she went back to her hotel room after lunch, she couldn't stop thinking about their conversation.

What they had shared was uncommon, but nonetheless, she was happy that they were open to even have such communications between themselves. she was convinced she had gained the kind of validation a woman needed to be open to a man. He career was important to her, but forming a relation with the man who was going to make it all possible didn't seem like such a terrible idea. Unprofessional to a certain extent but necessary nonetheless.

she imagined how her life would be if there was a child between herself and the doctor now. It wasn't like she didn't want one, it was just not the right time to do so.

Her career was soon to become overly demanding

and it would be impossible to reconcile her life as an actress with becoming a full-time mum. What Nicholas' ex-wife had done was unforgivable by all moral standards, reeling him in, marrying him, having the kids, divorcing him to marry another woman and then suing for a fortune. Plus, abandoning them for her own selfish pursuits. That was wrong on all counts. That was something Judith would never consider doing. The fact was, you had to find yourself in a position like that to truly test your character. she tried not to put herself in that position, as the ex-wife or Nicholas himself. The thought of it all had woken up a certain curiosity in her mind that demanded she sought clarity about herself. she hadn't particularly been protective during intercourse with the doctor.

After prancing herself around the hotel room and stewing over the possibility, she suddenly felt unnerved about it all. she had to get a test done immediately. she called the reception and the receptionist answered. she asked to know where the closest pharmacist was and if it was walking distance from the hotel. Her dinner event was in four hours so she had ample time. The receptionist persisted on running this errand for her but Judith insisted, wanting to keep the knowledge of what she aimed to unravel to herself. she left her hotel room and returned with several test packs determined to have a varied result.

she dashed into the bathroom and was there for about twenty minutes. All the while she conducted this test she thought of the doctor. she wondered if he was in or out of surgery. she knew in her heart of hearts that she had genuine feelings for him, but she also knew in her heart of hearts that she needed this result to all return negative.

Now the fact that she did not want kids at this point of her life was irrelevant. All her priorities were about to shift if the test returned positive. she was distressed as she used one stick after the other expecting a different result but to her wildest amazement, she was dumbstruck. she had her back against the wall in the bathroom as she waited for the final stick to reveal it's result.

she dropped to her knees in disbelief as the last test result was the same as the previous nine. she could not believe her eyes or her present reality. she was pregnant.

CHAPTER 9

The dinner event in Los Angeles put everyone in high spirits. A-Listers were in high attendance. It was expected to be a massive turn out and the moment served its course. There were mini gatherings across the hall and the conversations held amongst top-class executives were small talks about the big times. The Wright's company had provided answers for the relevant groups who had supported their families legacy.

By the time they approached mid-night, Judith had forgotten about her test results. she was certainly carrying the doctors child but this wasn't enough to cause her any form of distraction. she was going to need a lot more of these events to keep her mind pre-occupied.

Despite the test result, she was walking across the hall confidently, and had had a good time meeting some of her favourite actors/actresses. Judith had almost been talked into another role to pull he out the wrights family care with an offer of more earnings but Nicholas had talked her out of it. He told her It was a strategy most families used to test the loyalty of any promising talent set to lead a box-office movie. If they succeed in convincing them to leave their current sponsors, this only created a bidding war, which in most cases has led to major investors dropping out of the campaign. she focused on the advice he'd given her on how to play the floor. The entire occasion was fabulous. It was a white and Black dinner party. There was champagne clavier, high rise ceilings and chandeliers and a lot of cameras flashing.

Judith and Nicholas had fallen into a convenient camaraderie as they walked side by side. They appeared to be a power couple.

Everyone knew a thing or two about the wrights family and to the public, they knew all too well that Nicholas was divorced and hadn't remarried, on the other hand, they knew nothing about Judith's relationship status, past or present.

They were looking forward to the next two weeks it was going to be back to back meetings and presentations. There were award shows for the newly released block buster hits and Nicholas had arranged tickets, all front roll seats. As they met and greeted the entertainment personalities, they scheduled private meetings with them to discuss further investment opportunities in weeks to come. Things were looking great for their campaign and time in America. They were flying to New York In the morning and Judith was ecstatic. They covered their agenda for the evening, and now, they were certain it was OK to call it a night.

The following day they flew to New York, by now Judith was getting used to the routine.

Their first meeting was scheduled as soon as they landed at J.F.K. Kennedy. It was a meeting with one of Nicholas' old friends. They'd been friends since he was a fresh graduate from Harvard, Mathiaus Hummer was a close friends to the entire family and as a Legal counsellor, Nicholas learned to take good advice from him.

They had a driver waiting for them to take them to their new york hotel, and another to drive them to meet Mathiaus at his office. Nicholas was planning to make this trip alone for confidentiality reasons. He insisted that she needed to rest as it was going to be a long day ahead of them.

" I'll be fine you go on and I'll see you later on for the meeting with Rockhill Agency. That is Our six -pm schedule." Judith said, detailing the specifics as they changed vehicles while the concierge moved their luggages into the hotel.

" I'll be gone for at least three hours. But you must ring me if anything pops up". Nicholas said speaking to Judith through the window of the Limo he was leaving in. They were warming up to each other and were beginning to show concern for each others well-being.

" I feel guilty just abandoning you in a hotel in New York. A city you've never been in alone before" He said, with a faint smile across his face.

" Thanks or your concerns NIC', I think I can manage." she replied. They treated each other like old flames who had to respect their professional space to maintain a healthy working relationship, but if Nicholas didn't know any better, he would have ignored the warning signs himself. He was attracted to her and she knew it. she smiled at him.

" Enjoy the service at the hotel, it's the best in the city. I promise not to be gone for too long. Take a hot bath, or a shower whichever you prefer and I'll be back before you even begin to miss me". He said.

They laughed it off and she walked away.

They were meeting with a promotions agency that would take photo shots of Judith to run Social media/commercial advertising for new line of products. They'd agreed it would help boost her image to the public, so she was pleased to see it through. As soon as she got into her hotel room she called her mother.

" How are you love?" Judith spoke playfully.

" I miss you too mum" she said.

" Yes it was great. And I've only just arrived in new York to do it all over again". she replied.

" But I told you mum, You can't loose sleep waiting on me to ring you like I was in London. The time difference changes all that. Right now I don't even know what my time clock is any more. I promise I'll always ring ya, and If I don't get through, I'll ring again."

" I am Now. I'll have a bit of rest for the next few

hours before I'm off to my meetings." she said.

" Yes mum. it's going to be lovely I can Feel it."
Judith said with a smile. she wanted to tell her mother
about her pregnancy, but found the courage not to. she
always told her mother everything, but as this wasn't a
normal conversation to have with her, she wasn't sure
how to break the news.

" I do hope your taking care of yourself too." Judith
said.

" Of course I am Mother. It is all going according to
plan" she added.

" I can't wait to finish with new york, I should be on
the next flight back home. Perhaps not London at first,
but any where close enough will do". she said. she
laughed. she was always pleased to communicate with
her mother. The only family he felt she truly had left in
the world.

" That's alright mum. It's going to be OK. I can't
wait to see you as well"

" Yeah, It was so horrible mum, I wonder how the
survivors must be feeling now." Judith said. Her mother
had been following the Tour bus accident and she told
Judith about all the details she'd missed. The situation
was coming under control, according to her mother, it
was an unnecessary loss of lives. They chatted for a
few more minutes then, and Judith yawned for the first
time.

she was advised to take a quick nap and Judith
contemplated on doing just that.

" I'll ring you tomorrow. Alright love." Judith said.

" Good Bye" she said.
As soon as she hung up, Nicholas called wanting to
know how she was settling in.

" It should be comforting for you to know that I'll be
in the same hotel as you for a change" Nicholas said
sounding relaxed and friendly.

" It is part of me meeting your security requirement"

He added.

" Well that's truly comforting. Excluding the security in the building alone. That's double thanks. It's easier getting into Buckingham palace than it is walking through the corridor in this place." she said.

" I Know that's why I chose the hotel for this trip. You'll be happy to know that you could have you own personal guards escort you around town with loaded guns if you wanted."

" I don't think I will be needing that just yet Nic." Judith said." I am anxious enough as it is, I wouldn't want to be a walking paranoia as well. I don't think so." she added.

" Well the word is out on the street now, everyone and anyone in the film industry knows we are here. I'll like to think I've kept my relationships neat, but out here, you always find that its better to take that extra security measure. Just in case" He said

" We are here to impress and secure the interest of our investors and supporters, we are not here to pick a fight or settle an old score or nothing of that sort are we?" Judith asked.

" Don't be ridiculous. it's nothing like that. But the fact remains, that you make enemies just as fast as you make friends in this field. One thing I know for sure is, I get myself prepared for every possible eventuality. You can never be too careful". He said

" I can't say I am pleased to here that, but again, thanks for the heads up. I won't forget that on e in a hurry." she replied.

" Your welcome." he said in a gentle manner.
I could use the reality check quite regularly she thought to herself.

" You have made a lot of things possible Nic, I owe it to you for being incredible so far." she said.

" Oh please, I can't take all the credit here. You have been sensational. And I know that when we finally begin filming, they are all going to love you for you.

You'll see." He said.

" Anyway, I've got to go now. I've only just arrived at Mr. Hummers office. Ill be back in no time. Pamper yourself and do all you need to get yourself dolled up, we will chat a bit more later on". He said.

After all they had the entire night to be together and so she agreed.

After they hung up, she lay in bed thinking about him. he was a nice gentle man. Well spoken and confident the way he communicated with her. It was so obvious to her that he was currently single. It was more so obvious to her that he was guarding himself from falling victim to yet another dysfunctional relationship like the one he had with his ex-wife. Betrayal and unwarranted desertion wasn't particularly easy to deal with by anyone's standards, but that was the memory he was left with, and his kids were going to be constant reminders of this memory.

He carried himself well as it appeared but, Judith could tell he needed a woman in his life that would compensate for the emotional turmoil he had to endure over the years. It was an experience that was sure to destroy anyone, male or female, evidently it did result to the death of his ex-wife, but somehow, he'd managed to keep his sanity.

she admired his determination to deal with the situation the way he has. Thinking of it brought her mind back to her currently developing situation. she didn't know what to do about it, but she needed to make up her mind soon. With her present schedule, weeks could turn into months faster than one could realize, and this only meant that she fell into a more critical position whether or not she wanted to keep the baby. she let herself drift into sleep thinking about it. she was jet Lagged and was beginning to feel the change in time-zones.

she met Nicholas a few hours later at the

reception area around five-thirty as agreed. They chatted at the bar area, and then left for west new york for her photo shoot. Judith was amazed at how busy new york city was. she always heard it been described as the city that never sleeps, and she was eager to see it for herself. It felt good to see the city during the summer. she loved the amazing view as they drove through Brooklyn bridge.

" Like what you see?" Nicholas asked as he noticed she was enjoying the scenery.

" Of course. I wouldn't want to live anywhere else if I was born or raised here." she said. she was energetic and refreshed after her little nap, and she felt really relaxed. she briefly took her gaze away from the window and she turned to smile at him.

" Well perhaps you should consider moving out here for a while. You can see how it works for you." He said. He'd spent so much time here, he thought of it as his second home, and in that time people were aware of his accomplishments in New York city.

The photo shoot went well, they took as much shots as they needed to satisfy future work for when it was required. she had a chance to ask all the questions she needed answers to. They had a few of their sales agents pitch a few new proposals to Nicholas. He didn't mind moments like this, he was a firm believer in the saying that a good turn always deserved another. He had run a lot of successful campaigns with the executives of this company and they knew as much as he did that they were onto a winner. After four straight hours of the days presentation they were finished. Nicholas shot Judith a quick glance and then looked at his wrist watch. Immediately, she knew what he was initiating. He wrapped up the meetings and gave them his thoughts on the marketing strategy they intended to apply. With both ends satisfied, he left them to get on with it.

He was scheduled to see Mario Castolanio. This

was his fathers very good friend. They had been friends with the family for over thirty years and Nicholas never visited America without stopping by the Castolanio's resident to see the family. His children spent a lot of time with Marios grand children. Nicholas' children loved it in his villa. They were business partners but did a lot of favours for each other. Judith knew a lot about the Castolanio family and she was keen on meeting the man himself.

What she didn't know was that the invitation was extended to her before they hit he road. she had always been under the impression that it was good fortune for her to be a part of Nicholas' team and so she signed on to reap the benefits of meeting movie moguls she'd always wanted to meet.

But Mario Castolanio had done his home work before accepting to run the current project along side

The wrights family. He had a particular liking for Judith. It was rear. He watched all her childhood theatre performances. He saw all he needed to see to know what kind of talent Judith was turning into. So he wanted to be part of those who would bring her to The big screen.

" I think you might find out soon enough that this meeting would go down as perhaps one of the most important meetings we would be having until we secure all our rights to produce this film." Nicholas said.
she couldn't help but agree. she saw sense in what he said, and for the first time she was convinced that she was going to be made a star. she told Nicholas that she felt nervous. she felt she wasn't truly ready for all this. But Nicholas was insistent. he wanted her to come visit the Castolanio's. That was his primary mission to accomplish.

" Look have I let you down this far?" He asked.

" Of course Not Nic." she replied slightly taken aback by his approach to open her up to what was true ly on her mind.

" Well then, you do know it's only a bit of fear right! It breeds anxiety and uncertainty. And I do not know fear." He said.

" I want to believe that I made the right decision to choose you Judith". He said.

Judith raised up her head and Looked into the eyes of the man standing before her. He had her full attention now. His choice of words to her most times were captivating and always overwhelming.

He spoke directly to her soul at this point and she said nothing more but walk towards him. He held the door open as she got into the limo. He had enormous respect for her attitude towards things. she exuded the right charisma that always made people want to go the extra mile for her sake.

He was so proud of his investment choice. After all she was an investment to his family's empire, besides her beauty and good nature, he was convinced that had made the right decision to support her ambitions. she noticed just how passive she had become around him. It was almost like he'd figured out just how to bend her to his will.

Even though it seemed like this wasn't his intentions, she felt his power and authority very intriguing. It seemed rude to go against his will anyway, she thought to herself. she accepted it was the right thing to do to remain corporative. His mobile phone rang and he answered. she was amazed to see that he actually carried around a mobile.

It was almost impossible to ever reach this guy. And even if you did it was always through approval, and it usually was after nine -to eleven other delegates of his company. He chatted respectful to whoever was on the other end of the line. He was pleased to report that everything was going according plan.

" It's going fantastically well dad," he said with a broad smile, and a glance at Judith.

she had never met his father. He was on the top list of her favourite moguls to meet, but she wasn't in a position to disclose that to Nicholas just yet.

" They'll find it difficult to keep up that's for sure. I mean look at Ryan Mc Anthony. He dropped out with no meaningful validation whatsoever, it's embarrassing." Nicholas said, his egotistical side was immediately recognised by Judith who smiled at him faintly. He was a bright man, and had the upper hand of his fathers guidance. Judith would have hated to admit it to Nicholas, but his position was what she would have truly loved to be in. Even as a woman, she would have been just as good as him fundamentally. Maybe even better she imagined.

" I'll get him on the bandwagon in no time dad don't worry about it. That too has been handled, I should have a concise report for you by the end of next week." He said. Gazing straight ahead, and oblivious to the fact that Judith was mesmerized by his presence.

" I agree. It would speed things up a lot more for them. They seem to be very excited about taking on the responsibility so we would have to make it happen for them". Nicholas said.

" He maintains his reservations about the initial proposal, but I am sure I can make him see sense when I visit him again." He added.

" OK. Let me process all we have touched on now and I will ring you with positive feedback.". He said.

" I am sure it will dad,you leave it all with me. And tell the kids and mum I love them very much, I'll be home soon".

" Goodbye." Nicholas said, putting his mobile into his inner suit pocket."

" My father". He said, looking at Judith who he couldn't interpret the look on her face. For the first time she saw that His father was a major influence on his life.

" He is going to make shit loads of money on this one. he just doesn't know it yet." he said, flashing a broad confident smile at Judith.

" Your stakeholders must find you very charming all the time." she said.

" poor old sods, they have no choice in the matter. I have worked very hard to be taken seriously even though anyone of them might choose to oppose it, but It is fine as long as we can make things which are worth my while continue to happen. Then I stay happy" He said.

They talked about a few ideas and developed new strategies as they continued their journey to long island, all over again she was impressed by his initiatives. He was just as creative as she was and she liked that in any person. He was able to maintain a positive forward thinking approach to everything he did and she could see that this was key to his success. They both sat back comfortably and they shared more thoughts and ideas about the project.

He was very good at business developing and she knew this wasn't her strongest point. He was extraordinarily good at it, so it was always good for her to listen to him at times like this.

" That's a brilliant idea Nic." she said with a smile.

" I always believed you were great at this sort of stuff but yet again you've proved me right." she added

" I'm glad you see how you can make it work better for yourself." Nicholas said gently. " And if you do decide to get it started, I'd love to be the first person you call with interest to make partner. I just thought I let you know that." He said

" I am very pleased, and much so, very flattered indeed. I will be giving it some serious thought. I promise." she replied

" I do believe in you Judith. That is the honest truth." He said.

" Would there be any other kind of truth?" she said.

" I guess not"

" I think you have done an exceptional job, growing the families business. It would all be worthwhile if everyone was as robust as yourself. But the reality of the whole thing is, not everyone can be like you NIC, what happens when You decide to turn your back on all this? People like me who have been reeled in by your vision would be left high and dry, no protection, nothing. These guys have more power than I do, so whose mercy would I have to beg for to secure the next screen play of my choice."

" There isn't much to fear for Judith. By the time I show you the ropes, you will be running the whole bloody show single handedly." He said with a broad grin.

" Well that's just you been modest. But you know that isn't entirely realist." she said.

" OK I empathize with you a little bit there, I know how it feels when you just want in on a little bit of the action but you have people shutting the door in your face. That should only make you want it more." He said.

" I know a good thing when I am on to it. And this has all the indications of such good things to come. We have a similar way of seeing things and that darling is a given" he added

Again, he was able to boost her motivation. They worked well together and she believed she was bound to acquire a wealth of knowledge to handle things better on her own if it came down to it. He smiled at her and she returned one just as warm.

" As long as you keep your level of determination this high, you'll become a professional by the time the road show is over. I'll always be here for you." He said

" Soon you'll be on the road with the next hot sensation, showing them the ropes and angles of how to incite and commission a hostile takeover." He added with a roar of laughter. she smiled, realising that she was indeed in for something life changing experience, and right now she was a complete novice.

"I don't know how you do it Nic, But you do". she said admiringly.

" Maybe that's your gift or that is something you acquire on the field. But you get things done like no other I know. So I am just going to embrace it as it comes you. Maybe soon enough I'll be able to co-ordinate a multi-million pound film project. What a sight that would be." she said with a shy smile.

" Now, that's the spirit. I told you you would come around soon. See it's only been five minutes." He said jokingly. They smiled at each other. He was looking forward to spending time with her at the Castolanio villa tonight. He knew it would warm her up to the realisation of the prominence behind his campaign. It was going to be a late family dinner, they didn't have a schedule for another two days so it was fine for them to unwind. she didn't have to be up early for particularly anything, and she loved the thought of that. It meant she didn't need to get out of her bed until afternoon.

Although she had agreed to meet them, she had been told of Nicholas' relationship with their eldest daughter. Elizabeth.

she was the only child from his first marriage which ended due to his first wives poor health. she died of cancer after battling with the illness for over fifteen years of her life. Although Elizabeth now runs a successful modelling company in Europe, she had flown in just two days ago when she learnt of Nicholas' arrival to America. They always had a sweet thing for each other as they both graduated from Harvard, but they never made anything serious out of their relationship. It was open to both families and there was a lot of promise of marriage and both families were in support of it. Elizabeth always played a supporting role in Nicholas' life emotionally. she always made herself available to him when he needed it. she hadn't particular found a suitable suitor either so they felt connected in a sense of understanding each others challenges.

Judith was keen on meeting Elizabeth Castolanio. she knew as much as she did but intended to reveal none of it to Nicholas. she didn't want to impose anything on him, but she wanted to truly make her own observation . she wanted to make her assessment of them together from a woman's point of view. she smiled at the thought of her mischief, and was curious about this meeting a lot more than she cared to admit. she was enjoying his company.

" Are you sure they are going to be welcoming Nic? I don't do very well at family gatherings." she said.

" They would love you Judith. They are used to sensations like yourself. They don't pay attention to anything but your passion for what you do. That is how I've known them to be, and after thirty or so years, I doubt they would have changed very much since last Christmas." He said.

" They might someday," she said sceptically. " People change Nic".

" Everything in the world may change but if you are favoured by a family like the castalinios, it would take perhaps another big bang to change their interest in you. The truth is they know people struggle with this level of understanding, so they are even more forgiving when others let them down." He said. " So long as you remain true to yourself, they are prepared to go the extra mile for you."

They arrived at the home address of the Castolanios villa and Judith had enjoyed the ride there. There was a security check at the gate and then moments later the massive fifteen foot tall gates opened.

The sight Judith was confronted by was grandiose. Perfectly trimmed hedges, multiple acres of garden space with a maze made out of exotic flowers. she saw five stone houses with a large expanse of perfectly trimmed lawn in between each structure. she saw

Several statues and a massive swimming pool. It was at least fifteen degrees warmer in Long Island than it was in central New York, but she didn't mind the weather at all. It brought her life, if anything this time of the year was always her favourite. There were several young ladies in bikinis watching over the kids scattered around the swimming pool area. They also had a mini Disney land built inside the villa. The scene was idyllic and nothing like she had ever seen before. This was the sort of home she'd love to come back to every night no matter where she found herself in the world. There was a lot of beautiful smiles shown towards them as the limo pulled over for them to get out.

" Hi Juanne", Nicholas said as a young lady about eleven year old raced across the lawn towards them.

There was so many people inside the Castaliano residence. Especially children. Juane was getting a hug from Nicholas while three others followed. Matt, Simone and Sally. Sally was Castolanios youngest grand daughter. she was only five years old but could always keep up with her older siblings. Judith watched and listened to them make several playful remarks about each other. It was all amusing to them as they understood better what it meant, Judith remained silent and observant. For a while it was almost as if she didn't exist at that precise moment.

" Nice dress" she said. "Are you a model?", she asked playfully.

" No I am Not Sweetheart" Judith replied.

" My name is sally." she said, Stretching out her little hands to shake Judith. Their conversation seemed to catch the attention of the other girls.

" Well it's nice to meet you sally. You look so adorable. My name Is Judith". she said.

" Hello Judith. It is nice to meet you too." Sally

replied.

" Guys say hello to Judith. she is a colleague at work." Nicols said.

" Hello Judith," said , Matt, Simone, And Juanne. All three of them were intrigued by her beauty as he introduced her.

" Where is mummy and daddy, run along and go tell them I am here" Nicholas said. They stormed off and he smiled at Judith.

" I think you already have you first fans here", He said.

" Ohh they are so adorable!" she replied.

" Kids always know how to get you feeling that way. But when they choose to they can be adorable little devils." He said. They both laughed as they walked towards the main living area to meet the parents of the kids. He complimented her on her efforts and calm demeanour, and Judith accepted it with delight.

" Welcome to a place I did find very comforting once upon a time during my University days." He said, walking her through the lawn. before they reached the entrance to where The parents were waiting, they were rejoined by sally. she had become Judith's favourite at this point.

" Come on, Daddy has been waiting for you", sally said, pulling Nicholas by his trousers to hurry him up.

" OK, OK Sally.", Nicholas said playfully.
As hey walked into the house, they were met by the butler who ushered them into the area where Mr and Mrs Castolanio. As they entered the conservatory, Mario Castaliano rose to his feet, and spread his arms open with a smile on his face as Nicholas approached him and hugged me.

" Nicholas My Boy, I can't say it isn't nice to see you My boy". Mario said.

" Hello Mrs Castolanio", Nicholas said, reaching out to embrace Julie Castolanio." You look graceful as always," He said to the one time Miss America.

she was one of Mario's priced possessions. Only difference was, she kept his bed warm and gave him the peace of mind any man in his position could wish for.

He met her when she was just eighteen years old.

He sponsored her entire career with the promise of marriage if she worked hard to prove to him that she deserved his support. And so she did. she finished college and university, and at the age of twenty-one, she was one of the youngest graduates in her school year and the first ever to be crowned Miss America coming from a State University. she graduated with a degree in International relations, and straight afterwards they got married. At age thirty eight, Thirteen years after their marriage they had four beautiful kids with another on the way living in a home to die for.

" Nic you handsome devil. How are you?" Julie said, as they kissed each other on the cheeks. The Castolanios where from Italian backgrounds and they always exuded passion when they met with friends and families." How are your parents? I do need to visit England very soon, or else you mother would kill me." she said, forcing a smile on all their faces.

" she did extend her greetings, and yes she did say to remind you that the next trip was your to make." Nicholas said.

" Come on in my boy." Mario said as he turned to embrace Judith who was now been introduced to them.

" This is Ms Judith Meredian. Judith meet Mr/Mrs Castolanio."

" Hello darling, welcome to our home." Julie said.

" Thank you very much. You do have a lovely home here I must say" Judith said.

" It really is, I want to be buried here if I had my way." Mario said jokingly." Mario said.

"Oh don't be silly Mario. You are going to live forever." Julie said, forcing a roar of laughter amongst them.

" Nicholas hasn't stopped rambling on about you in the last month. I think I can see why" Mario said.

" I do wonder what he must have said" Judith replied, shooting Nicholas a puzzled look.

" Ohh don't you worry, he has been a perfect gentleman. One who speaks highly of you if I might add." Mario said. she smiled at Mario faintly as he offered her a seat next to him. Julie left the room momentarily and left them to it. A few seconds later she returned with the butler offering them wine.
They had talks about anything and everything and shortly afterwards they were in the back garden sitting on the lawn, drinking wine and chatting about what brought Nicholas to America.

" I understand the road show is off with a blast. how are you finding the rally this far." Mario asked.

" More hectic than I bargained for Mr Castolanio." Judith said.

" Please call me Mario." Mario said.

" Oh no sir, I wouldn't dare." Judith replied.

" Oh No I insist. Been called by my last name only reminds me of how old I am. I mean I am only fifty-nine but that's all there is to it." He said with a confident smile.

" You look in great shape if that is the case Mr Castolanio. I mean Mr Mario. I'm sorry, it's going to take a little bit of time for me to get relaxed enough to refer to you by your first name." Judith said modestly.

" I understand. So by you finding it hectic, Little Nicholas here hasn't just tossed you into the deep end to fend for yourself has he? Mario said, glaring at Nicholas with a questionable expression on his name.

" Oh no, I wouldn't say that. He has been brilliant. In fact, he has been the reason I've stayed on the bandwagon this long." she said.

" So you should Judith. The best is yet to come.

Trust me." Mario said. Nicholas smiled at her reassuringly.

" I've tried to get her to focus on that more than anything else she maybe experiencing at the moment." Nicholas said.

"It's the only way to be Judith. Plus Nicholas here is family to me. Nothing we venture into ever returns disappointment. It's unheard of". Mario said, sipping from his glass. From everything they had both aid to her, she was beginning to feel more relaxed.

" I mean, the industry isn't particularly kind to new faces, I mean let's face the truth. Only ones with the right recommendation and support some how pull through. Oh, they would have no choice but to welcome you Judith, the same way they did Marilyn Monroe."

Judith wasn't used to having her name mentioned in the same breath of the the success stories of a few of the names he'd just mentioned, and she was pleased to learn that they too had wined and dinned on this very same lawn at one point or another. It was hard to believe at first that this was actually happening to her, but she was beginning to take matters a lot more seriously. It made her wonder about her image, and sh came to the conclusion that she was going to give it all she had to respected for her contributions, however small or excessive it was going to be.

I do trust I am in good hand, I can't see it happening any other way but marvellously" Judith said.

They sat outside for a while, enjoying the balmy evening, and then he invited them to come inside to the large elegant living room separate from the one they were ushered in through when they arrived. There were four other parlours like this one in the villa but this was the one Mario enjoyed entertaining his guest in. It was filled with a mix of Italian and English antiques. There were large framed works of art and sculptures across the room. it was like a gallery on it's own with long hall ways filled with photos of award shows, dinner nights and ones taken onset of filming. There was a wealth of history in this very room, and at a glance, Judith could see photos of Mario in frame with the likes of Elvis Presley, Diane Keaton, June Clyde and Lucille Ball.

Whilst she was scanning the other pictures and admiring the magnificence of the room, she was startled by the voice of the butler who announced that dinner was ready. Mario walked ahead of them to join his wife who was getting dressed into a more appropriate evening dinner attire. Nicholas approached Judith, he took her by the waist gently and walked her into the dinning area. she had never seen a dinning table so long. It could hold seventy people easily, and there were candles lit across it. As they approached, so did everyone else present in the household.

" I hope your hungry Judith", Nicholas said with a charming smile as he noticed Judith was mesmerized by the wealth she was amidst.

The kids trooped in, so did their parents and others who had accompanied them. Nicholas walked slowly towards them and shook hands whilst having small banter with those he was more familiar with. He was used to this sort of gatherings. He remembered his time here, as this was what he and Elizabeth used to do for her parents several times in the year. They would both make sniggering remarks about the attendants, and when all the guest were settled for dinner, they would both go running into the maze laughing about it. Judith stayed close to him, flashing a smile when necessary as everyone walked into the room and sat around the dinner table. Nicholas pulled out the chair reserved for him and Judith. he held it until she sat down.

" I could get used to you been this gentlemanly Nic", Judith said with a smile whispering the words into his ear.

" I am a gentleman" Nicholas said. His warmth

made him appear very attractive under the candle lights. From what she could sense, he was genuinely a charming guy. And more than anything else, he was raised very well. Eloquent, intelligent and successful. Judith couldn't help but notice that there was a vacant seat to the right of Nicholas. it was the only vacant seat before the head of the table which was obviously Mario's position.   Across the table was equally the case. To the Right hand side Mario's seat was obviously Julie's position as it was clear to see her children had claimed their rightul positions.

Meredian could't help but wonder whose seat it was but then it dawned on her. It had to be. Just as she was about to draw her conclusion, In walked Elizabeth Castolanio. she was as beautiful as Judith imagined her to be. she stood about five foot nine from the floor. Jet black hair, piercieng hazel brown eyes and had the figure of an elegant young lady. she watched Nicholas rise up to embrace her and immediately she could see all she needed to see. she was exactly the kind of girl she expected her to be for Nicholas if they were to be labelled partners. she walked gracefully towards the table and Nicholas already standing, leaned in to hug her. It was along hug and the affection between them was undeniable. Judith couldn't help but feel like an uninvited guest at the table. Seeing Nicholas with

Elizabeth made her think of the doctor. she wondered if Nicholas was always this way with other women, but she shunned the thought for the moment.

The heads of the family arrived at the dinner table shortly after Elizabeth, and everyone remained standing until they sat down. Conversations were held between Nicholas, Elizabeth and her parents and or that while, it almost seemed as though Judith didn't exist.

After everyone was seated, Nicholas introduced the pair to each other. Afterwards, Judith couldn't help but feel like she was a threat been Nicholas' company to their home.

Dinner was served and conversation during dinner was awkward between Elizabeth and Judith.

Nicholas pretended he didn't notice. And Judith eventually gave up trying to engage herself in conversation with Elizabeth and Nicholas. The one thing Elizabeth made clear in so many ways unsaid was that she was territorial. Judith wasn't all that at ease with the atmosphere between them, but she composed herself thorough out dinner. After a while she settled for just faint smiles across the table, not responding much to questions that were not aimed at her directly. Even

Nicholas noticed her reservations but said nothing to address her mood. Elizabeth excused herself momentarily before desert, she left to use the facilities and so Nicholas used this opportunity to reach out to Judith.

" I'm sorry Judith, How are you finding it here. I mean we don't have to sat through it all. We can leave whenever you please."

Judith was pleased that he'd spoken up about her possible discomfort. It had been pleasant having dinner with the Castolanios. But with respect for Elizabeths demeanour, Judith felt the strained.

" I don't think she likes me very much." Judith said.

" Who, You mean Lizzy?" Nicholas asked trying to seem oblivious to the awkward reception between them.

" Of course." she replied Dapping her lips with a napkin.

" she is alright, Just give it some time she will come around. OK". Nicholas said.

The housekeepers walked in serving desert and Judith relaxed visibly. It seemed an odd emotion she suddenly developed but Elizabeth's responce towards her made her think a bit more of the details Of Elizabeth and Nicholas' relationship. They had been immencely intimate, and claerly hadn't made the time to develop their relationship into something more. she understood how Elizabeth must see her now, so she wasn't. If Elizabeth felt threatened in any way, it must mean that she still had deep seated feeling for Nicholas.

" I'm OK Nicholas. It's probably just me reading meaning into things wrongly," Judith said, smiling at him.

There was no point bringing them together if Nicholas had a choice. He didn't know she was in the country to begin with, if anything, seeing her tonight was an absolute surprise. He did slip into quiet thoughts about his relationship with Elizabeth. They'd always managed to get on well. They had shared a lot of intimate times together since his divorce, but they only saw each other when they were able to take a break from their respective businesses. Elizabeth always had a reason to be in England, so it was OK to be with the one person she trusted the most.

Nicholas had gotten use to having Elizabeth in is life without the added pressure of taking their relationship to the next level.

Elizabeth had been patient on his terms, appreciating that his divorce wasn't going to be an easy hurdle for his to get over. But seeing Judith on the dinner table was indeed a tough steak for her to swallow. Their history together was something Judith couldn't understand entirely, but she sensed it had substance and was always going to be this way for a long time to come.

she saw how possessive Elizabeth was towards him, and this ignited a certain desire for him that she couldn't comprehend a the moment. Elizabeth returned to the table, and her eyes had bored holes into Judith all the while they sat for desert. Judith was reluctant to say too much to her, but she was prepared to gain the best of Nicholas' attention for the while they were in the room. she was a guest after all, and it was expected that Elizabeth had to accept this much. she was healthly and very beautiful and appeared very intelligent.

The conversation on the table was now about the project Nicholas was commissioning and all the attention was on him and Judith. They talked about business, and this conversation carried on into the night with only the adults. All the children had retired to bed, those who were not staying in the villa left with their parents, and as the crowd lessened, Judith felt a lot more at ease.   They had more wine over the course of this chats and at about mid-night Judith and Nicholas left the Castolanio resident.

In the limo they spoke about the dinner gathering. Nicholas was first to communicate with Judith who appeared slushed, perhaps by the quantity of wine she'd consumed.

" It was lovely." she said giggly. " You have nothing to worry from me Nic, You do have very powerful friend I must say, and mario, he's just classic." Judith laughing.

" Do you think they saw us as an item?" Nicholas asked, expecting Judith to spill some intoxicated truth about her experience over dinner.

" You mean the parents or you girlgriend?" Judith said, unaware of how her insinuations might come across.

" I beg you pardon? My girlgriend. You mean Lizzy?" Nicholas said.

" Yes, I mean Lizzzzy. Your sweetheart lizzy" she replied.

Nicholas could see that she'd obvoiusly had one too many drinks. He too was intoxicated, but he could handle his alcohol intake. He wasn't a big drinker, but he never turned down a good bottle of wine or champagne every now and again, especially if the moment called for it. He didn't see the sense in entertaining Judith's plight. But she continued.

" Don't try to cover it up Nic. I saw the way you two looked at each other. I can see these things you know." she said.

" I think someone has had a real bender tonight" Nicholas said trying to detter the line of communication Judith was initiating.

" I am fine, so what if I've had a little bit to drink. I haven't had a drink in over six months. Surely, Just surely a girl can be allowed to let her hair down every now and again right?" Judith said, her words were getting slurred after every statement she made.

" So tell me then, what is the story between yous two?", Shes your sweetheart isn't she nic?" she said.

" look, we have been very close friends for so many years now. That's as best as I can explain this to you". He said.

" Well tell that to the tooth fairy, maybe she would believe you because I am not buying it. I'm not buying it Nic." she said.

" she clearly thinks we are involved. Maybe she thought I'd come to take her prince charming away from her" she said.

" Oh don't be ridiculous Judith." he responded shocked by her suggestion.

" Would you try to disguise the fact that there is a lot about you two than what meets the eye?" she said.

" Why would I do a thing like that? Elizabeth and I have been through a lot together. We grew up together, and she has been there for me a lot more than any other girl I know. But does that mean we are an unveiled item? No. Do I think she is beautiful and desirable? Yes. And are we actually together? The answer to that quite simply is NO"

" SO you do find her attractive then? she asked. Nicholas was reluctant to answer her question.

" DO you find her as attractive as you find me Nic?". she asked. Nicholas had suspected that she had noticed his desire to be with her in more ways than one, but he didn't think she would be putting him in a position to admit to it before he could explore his own feelings about the situation. He tried not to do the same thing by not giving her an answer to a more driect question like he'd done with reagrds to Elizabeth. But he was silent for a while.

" Look, I'm not sure where any of this is coming from Judith. But I think it's been a long day for the both of us" He said.

" Ahh, nice try mister, your not going to talk you way out of this one mate". she said.

He smiled and looked at Judith who was still keen on a direct answer to her question.

" It is late Judith. I think we can always talk about this when we both have our heads screwed on properly".He said.

" Oh No can do mister. I need to know. You can't just charm your way in and out of peoples lives without giving them an honest answer about you feelings Nic. You have managed to convience me to stay on board this project, now I insist you persuade me to believeing that what I think is nothing more than a figment of my imagination."

" Don't be silly", He said politely. By the time he could alter his next words, they were interrupted by the driver who informed them they'd arrived at the hotel. Realising she wasn't going to have this conversation extend any further in the car, she stormed out of the vehicle and into the hotel. she wasn't able to walk straight so Nicholas hurried to assist her.

" Let me help you up to your room. it's OK I got you" He said, allowing her to lean her weight on him as thye walked through the hotel lobby. It was pretty quiet at this time so it wasn't too worrying for him to escort her without the added embarrassment. she was excessively friendly to the staff, making it very obvious to them that they'd been out on a well indulged evening.

" You are a handful to deal with when you've had a bit inside you aren't ya Judith?" Nicholas said.

" Ohh Who cares, I do not need to be up for another forty eight hours if I choose to." she replied.
'Fair point." He replied.

" Somehow I can't imagine you getting slushed mister high and might. Ohh. That'll probably one big distater in the world of Mr Nicholas Wright ey. Tell me nic, when was the last time you went out and truely had fun. You know, like real fun, not conference dinners and god father family dinners." she said.

" Hey I'll let you know I do let myself have some fun every now and again alright. What I can't say I've done lately is try to walk a drunk girl to her room after a night out." He replied with an infectious laughter. Judith laughed at this remark knowing full well that his humour was directed at her.

" Hey cheeky, in my defence, I'm not drunk OK. Maybe tipsy, but not drunk." she replied as they gigged out of the elevator.
He walked her down the corridor, looking at the door numbers to determine which room was hers. Shortly afterwards he found her room.

" Well, here we are, safe and sound." He said.

" Well thanks mister. Sometimes I wonder if your always this nice to all your other female accomplishments". she said.

Nicholas tried to ignore what she could have meant by the remark, but the last time he checked, he was unaccomplished with her. If anything he wasn't sure if she desired him or not. He knew he was drawn to her, but it didn't seem appropriate for him to confess this to her. With her intoxicated state, and unbelievable ability to still make meaningful sentences despite it's slurred projection, it was hard for him to tell whether or not there was any real purpose for her inquisition. It had been along day for the both of them and they were visibly tired. As she struggled to find the electronic card that opened the door, he intervened in helping her with the search in her handbag. she left her bag to him as he rummaged through it delicately. she took her shoes off waitng for him to find the card to let them in. He finally did and opened the door. He watched her walk into the room, dashing her shoes and handbag across the room. Nicholas was standing at the door watching her in delight and amusement. Despite her line of questioning, he saw that she was happy. she turned around to see him smiling.

" Well don't just stand there looking smug. Come here and help me with my zipper." she siad.

He obliged as he entered the room and shut the door behind him. He ran his hand slowly along her back from her hips, through her spine and up to her zip. He realized with longing how long it had been since he had to do this for any other girl. The short flings he had had was mostly with girls who instigated and executed their desires with him, without the sort of practical involvement he was subjected to by Judith.

But she wasn't just another one night stand. Neither did he see her as any other one of his accomplishments. These were his thoughts as he lowered his hands unzipping her dress. When he finished, she turned around and looked into his eyes.

There were no words between them at the point she let her dress drop to the floor, only the passion that had been brewing inside them since the day they met.

There wasn't any clarity with what was happening between them, but even that wasn't enough to stop the progression of their current entanglement.

CHAPTER 10

Judith spent a quiet day in bed. she stayed in bed until 12 noon the following day, falling back to sleep after she realized that Nicholas had left her room. When she finally woke up to the day, it was 2pm. she found the note he left by her bedside. it was an invitation for her to meet him for dinner.

They met at the hotel lobby and there was a three course meal prepared specially for them. They talked about their visit to see Mario Costalanio within a more professional capacity. As they dinned they opted to say in the hotel for the night even hough there were a few exclusive invitations Nicholas had received from his friends.

They were social calls so it was easy for him not to make an appearance. And for the first time in months, Judith was apprehensive about their business ordeal. she was going to be tightly scheduled with the tour after the next day. Nicholas went over the itinerary with her.

They were going to leave New York on Friday morning, and they would stop in Los Angeles then Vegas for three days and then leave Tuesday night for Europe. They had received two more cities on their schedule to Europe, and he doubted if they might make it back to New York for the Oscar Awards. They thought through which cities to exempt based on their order of priority. As it stood, it was Paris on Wednesday, Thursday in Switzerland, where she will be for two nights. Sunday morning in London where she planned to see her mother in between events as she was going to be there for three days. she was going to be spending time in Liverpool afterwards where she would be over the weekend. Monday in Milan after that.

Tuesday in Paris for an all important fashion

exhibition, and then back to New York on Wednesday.

she sat back and took in the intensity of her schedule for the next two weeks. If they considered their Belgium and Spain visits on Thursday and Friday, they wouldn't make it back for the Oscar awards on Friday night.

Judith wanted to be there for it this year so she sat back and listened to Nicholas try to work his magic to pull his investors into Paris on Wednesday so they could leave Europe a day before the awards show. Nicholas was used to the back to back trips, but it all seemed unimaginable to Judith. Her schedule to travel in the next two weeks was more than she'd done in her entire life.

" I not sure I'll b able to function effectively flying in and out of time zones after the next two weeks" she said as Nicholas finished his last call.

" I thought as much but I think it's going to be a blast. You will get used to it. I function ten times better after I make trips like this. Sometimes I do this twice a year. I don't see myself slowing down one single bit." He said.

" Well maybe you should.", she said, but she knew that was just wishful thinking.

Nicholas talked to her about more specific details concerning their travels, and he touched on all the point that needed to be tackled before the deal was done. she appreciated their time together to discuss it. He figured it was her right to know what she was getting into. He had always wanted to involve her with other aspects of the venture which was not on the itinary but he was happy with the plan they had decided upon. He wasn't sure how much she was prepared to handle so he left the other issue for the moment. He needed to see how she would fare in the next two weeks first, so it was important for Judith to pull her weight on the next tour. They sat and chatted more as they went through their meal, They didn't want to get into discussions about their night together. They just wanted to focus on the more relevant aspect of the reason they were on tour and meeting with investors.

After dinner they sat at the theatre room in the hotel and Nicholas showed her a series of screen plays by some of Hollywood's leading actresses. It was a surprise for her to see classic recordings with a host of her favourite 60's to 80's award winning actresses. These were the sort of screen plays that made her want to become an actress. she watched as much as she could,delighted to carry on the viewing into the morning.

" I will see you just about lunch time tomorrow Judith." Nicholas said as he made his leave at about mid-night. she couldn't figure out where the night had gone. she had already spent six hours in the movies room.

" OK, I'll see you then." she said to Nicholas without making eye contact with him. Her eyes where glued to the screen as she fed herself pop corn and the best milkshake she had ever tasted.

she nodded as he patted her arm, and seconds later he was gone, off to attend the very last invitation he received from one of his primary investors. Mr Amir Sheek. Mr Sheek had come into knowledge of the Wrights family campaign for the next project, and as always he made an enormous contribution. Judith remained in the movie room until six AM, and then she returned to her room, made hot chocolate,checked her e-mail, and returned to sleep. By eleven o'clock she woke up and began to pack her suitcase. she packed for her trip to Los Angeles, Europe and London, leaving a few things behind for when she returns to New York.

They were going to be extremely busy within the next two weeks so she prepared to travel light. he wanted this trip to end successfully before she would know for sure if she landed the role, and now,she thought there was a good chance that would happen.

she was finished and packed shortly afternoon, and after that she got into the shower.

she wasn't keen on having lunch with Nicholas, she felt like she wanted to be alone. In the end, she decided to meet him. she could always learn something new from him. It was better than sitting alone in her hotel room.

she got dressed and contacted the reception to announce her arrival to meet with Nicholas. As she walked into the lobby Nicholas was there before she was.

" You look breath taking as always Judith."Nicholas said

" Well, Thank you Nicholas." she replied as she took a seat.

For about an hour they sat and chatted about his late meeting with Mr Sheek, his Saudi Arabian Investor and fellow golf club member. she sounded so pleased to hear that they'd secured another ten million dollars towards the movie.

" Well I must say, we are going to be over invested in by the time we meet all out prospective investors." Nicholas said with a confident smile. Judith laughed.

" The more the better. We will have enough to scare of the competition so we can get this show on the road soon enough." she replied.

" The man is a big spender, he makes the rest of us look like total slobs compared to him." Nicholas said.

" He actually asked Us to join him for a swing of golf when we return to New York. We played golf once, although I lost to him the first time, I don't think I quite fancy getting my arse clubbed again anytime soon." He added embarrassingly.

" You actually should take on the invitation, it will be a good way to redeem your self esteem Nic" she said Jaunting him.

"Oh come off it, I never claimed to be brilliant at

golf." He said in a tone that covered up his embarrassment with modesty. But he knew she was just kidding. Even at times when he wasn't the best at something, he was always open to admit it, and she respected him for it.

" No. You are just a perfect business executive. With the wits and charm of a genius, who has friends in high places you could just allow win you over a game of golf, so long as the hefty investment funds keep pouring in, you'll just consider it bad sport but good business. Truly ingenious, Nicholas" she said.

" Remarkable way of looking at it. If it were true, then that could be considered the work of a genius, but if it wasn't, I guess one could simply say that my passion for what I do in some things, does make up for my flaws in others." Nicholas said.

" That sounds really good. I must say." she replied. It was actually why she took a liking to him in the first place, he had his way of putting words together that was so refined and unheard of. He very seldom did it, but whenever he did, it was uplifting. They decided to take a stroll into Broadway to appreciate the city on foot. Neither of them was held back by the thought of this idea so they parted ways briefly to change into more suitable attire.

" she returned in knee high boots and a short skirt that showed of her lower thigh. she wore a matching cropped top and a scarf over her head and was wearing a 60's style sunglasses. she was indeed a beauty to watch. When Nicholas returned, he too looked like a model out of a men's wear magazine. He was wearing a baby blue polo top, a pair of black jeans, his well polished loafers and a pair of ray bans. They had the look of a power couple, and played on to the best of their amusement.

" Why do I feel like you would be turning more heads today's than I would Judith?" He said.

" That's just the natural order of things Nic, I though

you'll be used to it by now." she replied as she looked at him admiringly. she looked fresh and young and pretty. He did look well groomed as well, although she tried not to get into the habit of complimenting his good looks, she was prepared to do so just this once." You don't look too shabby yourself if I must say." He laughed at the back handed compliment.

" Coming from you, that would have to be the best compliment of the year." He said as they walked out of the hotel, laughing and chatting, like the friends they were gradually becoming.

They walked down Broadway, storming one clothing store after the other. After about forty five minutes they each had five different high end designer brand shopping bags in both hands. They decided to stop in a pizza restaurant a few blocks away, and they spent the rest of the afternoon deeply engrossed in conversation about her career.

By their conversations he was beginning to see what kind of character she wanted to develop her self into, on or off screen. He was fascinated by how she revealed herself to him, and he was intrigued to discover a rising star, one soon to be described as one of Hollywood's leading actresses. But at the same time, she was gaining a considerable grasp of the intricacies of the entertainment business.

As they shared ideas about how to execute their plans, it was gradually becoming apparent to Judith what she was truly in for. They finished their meal and hurried back to the hotel. A driver was waiting to take them back to the hotel.

They got into the limo at about 4pm, and shortly afterwards, they were off the strip of Broadway. Judith and Nicholas had to be in Los Angeles to attend their first meeting scheduled for 9Am.

Nicholas had given her pointers to handle questions that were going to be thrown at her by the media and movie critics. They both needed to get some sleep. she particularly needed to get as much rest as she could because she was going to be in the firing line.

The organisers wanted this to be a solo event, but Nicholas refused. He insisted that he would remain by her side, but acknowledged that he wouldn't interfere in the line of questioning and response only if it was necessary. Judith was going to take it as yet another presentation.

These sort of media conferences was usually how everyone got the inside scoop about the executive producing companies game plan.

Judith Knew that Oscar Reddington, The CEO of Colombia Broadcasting Service was going to attend this conference. He had flown in from London particularly for this conference. Judith wasn't sure of what to expect but she had been briefed by Nicholas that the man was a tough nut to crack. They both hoped that his knowledge of the influences currently pushing this project would help persuade his final decision to come on board. It was a strategy that the wrights family had used in the past, but it was surely one, Oscar Reddington was well aware of.

He hadn't been a part of their last few campaigns, and in an elaborate sense, Nicholas' father had long accepted him as an antagonist. The wrights knew that Osacr Reddington could single handedly provide them with 70% access of the broadcasting services in America alone, but without him, they had managed to gain sufficient coverage on their own. They always extended invitation to him, and Nicholas confessed his surprise to Judith as they went back to the Hotel.

" I had a long talk with the man for about four hours this morning. As a matter of fact, he called me. To say I was shocked is somewhat of an understatement. He told me a lot about his dealings with my father, and although there wasn't always mutual benefits for them in the past, he never disregarded my fathers business acumen." Nicholas said.

" And how does your father feel about him now?" Judith said.

" My father sees him as a rival. He said he couldn't understand why this man remains the one person who is fluid with all his other partners but always chooses to play the shadows. Nothing escapes his knowledge in the entertainment industry was what he once told me. Even at that, there was never anything he could put forward to him that seemed interesting enough to gain his complete attention." Nicholas said.

" But there isn't any kind of bad blood between them. Personally, I've come to accept him as one who would offer criticism, but only in ways to improve how families like us may choose to run our rallies. When we decided to take our company public, he was a major investor, but he wanted us to remain a private company. He even offered to double his offering and cut his steak in the company if we didn't go ahead with it, but my father insisted on his move. Once we gained the approval, He pulled out."

" So what you mean is your father sees him as a rival now, not an ally any more?" Judith said.

" Precisely. I mean they haven't partnered in any project for over ten years. I know he had tried to dissuade my fathers reluctance to remain in the private sector of the business." Nicholas said

" Even though he might be attending tomorrow, he is not going to play fair."Nicholas added. Judith remained silent as they arrived at the hotel. They said their goodbyes and she retired to her room. she was going to get only six hours of sleep as their private jet was set to leave New York at 2Am in the morning.

They arrived in Los Angeles just in time for the event. she had a short while to go through her presentation. As already hinted to her by Nicholas, it was a full house. They sat for the meeting and for the next hour Judith was taking question after her twenty minutes presentation. Finally, a male figure walked into the room and was usherd right to the front roll of the sitting area. Judith wasn't sure who he was but When he refused to sit down, she knew it had to be him. Oscar Reddington waited for the LA Times Journalist to finish getting her words out before he spoke.

" Well I've stood here for the last ten minutes listening to you rambling on behalf of a company that has not stood the test of time in this arena,so Tell me Miss..."

" Judith Meridian" Judith replied, not leaving him any room to address her incorrectly.

" I do beg your pardon. Miss Judith Meredian. Tell me, how are you coping with your substance misuse issues at the moment?" Oscar said openly hostile to her.

" Let me tell you. I understand perfectly why you think you can walk in here and throw your temper tantrums like a baby that has lost its toy. But let me remind you that we are here to discuss matters concerning a brilliant movie project not my private life." she replied incredibly defensive.

" I am not sure you understand what I mean. What I am trying to say is." Oscar paused briefly, very aware now that the entire room was paying close attention." I don't agree with anything you have said here the last ten minutes, or in the last twelve weeks for that matter.

This whole rally is been run by a company, who would dazzle you people with the dollar signs, so that they can turn your heads around not to see the bullshit that they are really competent of producing." Oscar said. In spite of herself, Judith looked shocked not only by what he said, but by the total lack of respect in the way he said it. He had managed to insult everyone in the room, and it was obvious that nobody could do a thing about it.

" Maybe if you begin to accept that this bullshit

production is going to go ahead with or without your direct involvement, maybe you wouldn't have your head screwed way up your arse to imagine any different. The best of my work is all the world should expect. Nothing more nothing less. Anyone can be a part of this if they choose to or not. The casting is going to go into production whether you like it or not, but unless you have a more privileged candidate to spear head this project, I can only suggest you bring them forward or stick around for us to establish our worth."Judith said with the confidence of a wild cheater gaining its stride in the jungle. she turned her gaze away from him and focused on the larger audience present, who were at this time puzzled and eager to hear what was going to be said next.

" I can assure everyone here present that this production is going to be epic. As you can see by the statue and by the remarks of our dear friend Mr Oscar Reddington, we are not dealing with any form of half baked measures. We are dealing with and up against the best, so be rest assured you would only receive the best from us in return. We only need you to figure out the best way to do it."

Nicholas looked startled by how she was handling the entire scenario. He saw the fighter in her and was convinced everybody else did too. This was show business at its best and he knew exactly how much of an impact the proceedings in this very room was going to have on the industry through the media. All he could say at that point was that Miss Judith was not going to be taking any further questions, and as they got up to leave, he asked to speak to Oscar Reddington in private. Judith could only imagine what that meant.

They were going to iron things out absent of the prying eyes of the media, and perhaps come to one or two agreements if necessary. The tone had been set and it could go anyway from here.

Everyone left the hall, and Judith was escorted to her car by armed security men while Nicholas vanished to discuss with Oscar Reddington.

she sat in the car in silence.

Photographers were taking endless pictures outside her limousine, press agents were in a frenzi trying to get a few more words out of her. she was sitting behind tinted windows so it was impossible for them to get through to her in any sense.

she thought Oscar was way out of line addressing her in public the way he did. In the midst of all the media attention she was receiving now, she was raging about him inside the car. she was happy to b alone at this very minute. A part of her wanted to be alone with the man himself but she was able to calm herself down following what Nicholas had told her the night before.

Suddenly, the door opened and the voices of the shouting reporters gathered around the car filled the inside of the vehicle. Nicholas managed to enter the vehicle after muscling his way through the crowd of gossip hungry journalist and paparazzi, who were sticking their microphones and cameras through the opened door trying to capture anything that would justify their efforts. As soon as Nicholas got in, he shut the door and ordered the driver to move.

" Oh my goodness, it is manic out there."He said, " You were sensational in there. He had no right talking to you the way he did." He added.

" Good thing I wasn't standing next to him then. I would have really given him a piece of my mind" Judith said.

" He is just a difficult one to deal with in this industry, Judith. No one gets it easy with him and there are certainly perks to having such intensity engulf a conference room the way it did. He is a big timer, and a very smart one too. He has seen things like this happen over and over again. It's nothing new to him." Nicholas said

" Well it is all new to me, so he is going to have to find a way to accommodate that." she replied.

" Well, you may be surprised, but he is prepared to make us an offer." Nicholas said.

" Stop kidding Nicholas, I am not in the mood." Judith replied despite herself.

" I am not kidding at all. He has expressed his intentions, and thats as good as it has been in over a decade." Nicholas replied.

" So what does this mean for us then?" she asked, enthused by the information Nicholas had returned with.

" We will have to wait and see, I wasn't expecting anything from him, I just wanted to pass on a message from my father. His willingness to get on the wagon at this stage could mean a lot of things. We were prepared to carry on without him, just like we have done over the years." Nicholas said.

" Well, if any good comes out of this, he is going to have to give me a public apology." Judith said.

" No one can persuade him to take public interviews. Everybody knows that." Nicholas said.

" Well, I am not impressed," she said.

" Look there are ways to build on these kind of things. There's really no point letting it bring down your mood. I think you were brilliant how you conducted yourself out there." He said.

" Well he had no right to speak of my past the way he did like he knows anything about it." she said.

" Look at it this way, Never underestimate the power of public sympathy. In a lot of ways, he has done us a favour. We can now capitalize on this opportunity before it dissipates." Nicholas said.

" Well, if you say so." she replied.

" There is a lot of time for us to win him over, and I know that what happened in there was a catalyst." Nicholas said." But in the mean time, you'll have to decide what you want to do after the tour. This isn't the time for wallowing, we have a long schedule ahead of us, and there are more sharks out there just like Oscar. So we still need to be prepared to throw them a bait every now and again. That way they lay off us for a while." He said.

" I know that," Judith said. Still looking angry. she felt as though she was been reeled in involuntarily, just she knew better. This was the way of life in this arena, just like Oscar put it earlier. she understood this much now.

They got back to the hotel, and called it a night. They were set for Vegas and Nicholas had made their travel arrangements. They arrived at Vegas right on schedule, and the order of the day rolled straight into play. Judith couldn't help thinking about the confrontation yesterday. she felt she could really get through the next couple of weeks without the added headache. This was all that had been on her mind since it happened but she was too angry to admit it. Even though he never appologises to her, she was convinced there was nothing she could particularly do about it.

Nicholas observed her quiet nature through out the day, and he knew she was finding it difficult to deal with things. she had gotten herself into a right hump over her confrontation with one the countries most influential men, and the symptoms of such experience was beginning to show. He could see she was passionate about her current role in this project, and being able to anticipate such occurrences, he was prepared to make sure she wasn't exposed to any of such propaganda that may occur.

After their third day in Vegas, they left for Paris. she liked the feeling of getting closer to home. she missed her mother, and her own bed. she was looking forward to her time in London so much that it distracted her from the upsets that had gotten the best of her the last three days. Their first presentation in paris went extremely well. she liked the atmosphere here better than she did in America. The people where much more welcoming. Although she couldn't understand a word of French, she was pleased to see that every other person could speak the English language moderately.

They had met their investment quota by the time they were prepared to leave Paris, but their investors in other parts of Europe still wanted in on the play. It was exactly the situation Nicholas wanted.

Everything was going according to plan and she was happy. Nicholas took her out for dinner to celebrate their achievement. He knew all the best restaurants everywhere he went so he took her to one of his favourite, Le Jules Verne. It had a three hundred and sixty degree view of the city and they could see the Eiffel tower From the inside. It was a beautiful and truly breath taking sight at night, and Nicholas enjoyed the reception by the locals.

They both had a talk about how she was coping on the road. Nicholas never did feel to meddle in her private life but out of concern, he asked one or two personal questions that Judith wasn't particularly keen on answering.

" I'll rather deal with my family issues with family OK. It is too much to bear if I have to some how compromise one aspect of my life for another." she said sensibly.

" The last thing I want is to make you feel like you have to go through all your worries alone."Nicholas said. she knew he cared about her as a person. understandably, he had to protect his investment, but there was a growing sentimental attachment with her.

" I appreciate your good will, but I'm a big girl. I can take good care of myself. If for any reason I begin to feel like this whole thing was getting the better of me, I'll pull out indefinitely. But until then, I say we should focus on Europe."she replied

" Yes Europe. I have prepared a few things for you

to read through. One is your contract. The other is a manifesto. I think you'll find the connection between the two when you go through it. Do not hesitate to contact me if you needed clarity on anything." He said

He handed over to her a brown A4 size envelop as they finished dinner. Judith insisted that she wanted to stay a bit longer to enjoy the scenery and the after dinner musical entertainment that followed. The locals did this for their customers as a way to promote their culture. He agreed to spend some time with her, he saw the idea made her happy and this was all he needed her to be. He considered it a way of adding a little levity to their work experience.

" I think you might love it after all." He said.

" Oh really. Why do you say that?" she asked.

" Because I was just like you the first time I came up   here."He replied.

" Ah. I thought as much."she said

" I think you do deserve it. After your display of bravado the other day, I see no reason why we shouldn't be celebrating our successful turn of events." He said

" I couldn't have asked for it to happen any other way". she said.

" Neither could I. My father wonders if you are having a great time on the road. He is extremely pleased how much we are getting done without him. He feels left out in a way."He said. They both laughed at what he said.

" You don't say. I would had thought he will be fed up of the whole thing by now. I mean he has probably seen it all and done it all right?" she asked

" Well, in a sense yes. But these runs always have a way of getting you reeled back in when you resist for too long. He said.

" Why not bring him out on the road with us. He could come out to Europe, or meet us in New york." she said simply

" I am beginning to think some one would like to meet the parents." He said jokingly.

" I can't say I haven't considered it. Maybe you don't want me to, who knows." she said.

" I have no opposition to that at all. but I'm afraid it's not that simple."he said.

" How difficult can that be Nic?" she asked

" Very. I mean I'm there to see the kids most time and I don't see him eye to eye. Although we communicate a lot, it still is a privilege to actually see him physically. Sometime I don't believe he is there like everyone says he is,"

"Oh that's a shame. And have you asked why?" she replied.

" What I've come to understand is not to ask questions you do not want the answers to." He said,

" So you just accept this as it?" she asked.

" Truthfully yes. After all they are raising my children, he still finds there to be something particularly dysfunctional about that" He replied

" You are damn lucky to have them still show you that level of support."she said.

" Yes I guess your right. I should be the one looking after the lot of them." he said.

" But not to worry I'm sure I can initiate a meeting soon,it's only right you get to meet the source of your investments. If he wouldn't make time socially, I'm sure we can make it about a professional obligation. he'll be sure to see some sense with that approach." he said.

" I'll love that. There is no real rush really, after all, this is just the beginning of better things to come right?

" Absolutely." He replied.

The local singers walked into the room singing as Judith and Nicholas settled for another glass or red wine.   Afterwards they left the hotel.

The next morning they were off to Switzerland, meeting with investors and taking on new sponsors. When they met the new prospectives, they wondered why it was that their offerings were shooting off the roof. Then it dawned on Nicholas after they were congratulated by a famous journalist.

Mark Hamburg gave them the scoop of the turn of events their Paris encounter with Oscar had had in certain major cities across Europe. He could understand this, but Judith couldn't. As far as he was concerned, she was responsible for that and deserved all the accolades that followed. But it was his family the world recognized. she had done what was expected of her and deep inside his heart, he was thankful to her.

" I told you these things have a way of turning on its head for the better didn't I?" he said.

" Yes you said so. Look we are all over the newspapers." she said, reaching for a copy on the roll of a news stand inside the convention centre.

" The stories differ depending on which city you find yourself. I suggest you don't indulge too heavily on the news at the moment. these guys know how to sell their papers, and they wouldn't be compassionate when it was their integrity at steak." he said.

" That's a bit harsh isn't it Nic." she said scanning through the local papers.

" Well that is just the nature of the business I'm afraid." he replied.

" Well. I think it's all getting pretty exciting now." she said with a smile across her face.

" We help them sell their papers so we get into the hearts of our fans. I mean it's a win win situation if you ask me."she said

" It is not just about the money for these guys you know. They have it within themselves to make or break anyone. They have done so with pretty much anybody who is somebody on this earth. I believe you choose to do this because you have a burning passion to share your acting talents with the world on screen. They will prey on you for as long as it takes to the point where you feel like you no longer have control over your own privacy." He said.

" That's all true. But there is no way I am going to let any of that stand in my way. If there is any genuine love in the business, then that is all I seek, if there isn't, then they wouldn't have to throw me kisses and rose peddles at my feet for very long. We could just see this as just another experience in life." she said

" I think they'll only get harder on you if they believed you could deliver more. It's almost like a test.

The only difference is, you don't know you are being tested until it is too late. And then the fat lady sings. Then there goes your entire career, flushed down the loo following some article about you by some fresh out of university graduate, whose desperation to keep his job and impress his boss, leaves you in debt, with mortgages,health insurance bills, over due credit card payments and high cholesterol, and worse enough in most cases, a broken home." He said.

" Ouch! when you put it that way, it sounds really awful Nic." she said forcing a roar of laughter between them.

"But it is true. I tell you this because You are a hell of a lot smarter than a few others I've come across in my time. I wouldn't want to see you end up like any one of those nut cases. It is like What ever you tell them goes in one ear, and shoots out the other." He said, forcing her to continue laughing at his description.

" Thanks for you concern Nic. You have been truly remarkable. I couldn't have asked for a better mentor." she said.

" I should be thanking you. I've had a great time working with you." Nicholas said. And more than that, they had come along way together. They were an honourable pair and brilliant together as a team.

Nicholas flagged for his limousine driver to spin the car around. They would head back to the hotel and re-visit their plan for the next day. she hadn't spoken to Doctor Oakfield in over a week now. she was beginning to worry about him. Even though she was approaching London in less than two days, there was no guarantee she'l; see him.

she seemed disappointed but not surprised by it. It was the nature of the life they Led, this was what she anticipated would happen, and she only hoped that he understood the situation she was dealing with it better than she could. she thought about the life growing inside of her and as they returned to the hotel, she forced the thought out of her head the best she could.

she knew it wasn't going to be easy for her to deal with the situation alone, but even at that, she wasn't sure who to talk to about it.
When they arrived at the hotel, they sat and went through the next days agenda. it was all down to Nicholas to have executive meetings with the clients involved but Judith was prepared to assist. When he was satisfied he had all the facts he need to address the chairmen as intended, they parted for their respective suites.

They were ready for the remaining two days in Switzerland and it all went past in no time. By Sunday morning they were both tired. Their next stop was London. Nicholas didn't want the hassle of taking a commercial flight back to London so he arranged for a private Jet. On the flight he sat next to Judith as they were in the company of Nicholas' European agents whom he needed to handle some work in London.

" I hate sleeping on planes but don't attempt to wake me up unless we are at Heathrow." she said.

" I don't blame you at all. You've earned it." He replied. His tone was kind and caring,and she could suddenly imagined how she was with her father. she missed him dearly. she knew he would be happy for her, seeing that she was making such remarkable strides. she had learnt to survive without him, so as it was now,she tried blocked out every painful memory she had buried deep inside her mind for the last few years.

she moved her seat back, put a pillow behind her head and pulled up her blanket. Nicola watched her in amusement as she tried to get herself as comfortable as possible. Moments later she was sound asleep. He picked up his briefcase and pulled out some papers. After an hour, he moved his seat back like hers and within minutes he was fast asleep too.

CHAPTER 11

The private jet arrived in London right on schedule.

Judith had woken up an hour earlier, as she couldn't bear the excitement of returning to London.

she felt like she'd been away for too long. It was 7am in London when they arrived driven by the chauffeur Nicholas had hired, so they had two hours to get themselves checked into Four Seasons Hotel in canary wharf.

Their 10am meeting was with the top executives representing Barclays bank. He had chosen Canary Wharf as a place to lodge specifically because of it's close proximity to location of the meeting. The Barclay's head quarters is a landmark building in canary wharf, and its high rise structure has a helipad.

Inbetween their journey from the airport, Nicholas requested for a private helicopter to pick him up and land him on the roof of the building. It was how all the top executives gained access into the building following security protocols, so Nicholas made sure all aspects of his arrival was announced accordingly.

As it had from the beginning, things were going according to plan. This made Nicholas all the more happier than he cared to admit. Judith was ecstatic when Nicholas handed her a copy of the projects business account. He wanted her to see for herself how much funds were been generated. As it was, they were now receiving funds in excess of a little bit over 10% of their intended budget.

This was an outstanding result.

This meant that they had surplus of funds to go into future production as soon as the current one was concluded. Nicholas' aim was to double the current capital figure by the end of this meeting. By the time they arrived at the hotel and checked in, he was yearning to get things moving on. He was pleased with everything. Everything on the books looked good enough to entice his banking associates to see the prospects of his proposal.

" Do you think it's necessary meeting with your friends at Barclay's?" she asked. Curious about Nicholas' real intentions to push for more investors. she was certain that any more investment coming in would be good, but she wasn't certain if they needed it.

" I'm prepared to go all the way with it. Besides their interest in our affairs, I do need them to secure all we have generated already. Think of it as an insurance cover." He said.

" What are you really up to Nic? I can sense there is a lot more to this project than we have discussed." she said.

Nicholas smiled faintly. He knew she would ask to know more about his ordeals, but it wasn't in his place to disclose his families business agendas. They had maintained a strict code of conduct over the years, and this was why his families proposals were always welcomed with added interest.

" I can assure you that everything to be considered at today's meeting will be of mutual benefit to us." He said.

" Is there any real sense of me coming along?" she asked. she felt beat. she did consider her baby and so she thought more of having a rest and perhaps a secrete visit to a clinic to have her body checked.

" It is entirely up to you. I mean you could relax at the hotel for a while and then when I do return, I could fill you in on the details over lunch." He said.
His suggestion was in line with her thoughts so she played into it.

" Yes, I would like the time out. I am so beat, I wouldn't want to ruin the meeting with my dull presence.

I think I'll be up and running again after a few hours of me time.

" There's no harm in that. I think you need your rest. After all you are going to be doing a lot more running around for the actual movie production than I would when this tour is over. So we do need to find ways to preserve your energy."

" That is very thoughtful of you Nic. I do need all the strength I can afford to pull this thing off." she said. The jet lag and excessive travelling was finally catching up with her and she couldn't deny it. she knew this was going to get even more challenging for her in time, so she needed to think long and hard about her developing pregnancy. When they arrived at the hotel, the porters took their things into their respective rooms.

Judith was pleased to have some time to herself. she was eager to attend their next meeting because it was a television talk show event. They had gotten an invitation to meet with Jonathan Ross on his evening show, and she had seen so many of his shows and loved it. England was where she wanted to make the most of her career count. she had noticed that she didn't feel as pressured here as she did in America or Europe. she would have personally entertained the British market alone if it gave her as much exposure as she needed to be recognized for her work.

But she could see sense as to how important it was to have others participate in their current affairs for the long haul. As much as she would prefer to be recognised as just a British actress, she needed the international market to also celebrate her existence.

she wandered back into her room after they had brought in her luggages. Judith remained with Nicholas before hand to make sure there wasn't anything left undone. A little while later, she received a call from him to say he was gone. she let her body give into the fatigue she felt and within minutes, she was sound asleep. Four hours later, she left the hotel and visited her Gynaecologist. He was supportive of her needs and most importantly the part of keeping her visit quite for the time been. Although Doctor Henry Barrington was the families doctor, and had always conveyed her medical reports to her mother, he was prepared to keep matters strictly confidential. she returned to the hotel feeling elated by the doctors all clear report. she slept some more, and by eight pm, she met Nicholas for dinner as agreed.

" So how did it go?" she asked him as they sat at the hotel lobby having champagne.

" Brilliantly. I still have some very good friends in there, so it was like a re-union." He said

" That sounds good.". she replied.

" Yes it does, and it calls for a celebration." He said.

" Everything calls for a celebration Nic. Where do you find the strength for this." she asked inquisitively. Even as tired as she knew he had to be, he had a way of not showing any form of weakness. Nicholas did like to work hard but play harder. It was one of his things. And it made him appear very unique.

" You have to do better than that to try and slow me down girl. Results like this is why we wake up very early everyday. If it isn't worth the celebration, trust me nothing else would" He said as he smiled at her.
He was in very high spirits and Judith could understand why. They chatted as they ordered their dinner. They had made considerable efforts to secure twice as much of all the finances they need to launch this movie project and indeed, it was worth a celebration. They were joined by one of Nicholas' European associate who arrived with them. He went on a separate assignment earlier in the day, and had returned with news for Nicholas. Nicholas collated all the information he returned with and insisted that he remained for dinner with him and Judith. Barry Alvez was obliged to

have dinner with them and after two hours he retired to his room. He had plans to return to europe the following day, so he needed to call it an early night.

In a well fashioned gesture, Barry wished them a complimentary fare well with the remainder of their tour, as his bit of work actually commences when the movie shoot begins. Judith allowed her self to warm up to him as he was going to be an assistant director. Shortly afterwards, Nicholas and Judith returned to their respective rooms.

They agreed to meet at the lobby before mid-night to attend a fund raising event for one of his old friends.

That wasn't on their planned list of things to do, but as the most part of the event had taken its course through out the night,Nicholas was compelled to attend because he had promised he would stop by. It was a good way for him to meet up with some of his British business colleagues. Naomi Weathers had been raising funds for a charity organisation she established, and her success story today was part of the reason Nicholas felt compelled to attend this event. Judith shared in his enthusiasm so she prepared her self for the function. she was deciding on what dress to wear when her mobile phone suddenly rang. she looked at it to see who it was, and with delight, she answered. It was Dr. Oakfield.

He had received her voice mail at his office earlier saying that she had arrived in London. she smiled even more the moment she heard his voice on the other end.

" Hello darling." she replied as they spoke. it was their first conversation in two weeks and she was delighted to finally hear from him.

" It has been fabulous, but very hectic I must add." she answered with a broad smile as she sat down by her bed side.

" Believe it or not London brought the most success. The MD of my sponsoring company has doubled our investment capital. Can you believe it?"

she replied.

" Even I still can't get my head around it." she said.

" And thank you ever so much, You did say it would turn out for the better. I am happy I made the decision to see it through." she said.

" How have you been coping at that Hospital?" she asked sounding concerned for him.

" That is good to know it has been a bit quieter in there since the incident." she said. she could hear in his voice that he was pleased to feel some kind of relief from work.

" I have been looking after myself." she replied, amused by his concern.

" There is so much I want to tell you, but it isn't a good time to talk about it all now." he said.

" Of course I will. I promise. As soon as the tour is over, I'll be more inclined to tell you all about it." she added

" He has been very supportive. In fact it would be good for you two to meet each other soon." she said.

" I can see why you would say that, but he is the only one pulling all the strings I need to move this project forward." she said.
I'll rather much be spending time with you too, but you know what is expected of me now. We need to make this happen, and like I said, it is all coming together." she added.

" I wouldn't mind you with me at all, but you and I know that this is not realistic." she said.

" I wish I could see you too." she said.

" I know how difficult it must be, I am doing my best to make sure I secure this role. it is not particularly easy for me either." she said.

" We have the next three days to secure all the final participants on this tour, and I would know for sure." she said.
Given all she had just heard from him, she knew he was

worried about her. she couldn't bring herself to tell him she was pregnant for him. she knew how important it was to share this bit of information with him, but she wasn't prepared to do so.

she wasn't sure she was going to keep this child yet. she believed it was all harmless, but the risk of revealing the truth to him was something she wasn't prepared to initiate. it just was news she would rather tell him in person.

" I will let you know how I am getting on in a couple of days." she said.

" Please do not worry. I will be fine.". she said.

" He is not going to interfere in my relationship choices in any way. This is just a procedure I need to be able to handle on my own. It will soon be over." she said.

" OK. I need you to give me some time until I return home." she said.

" OK take it easy. You know you work like a manic for that hospital." she said humorously.

" It's a shame you wouldn't be off this week. I would have made some time to say hello." she said, saddened by the prospects of her tightly booked schedule coupled with his.

" We will see then." she replied.

" OK chat soon.". she said. They hung up a few minutes later, and she suspended her parade of dress choosing and went to have a bath. she ran some hot bath water and dropped scented oils and lavender inside her bath water. she sat inside the tub and thought of her progress to this very moment.

It was funny to her that she had two very charming men at her beck and call. she couldn't fault them within any flawed capacity. They were both at a reasonable age, successful, good looking, and powerful within their field of profession. she prepared herself for her night out with Nicholas who picked her up shortly before Midnight. she was wearing a long black cocktail dress, high-heeled red bottom shoes, and a 24k gold necklace and matching bracelet. she was exquisite to admire and Nicholas couldn't take his eyes off her from the moment he saw her. she was truly beautiful, and he knew it. He was impressed by the efforts she made to make an appearance. she was young, sexy and full of ambition. This was all that was needed to keep Judith relevant in the industry and she was bent on making her impression felt.

" You look ravishing tonight, miss Meredian." He said

" Thank you Nicholas Wright." she said, blushing slightly.

It was fun dressing up to her best every now and again. she would have loved to be this elegantly presented before Dr.Bernard Oakfield, but the personalities she was informed were going to be attending tonight's event were befitting of her efforts.

They arrived at Ramson's Resort. It was an exclusive club Nicholas was a member of. They were in with the trend setters of the city,well know names in the British film industry, aristocrats and members of parliament were there. It was an exclusive gathering and the personalities Judith was surrounded by left her star struck.

Nicholas took her round the room introducing her to his friends. After the numerous chit chatter, they went to their table which was reserved for them. They were served with the best champagne on the house as they listened to a live ochestra.

They were surrounded by oil tycoons, Musicians, international bankers, corporate executives for major blue chip companies, Royals from Europe, movie stars and professional athletes. It was a star studded crowd,and this made Judith feel really special.

she some how believed that everyone present was aware of their ongoing campaign, so it was fair not to talk about business. she planned on maintaining a low profile however impossible it was going to be in a room filled with people who knew each other's business.

Except for the fact that she was Nicholas' companion for the evening, she knew she had to compose her self in a manner that showed she appreciated being in a place like this. A place she would have never known existed if it wasn't for Nicholas and and the pursuit of her dreams. she didn't have to worry about how people saw her, she knew she deserved to be here just like anybody else present. Everyone had their own intentions and agendas to foresee, but hers was simply to enjoy a nice evening with a friend.

" I can only imagine how you've come to know this many people." she said as she sipped champagne from her glass.

" This profession of mine will take a person far and wide, you just have to be open minded about things as they come your way." He replied.

" I am not sure I can be loyal to everyone on equal measures if I knew half the people you know." she said.

" What makes you say that?" He asked.

" I am not sure how easy it is for you but I know it certainly would not be easy for me. I don't think I can trust everyone just as much, especially when the next person is making one offer after the other." she said. He nodded his head in agreement. He could understand what she meant and he knew she wouldn't be wrong to hold such an opinion.

" Well,you decide who to trust as you get along, that is just how the cookie crumbles in this playing field. The sad part is, no one man can be an island in this. It just won't work. So you have to mingle regardless of whatever reservations you hold." He said with a smile, as they noticed the host of the occasion walk into the room in a black dress looking very stylish.

she was embraced by several people as she made her way round the room from one table to the next.

Everyone knew who she was and they all seemed to really like her. They watched her chat and laugh from table to table, Meredian asked her if he knew her personally, and he looked at her for a long time before he answered.

" Yes, she was my ex-fiancee before my last marriage." He said to Judith looking into her eyes.

" Now before you start criticizing me, It was an honest relationship. I wanted more out of it than she did, but I respected her life style choices. she is very social, and is well acquainted with all my London associates. We met in a fund raising event just like this one when she told me she had a passion for this sort of thing. Five years later she communicates directly with some of the most influential figures in the country." He said.

" I wasn't going to criticize you at all, but why did you two split up, that's if you both are not seeing each other?" she asked.

" Like I said, she didn't want the same things I did at the time, so we decided to remain just friends." He said bluntly.

" We have remained friends for all the same reasons she is friends with everybody else in this room." He added.

" I see. So there is no bad blood between you two, just the history of a brief romance.?" she asked.

" You can call it that yes. And it is unfortunate it didn't last for very long." He said.

" Unfortunate. How?" she asked.

" I had real intentions of settling down with her by way of having a family life together, but she had other things on her mind. Believe it or not, she was best friends with my ex-wife. When she decided she didn't want to go any further with the relationship, my ex-wife stepped into the scene, pledging to be a much better spouse than she would have ever been." He said.

" And You accepted her into you life." she responded.

" Yes. I was sceptical at first but she seemed really genuine in the beginning." He replied.

" I am sorry things didn't work out happily for you and the wife, but how did this woman take the news that you two were getting married?" she asked.

" she told me I was making a grave mistake. I thought she was just bitter about our break up, But little did I know she was trying to tell me something important at the time." He said.

" You poor sod. You've been a hopeless romantic. So I assume you two are on good terms now considering you've chosen to come here tonight." she said. Nicholas was silent momentarily so she wondered if they were going to say hello to each other or not, but as the thought crossed her mind the graceful, 5"11 blonde in the black dress was standing at their table, and holding a hand out to Nicholas, who was now on his feet, reaching for her hand as he kissed it.

" Hello Naomi. You did pull such a grandiose event tonight. I must say I am impressed with the turn out." He said, still holding on to her right hand.

" I am glad you think so. Thank you for coming. I heard about the passing of..." she was interrupted by Nicholas.

" Please don't mention it, it is all in the past now where it belongs." He said.

" So how are you? I didn't think you'll be back in town early enough for this." she said with a broad smile across her face. As she glanced at Judith who couldn't take her eyes off her.

" Ohh, and this is Judith Meredian." He said. Introducing her politely.

" I've heard a few things about this one. I hope it all works out very well for you Nic. Thanks for coming." she said as she moved on to the next table beside them.

It struck Judith after she left that she wasn't

particularly the warmest person she had met. Within the glitter, diamond rings and necklaces, there was a cold hearted person who only smiled at you as a way to disguise her true intentions.

she said something to Nicholas about how she was addressed by this woman, and he shrugged and looked at Judith with a weary smile.

" I told you, she is in a league of her own. After two years of being with her, I still saw her as a stranger most times. she knows how to safe guard her heart and interest, and I think there are some things to be learnt from her way of doing business if you want to be able to pull this sort of crowd"

" So all that interest her,are the gians she stand to acquire by knowing this people?" she asked.

" It is her business. After all, every one here has turned up for her." He said

" she is very powerful" Judith commented "And very beautiful" she added as she watched her meet and greet a few more of her guest.

It said something about the kind of women Nicholas was attracted to learning of his past involvement with Naomi Weathers. she could see he liked Women with status, power and beauty. It was hard not to be drawn to women like Naomi, and by the looks of things, she must have the brains to pull together such influential people on her behalf. Judith observed Naomi closely as the music playing filled the room. she could see Naomi liked all the attention her money and status afforded her. she had built something monumental for herself, and now, she could bask in the glory it yielded.

she was actually an inspiration for her at this very moment. Naomi was exactly who she wanted to become. she adored all the uncertainties her personality exuded, it was clear Naomi lives vicariously through them, and indeed there was a certain charm about this. Everyone was drawn to her, and Judith could see everyone's eyes was fixated on her as she circled the room. This was how she imagined herself becoming. Judith grinned following her present thoughts. The thought of it excited her, the thought of becoming a huge success, accomplished with the money and power to influence even the most influential.

she looked at Nicholas unassumingly, and at that moment she knew they would both make a lot of money from this project. Now, she wanted it to be more than just the money for her. she was passionate about her acting talents above everything else, and she knew she was brilliant at what she did. In the coming months, she would make everyone appreciate her more for this, then she would entertain all the accolade that followed. she let the pleasantries her brief encounter with Naomi Weathers settle into the depths of her guts.

" Are you enjoying your evening Judith?" Nicholas asked noticing she was distant.

" It is a marvellous evening Nicholas." she said in answer to his question." Much more so, that I get to spend yet another memorable moment of my life with you." she added

" The feeling is mutual Judith, I promise. I'd like to think that this is just the beginning of better things to come." He said, looking into her eyes. she understood what he meant, and at that moment, she wondered if Nicholas was falling in Love with her. she never understood what it was he saw in her, but she could sense his emotions were getting involved with hers. At least she wasn't married so it was fair to let herself indulge a little, except maybe not entirely, as she knew she was carrying Bernard oakfields child. Was this considered as cheating. she was confronted by a wave of perplexities, unsure how to process the moral dilema swirling in her head. Maybe it was time for her to speak up about this situation,she assumed it was the right thing to do, not only for herself, but for the kids' sake. It wasn't particularly the sort of conversation one would have at a fund raising event, so she considered a time when it would be most appropriate to do so. in the mean time, she would celebrate the evening in style.

" I'd like to think so too.I can't imagine having it any other way. Soon I would be organising an event just like this one." she said.

" Great way to think Judith. If I did not know better, I'll say someone may have been seduced by the great will of purpose inspired by Naomi." He said.

" I beg your pardon, No I have Not! she replied defensively." The woman seems to have everything going for her, but that's about it. I can manage on my own to create an empowering identity that would inspire the whole world thank you very much." she replied. With a faint smile.

" Oh, I very much believe that is truly possible. But there is no harm in admitting we get inspired by others first before we strive for our own accomplishments" he replied.

" What makes you think she has laid an impression on me in the way you speak of Nicholas?" she asked.

" I see the way you look at her. Remember I told you we met at an event just like this one a few years ago" He said.

" yes You did say this" she replied.

" Well, you sound just like her then. The host was interestingly an iconic figure. Someone Naomi had admired since she was a child. I remember her exact words to me, in fact I am forced to believe she must have been speaking her thoughts out loud at the time, because when I confronted her to repeat what she'd said, she thought of every possible trick of the trade to avoid giving me a direct answer." Nicholas said.

" Lucky for her then" Judith replied.

" I thought so too when I learnt that five years later she raised seventeen million pound for her charity organisation in one year."

" Wow that is truly remarkable." Judith said.

" I totally agree. Now she is a force to be reckoned with, and everyone she associates with, seems to think the same too." He said with a look of amusement, realizing that that included himself.

" I see your point Nic, But why are you telling me all of this?" she asked.

" I am, because I happen to think it is a great think to admit to this sort of things. When you genuinely confess them, the universe has its way of bringing them to you." He said.

" Then I would consider myself to be very lucky." she smiled warmly at him, and sipped from her glass. They both seemed to relax and watch the event unfold. For him, none of what he was experiencing now was new to him, if any thing, he was reliving the build up moments to any project he commissioned the best way he could.

For Judith, it was euphoria. It may well be a closed book for Nicholas who had seen it all, but it certainly was the very beginning chapters for Judith. He had sensed her tension when he confronted her with matters over Naomi.

He could clearly see that she had left a lasting impression on her whether she chose to admit it or not. They chatted easily as they watched the host give her final speech of the day. He ordered more champagne for both of them, and it was good for him to see that she was having a great time.

Nicholas was fun to be with, she admitted this much to herself, but she saw no way out of this entanglement without compromise. she hadn't been in a lot of relationships to draw up instances that could simplify matters for her on how to deal with the situation, so in a sense she felt stuck. He had been badly wounded in his previous relationship, and she wasn't prepared to be responsible for any further damage.

He was a wonderful guy full of life and energy. she might never amount to that much, but he was a good force to be around. he was immensely appealing, and she thought he deserved someone who would genuinely treat him the way he truly deserved With

Love, honesty and devotion. Somehow, his status did not seem befitting for only one man. he had everything he could ever wish for but a lifetime partner. she was sorry for him that in some ways he was still so bitter, although he had his children to fulfil a certain aspect of his life. in all the time they had been travelling, he had never mentioned a significant girlfriend or a companion, neither has there been any woman, desperately demanding for his time and attention. she couldn't help wondering why this wasn't the case. she imagined it was probably due to the nature of his work, but that did not satisfy her curiosity.

Nicholas was the perfect social creature. Every girl in her right sense would fall for his wits and charm any time of the day. she allowed her self relax more as they chatted and laughed happily. she wasn't uncomfortable with him for an instant, infact, she felt they were getting considerably close. An hour later they left. In the chauffeur driven mercedez, she realized it was past one Am in the morning and their time together had been an intriguing glimpse into his past and her future.

" Did you have a good time?" He asked.

" I can't say I didn't" she replied.

" I think you can really get used to outings like this. it will help give you the confidence you need to keep things moving." he said.

" I loved the atmosphere in there. The calibre of people in that room alone could conspire to take over the world, and I am afraid they could get away with it." she said.

" I must say I agree with you on that one" He replied easily.

" Are you psyched up for your TV interview later on?" He asked, reverting their focus to the project.

" Of course I am. Jonathan is my favourite talk show host. I can imagine a lot more invitations coming through after my appearance on the show." she said

" I think it would be great for you too. By the time you get on screen, people can identify you face a lot easier." He said.

" I can't think of anything I would like better." she said comfortably, and then added," I think we are in the business of winning souls Nic, If we win mother England over, every one else would follow suit."

He smiled. He saw she was embracing the turn of events positively. she was a whole other breed. she was a great deal and more real in comparison to a host of others he had worked with over the years and he liked this much about her. As they arrived at the hotel, they were ushered into the hotel by the concierge at the reception. Nicholas walked her to her room, and this time she was more composed than the previous time they returned later than usual.

As they stood in front of her door, they ended their conversation about their plans later on in the day.

" I had a lovely evening Nic, thanks." she said. It was really exciting."

" My pleasure, atleast now I know what kind of events you like to attend, I'll have to set up a separate agenda for you if that's the case." He said and she laughed at his suggestion.

" I'll see you shortly." she said.

" You too." He replied as she opened the door to her room and closed it behind her. she was tired, but she had had an amazing journey so far. she thought of speaking to Doc Bernard, but he was too tired to chat so she decided to call him later on in the day.

she tossed her dress on a chair, kicked off her shoes, and jumped into bed in her underwear. Within minutes she was fast asleep.

she woke up at nine-thirty Am, brushed her teeth, and slipped on her lounge robe. An hour later she got on the phone to her mother.

" Hi Ya" she said, delighted to hear her mothers voice.

" Hello my love, how is everything going?" she asked.

"Mother, it is all going very well." Judith replied

" And Last Night? I called the hotel to get through to you but I was told you were out."

" I was Out with Nicholas. I am afraid I haven't been informed you tried contacting me." Judith said.

" Well I did. And what was this late night putting with Nicholas all about? surely it wasn't part of your movie campaign was it?"Adriana asked

" Not precisely Mother. We attended a fund raising event together." Judith said. she kept no secrete from her mother. Although lately, it has been impossible for her to open up to her like she always did. she just didn't want to worry her.

" By the sounds of it, you two seem to be spending a great deal of time together."Adriana said, implying as though there was more Judith wasn't telling her.

" It is the nature of the tour Mum. He has been very helpful." Judith said.

" You know you can tell me anything Judith." she said, believing there was a lot more to learn from her daughter since she had been away.

" I know. It hasn't been a walk in the park, but I am doing just fine." Judith said.

" I understand. I do hope you have been taking better care of yourself. I have never liked it when you go away for too long."Adriana said.

" I know, it will only be a couple more days now, and I promise. I will see you before I Leave the country." she said." I know you are worried, but everything will be OK." Judith added.

" How about your doctor friend. Have you been in contact with him?"Adriana asked

" Yes I have mother. he has been a perfect gentle man, it's a shame I wouldn't be able to see him before I leave." Judith said.

" So why don't you invite him for dinner on the day you plan to visit home. We could all get to spend a bit of time before you leave again."Adriana said.

" It would be perfect mum, But I am afraid he has such a tight schedule with work, it would be impossible to see him on the very same day I intent to come home." Judith said.

" How do you know this, have you asked him?"Adriana asked.

" No I haven't" Judith said.

" You did sound like you had a liking for this gentleman. Things happen when two people who may want to share a long lasting intimacy together but allow their hectic lives come in the way of their happiness."Adriana said.

" I understand what you mean. it's just unfortunate this is the way things are at the moment. We seem to understand each others commitment to work. Trust me mum, I wish it was any different." Judith said.

" Well, if it means much to you, I know you will do the right things by each other."Mrs Meredian said.

" It seems as though you like the doctor." Judith said with a faint smile on her face.

" I've seen the way you speak of him. I'll be shocked if you told me that you didn't fancy him as a partner."Adriana replied.

" Mother, This is so embarrassing." Judith replied blushing as she listened to her mother pass on words of advice.

" All right, Judith, I am sorry. I believe you know what your are doing. So what is the plan for today then?"Adriana asked.

" Nicholas and I are going to be on the Jonathan

Ross show tonight. It is going to be televised Live"
Judith said.

" Well then, I suppose you and Mr. Nicholas are
getting very much acquainted then." she said.

" He had been awesome mother. He has been
making all the bookings on my behalf. I don't think I
would have come this far if it wasn't for him. Plus we are
both stuck together until the tour is over, so it only
seems fair that I get to learn as much as possible about
the movie industry from this man" Judith said.

" Well don't get attached too soon. I just want you
back home soon, in one piece."Adriana said, sounding
antsy and worried, and she had good reasons to be.
she couldn't go through the emotions of how she felt
when she thought she was going to loose her only
daughter. she was way too fragile now, and
understandably too.

" I understand what you mean. I can't wait to see
you too. Everything will be fine" Judith said.

"I hope you get to accomplish what you set out for
",Adriana said sounding mildly worried again as
she listened to her daughter speak.

" It will, Nicholas knows what he is doing. We now
have more investors than we anticipated. The result at
this stage is truly outstanding. We couldn't ask for it to
be any other way." Judith said.

"All right, I am sure you a going to be sensational.
just be very careful out there."Adriana said.

" OK mother I will. I am going to be on the BBC
with jonathan Ross at tea time."Judith said excitedly.

" I'll have my cuppa ready, and glue meself to the
telly later, and your aunt Regina is coming round in a bit
aswell, we will both be cheering for you"Adriana said

" Thank you mother" Judith said.

" Well you do sound happy, so I'm glad you'll be
home soon."Adriana said and they both laughed.

" I will be back home soon. I miss you." Judith

replied.

They ended their conversation and Judith seemed nervous by her mothers concerns, which was normal for her.

she never disregarded her mothers feelings and concerns because she knew they always came from an place in her heart. If only she could confront her with the full details of her present development, perhaps then would her worrying heart really be at peace. she was usually unconcerned about how people interpreted her opinions, so she would usually confront a person when ever she had to get her point across, but with an issue such as her pregnancy, Judith couldn't summon the courage to do so.

Things were obviously different now.

Maybe it was time for her to think long and deep about her decision. The newspapers would have a field day if this story got out now. she wasn't ready for whatever counter effect that would have on her career, not while she hadn't finally secured her role for the movie. she dragged herself out of bed and into the bathroom, then thirty-minutes later, rushed back into the room to get herself ready for the show.

They arrived at the BBC studio, and sat upstairs in a private room, and they watched other dignitaries who were on the show on a big screen TV. Judith was anxious to get through the night as she had always dreamt of being on a highly credible talk show. They sat through the show, and they both thoroughly enjoyed it. Afterwards, they went out for drinks at the Light House which was one of Nicholas' exclusive members only club in Oxfors Circus.

By the time they left the club, it was 3AM in the morning. They returned to the hotel and retired to their respective rooms.

By 9Am later that morning, they were both busy taking calls and re-affirming all their scheduled appointments for their tour in London for the next two days.

They spent the entire day communicating with all their active agents and representatives, and by the end of the day, they had passed on all the relevant information needed to be processed, and given directions for all other aspect of work to be done.

Judith passed on dinner with Nicholas and decided to go to bed early. By the next morning, they made their presentation to their London investors and Nicholas was pleased with the progress they were making in London. He was in a a much better mood and was incredibly pleased with Judith's effort since they arrived. It was their last day in london and as promised, she went home to see her mother after her last meeting for the day.

she arrived at her home at Five o'clock, and by 11pm, she was on a plane to Liverpool. Nicholas and Judith were surprisingly congenial on the trip, which led Judith to believe that Nicholas was finally beginning to have high hopes for the outcome of what she was going to do for his project in the end. she noticed his endearment towards her had been considerably enhanced by the utmost level of sincerity between them.

They arrived at their hotel, and after breakfast, they were on the road to make their next appearance at the National theatre of performing arts. Afterwards, Nicholas informed her that he had made reservations at their favourite restaurant. Judith didn't have an excuse not to attend dinner, so she obliged. They arrived at the restaurant and a number of heads turned, and it was becoming a reality that people did notice her following her numerous TV appearances.

Dinner was pallet able , and they spent the most of the evening talking business, despite the sumptious meal and very well decorated dining hall. They wanted to be super prepared for their next few presentations.

They had been massively favoured, and news about their success was spreading through the media like wild fire. They considered taking on more investors nonetheless as investors were willing to get on their bandwagon upon further consideration. Nicholas didn't have any problems with the idea. The finished their dinner and Judith was pleased to call it a night.

The chauffeur brought them back to the hotel, and they walked to the main lobby of the hotel which was at the fifteenth floor of the twenty storey building. The view was amazing and Judith could feel the evening summer wind.

It was a beautiful balmy evening and the skies were clear, with only a distinctive star and the moon. As they stood outside the balcony geting some fresh air, Judith began to feel the chilly evening breeze in the thing red dress she was wearing. Nicholas tried to keep her warm by embracing her, but she put a stop to it. he noticed she didn't want to make close contact with him in that sense so he reserved his gesture.

"Even though it has been a very pleasant evening, I do not plan on been out here very much longer." she said. They were going to remain in Liverpool for the weekend, then they would fly out to Milan for their Monday schedule, And then return to Paris for the fashion exhibition. The weekend passed her by in a jiffy, and by Monday, she was well rested for the days events. By the end of the day, they were on the next available connecting flight to Paris.

This was more of an entertainment plan for Judith, but she was keen on meeting one of her French designers who was going to take care of her wardrobe during the movie production. she was pleased to see Paris again, but afterwards, she was prepared to move on. The following day, they returned to New York, in time for their one of two final presentations before

Nicholas would have to make the last call on the

standing of the project. As soon as he could receive the approval he needed, then, he could set a date to begin production. The tour was nearly over, and it was amazing for Judith to realize that she'd coped fantastically. she seemed to feel almost nostalgic about her return to New York when she returned to the hotel room where she spent her first night in America.

" I can't believe we have come this far together." Nicholas said as they walked through the reception lobby.

" I do not want it to end." she said.

" No,for you it won't. For me it stops after my Los Angeles trip. Which by the look of things you wouldn't need to attend." He said.

" Awww. That's a shame. I was looking forward to the end of the trip together." she said.

" Well, my point exactly. How were we to know how well we were going to get things done before now. You have been exceptional, and I think I can deal with my shareholders and all their needs without having to hassle you for very much longer." He said.

" It has never felt like a hassle." she said.

" Well, why do I feel like I'm being pushed away?" He asked. He knew what he was confronting her about, but Judith was worried this conversation wasn't going to end too well for the pair of them.

" I do apologise if you feel that way, but it is not as simple as you think for me to deal with the intensity of our time together." she said.

" It wasn't intended to make you feel this way. I have just gotten use to having you around." He said.

" You have been doing so well without me before you met me," she said confidently,besides, you always knew that this had to remain strictly professional between us." she said.

" I never lost sight of that. It has been a frightening thought to deal with knowing that it was always going to come back to this very conversation." He said.

she noticed his handsome face under the beaming lights of the hotel corridor, but forced her mind to remain neutral on the subject matter. He always looked impeccable, and she knew it had always been the initial point of attraction for her. He was the heir to one of the most lucrative and successful businesses in England and America, but even at that, all it did was make her think of Dr Bernard. There was no doubt that Nicholas was the right kind of man for a woman seeking the returns being in this position,but she walked into the room of their very first meeting with only one thing on her mind. As that purpose was rightfully established, it was impossible for her to find that there was more to deal with now than the prospects of their plans for the project.

" I wish it was a different time and place, and perhaps occasion,but it isn't Nic. You of all people should understand that." she said.

" If you can't tell me the moment we shared together here meant nothing to you, then I can't possibly begin to comprehend how difficult this must really be for you." He said.

" I can't say it meant something, just the same way I can't say it didn't either. I pleased for you to see it as nothing more than what it was." she said.
" And what would it be that you see it as Judith?" He asked.

" A flawed moment that should never have occurred to create a disruption to our working relationship." she said.

" it is a real shame you see it that way." He said.

" It's a real shame that we had to engage with each other recklessly the way we did that may now lead you to see it any other way. Please do not misinterprete my point, I just think we could have achieved the same results we did without the existence of that aspect of our journey." she replied as they carried on walking down the long corridor.

They arrived at the front of her hotel door and they stood opposite each other. It had been a lovely experience until now, but they both had to come to a firm understanding that they did cross the line professionally. she admitted and accepted her portion of blame.

she felt that she'd perhaps led him on, but there was no need crying over spilled milk. They both had been impressive working as a team and these sort of situations were always bound to present itself in more ways than one.

she loved dining in fabulous restaurants and lodging in five star hotels and resorts, but there had to be a balance. And right now, she was convinced that scale of balance had tipped disproportionately, even when it didn't have to.

They agreed to meet at the lobby in the morning to conclude their New York schedule, and this was the only thing Judith needed to comply with. They parted for the moment, and in the morning, they met as agreed and took matters seriously enough to secure their reasons for returning to the big apple. Their new york partners were anxious to invest in the project. they saw it's potential just like everyone else had right from the beginning. Their results so far had been beyond what all the critics had speculated and that in a lot of ways was a good reason for them to remain cordial towards each other.

They were going to make an impressive entry onto the movie scene when the current project goes into production, but until then, they had to remain pleasant about being seen together.

Despite the tension between them at present, it was yet another successful day for them in New York. By the time they got back to the hotel that evening, it was clear that they had to regain a mutual focus.

Nicholas proposed dinner and she obliged to join him. Although she had promised herself not to give into her desires solely based on physical appearances, she knew him well enough now to know that he could talk himself into having whatever he wanted to accomplish, she was mindful of this when they sat for dinner.

He commented to Judith that she was truly an extraordinary woman, and that any man would be lucky to have her as a partner. He even commented on her dinner dress as they sat on their candle lit table sipping vintage wine. They congratulated each other on how well they had done on the tour to date. He had to take it on all by himself after tonight, although he did promise to return for the Grammy awards show.

Afterwards, Nicholas would have to sit with a certain entertainment board to receive a general consensus that their project had been approved. He re-assured her that he would deliver, and after she returned to London, it wouldn't be too long before he gave her his final say. it was going to be a long wait for Judith, but despite how excruciating this was to be, it was a wait well longed for.

She looked pleased and happy that they had done an outstanding job. That alone was enough to write home about. she loved all that had happened before this very moment, she would cherish the time they'd spent together travelling. He on the other hand had enjoyed her company more than he had with his other clients.

They worked well together, and it was only reasonable to expect that either one of them would have wanted more than they'd bargained for. They shared a number of views about the movie itself and this was always something they both shared in common.

Their love for a good movie. she was always excited about this, and in time, she knew she was going to be crowned as the lead character of this project. she had waited patiently enough for this long, and had studied very hard for the role, so she made it clear to him that she was unwavering in her passion to deliver the best performance possible. he was pleased to see that she was still eager, and this made him vastly impressed.

He alerted himself to the fact that his emotions where only involved because he saw the potential in her, in some ways he wasn't convinced she could see in herself just yet. But he was pleased to listen to her present thoughts on the manuscript. Her translation of her role made him believe that she truly knew her stuff, and he admired her for it.

As they chatted, people could observe that there was great camaraderie between them. If one wasn't too sure, they could easily be seen as a couple in love, but the only love that existed between them was the love for making a box office smash hit. They shared more ideas on the manuscript and what to do next, and as the evening dinner came to an end, they'd tailored the prospects of future productions she wanted to develop.

They chatted about it for a while longer, and it was surprising to learn that their thoughts had shifted away from the tension that was initially brewing between them. They were full of great ideas, and he wanted them to see that it wasn't going to end as just another idea. they weren't the kind of people who rested on their laurels, and this much was what they shared in common.

He let her in on some financial loop holes, and she was excited to learn about financial terms she never knew existed. Nicholas had pretty much familiarised him self with all the corporate jargon he'd acquired over the years, and he knew his stuff very well. He warned her she would have to re-educate herself if she was to become able to use them to her benefit. Regardless of her deficiencies, he told her of all the vital processes.

she gained a fairly good idea of where he was heading with his families business, and she could see he was working towards accomplishing his plans.

They were still talking about his plans when they got back to the hotel, and sat in the lobby for a little while. He ordered a bottle of champagne, but she only wanted to listen to what more he had to say.

They chatted comfortably for a while till she decided to return to her room. There was always so much to talk about, share and execute, but this was what she enjoyed the most about his company. They agreed on a lot of things, but she asked all the right questions to satisfy her inquisitions. They shared a lot of information only a few people were privy to, and he only wanted to do so to see her grow.

By the end of their conversation she was fully knowledgeable about the financial terms and their functionality. she was impressed by the way Nicholas used them. she smiled at him as he finalized his instructions on what was going to happen next. she was truly grateful to him for that. Sometimes it was hard for her to believe he had actually made this much time available for her. Judith informed him that she would be fine on her own until he returned.

The next day, he was going to leave for Las Vegas, and needed to make sure she had everything she needed. They commended each other for their joint victory and the mutual interest they both shared. Knowing that it didn't surprise her when he touched her hand and hair a few times, she could see he wanted to be with her intimately again.

" I want you to know that If given a chance, I would make this trip happen all over again just the way it has been." He said.

" I've enjoyed working with you, Nic." she said.

" I have also learnt a lot from you." she added.

" I hope we remain good friends to make it happen again." he said.

" If by the time this is over and we were serious about the next possible film, I would be the first to sign up for the project." she said with a smile.

He smiled realizing that this was almost the only way they needed to see each other more if they chose to. He walked her back to her room, so as not to ruin the evening, he kept his distance from her when she got to her door. she opend it and turned around to look at him.

" Have a goodnight NIC." she said softly. Afterwards, she leaned towards him and gave him a kiss on the cheek and then took a step back.

" Goodnight Judith." He said, looking into her eyes for a long moment before he walked away. she closed her door, took off her clothes and went into the bathroom. While she soaked in the tub, she thought about all that happened in the past nine months, and she hoped that, after all she was going through, she would finally accomplish her goals.

CHAPTER 12

The following morning Nicholas was on his way to Las
Vegas. When he arrived he was met by his assistant
director, Jergens Smith as soon as he walked through
the revolver doors of the building where he was meeting
with the board members as scheduled.

They have been partners for the family business
since he took over as the chief executive from his
father. He presented Nicholas with a stack of papers
that Nicholas scanned through as he walked through
the reception hall towards the elevators.

Nicholas asked him specific questions and Jergens
smith responded accurately. It was his briefing for the
day, and a few other relevant information he requested
for. He looked at his watch as they rode in the elevator
and realized he was right on schedule.

" The meeting would commence straight away."
Jergens Smith said, observing his superiors
apprehension.

" That's fine with me. So long as it dosen't take
them all day to make up their minds."

" I don't see that as been the case at all today. If
anything, they would make their minds up quick
enough, but they might spend all day congratulating
you." Jergens said as the elevator doors opened.

As he entered the meeting room, there was a
round table with twenty men and women sat in
anticipation of his arrival. Nicholas sat down with
Jergens sitting to the left of him. Within moments, the
head of the board commenced his speech, and by the
look in Nicholas' face, he knew it was going to be a long
day.

After six hours of deliberations with the senior
partners, Nicholas emerged with a broad smile across

his face. E

veryone was shaking hands with him, and others were clapping and cheering him on. They congratulated him and each other.

In the melee of people in the conference room, Nicholas thought of Judith. He had made a point of telling her that she worked extremely hard to realize this moment, and now he felt like she ought to have been here with him.

People present were intent on talking to him about his next move, but this was something Nicholas wasn't prepared to disclose. The older senior partners were used to this sort of outcome., so it didn't move them as much. They were classed as the overseers, and everybody they appointed was given supreme power for the tenure of their proposed project. Knowing what this meant, Nicholas knew it was a great deal for him and the business.

But as Judith had put it when she asked about what his real agendas were in one of their many conversations during their travels, he knew there were answers he would have to provide her with when the time comes. This of course would be against his will, but this circle was an elite society of sorts, he would be offending a lot of families if he was to ever disclose their inner dealings. For the moment, he would savour every gaul that has brought this fate upon him.

He smiled at what he thought Judith would say when he tells her of the outcome of today's meeting. He had something in mind now that he would have loved to see change, so for the while he chatted with the people in the room, he pondered on how to make his offering.

" Today has truly been the break of a new dawn." Nicholas said, positioning himself at the front of the room with all eyes on him. The person we have all decided to be cast for the lead role of this new project just happened to be absent of this meeting today, but I am sure she will soon be thrilled to learn about your decisions made in this very room." He said.

" she is a fresh, bright, young mind, and is absolutely incredible. when you think of how we have come to be elected today, it may become necessary for you very fine people to hear her express her delights in person, but until then, I'll like to say, thank you all for believing in us. I have heard tales by my father telling me of times when he stood in this very room, stating his plans and visions. I must say, that I too stand here before you, sharing those same plans and visions indefinitely."

Everyone seemed particularly interested in hearing what he had to say, and this brought out the best in him.

Nicholas adressed the figures in the confrence room with bespoke eloquence, revealing some minor details on how they intend to handle the anticipated project. He did not fail to let them know know how driven he was to satisfy all his investors and the partners present who have voted for him. They were all pleased to hear that there would in fact be a handsome return for everyone who has come onboard, and the only thing left to do was determine how the stakes were going to be distributed.

Nicholas presented an excellent closing speech exuding genuine qualities of an appointed leader. Given the tremendous budget surplus they had, the projects was bound to be of premium standard. Nicholas gave a few hints of what to expect from the project it self and he knew this would keep everyone on their toes. It was the perfect turn of events, and it had come to a satisfactory conclusion for him. Nicholas had no doubt that his father would be thrilled for his success following the end of today's meeting.

He left the building and inside the limo he chatted with Jergens about the intricacies of the projects development. He was on his way to the airport to catch the next flight to New York. The most difficult hurdles had been scaled, and this was when he had to recruit the best in the trade to move things ahead. He felt accomplished, but he knew thee was still a lot of work to be done.

Jergens was very vocal about their success from beginning to end and he supported his ideas on an expansion of the family business. He was prepared to stick to what ever Nicholas indicated as the best approach to take with respect for his stake holders shares. he was happy to be taking the led now on this project now, but he wasn't prepared to be taken for granted. He could have decided not to pursue this campaign, or even treated it with less viguor, but he didn't do that. He was recognized for his impeccable work ethic, and anything less than that would only devalue his families prominence. The least he could do was maintain intergrity, but have the most fun while he was on it.

" OK, I am happy with the position of things." He said simply.

" You have set a trend that would be very difficult to superceed in another ten years atleast. I'll be kicking myself in the teeth right now if I was anyone of your competitors."

" Ha Ha Ha." Nicholas laughed out loud at the reason behind jergens thought." I am fine with that, so long as they stay out of my way from here on." he said.

" The results are going to be astronomical, I can predict that myself. Stock prices are going to be at an all time high." Jergens said.

Jergens had pulled his weight for the company and Nicholas recognized his efforts. He knew his job and Nicholas could only imagine maximizing his productivity.

He had once made a lot of fuss about him when he first joined the company, and Nicholas was pleased to see that that wasn't a decision he would live to regrete.

They had both handles major deals over the years,

but nothing like the magnitude of this project.

" I expect that too. After all we've made it affordable for them. I'll like to see them carrying us around on their shoulders by the time I make my next offering." Nicholas said.

" Won't that be a sight to watch." Jergens said, forcing a roar of laughter between them." Nicholas recognized his worth to the industry, he felt that they owed him more than just cursory thanks for his hard work, but he wasn't the kind to fish for compliments.

" Have good flight back to New york," Jergens said as the limo stopped at the designated location.

" I'll call You when I return to London." Nicholas said as they shook hands.

" I'll be looking forward to seeing you at the office when you return." Jergens said

" Me too." He replied. Jergens left the car and the limo sped off to the hotel before they left for the hotel.

Nicholas was in quiet contemplation as he now that his mission was accomplished. He thought of breaking the news to Judith but he held back. he wanted to look at her in the face while he told her all about it. He was pleased and he knew she would be as well. He called his father instead and the news was beautiful music to his ears. Nicholas arrived at his hotel, and less than an hour later he was on the plane to New York. He arrived at the hotel in New York and his mood was on an all time high. Nicholas had contacted the management to announce his arrival to Judith and they prepared a table for them to have lunch. They met for lunch and Nicholas could see that Judith was eager to hear what news he'd returned with.

" Welcome back Mr Wright." she said as she approached the table.

" it feels good to be back." He replied with a smile.

" How have you been faring in my abscence.?" Nicholas asked.

" I have been OK. I haven't left my room since I last

saw you. it's been T'v and sleep, nothing exciting." she said.

" Now, why don't you tell me what exciting things you've been up to in your part of the world?" she asked. " It has been a marvellous trip. Besides the uninterrupted corporate contribution of our sponsors, I'm please to announce that we could be off the road for now, while I focus on other things." Nicholas said. it felt good to him to deliver this news to her, and he was fulfilled by the excitement on her face. They were finally going to get the project on the road, and they both couldn't wait.

They chatted fitfully through lunch, talking about the outcome of his meeting. It was just as she expected it to be. Her name was going to be on the cover of all their campaign ads which indicated that she was leading the casting role, and Nicholas' company was going to have their names above all others as the executive producers. They could finally fly their colours and could choose whoever they wanted to work with. Everyone was talking about their deal. it made her feel important to be a part of something huge. It was all she had been dreaming about and it felt so anticlimatic for her to be at this point now. she was feeling pleased about it all as they chatted some more and ate their lunch.

" So what do we do next?" Judith asked with a smile.

" I would have to return to London to know for sure, but until then, we should make best do of the remainder of our time here." Nicholas said

" So what do you propose we do?" she asked.

" It may seem like it's over but we are only at the half way point of this journey but there may be one or two other things we could do before we leave for london. Thanks to you, it has been smooth sailing this far. And I made it clear to the partners that you have been tremendous.

" I am pleased to know you did speak well of me in my abscence, but I'll need more information on what you'll be expecting to be done." she said.

" I'll think of something and get back to you. we would be in a better position to strategize soon enough." He replied

They made more plans for the project, and Judith kept a mental note of all his suggestions. There were no specific meetings to have in new york, but he was going to squeez in any last minute offers he received. They seemed like old friends when they agreed to disagree on any issue. They agreed on one particular client to meet and Nicholas called him to book a last minute appointment. They were his jewish connections in Long Island, and he felt he owed them a well deserved visit. Judith listened to his conversation with Mr Morris bethloven, and he sounded poetic as they spoke.

" I will be there." Nicholas said, scheduling a meeting with him the following morning.

" Goodbye for now Mr. Bethloven. " Nicholas said as he got off the phone. He explained to Judith that Mr Bethloven had remained ornery right up to the very last minute of several other projects they'd handled in the past, but he'd always been gracious whenever Nicholas contacted him to offer a piece of the action.

After lunch, they returned to their rooms as Nicholas admitted he was tired from his travel. he had been hungry to give her the news, but now that he had done so, he was exhausted.

The next morning they both set out to visit Mr. Bethloven. They arrived at his office, and Nicholas was invited into his meeeting room alone. Judith was waiting for him in the reception area having her first cup of coffee. As soon as they finished, they went out to pick their attires for the evenings award show. Following the positive turn of events, it was an idyllic moment in both their careers. They talked and laughed as they went from one designer clothing store to the next looking for the perfect combination of clothing to wear for the evening occassion. Nicholas had friends in the clothing business, so it was easy for him to lead them in the direction of those who would appreciate their point of need. What Judith settled to wear for the evening was a far cry from her intial choice of Harry winston, but she was just going to have to make do with christian dior.

They both managed to get all the assistance they needed, and shortly after they'd finished shopping, they were picked up by their limosine driver. Everything was perfect, she was going to be live at the one of the worlds most popular award show and she couldn't ask for anything more.

They returned to their rooms to get ready and at about six o' clock, they were in a black chauffeur driven Rolls Royce. When she got into the car, Nicholas was pleased to see her in her dress. He was thinking of all the nicest possible things to tell her, but he managed to keep it simple.

" You look splendid in dior Ms.Judith." He said with a warm smile. she blushed at this compliment and returned one just as pleasant.

" You do too Mr.Wright. Balenciaga should send you a Loyalty cheque every month for making their tuxedo look this good." she said briskly as she pulled her make up kit out of her purse and re-touched her lipstick. she was indeed spectacular to look at, and Nicholas couldn't take his eyes off her.

" Well, other things may have been communicated with my partners that I haven't brought to your attention yet." he said.

" Oh really?! Like what?" she asked, still peering into the mirror in her hand.

" it wasn't difficult for them to see that things had been moving brilliantly for us in the last few years, and now we have this projects potential to show for it, we've announced to expand our workforce." He said,

" Well, that sounds promising NIC." she said, intrigued by what he was telling her. she put her kit into her purse and turned to stare at him.

" Promising for the right candidates yes, but this is something that I believe I have to be very tactical about." He said. " I only want to bring in people who would keep our steak holders happy, not some waste of space. Jergens and I had a long chat about this before the tour, but now we have the upper hand in this deal, it would be a perfect way to maximize our earnings by way of expanding the business." He added.

" I see your point, after all, you are a public trading company. The alliances you make now would certainly reduce the lawsuits you may encounter along the way by those who oppose you." she said." Why do I sense your planning some kind of aquisition? she asked.

Nicholas smiled at her. He knew she was now capable of detecting his mode of operation and he was overwhelmde by how quickly she could put things together. Nicholas nodded as he answered to her.

" That may be a possibility. Hence the need for the all important structural re-arrangement." He said.

" Well, you need to start finding the candidates you need it is a move that has to be acted on immediately." she said, enthusiastically. "Do you have anyone in mind?" she asked.

" To tell the truth, I do, but I am not certain how it would be accepted by this candidate." He said simply.

" I can't think of anyone who would pass on such a wonderful opportunity by your company. What positions do you have open to be filled? she asked.

" There is the all important Assistant Managing Director position." That is my main position of consideration and I think the elected person would be tactical enough to build the rest of the team without my direct involvement." He said.

This was what he had been itching to tell her all

along, but even now he'd opened this conversation he wasn't sure how to follow through. Judith knew she would stick around for the long haul, but she hadn't thought about the prospects of actually becoming part of his organisations work force. Her thoughts were solely set on the movie, and even now, this was all she seemed to be thinking about. Nicholas knew that, and he'd been skeptical to initiate any offering that may hinder her performance.

" Would you be considering someone from within, like bringing them on board on the basis of a promotion?" she asked.

" That is the tricky part. I wanted to bring in someone fresh. Someone the others were not too friendly with to shake things up a bit in there." He said.

" That sounds like a solid plan. They wouldn't see it coming." she said with a smile.

" Exactly. You see, I knew you would understand my approach. Jergens advices I use a familiar face from within but I think the opposite should suffice." He said

" have you made an official notification for this position?" she asked.

" Not yet. But I am about to." He said.

" Well, I say go for it. it might be the ove you need to achieve your new set of goals." she said sounding interested. she was pleased that he was sharing this bit of information with her, but she couldn't get her thoughts past the fact that she was going to be walking on the red carpet very shortly.

" I intend to, infact, I think this person would be supportive of Jergens who has told me of his possible plans of moving on to begin his own entertainment business."

" What are the odds, I know you have a history with him, who would have thought he would leave at a time like this. " she said.

" I think he has always had in the pipeline, but

despite his intentions to move on, he proposes to remain in joint adminstration with our company." He said.

" Like a sister company?" she asked

" Exactly like a sister company." He replied.

" That makes your offering a lot more valuable to whoever gets onboard now I assume." she said.

" Precisely." He replied, realizing that he was finally getting her to see the bigger picture.

" I am not sure I know who would be more deserving to fill that position Nic. I wish I did, I'll recommend them in a heart beat." she said.

" I don't think there would be much use for wishing now Judith." He said simply.

" I am not sure I understand what you mean." she replied.

" What I mean is, I'll like for you to come onboaar to secure that position." You are exactly what I am looking for. You have all it takes to see this project through, and many others alike, and I want you to give this some serious thought." He said.

" You can't possibly be serious right now Nic. This is insane." she said sounding startled.

make " I am dead serious Judith. I'll like for you to become the companies next assistant managing director. We share similar visions and goals, you are a quick learner, and ive invested heavily to sure that you could acquire all the knowledge you need to run the company with your eyes closed. I can't think of anybody more deserving than you. You are the prefect candidate." He said.

Judith was shocked as much as she was flattered, but she was rendered speechless by his proposition. she couldn't think of any possible reason to decline and there was no way she could imagine being any good at a routine job.

" what you are offering is truly flattering Nic, but I can't see the sense in this. I mean, I can't possibly say I know the first thing about running a business as big as yours."

" Don't be silly. You have all it takes to make this a work out for yourself. You would have me to guide you through the process so you have nothing to worry about." He said.

" I am an aspiring actress Nic. My job is to make your business look good on screen not to run it for you." He said.

" Well, that is a point of common misunderstanding. I wouldn't want you to run it for me, you would be in a position where we can run it together. You wouldn't be working for me but with me." He said.

As scary as it was for her to admit it, he was making a lot more sense now he made the distinction about his proposition. she thought about her mother, the doctor and her growing baby. Her priorities where bound to be extremely muddled up if she was to accept his offer.

" Look I can't just jump into making a decision like this without giving it some serious thought. I mean if I wanted a Job, I would have been in a pharmacy somewhere in london selling viagra to a bunch of old age pensioners. No offence to the lot of them but, you see what I mean right?" she said, forcing a roar of laughter between them.

" It isn't uncommon for people to make these sort of career choices. it is just part of life. considering how well you've been so far, I have no doubt whatsoever that you wouldn't be great at this." he said.

" You might have witnessed how exceptional I may be, but I would be invaluable to you as an employee with a job title. Don't get me wrong, it is a fantastic opportunity, but I just don't think it is for me." she said.

He was disappointed to hear her speak in the manner she did, but he knew it wasn't going to be easy convincing her. she wasoverwhelmed by the prospects of this job offering but she avoided giving him any direct answers despite his persuasiveness.

" Look, I don't expect you to give me an answer now, but I need to know you would be taking this offer seriously. this is one of those sort of once in a life time opportunities you wouldn't want to miss." he said.

" I know what you mean, it is an enormous decision. I'l have to talk this one over with my mother. Morover, I do have a private life that I do not intend to undervalue in any way whatsoever." she said.

" I am going to assure you right now that this is the best thing that would come by your way in a long while. you do want to learn the ins and outs of this business right?" He asked relentlessly.

" You know I do" she replied sounding panicked. it was the first time she had ever been put in a position like this. And frankly, she wasn't sure how to handle this situation. Nicholas knew how to get what he wanted and he was determined to win her over.

" Then what is holding you back?" He asked

" Do not push it Nic. I am not ready for this. I have a life of my own to worry about you know. How would you feel if someone decided to take you away from everything you have built over the years," she said rethorically.

" I am not trying to take you away from your life. I am simply trying to put you in a position where you can take real command of everything you've ever dreamt of. Look, The fact of the matter remains that, I intend to move my operations to New York. That is exactly what is on my mind. If you fancy a real shot at your career developig into what you really want it to be, this is where you need to be." He said.

" Now that is a different twist to this whole thing. You can't just do things like this Nic. It is a life altering decision. As much as you know I need to grow into someone reputable, you are asking too much of me as it stands." she said sonding irritated.

" Look it is not my intention at all to get you irate. I

am only loooking to make the best calls on your behalf. It isn't until they see you are very serious about your career that they would give you the access you need." He said.

" Nic you are impossible to deal with at times. Do you know what you are asking of me?" she said sounding worried. He knew she could throw every sensible objection right back at him but, for the first time, he could see that there was something more that hindered her immediate decision. but he didnt know what it was.

" I am not trying to make things difficult for you at all. If it seems that way then I apologize. I just expect you to see an amazing opportunity when it comes by. I mean, at first you thought the candidate would be lucky, now it has been put to you as being that that candidate, you want to find every reason under the sun to dismiss the idea. I don't get it Judith." He said.

It had been one of her dreams to live in New York. she was beginning to feel that Nicholas was in her life to turn it up side down, despite his good intentions.

" Besides the offer it self, there are a lot of perks to go with it. I just need to know you would give it some serious thought atleast." He added. New York was a long way from london, if things were not as complicated as they had turned out to be, she would jump at this offer at the drop of a hat.

" Look Nic, I am sure your intentions are good, but I feel conflicted enough as it is. Please do not question why, just understand that It would be better for us not to discuss this offer any further at the moment." she said.

" Does this mean you would think about it atleast?" He replied.

" Your offer is incredible Nic, and it is a huge favour, I will think about it, perhaps when we do return to London, I'll know forsure." she said.

" Now that's the spirit. I do respect your approach

Judith. I'll do the same if the shoes were on the other foot. it is all about making Big out of a fantastic opportunity. You stand a chance of making some good money and a name for youself if you wish." he said.

" I understand this perfectly well nic." she said, laughing." But carry on your search regardless, I am one to declear false hopes to people." she added.

" I respect that too. No one can deliver the way I believe you can. But you can take out as much time as you need to think this through." He said" But the sooner the better Judith." He added

" You have no choice in the matter. If you are certain it is me you need, then you'll wait." she replied. she seemed flustered about the entire proposal. she wondered if this was one of Nicholas' plots to have her within his graspe. it was beginning to sound too good to be true, but nonetheless, it was intriguing.

" Besides the proposal, I want you to know you've earned it. I would not want to wait too long for an answer from you, but you know me well enought to know that I am a patient person. you are diving into a world where you need as much leverage as you can acquire to make things happen the way you want it, and it's not going to be that way until you are able to grab the bull by the horn." He said.

" you have a fair point." she replied.

" It is the truth Judith. And you know it. I have no intentions of lying to you. Once you find yourself in a position where you feel more appreciated, then you would see things differently." He said." I trust you would find it within yourself to make the right decisions." he added.

" you make it sound so simple." she said hesitantly.

" it would be if you are prepared to follow my lead on this one." he replied.

" You do know you are asking me to make the ultimate sacrifice here. I'll be pulling my life out the roots of my upbringing just to make this happen for myself.

Have you thought of how this might affect others in my life?" she asked.
Nicholas was hesitant to reply.

" Tell them this would mean the world to you if you were to make this move. If they don't appreciate that it is in your best interest, then they do not have your best interest at heart." he said.

" And you happen to think that you have my best interest at heart?" she asked

" Yes I happen to think I do. I believe I treat you right, and most of all I think you deserve this break." He said. He looked at her intensely, observing her counternance.

" This is all I've ever wanted Nic, You know this more than anybody else. My mother is all I have left in this world, and if I have to do this, I'll have to move her out here with me too. I'm not sure how she would accept that, besides, she has lived in London all her life" she replied.

" Perhaps it isn't fair to ask you to leave her behind, so you are going to have to convince her to move out here too. Convince her that it is a career move for you, but a retirement gift for her." He said.
The thought had crossed her mind in the past to do something very special for her mother, but now the possibility had presented itself, she wasn't sure how to put things in order. she thought of her growing child. Her mother could play a perfect role as a nanny, and this would suit her perfectly. she pondered on how to make it a win win situation for all but her thoughts were clouded at present.

"That sounds perfect." she said sounding delighted. she knew it wasn't easy to relocate, but she knew it was going to favour her massively. Although she wasn't sure what to think of this situation, she was convinced that with his support, what may seem as an obstacle now, may just turn out to be the best decision she'd made in her entire life. But before she would make this decision she knew she had to speak to her mother in person. Everything was indeed happening so fast, but she understood now this came with the territory.

" I hope you are right about this one Nic. I really hope you are." she said feeling uncertain, but willing to see this through. she had never done a thing like this on her own, but she knew it was going to be an exhilirating experience nonetheless.

" Well, don't let me spoil the evening for us with this talk. I know you need sometime to think things through. But do not hesitate to ask me anything you weren't sure of OK?" HE said.

" That's fine with me. I will have a lot of questions for you to answer to when the time comes, I just hope you'll provide me with the right answers." she said.

" I promise I would." He replied with a smile.

He was a very persuasive man and brilliant at what he does, and Judith could not undermine him in anyway. They worked well together, and some where in her heart she believe it was going to be the right decision to take him up on this offer. she was prepared to take this risk if it meant that she received the right returns. she had to look out for her best interest despite his intentions, so she was inclined to make this happen for them. she had never imagined herself to make it this far, but considering she was taking control of her own life, she wasn't going to let this opportunity pass. she seemed almost providential about the entire prospects of things, but she hoped she was making the right decision.

Not just for herself now, but for everyone she loved. she smiled back at him but reserved her response as their vehicle pulled to a sudden halt. As the door opened, she was met with flashing lights by the photographers on both sides of the red carpet entrance. Her heart was pounding uncontrollably as she got out of

the vehicle. she was met by Nicholas who held her
hand and took the first couple of steps onto the red
carpet. Momentarily, he left her to it, realizing that she
had come into herself as she twirled and smiled for the
cameras.

CHAPTER 13

The award show was all Judith wanted it to be, and for the first time, she was feeling like she was part of the elite minds in the industry. Her flight to London went easy, and Marcus Billingham was wiating to welcome her at the arrival gate. she came off the plane pulling two suitcases, and when their eyes met, they both sprung into a bubble of excitement.

" I am actually amazed that you've returned to us. I thought the Americans would have loved you too much not to let you go." Marcus Said, as he took one of her suitcases.

" I can't say they didn't try." Judith replied with a broad smile across her face.

" I can't say I am surprised at that. I know you went out there to make a killing." He replied

" Yes I did. It was high time I made my impression felt, moreover, it would seem pointless making this trip if we didn't have the right attitude to win the world over." she said.

" I was worried about you, but judging by the glow on your face, I guess my worries were pointless." Marcus said.

" Awww, that is good to know. Well, here I am, back in the bosom of mother England. I would have made plans to meet with you when we came in to see Jonathan Ross, but we didn't have the time to mingle much." she said

" I understand, I watched it on TV. You were truly sensational. If I didn't know any better, I would have believed you were already in the league of the Julia Roberts of this world." He said.

" And who says I ain't already." she replied, forcing a roar of laughter between them as they walked out of the airport. They got into a black cab and chatted some more about everything that had happened on her trip. They spoke about Nicholas's offer and it seemed important for her to discuss matters with the one person who had experienced the inner dealings of the wrights family business.

" I couldn't believe my ears when he mentioned it." she said. " It just never occured to me that he would make such a proposition. What if I don't deliver?" she added. she was still concerned that her agreement to take on the position would do more harm than good to their relationship if she was to accept it.

" These things have a way of working themselves out. I wasn't granted the opportunity to explore the depths of their organisation, but, by the looks of things, you would be right in there to learn a great deal about the business. Besides, you may have just been offered a position that many would kill for." Marcus said. Judith knew that, which was why she was willing to consider this offer with intentions of making the best out of this new found opportunity.

" Judith, offers like this don't come around very often. It would be the most important decision you've ever made about your career, and I don't think you would live to regret it. If I were in your shoes, I would grab it and sing to the world about it any chance I get." Marcus said.

" I know what you mean. It is just so over whelming to see things change so fast. He also proposed relocating to New York. Can you begin to imagine what that would mean." she said.

" I know you are worried about your Mother and your partner, but if you thought about it critically, New York has one of the busiest Hospitals in the world. With his remarkable work experience, the Americans would jump at the chance of offering him residency in any of the prestigious hospitals." He said." And as for your mother, I bet she would be thrilled to learn that she could retire in one of the finest homes in the world, with dozens of maids running after her." He added with a broad smile.

" I know there are a lot of options out there, but would he consider it? Besides, my mother hasn't left London in over twenty-five years, how much more leaving the country permanently" she said.

" It may well be the move you all need to begin a new life. You are going to be earning so much to retire her and the good doctor if it came down to affordability." Marcus said.

They talked endlessly about how important this decision would be for her, and Marcus was enamored of the prospects, shining new light on the matter in ways Judith hadn't thought of. On all grounds it was a massive once in a lifetime opportunity and she couldn't deny it.

They stopped for lunch, and chatted some more over the entire project. she was able to communicate to him that he would be part of that move if she consider to take on the offer, and she was pleased to know that he was prepared to go all the way with her. They both had the same work ethic and Judith knew he would be a valuable asset to her. His passion for what he did exceeded the requirement of an average agent, and Judith appreciated his drive to be classed as the best at waht he did. it was almost obsessive but she recognised it had to be this way to achieve the sort of results their profession required. They spent the rest of the afternoon detailing new plans for the project and Judith was pleased to see that Marcus had done some home work in her abscence.

" Judith," he said, looking intensely at her. " It is not going to be particularly easy working with Nicholas. I wouldn't be such a good friend or colleague if I do not mention this to you now." He added.
" How do you mean?" she asked.

" He could be very demanding on occassions when he wants what he wants. Being a part of his work force might just put you in a compromising position." Marcus said.

" I gather that much about him." she replied quietly. But this wasn't her immediate point of concern. she wasn't sure how to break the news to anybody that they had shared a night of sexual pleasure together. she had loved everything else about her trip besides the guilt of their encounter.

" I do not want you feeling discouraged about this. My only point is, I want you to remain aloof in your dealings with him. Besides that, I still think there is a lot to gain from taking on his offer." Marcus said.

" There is a lot to consider, and trust me,I am cautious as much as I am weary of the entire progression of things. Having an illustrous career would always be something to take away from all of this, but is it worth the added hassle, short comings and disappointments? I think we are soon to find out. So long as Nicholas dosen't choose to deny me access to the resources I'll neeed along the way, it is only fair that I give him the benefit of doubt for now." she replied.

" If you ask me, I would say nobody deserves this opportunity more than you do so I will be around to share it all with you." He said.
" It would be nice to have you around, I don't think I can manage this without you."she said.

It was easy to see that she was incredibly torn between an important career decision, and her private life. she felt concerned because she wanted to make sure she was making the right decisions all the time. It was something her father always told her to do since she was a child. she remembered him saying that the most important decisions were never easy to make, and sometimes you make them not realizing how important they were to begin with. she understood the importance of that lesson now because she could see how it applied to her life. There was no question in her mind that she was going to accept Nicholas's offer sooner rather than later. she remembered Dr Oakfield saying that he would consider a career overseas but there hadn't been any real need to consider such a move. she believed she could some how convince him to see that such a need had presented it self, so this way, they could live out the rest of their years together. He was her only real problem, eventhough her mother decided not to accompany her, she was prepared to leave the nest. she knew her mother wanted the best for her, and would do everything she could to support her. If she had her way, she would have loved to have her mother with her when she finally hit the glass ceiling to acclaim her name in the sky.

Marcus gave her good advise when she needed it and she appreciated his point of view. He knew she wanted this opportunity more than anything else in the world. They shared the same visions, and given the perfect opportunity, they both could be making a name for themselves respectively. she recognized that he wasn't trying to pressure her into this decision eventhough she could see how much he could benefit from this move by her acceptance of the offer. But seeing the direction the project itself was taking, she was convinced it would be good for them.

" I would be glad to be of service Judith. I won't regret any moment we share together." Marcus said." Judging by how much fun I am sure you've had on the road show, I don't think I want to be left out on the next one." He added.

" There would be a lot of surprises waiting for you when the time comes, I can promise you that much," she smiled at him benevolently.

Marcus was a pleasant young man, easy on the eyes and a good listener. she treated him like her brother as he reminded her so much of her youth. Judith spent a lot of time with her brother before his death, and she could see a lot of his traits in marcus if he was still alive to mature into a much older male.

" I have always worked hard enogh to be treated with surprises. so if hardwork is what it takes for you to grant me promises, then hard work is all you will get from me." He said,

" You are young enough to enjoy all of it. I know I'll be focusing a lot of my time and energy on the movie production so it will be best for me to latch on to you now so that when the time comes, I know I have someone who actually knows what they are doing to look after my affairs when im on the road. What do you think?" she asked.

" I think we are on to great things to come. And I'll love to be in the front row when the drums start rolling." He replied with an infectious smile.

she was pleased to observe that he didn't feel so pressured about her invitation like she did with Nicholas. she appreciated this much about him. They chatted some more about their next point of action and after half an hour, they went their separate ways. Marcus left to attend a book signing event, while Judith returned home, pleased to be in the company of her mother and the warmth of her own bed. she had as much time to herself and by the following morning she was pleased to be woken up by a call from Dr Oakfield .

" Good Morning sunshine, How would you like your scrambled eggs this morning madam?" He said Jovially.

" Sunny side up please, and a double creamed latte and freshly baked crossants, thank you very much" she said, cosying up underneath her duvet. They were used to this playful way of waking up to each other, and she told him once that, she'll do anything for him when ever he could serve her breakfast in bed. So he uses it to gain her affection at times when they are apart.

" Sorry dear, I could have called you much sooner

before your bedtime but I've been in surgery through out the night." He said.

" How is it going?" He asked.

" Better now I can finally get to hear your voice." she replied
she had been pondering on things she wanted him to be aware of as a part of her did not want to experience any form of unhappiness with him. she found herself wanting more of his opinion about certain things than she cared to give her sound judgement credit for. she felt she owed it to him to try as much as possible not to interfere with his career and stick to what she was doing, but she felt guilty keeping it to herself. she had come this far, and now she had to pour her heart out.
" I haven't been doing very well without you." she knew she had let her guards down even putting the thought out for discussion. But she had learned to always share her emotions with him. They had both decided to be this way from the very start of their relationship. she knew he deserved to be treated with respect and it didn't seem uncomfortable for her to let him know how she was truly feeling.

" That's OK sweetheart. You have been terrific. And I think that every normal person would feel enstranged from their loved ones when they are on the road for too long." He replied.

" It is more than just that now. I can't bear the thought of being away from you any longer than I have on this road show. The job is the real draw for me, but as much as I could get use to it, I have no idea how you would cope without me next to you." she said.

" You need to think about this carefully Bernard," she replied, comfortably addressing him on a first name basis. she sounded tormented and he was very concerned for her. One part of him wanted to leap at the chance of proposing marriage, and the other told him that he owed it to her to support her through this challenging phase first, and then, when they find themselves in a more comfortable way of life, then marriage could follow. But there was sufficient time for all of this to happen if it was their destiny.

" I have no idea what I am suppose to do to fix this eminent issue, but I am prepared to hang on until we figure it out together. I think it is something I'll really have to do if I want to save our relationship." He said.

" I love you and I want us to always be together. So whatever decision you make, I'll supoort it 100%." He said.

" So would you be prepared to take another job in new york?"she asked directly. He was silent momentarily, but responded without the emotional attachment she was concerned about.
" If that is one of what it takes for us to remain together, yes I would. After all, doctors are always needed all over the world. He said.

" But what if you do not like it out there, and you decide to leave, I'll be all alone without you." she said. " I know life could be a bit better for us in America, but a part of me still feels it would be too much to ask for simply becuase it is my career path that brings this upon us." she said. He could sense the sincerity of her words, so he was committed to make things easy for her. He admired the fact that she was very thoughtful of his opinion.

" I love you Judith. That is all that matters. Besides, I am no stranger to the streets of New york, it wouldn't be too much of a change for me. It is you I should be worried for more." He said. He was only half kidding and she knew it.

" I love you too. I love you so much more for being so understanding. I'll do my best to make sure you do not regret this decision because it would mean a lot to me if you came along with me to America. " Judith said with tears in her eyes.

" OK, so we can begin our search for apartments

and start looking into other major aspect of this decisions as soon as you are settled in." He said.

" Oh, thank you baby. I can't wait to see you." she said. They had a solid understanding, and she wasn't prepared to jeopardize that for either of them. she was determined to keep it this way for as long as they respected each others feelings.

" I'll be off for a week from tomorrow evening, so we will be glued to each other soon. then, you can tell me all about your trip." He said

" I will tell you all about it. it is looking very promising now, and I can't say I am not nervous. There are some fantastic ideas lined up for the future. Moreover, Nicholas plans to triple the size and impact of the company as soon as the project begins. He believes he could use the momentum of this on going campaign to maximize his market share within the next 3-5 years.

" That sounds like a truly promising business move, and a lot of profit to be made. Perhaps you are positioning yourself for some serious earning potential in that time. You should not worry too much about it. The world is yours for the taking. I can't wait for my sweetheart to become a mega star. Just tell me what you would like me to do, and I'll have it done." He said.

" Thank you very much. You have made this a lot easier for me to deal with than I thought." she said. This made her love him a lot more. He was understandably unselfish, and had been such a decent person with respect for her emotions. This was how she had always imagined her relationship to be. He was smart, and was astoundingly patient with her. This made her all the more intrigued by him. He understood her completely and she could tell that he really cared about her. No matter how different their careers were, it was undeniable that they were an unbeatable combination.

They were both very beautiful specimen of their gender, and they seemed to compliment each other very well.

" Actually, if it's OK with you, I could book a flight for two straight away. I have the entire week off, and I could extend it too if I needed too. You are one of the best things that has happened to me, and if America is where we need to be to find our future, then America it is. I know a few places on the outskirts of new york that would be lovely to raise kids." He said jovially.
Judith ignored the latter comment but was astonished by his zeal to get onto the preprations immediately.

" Swetheart, there really is no rush you know. we can do this in the coming months." she said, concerned that she may have pushed the envelope alittle too hard.

" No, it is fine darling. Look, I want to spend the rest of my life with you, and I know nothing else could feel like the best thing to do for us to realize our dreams. I am an accomplished doctor as it stands, anything more would be added bonus to the long list of awards and doctorate certifications I have amassed over the years. What I am passionate about now is you. And God willing, having a family I can call my own with you. Besides, I did plan to retire very early. And I'm pretty certain I have not too long left on that clock."He said.

" Then, Let us do it. If you feel this strongly about it, I would be there with you all the way. You do not know what it means for me to begin this chapter of my life with a man like you. Thank you for being so kind to me" she said gently.

" Don't worry about any of it. If does feel like the right thing to do."He said. I'll ring you in a few out to give you some informtion after I talk to my people at the travel agency." he added.

" OK sweetheart." she said. As they ended their conversation. she could feel a different level of bond between them that she never thought existed. she made no comment about rasing kids in New york when he mentioned it, but she knew this was now going to be inevitable. she had dismissed the idea for too long, but now, it was one she wasn't going to be able to escape so easily. she just couldn't tell him, and this was mostly because she still couldn't believe all this was happening to her. it frightened her a little bit, but it was also incredibly stimulating. she would wait until they were settled in America before she told him, this was her decision.

she spent the rest of the day with her mother, and by tea time, she arranged a meeting to meet with Marcus Billingham the next morning. The following day, marcus accompanied her to a few meetings that Nicholas had appointed her to attend. she had a new found source of energy to pursue and retreive all the relevant details in preparation for the movie production, and now, she was beginning to enjoy what she was doing. she was gaining far better insight on the necessary steps building up to the actual production, and by now, she had a better sense of Nicholas's business organisations and some of their clients who had worked with him for years. she checked in with his London office and reported all she had collected. When she finished her assignment for the day, she received a telephone call from Nicholas who was pleased to hear about her progress since she returned to England.

" I have always been confident in your ability to handle things on your own. I can't thank you enough." Nicholas said.

" Dont thank me, You hired me remember?! I should be the one saying thank you for giving me a shot at this." she replied.

" Well, I guess you have a fair point. But it still dosen't stop the fact that It wouldn't turn out this way if we didn't do it with you on board." He said

" well, if you put it that way, I guess you have a fair point as well." she replied, forcing a roar of laughter between them.

" So how is London treating you, are you missing it

here already?" Nicholas asked.

" London is fine. I can't say I've been given enough timeaway to miss it, especially considering that I could be on the plane to New york within the next 48hours." she replied.

" What do you mean, are you trying to tell me that you've made your decision already?" He asked, intrigued by her response.

" Lets just say that it is more of a possiblity now than it   was when you first made your offer." she replied.

" WoW. That is awesome Judith. I knew you would come round to it eventually. Congratulations." he said

" Thank you very much Mr. Wright," she replied.

" I think this calls for a celebration." Nicholas said." I am going to make dinner reservation. The kids are making their way here too,a few good friends are coming into new york in a couple of days too, so we could all get together and break the good news to them. I think it would be awesome Judith." He said.

Everyone Nicholas chose to invite for any occassion attended. All he had to do was make the call. He had pointed out to her that, the quality of life in America was always more tasteful. People seemed to enjoy taking care of their health, meeting new friends, building new businesses, or just partying with friends.

The average person was happy earning a living, but once they had some time off work, they would be having the time of their lives. They all seemed happier and ambitious, always willing to help others along the way. In London, the people she interacted with looked as though they existed inside a cave, they were moody, pale, tired and always stressed. Most of the time they looked frantic and less interested in anything that didn't interest them the slightest. It was certainly a turn around point in her life.

" I think it would be. But I'll have to finalize with my mother first, then once the dates are set, I'll bring you up to speed. It should be no longer than two days really."she said.

" Well that sounds terrific, I'll have to call my friends in the medical field to schedule a few meetings for him."

" That would be very kind of you." she said," he still has friends there from his student years, so it would be interesting for him to re-unite with most of them. But as for my mum..,"

" I am prepared to arrange for a countryside home for her straight away if she needed certainty of any kind about her accomodation." Nicholas said.

" That's good to know, but I do not think that would be necessary. she is still going to need a lot of persuasion. she might not jump at it immediately, but I am prepared to support her whatever decision she chooses to make. For now it would just be Bernard and Myself. And a hotel accomodation would do us just
fine." she said.

" OK, I would look into reservations." He said.

" Oh dear, Please do not trouble yourself. He would be happier if he made his own arrangements. I think you should focus on getting the gathering plans in order." she said.

" OK. I'll do just that. Do you need me to arrange a chauffeur to pick you guys up at the airport?" Nicholas asked

" You don't need to do that. We will take a cab. Perhaps after we've arrived at the hotel it would be more suited then." she replied.

" OK. That's fine," He said. He had made several calls directly to his friends practicing medicine, and a few appointments we made for dr.Benernd Oakfield. He also made other arrangements for them courtesy of his company. He wanted their trip to be very relaxing because he knew they were both going to have busy schedules running in the week they were going to arrive in New York. Nicholas had hinted he was going to set-up some official meetings with some of his important clients, so he wanted her to meet them. Meanwhile, he had heard that the media was highly interested in this campaign more than they anticipated, so he warned her of the paparazzi at the airport on the day of her arrival.

Everything was coming up roses for the project, especially for them now that she had considered his offer.

" OK, I'll give you the heads up if anything changes." she said.

" Gotcha!" He replied. He was intrigued about the present turn of events. It was her willingness to reach out and make honest attempts to exel that got him drawn to her. He too was once an aspiring executive, he understood the entire process, its challenges and setbacks, so her reputation was so out of sync with the determined voice he heard from her. He knew she wasn't going to be very much concerned about what the public had to say about her.

She is currently a highly bidded actress newly commissioned to run a multi-million pounds movie project. she was prepared for good and bad publicity. she didn't mind which came first. He knew enough about her now to believe that she would do the wrong things for all the right reasons. He didn't think his family would mind having her around, but he acknowledged her relationship with the doctor. He envied them in a sense. He wanted their sort of relationship for him and his ex-wife but ended up divorced. This was his creation. He had the perfect candidate listed to show case a major film, so this made him purged to deliver.

He was prepared to give her all she needed in return for her loyalty. The most important thing for him was that she agreed.

Judith ended her conversation with Nicholas and returned home to her mother as they were preparing to have dinner with the doctor. They had spoken earlier about a possible flight departing London for New York the next day.

Dinner was her way of officially introducing him to her mother. It would mean a lot considering they were making such a huge decision, so it was important for her to see and hear what her mother had to say about it all right in front of him. she had worked hard and enjoyed her road show but dinner with her mother and lover was going to prove a lot more daunting for her to deal with.

A few hours later, she heard the door bell and hurried to to front door. Judith remembered all her trip to his flat, it was decent having him round for a change. she welcomed him into her home and led him into the living room. Moments later, they were graced by the presence of Adriana . she remembered and smiled that he was a doctor. They both shook hands and pleased to see her again, he planted a warm, gentle kiss on both of her cheek. He was pleased to see she was in good health considering the state he first met her in. Judith was pleased that her mother liked him. If her father were still alive, he would have been the only holdout. He was always very fond of his little girl, and always thought no one was ever good enough for his daughter.

Adriana had looked pleased the moment she saw her daugher happy in the arms of another man. she gave them some privacy , and disappeared upstairs to her room moments after. she came back to join them downstairs again for dinner, long enough to hear all she needed to know about his background. Judith looked startled as she saw him answering to her mother politely. Dinner was perfect and as always, he thanked them both for a wonderful meal. Him and Judith returned to the living room, while their housekeeper cleared the table.

Adriana could see the bond between her daughter and this dashing young man. Following her survival after that terrible trauma she sustained, she believed the doctor was godsend. Other parents may feel some kind of rivalry with the doctor, now that he is getting close to their child, they would be hard on him.

Adriana was just grateful he speared her life that day. she took it the hardest when they arrived at the hospital and she didn't know what to expect. she understood her daughter was dealing with some severe level of anxiety and depression mixed with the fear of loosing her father and brother. It was never easy for children like herself, those who relied on drugs to cope with such trauma, end up in the same postion over and over again. Judith on the other hand was doing just fine at the moment, and her mother could not think of anybody more suitable to be seen as the man in her life.

They got along terribly well with each other. He understood that she was dealing with a lot, and it wasn't easy for her. He wanted to make her happy and that alone was easy for her mother to see tonight. she felt good for them both. Eventhough she would have loved to have her husband alive to witness this, it was just fine that she got to witness it herself. Eventhough she wasn't particularly welcoming or polite to people at times, she was undoubtedly welcoming and polite to Dr. Bernard Oakfield.

They all talked about the trip and how exciting it was going to be for them.Adriana felt sad suddenly just like any mother would feel coming to terms with the fact that their child was fleeing the nest. It was her dream to see her daughter happier and she was pleased to see this dream coming true.

After dinner, they arranged to meet at his flat to leave for the airport. Nicholas had invited them for dinner the following night, and both Judith and Dr Oakfield had no reservations about attending. He was anxious to meet Nicholas as Nicholas was anxious about meeting him as well. Judith didn't need want this to turn ugly for either of them, but she knew Bernard was the calm sort. It was Nicholas she wasn't so sure about. she didn't want to keep anything away from him, but she also didn't want to loose him to the knowledge of such mindless encounter between them. she knew she would loose so much if they fell out with each other so she didn't want to risk it. she could tell that Bernard was suspicious of her, but for the most part, she knew he didn't know very much about anything that had happened. she would tell him, but she didn't want to be the one to talk about it because it wasn't important to her for a variety of reasons. she trusted herself more now not to allow it happen for a second time. she suspected that the two men would get along with each other, and Nicholas would learn to keep his mouth shut, but she wasn't convinced it would plan out that way for them for different reasons.

When they arrived in New York, they looked like they would never be seperated from each other. There was always something so youthful that came awash him whenever he visited this city. He remembered one or two old flames during his time at medical school and that was always something to smile about. she never bothered asking because she thought she would never hear the end of it. she was just happy to see that they were both here.
she was pleased to have him around her so that
Nicholas could get the picture clear in his head. she needed him to see that they were taking their relationship very seriously. It was all she expected him to see.

" So who's idea was this dinner party tonight?" He asked

"Oh, it was Nicholas's. I don't think it is anything too fancy so don't bother about going heavy on the evening attire. It's not a black tie or red carpet event, it's just a little gathering to announce to some of his friends and family about the tour/movie productions success." she replied.

" Is there anything more I need to know before making this attendance." He asked.

" Don't worry about a thing sweetheart. We are just going to mingle a little. There maybe one or two famous personalities but if you point them out, I'll kick their butts for you." she replied Jovially.

" That's re-assuring. I'll have to get myself in trouble first to need you to kick ass for me." He said.

" Well. I am not banking on you not to start any trouble, but if it so happens, I'll be kicking ass for team Oakfield." she said laughing. He laughed with her as they left the airport terminal. He was happy to be with her a this point in time,

" Well, no need to get yourself worked up. Leave it up to me, you won't even notice me in the room." He said.

" I some how find that impossible to be the case." she replied with a smile. he grinned at her and leaned over to give her a kiss as they wheeled their luggages to the taxi waiting area. In truth he had waited to be back in America. He was enthusiastic about the prospects of living out here. Judith saw that he was a brilliant doctor and very elegant, she was convinced that the lifestyle here would suit him more.
" So tell me, is it going to be like this from here on?" he asked.

" Yes, I think so. It would be better than before I promise.," she beamed at him and talked animatedly about their love for each other. she expected this move to bring them closer together. As they rode to the hotel, they spoke endlessly about how they wanted their first accommodation together to look like, and this conversation carried on until they were on the road heading to Nicholas's dinner party. A black chauffeur driven Mercedez picked them up from the hotel at about

7:30Pm as arranged by Nicholas. They were both relaxed and sounded surprisingly enthusiastic. He could hardly wait to begin his visits to the hospitals he had an interest in practicing. Two of which ran the hospital similarly to how they did in london. He knew the chief resident at both of these hospitals and they were both interested in him. They were intrigued by his credentials and it was important for them to find an opening that was more suitable for him. He was more superior and way too experienced for them to place him in just any trauma unit. But this did not bother him very much. He was happy to find anywhere that would accept him so he did not pin his hopes on anything in particular. He was just happy being with his girl. He smiled at her and he could see that she was very positive about their move to America.

" I am thinking I like New Jersey better." He smiled at her, they both had a liking for the same things. It's not like New York, they are not as fiesty as the people here. But if thats what appeals to you more, you know the constant thrill of living on the edge, then maybe this is where your truly want to be. So lovely home are scattered across long island, you can get yours and handle your business across the five boroughs and still live good." He said.

" I can imagine you having your own private practice, you could turn it into one of the best hospitals in the world." she said.

" To be honest with you, I can't say I haven't thought about it one or two times." He replied." I 'll love it, Judith. it would be like a dream come true." she suddenly felt as though a whole new life were opening up for them, and there was something so promising about it all. The one problem was that he had to get himself situated first, then they would properly be able to weigh in on their options.

" There are a lot of ways to level out the playing field if you so desire. This is America, where anything was possible." she said casually, as though the pair of them had already made this decision and plan before now, or as atleast as thogh they we already certain they were going to attain all the favour they needed to realise their dreams.

" I can see how you are looking at it now sweetheart. I actually would like it out here and I wouldn't mind having as much homes as I can collect. That way, we wouldn't have to commute much." He said

" That would be easier for me too. I'll second that motion all the way through. it would be nice for us to always get around." she replied.

" I really do like the idea of a house in the suburbs, and," he paused dramatically, searching her eyes cautiously for a reason to discontinue their new plan, but nothing was forthcoming from her.

" I think Long Island would be a great place to raise children. This might be the right time for us to do it." He said, holding his breath as he waited for her to speak openly about what she thought about his idea. she remained silent for a while seeming to weigh what he'd been saying. she hated to keep the truth away from him,now just wasn't good timing. she needed to be sure about their decision before she told him.

" I'll consider that thoroughly." Was what she finally came up with, but she didn't want into that discussion with him. not yet anyway. There was still a lot of other important factors to think of.

" Thoroughly. Is that all I am going to get out of you.   Thoroughly?!" He said, sounding hysterical," Why does it seem like I am the only one excited by the prospects of becoming a parent, what better life to live than to be a happy family in new York." He said.

" To be a happy family in New York.", she smiled at him, and then seemed to relax a little bit, It always brought down her defences whenever he spoke about having children. But she had to admit it, it meant just as much to him as it did to her. she rubbed her stomach discreetly as she listened to the love of her life babble on about his plans fot them as a father. They were both happy having each other, this much was very plain to see.

They arrived at Nicholas's New home in New Jersey. it was about an hour away from their hotel in New York and Dr Oakfield had a chance to see what the homes around the neighbourhood looked like. They arrived promptly at about 8:15pm. Nicholas had brough in maids to attend to his guest for the evening. His new home had a pool so he made it a pool themed party. His maids were dressed in bikinis and swimsuits, as well as some of the guest. he was waiting for them in the living room waiting to serve them Magaritas, Mojitos or champagne caviar. There were kids around the house and this made the environment a lot more relaxing.

Nicholas called out for Judith as soon as he spotted her walking through the door. He was as handsome as usual in a perfectly pressed white shirt, and baige gabardine trousers, with his feet covered in salvotore feragamo loafers. The doctor was casually dressed in a tasteful Ralph Lauren Sweater and and matching jean slacks. she loved the way they both dressed, this was what attracted her to the doctor the more, but she knew it was also the same reason that got her entangled with Nicholas. As the two men met each other,Judith reached for two glasses of magarita.

Nicholas was telling him how much he had heard about him, and how much he had looked forward to meeting him as Judith spoke so highly of him.

" Judith I can see you didn't miss a spec of your description of mr. Oakfield. I can see why you never stopped talking about him, truthfully, what a remarkable job you guys pulled after that tour bus incident." Nicholas said. It was a warm way to break the ice and it seemed to work magic on the doctor who was always open to talk about his work.

Dr Oakfield entertained the conversation and it moved with ease as they talked about a variety of subjects that seemed interesting for them to discuss.

They talked about sports and business, but the football conversations seemed to be the favourite topic.

Dr Oakfield asked about their family business, and although a lot of the answers he received were not too far from what Judith had told him, he still listened with interest and gave a critical assessment on some of this business models in relations to health care. Their family had invested heavily in the private sector of the health system, and Dr Oakfield recognised some of their cintributions over the years. He offered his honest advice from a physicians stand point, and encouraged him to remain committed to his good will towards helping others. Nicholas was pleased to hear what he was saying but Judith took a liking to it more.

They moved inside the dining room after an hour, and they were served with fillet mingon for dinner. At about quater to midnight, they decided to leave. Judith was impressed that the evening had gone well, and there wasn't an exchange of any form of distasteful comments amongst both men.

"So Tell me the evening was fun for you as it was for me." Judith said. They had a driver waiting to take them back to the hotel so neither of them had to drive or hail a taxi. she was interested in what he had to say about Nicholas.

" He sure does know how to have a good time that much is evidential. Is tis what you two get up to when you get on the road together." He asked presumptuously.

" Come on darling, I wouldn't expect you to see it like that, although I would have to agree with you on his party antiques. He has got so many innovative ideas and whenever he makes any of it come to fruition, he celebrates like it is his last day on earth." she said.

" I can see why you two would get along. You both happen to like the aventurous ways of life." He said smiling sheepishly at her.

" He is totally the adventurous one, I'm just tagging along for the ride to my destination. As soon as we get to the production stages of this campaign, I wouldn't need to make as much appearances with him, and that means Public or privately. He would have to find him self another beautiful masscot to troll around town with.

But until then, this is what I have to put up with.

Truthfully though, his parties are always a way to unwind. Trust me, you would too if you have to sit down and listen to some wise ass journalist ask you a million and one questions under an hour. I would have to invite you to the next one so you can make an assessment for yourself." she said.

" Well, you seem to care about it enough." He said smiling. He was proud of her regardless of his reservations about their working relations. she was really stunned by what he said next.

" I think you have an amazing opportunity to grow with his company. If you really want it that much, I think you should close the deal and accept his offer. I just think you'll be beating yourself up for the rest of your life if you didn't give it a shot." He said.

" You know there is no turning back right?" she asked.

" Look how far we've come, do you think I have any intentions of turning back now?" He asked.

" I love you Bernard. And thank you for being so understanding. We need to get you working too, so you don't spend too long inactive." she said.

" I am sure I would in time, but until then, your career is our priority. I want to see you very happy doing this. This is all that matters to me now." He replied. There were tears in her eyes as he spoke to her. He always knew the things to say that would get her emotional. It wasn't like he did it intentionally to upset her, it was only because she felt just how good a man he was to her. He was kind and generous and more so, she could see that he wanted to spend the rest of his life with her.

" I want to make sure this goes well for the both of us." she said.

" I understand and I agree with you." He said. Nicholas had offered to pick them up and give them a tour of the city the next day, but Bernard Oakfield had declined his generous offer. He wanted to spend time with his partner alone for the next few days, but he agreed to take on his offer towards the end of the week.

Bernard Oakfield had accepted for them to meet, but solely on his terms. He would decide when and where they were to meet and it would be at his expense. He was very successful and could afford the bear necessities that came with such inpromptu plans.

The following day the drove across brooklyn bridge, took photos next to the statue of liberty, and after wondering around the shops, they had worked up an appitite. They decided to have lunch in Long Island, and afterwards, they strolled into an irish coffee shop for dessert. They spent the entire evening catching up on their times apart, and after long day, they returned to their hotel.Everything thing was peaceful between them and they had loved the homes they saw across the city.

Bernard Oakfild was fallig in love with the city all over again since his youthful days, but for Judith, she was one day closer to realising her dreams. The following day, they went into the heart of the city to see if main stream newyork was where they could settle into living, but they were overwhelmed by the fact that it was completely too hectic for them to consider having a home in the centre of one of the most busiest part of the world. As the weekend approached, Nicholas was pleased to remind them of his offer, and they both obliged to meet. Infact, he had some how managed to convince them that he wanted to host them again, so in the spirit of sports manship, Bernard Oakfield agreed following a little bit of persuasion by Judith. They arrived at Nicholas's home in jersy for the second time, but this time, it was less busy than it was the first time. Infact they were alone with Nicholas's youngest child, who had refused to go out on a picnic with the others. Bernard Oakfield was pulled into the swimming pool with her, while Judith and Nicholas chatted in the conservatory.

" I think she likes him a lot. If she wasn't young, I'll be facing a possible break up by the time they were done with their swim." Judith said softly as they watched them splash water at each other.

" I am actually amazed. she usually is more reserved around strangers compared to the others." Nicholas said.

" I can't say I am surprised at all. He works wonderfully well with kids. That is certainly one thing I am going to have to work harder on." she said.

" So nothing else shakes the core of your relationships foundation besides my little angel digging her claws into the heart of your man?" He asked.

" Well, it seems like you Wright's have away of having it your way more often than not. What I mean is, I started off just wanting to land a leading role in a movie, but it hasn't stopped there, I am now soon to become the Managing Director of your company, and about to start a whole new life out here, all thanks to you." she said smiling. He was pulling a lot of strings to reel her in, he knew how persuasive he had been, so he accepted his notoriety.

" how ever way you choose to look at it, you are an amazing introduction to my life, and perhaps the business aswell. I want to see things work out for us. I mean how can you not see that we are brilliant together.

Who would want to pass on that?" He said

" It is a wonderful opportunity, there is no doubt about that, but if you are still refering to what happened between us, I still maintain that it wasn't suppose to happen. The sooner we move on from that, the better it would be for us as working partners." she said.

" It's easy for you say so considering that you have your lover ready to jump whenever you say so. I'm a single parent now, the rules are different when you are in my position." He said.

" You are a nice guy Nicholas, I would be seeing things differently if I was single too, but I am not. I wouldn't want to do anything to jeopardize my relationship with Bernard. If that was to be the case, it would be an easy choice for me for give up on all of this just to be with him." she said

" it's not like you are married to this guy. I mean think about it, what can he provide for you that I can't?" He asked.

" Well, unfortunately it isn't about my needs here with Bernard and I, he saved my life, which is something no amount of money can compensate for." she replied.

" I am a workaholic, like I presume you could be. WE are like two peas in a pod. We need our kind of people in this business. I want to see us enjoy all the benefits that comes with the kind of success we can have." He said, glancing at his daughter playing in the pool. " You are lucky. He seems like a nice guy, and it is obvious he is in love with you. How could you then blame me for wanting that too." He said.

" Well, it is impossible to love two people with equal measures Nicholas. It dosen't work. Someone always gets hurt. And I wouldn't want to be the soure of anybody's pain." she replied. Nicholas was silent for a while as they watched the pair in the pool playing. she looked at Bernard intently and smiled at him. she didn't want him to feel used in any way and the last thing she wanted was to see him unhappy.

" So how is the job haunt coming along for him? " Nicholas asked.

" Nothing yet. He is driven to make it happen and I trust it would happen soon enough. He has a keen interest in a few hospitals and he is confident they would create an opening for him soon." she said.

" Which hospitals are you refering to?" Nicholas asked.

Judith replied detailing a few of the main hospitals the doctor had mentioned in the last couple of days and Nicholas made a mental note of them. He just so happened to have friends in the hospitals she mentioned who could make an opening available immediately. he sumurked as he spoke.

" I hope it works out soon enough." Nicholas said fervently.

" I hope so too", she replied.

He was keen on making things happen for her the best he could. He was desperate to have her in his life so he was compelled to pull a few strings absent of their knowledge. The last few days had confirmed everything he needed to know about her, and getting her partner settled in the country would see that he had her right where he needed her. Knowing exactly what he could do, he dismissed the discussion and reverted his attention to his little girl flapping in the water.

" Come on in daddy, the water is lovely." she said, splashing some water towards him.

" Oi cheeky." He said playfully, as he threw the ball into the water and she squealed with pleasure. As relaxing as the mood had been, they all seemed at ease enjoying each tohers company. Judith could see how it would be having a family of her own, and the current view of things made her long for it even more.

It was an easy afternoon for them, and doctor Bernard,

Judith and Nicholas got into long, interesting discussions, mostly about life living in America. It wasn't a new experience for Bernard, but it seemed particularly fasinating for Judith who was experiencing it all for the first time.

They also discussed about business, and Nicholas had his own pet peeves in so many lucrative ventures that caught the doctors attention.

He talked openly about what sort of businesses he would have loved to own if Medicine didn't quite work out for him. After a few hours of exchanging points of view, they left his home. Nicholas wished him well with hos job haunt, and told Judith he would be sending her some useful information for her to study regarding the up coming project. They left feeling exhilarated having spent a relaxing day with Nicholas and his kid, and by the time they returned to the hotel, they spent the rest of the weekend in bed ordering room service and not leaving the room.

By monday morning, Nicholas was out on the town meeting with people in the medical field who he'd hoped would give me a chance to begin his work. Judith was with Nicholas going over details of their project when doctor Bernard called. He sounded exhilarated.

" Hello darling." He said as soon as he heard her voice." I hope I haven't caught you at a bad time" He added.

" Not at all, I am just going over some projections for the project with Nicholas." she replied." You sound over the moon, what's up?" she asked, smiling, as Nicholas watched her intently.

" I have a Job. You won't believe it. They want me to start when ever I am settled in and ready." Plus I would have the ame exact position as I did as head of trauma, with the promise of half of what I am earning added onto my current wages. Plus there are other

incentives and benefits that come along with it if I was prepared to serve for atleast another decade." He said.
" Wow! That is awesome news. Congratulation love." she said as her eyes met with Nicholas who was smiling mischieviously. " I am speechless Bernard. I told you it would all fall into place soon didn't I?" she said.
" Yes you did. I guess it was suppose to be this way after all." He said.

    " We should celebrate." He said.

    " I couldn't agree more." she replied.

    " OK. I should be at the hotel before you. When do think you'll be finished at your meeting?" He asked.
" Very soon, I'll round up here as soon as I can." she said excitedly. Happy to hear the news she was receiving.

    " I guess this is the beginning of our life in America after all huh! I didn't see this on coming at all I must confess." He said.

    " I always had a feeling it would be this way. I would have to make my final decision about my offer as well." she said, finnaly gaining Nicholas's full attention.
" Yes you should, you'll be out of your mind letting it pass now." Dr.Bernard replied.

    " OK. It is done." she said.

    " I will see you very soon." she added

    " Wow! he's got it." she said smiling broadly at Nicholas, who ws trying to mask the fact that he had been eavesdropping on their conversation.

    " Oh really. That's awesome. Trying not to give away too much of his excitment for them. " I am happy for you guys." He added.
Now they both had great new jobs to start off their lives, and it lifed a ton of weight off her shoulders. she was willing now to accept Nicholas's offer knowing this was what he wanted so badly, perhaps more than she realized he did.

    " I can't believe it is finally happening." she said feeling grateful and releieved that it didn't take too long.

she was still smiling while Nicholas silently applauded himself for making this happen for them. His phone call to Doctor Albert, the owner of the private hospital Doctor Bernard was just accepted into clearly created it's desired impact. They would carry on beleiving he landed the job out of his own merits, but little did they know Nicholas was the master mind behind it all. He wasn't certain how long it was going to be a secrete for, but he was prepared not to metion a word of it to neither of them. Nicholas was watching her closely as she couldn't mask her excitement.

" So much for taking a leap of fate." she exclaimed as she beamed at Nicholas.

" Yeah, so much so. These things happen all the time, just for a select few though I must add." He said as his face broke into a broad smile. he was as relieved as she was but only because he was one step closer to fufiling his objective.

" Where does that leave us, Judith? He asked.

" Where would you like me to begin Nicholas.?" she said directly, her eyes dancing with excitment. It was like their mind were working in synchrony, only difference was, he was the facilitator of all this.
" Well, you can begin by telling me I was right to make you see reason for coming on board, then you can tell me how much you would love to be my new Managing Director." He said

" OK, you are right for making me see sense, and yes, I accept your offer coming on board as you new director." she replied.

" Well, double congratulations miss Meredian, welcome to the success club." He said with a smile.

"Well' thank you very much Mr Nicholas Wright." she said.

She was sure now, it was almost like getting your accepted into for first choice university or being inted to prom by your high school crush. For Judith, it was all that and then some. He held out his hand and they shook for a while, looking directly into each others eyes. Three weeks ago, she had nothing to begin with just her hopes and dreams, now, she had gotten twice as much than she'd hoped for. He called one of his assistants to bring them both a bottle of champagne and two glasses.

" You deserve it sweetheart." He said. It was all too much for her to read into the true nature of how things were turning out to be, but none of that mattered now. she was smiling from ear to ear and it was worth the celebration.

They toasted each other, and sat drinking champagne and talking for a while about all the relevant details to get them back on the road.

" When do you want to begin your job duties?" He asked, wanting to assure her that there was no added pressure whatso ever.

" Well, this becomes the tricky part. How do I swing both obligations at once?" she asked.

" Well, you can begin by getting yourself an assistant." He replied.

" OK, I think I might just have the perfect candidate for that." she replied.

" Well then, it's sorted. You bring them on board, we screen them, and they can begin organising your work load for you when ever you are ready." He said.

" That's eactly what I'll do. I would need a bit of time to tie up loose ends on my part, then afterwards, I should be set to go." she replied confidently.

Nicholas knew he could apply a bit more pressure to get her up and running as soon as possible but he was cautious not to over work her. The shrewd businessman that he was was ready to rise to the fore, but he put aside his own personal interest for the time been. He was going to wait until they were properly settled in before he made his next move.

" You can take as much time as you need to sort

out your living arrangements and whatever else is necessary." He said.

He didn't want to startle her, and he also didn't want her to feel like he was been too hasty. It wouldn't be fair to either one of them, and he understood this better than either Doctor Bernard or Judith.

She knew she would have to attend to his needs but she was pleased to see that he was very considerate. she knew he needed her and she was prepared to do everything to keep him co-operative.

" Are you sure you could manage without a managing director in the mean while? I'm sorry this would have to be a graudual transition, but I wouldn't want your business suffering any longer than it should while I am still trying to put things together." she said.

" That is very thoughtful of you Judith. But seeing that you are concerned, I do have an acting assistant on seat at the moment. It should all be fine until the final handover." He replied.

" Thats nice to know." she replied, releived to learn that she wouldn't be pressured into the position just as yet.

" I would like to let you know that a cheque of a hundred thousand pound has been drawn for your expenses through out this moving period. Consider it added benefit to incentive our future partnership." He said.

she rendered her speechless as there was no way she could say no to that.

" I am also prepared to make living accomodation ready for you atleast for the first year all paid for until you two love birds decide on where you want to reside permantly." He added. Nicholas knew exactly what he was doing and he was an expert at this. He was doing more than she could possibly ask for and they both knew it.

" It's all very thoughful and generous Nicholas. You

make it impossible for me to turn down your offerings, but I am just a little bit stunned why you are doing so much for me. I truthfully didn't expect this much." she said, a bit worried about it all silently, in spite of the cheque and job offer, which was more than handsome, it was an outstanding platform for her to begin her many steps to come.

" I am sorry if it feels like I am being pushy, it is just that I want you to know that I understand how importsnt it is for me to you well suited through out this entire process. it is the best I can do." He said.

" I can not thank you enough. We will work things out gradually. she wasn't sure how Doctor Bernard was going to take on his added offerings but she let the thought pass momentarily. she was meeting him at the hotel soon to tell him about her good news but ofcourse, she was almost certain that their excitment was going to be overwhelming enough for them to worry about every single detail.

Nicholas and Judith left his office an hour later. He returned to his family while she hurried to meet Doctor Bernard. They huged each other and went their separate ways.

" I hope everything goes smoothly for you from hereon Judith." Nicholas said, planting a kiss on her cheek.

" I hipe so too." she replied.

" Call me as soon as you run into any difficulty what so ever." He said before they parted. He knew he had her, but as far as he was concerned, he was handling his business, and this ofcouse was necessary evil to ensure future success. Sooner or later he would have her wrapped around his fingers but until then, he would wait.

As usual, she was intrigued by the rapid effect the changes in her life was presenting. she had to go all the way with this now. There way no turning back for her. Life wasn't going to wait for her to catch up. For the first time in her twenty-seven years of living, she considered herself truly lucky.

When she arrived at the hotel they were both over the moon. They made sweet passionate love to eachtoher, and afterwards, they talked about their new found purpose in life.

He proposed selling his apartment to raise some funds for their immediate accomodation. she realized that accepting Nicholas's offer was a great way to soften the financial blow they were bound to encounter one way or another, but telling him she had been given added monies would only be an even bigger blow to his ego. she knew he could afford this move, perhaps not entirely with the extravagance the likes of Nicholas would, but she didn't want him feeling any less inferior compared to the calibre of people Nicholas associated with.

" You know, I am starting to beleive there wasn't any coincidence how and why we met each other. The writing is clearly on the wall." Dr. Bernard said.

" I am a true believer of that too darling." she replied, kissing him strongly as they snuggled up to each other.

" That brings me to the point of this Nicholas guy. He seems like a nice guy and all, but I am always sort of weary about people most times, especially when they go out of their way to do so much for you." He said.

The statement he made made her heart skip a beat, and it made her a bit uncomfortable knowing eaxctly what she knew about their time together. she knew Bernard was clearly onto something, but there was no way of telling exactly what he was implying, so she was particularly cautious of her response to him.

" The man feels threatened by you in some ways." she said abruptly.

" And what do you mean by that?" He asked curiously.

INNOCENT NLEWEDIM

" Come on baby, have you not noticed how he seems so intrigued by your profession and your views on certain matters. If he could trade places, he would do so with you in no time. He believes your line of work is honourable. He even made a joke once saying that, all his friends and clients always need a good doctor to call on incase of an emergency, like when the stock market crashes, or theres been a declaration of a hefty loss of investors funds. People find themself in the hospital room somewhere battling with a heart related trauma of some kind." she said, forcing a roar of laughter between them.

" Well, if you put it that way." He said. " I would have thought he would have been onto you by now." He added humourously.

" No chance dear." she replied, eager to keep their conversation moving along without diving into any specific of the intended nature of their existence together as colleagues. They had considerablely gotten close to each other, but he chose to see their relationship as strictly professional and chose not to buy into the thought of suspision that there could be anything more.

" He is a fun guy to be around, plus his kids are to die for." she added.

" Yes I agree, kids could be a bundle of joy given the right circumstances." He said in agreement. Judith nodded, glancing out the window, haunted by the thought of one growing inside. she still couldn't bring herself to tell him they were expecting. He smiled at her gently, expecting her to play into his fram of conversation, but realizing how she responded to the subject, he refrained form talking about it, suspecting it might ruin the mood.

There was no denying the fact that it was going to happen sooner than he expected. The considered the thought of an abrtion momentarily, leaving it down to their added fortune if it happened much later in her career. she always said that if she wanted kids it would be when she had secured all her financial troubles, medically, she didn't want to leave it any much later. she was getting on now, soon to be in her thirties. perhaps she had some time to let this one go for now. It was terrible dealing with this matter alone, it scared her to think that she would loose him if she confessed her pregnancy to him now soley because she wasn't financially prepared.

" Why don't we see how things go," she said vaguely, not wanting to give off the impression that this wasn't as important to her as it was to him. It was an improvement from her usual dismissive response, so this made him happy with her answer.

" I don't think there would ever be a perfect time Judith. Think about it. We seem to be doing just fine learning to adjust to drastic changes. I am sure we would be able to handle that challenge when it comes." He said.

He knew she was frightened about the possiblility of being pregnant more than any thing else anyone could choose to throw at her, but it was more about the commitment a baby would require of her that frightened her the most, plus she hadn't gotten over the loss of her father and brother.

The thought of bringing new life into the world that was susceptible to a premature death death or the definitive eventuality of death wasn't particularly her favourite pass time thought.

" I know exactly what you mean Bernard." she said, sounding disturbed. she knew she owed him a lot after the sort of committment he had submitted to just to see her happy. Right now would have been the perfect time to tell him they were expecting, but she wasn't sure she was ready for this.

" I want you to know I'll do everything in my power to make sure you get all the support you need once your mind was made up. I promise." He said, planting a kiss on her forehead.

" I am sorry it seems like I am holding you back in any way, I just don't know if I am ready for that stage of my life yet." she replied sounding upset.
' Maybe you'll never know until it happens." He said.

" What if it never happens for us? What if it does and we can't handle it. When a child comes in the picture, there is no taking it back to where it came from. Our lives are going to get pretty busy trying to adjust to life here, what if we get to busy to make time for our child. it is called neglect is the court of law Bernard. Even the most successful parents struggle with this mostimes." she said

" It is a scary thought I know. I am not trying to pressure you into this at all, but I want you to know it would not be such a bad idea to have a mini you and I running around the new home we would be moving into soon." He said, forcing her to laugh at the thought of the image he projected in her mind.

" OK doctor, I see what your trying to say, we would talk about it some more when we are settled in properly." she said dismissing the thought as summarily as she always had since they had this conversation for the first time. it always made her anxious and on the edge.

" So when will you tell your mother about the current advancement of things?" He asked, voluntarily changing their subject of discussion.

" As soon as I sign the dotted lines with Nicholas, I guess. I want to make sure it is no longer a dream. that way I can be out of the nest once and for all." she said,

" That's fair enough, I bet she would be proud of your accomplishment in such a very short space of time." He said.

" she certainly would, no doubt about that." she replied.

" No matter what, I want you to know you have

earned it." He said.

"Thanks a lot. It means so much to me hearing this coming from you." she said. It did make her feel less guilty following the thought of infidelity that haunted her. she was beginning to see just much she appreciated him. Particularly seeing that he was with her through this very important stage of her life. After a while she was beginning to let the reality of her life wash over her. she had to accept this unprecedented changes, it was part of her life as it was and she didn't want to fight it for much longer. As she sat in the hotel room with him, she looked around the hotel room amazed at how far she had come in life.

"I am glad you are here with me." she said to him.

"I am too sweetheart." He replied with a grin. He was particularly happy about it all because he could see she was finally moving on with her life and he was there with her to give her the love and support she needed.

The one thing he had promised her was that he would not leave her on her own, and now, she could feel his determination like a force to be reckoned with. she was more confident now and he was glad to be her strength.

They both allowed themselves to relax more now. He was going to ring the hospital in London to tell them of his immediate plans. He knew the chief at the trauma unit would be devastated about his news but it was a sure banker now. He was moving on and there wasn't much that could change the outlook of things. He would miss some of his friends, but they too would have to deal with the saddness of his departure.

He tried not to think about the emotional attachment he had for the life he'd built in England. He smiled at Judith, and with a firm kiss, they warmed up into another steamy love making seccession which was all they planned to do for the remainder of their time until he returned to London.

CHAPTER 14

The turn of events was everything Judith had hoped it would be. It was life altering, and finally getting her life back in order was something she didn't expect to happen so soon.

Professionally, she was going to become a seven figure earner in wages only. she hadn't added the endorsment rights and commissions from numerous projects she was going to be running independently. It was a chance of a life time and she wasn't prepared not to let it go.

Judith and Nicholas maintained their vigour attending follow up meetings with the wrights associates.

They worked very well together, meeting after meeting, drawing up new plans for their current projects. They were both meticulous so it was easy for them to process information seemlessly but still get the best result. They were finished with their assignmen for the day, and Judith was pleased to return to her new appartment.

Nicholas had rented it for her and it was just spot on luxirious. It was spacious and had the warth of a real home. she called her mother as often as she could, to let her know what was happing since she left London. she tried calling Dr Oakfield a few times, to let him also know how she was getting on in her life, But as always, it wasn't easy to catch him in between surgery.

He had to be in London for atleast two months to finalize his move to America. Judith was always happy to hear from him on the days they could manage to speak to each other instead of leaving voice messages.

They both had too much work to get away and chat

over the phone for hours like they do when he is off
duty and she hadn't gone on tour. she was still trying to
get over the fact that she was pregnant by a man whom
she hasn't know longer than a year. she did love him
but having his child was certainly frightening for her. she
always seemed to find peace in her heart that made her
believe him whenever he said he was going to do
something for her. she saw focused on her duties and
was determined not to let this pregnancy get in the way
of her daily aganda. Now it wasn't so difficult for her to
put a hault to on-going productions if she wanted an
extention of time or a break if she needed to catch her
breath. she knew that doctor benarnd would seek for a
home that suited his taste more than hers.

Eventhough it didn't bother her much about where
they would live together, this apartment was one she
was going to keep off the books. it was going to be her
sanctuary.

Even after the baby comes, she imagined herself
returning here to escape the outside world. Nicholas
had offered it to her in good faith as he understood what
her work pattern was going to be like in the near future.
she didn't need to worry about the rent or any other
bills. It was all taken care of by Nicholas. They had
agreed that since they would be in and out of town a lot
they could both share the apartment, using it whenever
the other was away. The house was a good
comporomise for them, and Judith had agreed to it.

"Hello mother." Judith spoke as she heard her
mothers voice for the first time that day.

" work was good mum, I told you things were going
to work just fine." Judith said. she had been going into
the office with her new assistant to learn about her role
as the new managing Director of Nicholas company.
Her predecessor had left her with a ton of unfinished
work, so the sooner she could begin to get her head
wrapped around it, the better for her. she was a fast

learner and this was working out to her advantage. she knew she was going to get busier, so she managed to convince her mother to come visit before Doctor Benarnd returns.Adriana had refused her offer once, but this time she was prepared to make a trip to go visit her daughter. she had been told how marvelous life was for her daughter but she needed to see it all for herself. Nicholas had made arrangements for them to have dinner as a way to show his gratitude towards her for accepting his offer. Judith didn't mind him meeting her mother.

They were getting used to each other, and after meeting steve, he finally understood that he would have to do so much more to win her affection in the ways he desired.

Every passing day was a test for them and after the first week, she was sure she could do this all on her own. she was pleased to get things going. she was grateful to be able to get the kind of support she was receiving, especially from doctor Bernard. Although they were both busy at work, she always thought about him. she missed him even more now and she couldn't wait for him to arrive. she knew how important it was for her to keep him closer since she found out she was pregnant. Her second week on duty was just as good as the first, and by the end of the first month she was really beginning to miss doctor Bernard. By this time it was Bernard who called. He was going to be in london for another 3weeks before flying to new york. And Judith was as disappointed as he was.

" That is just terrible news Bernard." she said, sounding midly depressed about it. He had been busy at work, so he couldn't finalize the sale of his flat on time for their orginal schedule.

" I know sweetheart. I didn't expect it to get this windy. But I've accepted their offer and I think this process should be concluded very soon." He said.

They promised each other than nothing would stand in their way of having a life together. It had been four weeks since she'd lst seen him, and it would take another seven weeks for them to see each other again, but she had missed him. she knew it wasn't going to be smooth sailing for him, so she managed to cope with the anxiety the situated created.

" I know we had made plans but it will just take a little while longer OK?" He said apologetically.

" Of course, darling," she said, without hesitating. she knew how challenging it was for him, but she also trusted that he understood how important it was for her. she could do away with her worries and just count down the clock.

" It is OK dear, it's been four weeks, im sure I could wait a bit longer. I have no choice but to wait until I see you." she replied.

For once he coud feel the intensity of this decision to move to New York. It was a major step in his life, and most of all, Judith's. she felt a little guilty about her role in the entire move, and it made her submissive.

" I'll wrap up somethning special for you when you get here." she said.

" Hmmm. And what might that be?" He asked inquisitively.

" Now that would be telling wouldn't it?" she said.

" I guess so. Now I can't wait to get to you baby." He said.

" Well then, you know exactly what you need to do to get get here sooner." she replied.

" Great, well, I guess you got me waliking on a tight rope here. I'll have to work through this as quickly as I can baby. I wish I could get it out the way any sooner." He said.

" That's OK. you have been a good boy, so I'll keep your prezie for you nonetheless." she replied

" I'll be with you in less than seven weeks. I swear,

hand on the bible." He said. He wanted to be with her and he was prepared to do all it takes. But for now, it was a waiting game and there was nothing he could do about it. They ended their conversation and she was delighted to have the evening to herself.

The following day she attended a dinner function at Nicholas's home. He had invited all his chosen affiliates for the project to meet each other officially. It was planned to be a very pleasant evening. He asked Judith to come before the other gust arrived, which she failed to do. Bust she attened a few hours later in red cocktail dress that was sleek, sophisticated and very sexy. she immediately caught the attention of everyone in the room as soon as she walked in.

" You look marvelous, Judith." He said, as they huged and kissed each other on the ckeek. He walked her round the room and briefed her quickly on the background details of some of the people she wasn't already familiar with. she was happy to see one or two faces she'd already met with at the beginning of the campaigne tour, but most of all, she was pleased to meet those who she had only read about entensively on the company records.

Now she had arrived, Nicholas could appreciate her essence, she was a very gracious hostess for him. They both moved easily among the guest, talking to them about business issues. It was a well balance crowd of male and females with interesting point of views on their respective subject matter, and indeed, as Judith drifted around the room, she appreciated that it was a well-reserved business conversation. Nicholas beamed as he watched her, she was a joy to watch and indeed the perfect female business partner he'd ever worked with.

When the guest finally left, they both agreed that it had been a successful evening, great company, great food, new business proposals, more investment intiatives and promises, and everyone just couldn't wait to see the final piece of the movie.

" You are getting absolutely remarkable at this Judith" Nicholas said with a look of admiration.

" You can say I had good lessons from the master himself." she replied with a smile.

" Thank you for being a part of this. I can truly see how important all this means to you." He said.

" You can't begin to imagine." she said simply.

" Well, I glad to see you are getting a swing of things so fast." HE said

" It's just ike riding a bicycle really. Once you learn how to get on it and find your balance, it becomes part of who you are." she replied.

He had realized that it wasn't as easy getting things to work out the way she expected without some real struggle. But she ony had to do it for two more months. It wasn't forever. Doctor Bernard had to be understanding about it to still want to see it through with her, and this was all that mattered to her. she was establishing herself in a new business and things were looking up for her.

" Well' you know I am here for you every step of the way. I'll do anything to see that this works out just fine for you. " He said.

" IT sounds re-assuring to hear that coming from you." she said sincerely.

" You deserve it Judith. You really do." He said.

" Thanks. It feels good to know you think so. I'll like to use the rest of the weekend to go house hunting. Once Doctor bernard finalizes the sale of his flat, he would be in a position to make a payment for the home of his choice." she said as they walked slowly towards her taxi in his driveway. she was pleased that the evening had gone so well for him.

" Can I accompany you? I happen to know a few places you two might like." He said unexpectedly.
" It's too much of me to ask of you. I am sure you have far more better things to do with your time over the weekend." she said as she opened her door to get into the car.
" As a matter of fact, I don't. The kids are off to florida for two weeks, we've managed to set things up way ahead of schedule. So I do have ample time to while away as I choose. SO I choose to help you find a house." He said.
" I guess you chauffeuring services might come in handy after all." she replied.
" Alright then. When do you want me to pick you up?" He asked
" Around nine am. I have an agent willing to show me some places in the city first." she said.
" OK, I'll be there at eight-thirty just to be on the safe side." He replied with a warm smile.
" OK, that is fine with me, I'll see you in the morning." she said, and minutes later her taxi drove off. she arrived at her apartment an hour later and ordered Pizza for dinner.

The next morning, Nicholas was at the front door as early as planned. He did ring her mobile phone twice, so with no answer, he let himself into the house. He had his own set of keys and made his way into the kitchen to make himself some coffee. He could hear her in the shower, so he left the coffee brewing as he walked down the corridor leading to the bedroom. she had left the door open, so he could hear her singing along to the music playing on the radio. He could see the steam emanating from the bathroom as he approached the door. He wanted to announce himself, but held his breath. A part of him did not want to frighten her, bit the most part of him had longed to see her beautiful body again. He felt perhaps a glimpse of her in the shower would extinguish the desire burning inside of him. As he took a couple more steps towards to door, Judith emerged, holding a small piece of towel over her chest. Unawear of his presence initially, He was intrigued by the sight of her wet body and hair still dripping with water, but Judith was startled when she saw him.

" Oh My God! You scared the Jesus out of my." she said,placing both her hands firmly across her chest with the towel.

" I'm sorry, I didn't mean to frighten you." He said.

" How long have you been in here?" she asked, confused as to how he got into the house unannounced.

" I did call your mobile coulple of time. Besides, I've got my own set of keys remember?" He said, Removing them from his pocket and dangling it in front of her.

" I thought you would have been ready by now." He said with a faint smile.

" I woke up an hour late. I guess I must have slept through the alarm." she said, looking puzzled by the awkwardness of the situation.

" Well then, get a move on missy, otherwise you are going to be late." He said." I'm making coffee, I'll make it a double to go." He added as he turned around and returned to the kitchen. she watched him until he was out of sight before she entered her room. she was beginning to wonder that there might be a lot more to Nicholas's character than he was giving off. she knew he was still interested in her in more ways that she cared to acknowledge, but whatever else more he wanted was hard for her to imagine. she got herself ready, and after thirty minutes, he drove her to the city, as they chatted comfortably, about business, as usual.

The first house they saw had unfortunately been taken by a client of the agency she had contacted to show her a few properties that were on the market. she was disappointed because she actually did like the place, and she knew doctor Bernard would have loved it aswell. But after that, they saw two more but they did not match her expectation.

" Do not trouble yourself, there are so much properties on the market around town. Trust me, sometimes you end up finding the right one even when your not house hunting." Nicholas said as they got back in the car. It was lunch time and he had suggested they have luch at a restaurant on the upper eastside called the Grandiose Restaurante. It was a new italian opening and as always, he wanted to be one of the few who dined there first. she was starving so she agreed.

" It is mentally exhausting having to deal with work and find a home at the same time. iamgine if I had kids. I'll have to drag them along to these viewings. Can you imagine how stressful that would be for them." she said.

" Well that depends on if you plan to have kids," He said

" I have your company to run, isn't that enough for me to worry about as it stands? afterall, it does seem like I'll be baby sitting some of your clients just to keep them in your books. Thats enough motherly chores to deal with thank you very much." she replied.

" I am not sure how your partner is going to deal with all that when he finally moves." He said.

" How do you mean?" she asked

" Well, if you consider my business operation to be a motherly chore, that would leave no room for him if he did want to have children with you when he is settled in." He said.

" I know." she said uncomfortably. it was a sore subject. " He and I have had this conversation several times, and I still don't know if I am ready for it. I won't be able to escape his demands for very much longer when he finally moves out here." she replied.

" I think your just thinking too much about it. But I don't mean that to say it dosen't require a lot of thinking, it's just that, if you can't see it happening with him, you need to let him know, so he can move on with his life." Nicholas said. it was one of the most reasonable remarks she has heard him say in reference to her relationship with the doctor. But if only he knew that her pregnancy clock was ticking. she was far along a month now, and she was beginning to see the changes in her body.

"As much as you might shine some reasonableness on the matter, it is not in your place to make suggestions on the count of my relationship. I want it to work out for the both of us. he is a good man, and to suggest that it is my lack of committment to him that brings up my indecisiveness is nothing short of your total misunderstanding of my feelings towards him." she replied defensively.

" I am not saying you're not committed to him," he said, attempting to correct her as he realised he'd struck a nerve.

" I actually think you are committed, more than ever now, I just think maybe your are not ready for this sort of committment. it is two different things. Or perhaps, you just don't trust the relationship, or the future you two may have together." He said.

It was Nicholas's way of trying to get her to feed more into the idea of playing the single role in other for him to explore his chances with her without the guilt that festered in heart knowing very well that he was over stepping his boundary.

" After all we have been through. it would be cowaardly for me to cut him loose. I don't intent to do so, and I am pretty sure he feels the same way." she replied, knowing that this wasn't what he wanted to hear. I know my self, and I am trusting my gut instincts on this one, so trust me, I am not about to go against that." she added.

" But that wasn't what you had your mind set on

doing from the beginning. You were prepared to make sure nothing came inbetween you career pursuits as an actress, don't you think moving into a serious family life would compromise that, tell me Judith what has changed?" He asked.

she hesistated before she answered. " a lot has changed Nicholas. that is the issue. Only about a couple months ago I was uncertain how things would pan out, but not, it all seemes to be happening so fast. I mean, I am not particuarly getting any younger. The younger me didn't know how to handle been in a serious relationship, but now, it seems to be the order of the day. I can't keep trying to avoid the inescapable. I never thought my career would come to mean so much to me, but I have to find a balance now, or loose it forever." she said claerly and firmly.

" I know that, but there's usually more to it than just finding a man to call your husband. I made that same choice once upon a time but look where it landed me. With lovely kids ofcourse, but a broken home in the end." He said.

" I don't know what you mean when you say that Nicholas, but just because you life played out the way it did, dosen't mean it would play out the same way in my situation. I know people can be with the same partners for years out of just cheer security, but then year down the line they figure out that they are not happy, Be it either to the absence of kids, or just the mere fact that they might have rushed into it.

Some may want out, and before you know it, they fall for someone else, they get married, and bang, they are pregnant which ever comes first. it is just the nature of life. I do not want to be caught up in that frenzy. No offence to you, I do not intend to get re-married, or get tied down to a loveless relationship in the name of feeling financially secure. No offence to you in any way but, but I want to be with the father of my children for the rest of my life, and I certainly wouldn't want it to be with a man who already has been married." she said matter-of-factly.

" Are you saying that If I was your only option, you would pass because I've been married and already have children?" He asked.

" Yes, Bu that isn't the point I am trying to put across here, what I am trying to say is, I think I may have found the one. And I want to make it work out naturally. I am sure you of all people would understand this." she said.

" Now don't get me wrong. I do not mean to suggest that your onto a doomed relationship, I guess what I'm just saying is that nothing is predictable in life. I mean look at Us for instance." He wss immediately interrupted by her.

" There is no us in that sense Nicholas." she said abruptly. It was an old theory with him, she had heard it while they were on tour and here it was again.

" Just hear me out would you. if you look deep enough, I'll bet there are other reasons why you didn't want to make the ultimate committment to begin with. I know it certainly wasn't all work related then, so it certainly wouldn't be now. But what ever it was gave room for us to share such a wonderful time the way we did on tour. That surely isn't something your going to forget in a hurry Judith. No matter how you choose to deal with it." He said.

" Maybe you are right, but we have both established it wasn't supposed to happen. It was a moment of weakness, and that might just be one I might live to regret considering that I am in love with Bernard. Maybe I felt insecure to a certain degree that made me drop my guards then, but that isn't enogh for me to throw away everything else I have shared with him. We all make mistakes, I agree, but this is one mistake I am not going to allow define who I am. people seem to find ways to move on for these sort of things and I am hoping that you would do the right thing now to help us move on from it." she said.

" How, by pretending it never happened?" He asked.

" Yes, if that is what it take. No matter how wrong the circumstances were or how bad the timing was, if we made our choice then, I am almost certain that we could apply the same logic not to let it happen ever again." she replied.

" How about if I chose to apply the same logic that got us into it in the first place?" He said.

" That was work related Nicholas and you know it. If we didn't have important issues to deal with, we would have never have a reason to meet each other." she replied.

" Well, here we are Judith. It isn't particularly going to be easy fpr me to overlook the nature of what we have become. it is always going to be there in all manners of grey, no matter how you choose to sugar coat it. Unless ofcourse there is a more valid reason why you think this is a lost cause for us, and if there is, I'll like to hear it, until then, I can't ignore the fact that there is genuine chemistry between us, despite your moral view on our co-existence." He said.

It was all getting a lot more intense between them, and a few of his points were worth a closer look, and she wondered if Nicholas was closer to the truth than she wnated to believe.

Lunch at the grandiose was fun, it helped neutralize the intensity brewing between them. They owed it to themselves to be cordial and professional and the spectacular view and Service at the restaurant helped them relax. And afterwards, they drove around town to view more houses. They walked around for the most part as a few of the houses and apartments were within a block apart for the other. And when they finished, they had both worked up an apetite. He initiated dinner and she couldn't resist. After all, she was feeding for two now, so it was no surprise at all when she agreed.

" I am going to be as fat a a pig eating two to three time everyday while I am with you." she said humourously.

" Seeing that you seem to enjoy eating more these days, it's the least I can do." He said.

Besides their struggle finding a common ground to deal with the affair best known to them, she was having such a nice time with him. he was so easy to be with, and they always had so much to talk about when it came to the movie business. Nicholas's phone rang momentarily and he was informed that his kids where arriving shortly. He didn't need to pick them up, but they were keen on having dinner with him.

" I guess we have inherited comapny for dinner. The kids are coming back home tonight. it is going to be our last weekend together before they return to England." H said.

" Well, I think You should Go spend time with them. I wouldn't want to interrupt your family time together." she said with a smile.

" Oh don't be ridiculous, the Kids love you. You should come with me. We could skip eating out, and have my cooks whip up whatever we all want." He said.

" Well, if you insist." she said.

" Well, I do." He replied.

The kids weren't surprised to see her that night. When they all saw her, they greeted her warmly with hugs. They somehow managed to convince her to join them for movies at the cinema as it was going to be their final outing before they travelled. Somehow Judith got swept away by the tides of their enthusiasm, and the next thing she knew, she had given in.

" So long as your daddy woudn't mind." she said

" Ofcourse not." They all said in uniform.
she shot him a quick glance, and with the admiration
he felt his children had for her, he was inclined to
support their wishes.

" Who am I to decline. I am perfectly comfortable
with it. I think it would be a ripping adventure." He said
with a broad smile. They all sat for dinner, and Judith
was awed by them. she let her self warm into their way
of life and the jargon they used to communicate with
each other. It was something Nicholas was very familiar
with.

They had a way of speaking to each other about
people present without the subjects knowledge. On few
occassions, it was about Judith and Nicholas could pick
up on it. she thought it was cool, but little did she know
that they were talking about her. Her mind drifted into a
time where it was her family sat at the dinner table with
friends of the family having a laugh. she missed that
with her own family. things had changed a lot in her
home since she lost her father and brother. Infact,
things had never been the same. I took a lot for her
getting used to it, but she had found some ways to deal
with it. The kids were laughing now when Nicholas
called them to order, and she mind returned to her
current environment.

" I think you are going to be sentational in the movi
Ms Judith." The youngest out of the lot of them said.

" Oh, thank you sweetheart. It isn't as easy as one
thinks initially, but I am looking forward to it." she
replied.

" I hope to become a famous actress too some
day." The little girl replied.

" And so you would." Judith said, and then touched
her hand gently.

" You are a beautiful and smart girl, I think the
world would love and adore you." Judith added.

" You really think so? My daddy happened to think
I'll make a better doctor than an actress. it's nice to hear

an actual actresses point of view on the subject." she
said,
" You know you speak very well too, perhaps that is
something that your father would have to re-consider
when you are all grown up." Judith said.
Nicholas was pleased to see them tlak to each other the
way they did. He knew how important it was for adults
to help shap the dreams and aspirations of the younger
mins and she seemed to be doing so effortlessly. I didn't
bother him whatever anyone of his kids chose to
become in the future, he was only concerned that they
got the best out of life. He had enjoyed her company all
day. they had even laughed when the real estate agent
thought he was her husband, and now seeing her with
his kids at the dinner table made him see her so much
differently. He wondered if she could sense that she
was playing the role of a mother figure to his kids
eventhough they knew better. she knew it was a
concession she was making for her own family life, but
he was beginning to suspect there was more to the
changes he saw in her than what met the eyes.
' How are you liking the food, are you enjoying it?" He
asked.
    " I love it." Judith admitted. " I should hire them now
and again when I am settled in. I am sure Bernard
would like it." she added.
    " Oh, you mean the handsome doctor?" The little
girl next to her said in response to her comment.
    " Oh yes dear. He would be moving to New York
Soon". Judith replied.
    " Finish your food sweetheart, and let ms Judith do
the same." Nicholas said in attepts to bring an end to
the conversation about his rival in the matters of the
heart concerning him and Judith. she realized he was
insecure every time Doctor Bernards name was
mentioned.
    " I bet you can't wait." His oldest son said.

" Yes, it is exciting and nerve racking at the same time." Judith said admittedly, forcing a roar of laughter across the table.

" But first We have to find a place to live." she said.

" I am sure she will figure it out soon enough." Nicholas said. Realising that all attention was shifting away from him.

" Now finish your food guys and go brush your teeths." Nicholas said.

Making it seem so easy handling all of them on his own. He ordered one of the maids to pour him and Judith more wine after dinner, and they say in his living room chatting comfortably. it was finally just about midnight when she decided to call it a night. They arranged to meet the following day for their cinema trip and by noon the following day, him and the kids were at her front door. They swarmed into the house like little bees as soon as she opened the door, and moments later they left the house and drove into town. They had a fantastic time together, eating hot dogs, pop corns and nachos. And when they left, even without thinking about it, she returned to his house with them. It was nice seeing how he kept them in line while they were in public. He was a good father to them and he played his role very well.

" It was such a lovely day out with the kids, You guys seem to get along like a house on fire." she said.

" I can say the same for you Judith. This is the first I've seen them so happy around any other person since My ex-wife and I divorced.

" It's good to see they are dealing with all that has happened very well." she said.

" Well, there are down sides too, but I try not to make it too overwhelming for them." He replied.

" You set a great example for them, you seem like the perfect role model for them. Especially the girls." she siad.

" It is fun when they don't think you are old

fashioned, dumb or pathetic most of the time." He said, forcing a smile between them.

" That must be heart breaking. I know the girls must be the harder ones to raise without their mother." she said.

" Yea, you can say that again, especially when the house turns into a war zone when you stop them from painting their toes, fingers and lips." He said jovially.

" That is adorable. you should learn to leave them to it, becuase it would become their way of life invouluntarily." she replied,

" Well, I'll take note of that next time it happens." He said.

" Well, I have enjoyed myself thoroughly. Please wish them a safe trip to ondon for me. And thanks for a lovely day out." she said.

" I will do, but really, I should be the one thanking you Judith. You are a breath of fresh air, and I hope you know that. You've made it easy for me the las two days, I am sure their nannies would be relieved that we gave them a break from the kids." He sid.
It seemed a serious moment for them, but Judith was quick to swith the mood.

" You deserve all the credit Nicholas not Me. I am sure in time you would find someone who would fit in just perfectly for the sake of the kids." she replied. They arranged to meet t the office the next day wich was the start of another week, and after they shook hands, a few minutes later, she got into a taxi and returned to her apartment.

A few minutes after she got in, she called Doctor Bernard. she saw a few missed calls from him when she picked up her mobile phone. she'd realized she left it in the bedroom as she was in a hurry to leave the house when Nicholas and the kids arrived in the morning.

" Where the world have you been Judith, I've been trying to reach you all day." Dr.Bernard said. she was surprised by his tone. It wasn't as gentle as she'd gotten used to hearing him talk. But their current plans was putting a considerable strain on him particularly, and she was willing to be passive about it.

" I have been out in town with Nicholas and his kids. I Should have told you much sooner but I left my mobile in the bedroom this morning.I just walked in the door a few minutes ago." she believed it was an accurate count of event to help him understand what had happened, but it ignited his fury even more.

" You've basically spent the entire weekend with him. Why don't you too just move in together while you are at it?" he said

" Come On Bernard, there is no need for the ill sinicism. The project schedule was free for the entire weekend, howelse am I supposed to bore myself to death being here alone." she said

" That's besides the point. You two are always together on one staple or another. I must say, I am starting to find the whole thing absolutely ridiculous." He said.

" Well then, be my guest. Laugh it all up. I have made a conscious decison to make this work for us, but it would not be easy for either of us if this is how we choose to deal with this situation." she replied.

" I don't intend to ridicle your efforts, I would not sit here and pretend that I don't see the way he looks at you. He is always making sure he gets the best of your time, if I didn't know any better I'll say he's hitting on you." He said.

" OK, now you are starting to sound ridiculous. Why have you chosen to make a big deal out of this?" she asked

" I think a more appropriate question should be why shouldn't I make a big deal about it?" He said. she didn't like the tone of the conversation, and wondered if he'd had a bad day, or just exhausted about the entire prospects of changing his life for her.

" And I would answer, NO sweetheart, Do Not make a big deal out of this. If there was anything I couldn't handle on my own, you'll be the first person I'll call." she replied

" Well, at what point are my suppose to know that when you two are always everywhere and nowhere to be found." HE said." Then to top it all up, I get worried sick when I can't reach you, then you turn around and confirm to me that you've been out in town with Mr. Wright. The fact he has got money to throw around dosen't mean he should pre-occupy your time as well. The priority right now is for us to get a home to move into. Have you found a place yet?" He asked, sounding shrewd.

" Not yet. Still looking." she said.

" Well maybe you should look harder in your spare time that taking trips with your boss." He said.

" Come on Bernard, Don't be silly. I haven't liked anything I've seen, and I know you wouldn't too. Please don't get yourself worked up about this. We will find a place we would both love. We have time. Atleast I have a good enough place to stay instead of hotels. We will find a place you'll see." she said

" OH! A house that he had made private arrangements for you to live in for as long as you are searching. Well, I must say that is really comforting Judith. It really is. It is OK for me to sleep evernight knowing that my partners entire existence is surrounded by this one man."

" Would you rather there were more than one man Bernard?! Because the last time I checked we were doing this for us. For christsake, I am here to go into full time business with this same man. it is part of the plan remember? Please don't make this any harder for me than it already is." she said, she was startled to realize that he was jealous, but she couldn't blame him.

" Well, I certainly don't feel like the only Man in your life. And as a matter of fact I am not. you are practically living off this man. It is going to be months before you shoot your movie, any other from of earning would still come form this same man eventhough he has some how manged to employ you. Come On Judith Can't you see my concern" Or am I just been a fool here?"

" Of course not. We are just going through the early stages of this transisiton sweetheart. We are just friends Nicholas and I. I expect you to believe that. It was Important for you to meet him so you can see for youself that he is the one responsible for the project. he is going to be for quite a while too, so trust me, I am trying to deal with this situation the best way I can." she said

" Well, you should try ten times harder." He said, almost shouting at her." he would get to spend more time with you than I would, and I am supposed to be rational about this. Listen to yourself."He added.

" Sweetheart, calm down. I told you, I am not going to let anyone or anything come between us. Especially not Nicholas Wright." she said.

" well, I am not too sure of that. I saw the guy. He is handsome, succussful, charming, and he looks like he'd pounce on you, given the slightest chance. I know his type. They let all that money and power get to their head that they feel they can have anyone and anything they want, and most times it is usually vulnerable females who at most times are prepared to do whatever it takes to catch a break." He said.

" Now that's alittle below the belt Bernard. I expected you to be a bit more accomodationg about this entire situation. I am not sure who I am talking to right now. I am not about to throw away all my efforts for us just because some wealthy business man decides to want a bit more than he can chew. If this is getting too heavy for you please tell me, I really don't want to keep thinking I am still in this with you when you are not." He said.

" I don't know what I know anymore. This is just becoming too stressful for me to deal with, and I do not like it at all. You are practically living like a single woman almost like bait in an ocean full of predators. And then there is Mr,Wright who in my opinion happens to be the biggest of them all, just waiting for the next opportunity to open his jaw for the next kill." He said

" That may be the case, but I am making just as much a sacrifice trying to do this for us OK. Whatever it is you are thinking, I want you to know it is not easy for me either. By holding views like this, you are going to make it a lot more difficult for us than it really should be." she said.

" But you know that is the last thing I want. I do not want this to get any harder than it should. This just isn't working well for us at the moment. one moment it is good, the next I feel like someones bored a big hole in my chest. How long is it going to be this way for?" He said, sounding more depressed than angry.

" It is OK baby. It will not be for very much longer. I know how you feel. Come hell or high water, I will remain yours. No one is going to take me away from you."

" And how do I know that?" He asked.

"Because I promise, And you know how I feel about making promises." she replied. He didn't say another word. she said her goodbye to him, and she slumped into her bed. she didn't have the strength to take her clothes off. It was only for another seven weeks, she thought to herself before she lost consciuosness. it seemed like forever, and it did, to both of them, but there was absolutely nothing they could do about it. They just had to grit their teeth and get through it. she could plan a random trip just to be with him, and the thought to do so never felt more overwhelming as it did now. It was truly lonely for her without him , and missing him was almost a physical ache. she was right to say she understood how he felt. she hoped he believed her. she lay in her bed and nearly cried when the intensity of her passion for him came over her. Moments later she was fast asleep.

The following morning was the beginning of a new week for her at he office. Monday mornings always had its way of making her feel reluctant to do anything. she looked as terrible as she felt. she was having to deal with her morning sickness in silence and she was coughing and sneezing. Her lack of proper rest was starting to weigh her down, and she felt awful.

Nicholas had just finished a briefing in the confrence room and was walking through the corridor to his office as Judith stepped out of the elevator.

" Hello Judith. You look a right mess compared to yesterday. Don't tell me you've kept yourself up all night doing some kind of work have you?" Nicholas asked

" And even if I had been up all night doing some work, isn't that what I am supoose to be doing to get the work done? He asked in return, walking a few steps ahead of him to get to her office.

" Whoa, whoa, whoa, now slow down a minute Ms Judith. First of all, You are not looking too well. Secondly, As your boss I am in a position to have you placed on leave until you are fully recovered. He said when he finally caught up with her.

" And thirdly, if this project was moving too fast for you, you know I can slow it down or bring it to a complete halt if necessary. I am worried Judith. I think you ought to take your health matters very seriously. " He said with utmost concern in his tone.

" I know. There is too much at steak to play sickly. I'll be fine. it's just alittle cold that's all." she reassured him even though she felt rotten all morning. The last thing she wanted was to ruin the big meetings they had ahead of them. she knew Nicholas would find some way to forgive her, but she would never forgive her self.

" Just so you know Judith, you are not alone." He said kindly. And she thanked him for understanding. Although she accepted it well, he only had intrest in keeping her to him self. He knew the doctor was far away to administer any form of procedure to comfort her. He was her doctor now as he wanted to be forever. He walked her to her office, and ordered some tylenol.

" You probably shouldn't have come in this morning. There really isn't much to do around here for another week atleast." he said, feeling guilty.

" Your right, I probably shouldn't have." she smiled at him." I am sure I'll be fine soon." she added. He left her to it and the next few hours flew by, what there was of it. she couldn't get much work done that day. she returned home just after luch time, and three days later, she was over her cold, and looking forward to returning to work. It was the last day of the week and she was more excited about spending the weekend in her apartment glued to her television remote. Doctor Bernard called her on her way in troubled that she hadn't recovered well enough to return to work. But he had other devastating news.

" You are not going to believe what happened" He said grimly. There was a report of mass assault by the use of deadly weapons which has just been brought to my attention. There are currently fifteen casaulties. One pronounced dead, eight are critically injured and the other six have just been evacuated from the scene by the police after one of them was able to make that all important 999 call after narrowly escaping their death. I am actually racing to the scene as we spaek." He said.

" That sounds terrible. Well, good luck, and call me as soon as you can speak OK. And be careful out there." she said,

" Don't worry about it." He said cheerfully, " It is

your health that I am most worried about. Are you sure you really want to be going into work today?" He asked

" I will be fine OK, don't worry about me. I'll relax over the weekend. I am actually going to bring some work home so I can keep my mind busy instead of worrying about my poor health." she said.

" Work may have some how become therapuetic for you, but rest is just as important as work, if not more important." He said.

" Thanks doc. That is rich coming from someone who dosent's get up to six hours sleep every other day while on duty." she replied cheerfully.

" It's different for me, I am a trained professional. You have no real excuse. As the star you are soon to become, you need your beauty sleep as often as you can." He replied.
This made her smile. she was blushing infact, and he could sense it.

" OK, look, I've got to fly, I'll ring you as soon as I'm able to." he said.

" OK, be careful." she replied, endidng their conversation. he had promised to see her for a couple of days eventhough he wasn't ready for his final move. she was near ears when she got off the phone to him. These days it was such a big deal when either of them traveled across the atlantic to be with the other. It was though they were walking a tight rope, but she didn't let the thought of it delude her. she made it through the day and was delighted to return to the apartment. she spent the weekend indoors and by monday morning she received a call from doctor Bernard. she hadn't heard from him since the incident and she was still floating on air when he called her.

" How are you getting on sweetheart?" He asked as soon as he heard her voice.

" I am doing just fine. I thought you were never going to make it out of surgery." she said.

" I wish I didn't make it into surgery in the first

place. We lost three of our critically injured, and that was mostly because we were under staffed." He said. she couldn't begin to imagine what he must be going through. he hated the concept of loosing patients. it had to be bad for him the way he said it.

" Moreover I got some news from the prospective buyers, they've pulled out of buying my flat. Their agent said they found something more suitable for them at the last minute." He said.
she felt as though she had landed on a grenade when she heard his last remark.

" What?! are you kidding? the miserable old sods. What could they have found better than your flat. I can't believe my ears. it's just like one bad news to another." she sounded devastated.

" They changed their minds and there is nothing I can do about it." He said. Judith couldn't bear the thought of their plan enxtending for any much longer.

" They were very apologetic about it , when the agent called, he even made me speak to them directly over the telephone, but I just had to be a gentle man about it." He said,

" Oh dear. What are you going to do now?" she asked.

" Wait I guess, I am sorry it is not what you want to hear, but I can't leave the country for good without selling off that property." He said.

" You are right. I don't know what to say Bernard. I never thought that would happen." she replied. If she had thought it wasn't going to be a lenghty process, she could have given him more time to think things through. Now they were stuck with a miserable situation, she blamed herself immencely. There seemed to be so much she felt she hadn't taken into consideration so far.

Unless she and the doctor were going to end up living in Nicholas's apartment at the cost of him forfeiting his

INNOCENT NLEWEDIM

london flat, she was just going to have to be patient. she had been wating patiently enough for the past few months and now it seemed never ending how much longer she was going to have to be patient for. This was going to add further stress to their situation, and travelling back and forth England and America wasn't going to be an easy deal as they'd hoped for it to be. It could take several months to begin another selling process for his flat, and most times up to a year to finalize it.

Their lives were just beginning to get too challenging the way things were.

she was miserable about it for the rest of the week, and the doctor was dismissive to all his junior staff members at the hospital. They had never seen him that way in all his years as their head of the trauma unit. They suspected something was wrong, but no one got close enough to communicating with him to understand what was going on in his life. she was suppose to see him one more time before he finally moved to America for good. But everything was up in the air now. All she could do was hope that he dosen't loose the job offering he had secured before he returned to london. it was going to be a gureling process to make this transition for them, as it turned out. At work, Nicholas was depending on her full concentration and availability.

They had a lot of loose ends cripping up that made Nicholas restless. He couldn't blame her much, but now, he had to scrutinize her work much closer than he intended to.

In London, there had been a structural re-assignment of all staff at the hospital. Doctors Bernards plan to leave had brought about this change. Infact, there had been promotions, and a few others had been made redundant. With respect for those who may have transfered or quit their jobs voluntarily, a few openings

had become available within the hospital. Doctor
Bernard was finding it difficult to function at his best
without an assistant. Sussan Oregon had a bad fall ice
skating over the weekend, and broke her hip and pelvis.
she was going to be out of commission for twelve
weeks, so they had to find a replacement immediately.
Maria Lopez had been employed to work for him for the
duration. she had worked part-time over the years doing
these sort of fill-ins, and this opportunity would register
her first full time job since she arrived in America from
Cuba five years ago.

The Agency who'd sent her said she was smart
and would be suitable for the Job position for as long as
he needed her. He needed her to be at her best as they
claimed, as she would be the only thing making life
bearable for him at the hospital. she accepted to begin
work straight away, and now, she was his new full-time
assistant, while Doctor Bernard took back full operation
of the trauma unit.
So what seemed apparent now for Judith and doctor
Bernard was that, whatever happened, they had
another twelve weeks of seperation ahead of them. It
may infact take longer as they'd already been apart for
over two months.

" It would be a lot more easier for you to deal with
your duties around here as I've been told this is not your
first gig within hospital premises," Doctor Bernard said.

" No it isn't at all. I've filled in over the years with
ten years experience under my belt." Maria Lopez said.
she was twenty-six years old and very beautiful.

" Well then, get on with the most you can, and if
you need any help do not hesitate to ask. The last thing
you want to do is presume you can do it all on your
own." He said.

" OK, thanks. I'll remember that." she replied as
she left his office.

For the next few days, Judith did everything she

had to do, and got herself ready for the all most important meeting that Nicholas had scheduled for them. she was feeling a lot better and had preped herself not to allow her personal life come inbetween her and work. Understandably, she knew a lot was expected from her now and she was driven to deliver.

Their plans at the office were well executed for the day and Nicholas was well impressed by her attitude towards work. Althought her and doctor Bernards life at the moment seemed to be filled with nothing but problems and disappointments, she was glad she had something doing to distract her alittle bit. For the moment, her job was overshadowing her worries, but it somehow surfaced again and again whenever she thought about doctor Bernard. Knowing they would be apart for several more months, she was beginning to worry about her relationship standing the test of time. Although she tried to mask it, It was obvious to everyone one that she was troubled, and Nicholas was the first person to put up on it and speak to her about it. After work, he took her to dinner to talk about it.

" You two just have to talk and hold on for just a while longer. The situation is circumstantial, it's going to fade away and every thing will be back to normal again. If the property is good enough, it is bound to sell pretty soon." Nicholas said. He was worried that she would feel pressured into making an unreasonable decision, like, calling the entire project off, and returning to her partner in london.

" It is all too much for me to bear at the moment." she admitted to him, looking depressed about it.

" These things happen all the time. it isn't enough to weigh anybody down. You just need to focus on finding a solution to the whole thing. I am confident he can always find a home and something else to do for a living if he really wanted to. The only important thing is, how you deal with the situation together. I believe you can get through it." He said.

" Well, I feel as though I've deserted him since I came out here. And I think that is the real issue I am struggling to deal with. I know it must be hard for him too."she replied.

" He is a big boy. He knows how important this career is to you. And in the end, he wouldn't want to be the one to ruin this opportunity. I am sure he is going to make his equal share of contribution for your career. I can tell he loves you very much. People reach these sort of junctions in their lives, and it's only when they decide what to do next and stick to it, that they find themselves living the life the've always wanted." He said." For instance, if you were my partner and soon to become wife, I would have made sure you had everything sorted out by now." He added.

" I am strating to think I've made the wrong decision coming out here in the first place, and I think he is beginning to feel the same way too." she replied. she wasn't sure what The doctor wanted anymore. she knew that she was carrying his child and that would be the oly way she could get him to dance to her tune. she hated for it to be this way, but she hadn't anticipated this very turn of events. Nicholas was intrigued to learn that they were both getting closer to a point of disrepute. He knew that she was committed to her aspiration as an actress now, so it would be better for him if they didn't get back together. He put a sympathetic arm around her shoulders. He thought of several things to do to cheer her up so he decided to take her shopping. A few hours later they had bought each other gifts.

" Here, open mine first." Nicholas said. He handed her a small bag with a box inside, as he said it. They stood opposite each other as she reached for the box inside the bag and opened it. And as she opened hers, there was a sharp intake of breath. He had bought her a beautiful 3k diamond bracelet at Tiffany's. It was exactly what she could have bought herself if she was as wealthy as Nicholas.

" WoW, it is so pretty. He took it from her and put it on her wrist. It was a perfect fit and it made her smile. He was pleased that she seemed to like it.
she had something for him too. she raised the white bag in her other hand and handed it to him. The instant he saw the box, he recognized the company. It was from Hermes. He had bought so many gifts for his parents over the years from their branch in the city and he had spoilt himself a few times aswell. He was equally impressed. she had bought him a very handsome leather Hermes Briefcase. The finishing was superb, and it was every bit as elegant as he was. He loved high end quality clothings and she'd picked up on this very fast. He gave her a big hug and kiss the minute he saw it.

" You read my mind on this one. I've already made enquiries to pre-order one of these." He said.

" Oh really. I guess it must be your lucky day. The sales guy said it was exclusive and the final piece, so I thought, why not go for it." she replied.

" Good call Judith. I know you had it in you to spot the latest of fabric/leather." he replied.

" I happen to know a thing or two about fashion." she said as she twirled in the pant suit she was wearing, it was business like and at the same time it made her look very chic and elegant.
They returned to the apartment together, and she was pleased to have some company. she appreciated his view on things when she talked to him over dinner, and so she felt she could talk to him about how things were going with her and the doctor.

" Well I hate to say it, but I'm not sure it is going to be wise to leave you on your own these days. Atleast until you know when he would arrive. He said.
" He would kill him if I told him you were spending more time at the apartment. He would argue that it is already bad enough that we spend too much time together

during work." she said, glumly. It would certainly be the topper on an already messy situation. she had to admit it to her self. she really missed him.

" It wouldn't be your fault at all. You need to be cared for. He has to understand that." Nicholas said. she knew he had a point. she thanked him for the gift. it was the first time any man had bought her diamonds.

" Thanks for the bracelet Nic. It is a massive gesture. I am not sure what Bernard would say about this." she replied as she admired it again.

" Well, why don't you keep it as our little secrete." He said

" I am not sure I do too well with keeping secretes, especially not with him. It' going to be too flash for him not to notice, and not telling him how I got it would be a lie no longer a secrete." she said.
" In that case I'll have to own up to it when questions are been asked." He replied.

" You had Better." she replied, and then laughed ruefully. " I hope it dosen't get to that point anyway." Se added

" For now, I do not want you feeling negative about your decision to be here. It would kill me to know that you are sitting in here alone feeling sorry for yourself." He said.

" It wouldn't get that bad, I'll do my best to defend your honour." she replied.
" DO it for yourself first OK. I thik you have earned it." He Said.They both laughed, but she realized they were both getting extremely comfortable with each other. But no matter how comfortable he intended to get, she did not want him to remain in the house any longer.

" If it is OK with you, I would like to get some work done tonight so I could get enough sleep to be up for work early in the morning." she said.

" I didn't think you would follow through with bringing back some home work." He replied

" it's the best I can do around here, besides staring at the walls and ceiling all day" she said.
She was pleased that he accepted to leave her to it, but on one condition.He'd managed to invite her to have dinner with him tomorrow night. she remembered that doctor Bernards tone of voice wasn't overly pleased about her visiting his home. Even with the kids present, he found it too excessive. But now the kids were gone, she knew it would only be her and Nicholas. He set a date for 9pm, and on second thought, she agreed. she knew that doctor Bernard wouldn't advice her to spend all her nights alone. Although he was working up to eighty hours a day at the hospital, he admitted to her once that he always found a way to get by because there was always someone to talk to in the hospital, be it his patient or staff. He certainly didn't want her to be alone. Nicholas understood their predicament more than she did so the predator in him was going to take full advantage of it's prey.

The following day went by a breeze, and at eight o' clock, he sent his chauffeur to pick her up. He drove her to his house and she was pleased to see that he had made a real effort to set the mood. The lights were deamed, and there was candles lit around the room.she arrived with some red wine, and Nicholas opened it and served them both a glass each with glee. she shared a marvelous dinner with him that night, and afterwards they sat by the fire place.
They told each other stories about their youth and teenage relationships. He told her about trips he'd made with family as a child. He told her so much about his mother, and she began to understand how loath he was to make a life time commitment to any other woman since his divorce. As far as he was concerned, although he didn't express it that way, he always felt women always deserted him, at one point or another. His mother, been the only exception.

" It dose take quite an effort to find the ones that stick around for as long as you want." she siad, enabling him to see that she happens to have made that decision to be with Doctor Bernard. For what ever guilt she felt leading him on initially, she wanted to make things right between them. But it was too late and too difficult.

" I have a family to hold on to. That is always a plus, but nothing replaces the need for a man to be with his ideal woman. one he could raise a family of his own with. I have the kids I've always wanted, I just picked the wrong wife. He said, sipping long from him glass until it was empty, then he re-filled it.

" Your kids are awesome." she said, sipping from her glass too in order to avoid forming any sort of opinion about his ex-wife. He looked at her from where he sat, the room was warm, and the fire was crackling softly.

" You are pretty awesome, too," He said gently. he didn't expect her to be here with him. it was nice to have her around him especially when it was peaceful and quiet. He could hear his thoughts clearly now, and all he thought about was ways to make her fall for him. Their eyes met and noticing how he must be feeling, she hurriedly took her gaze away from his eyes, and then stared into the fire, thinking of doctor Bernard. she really missed him.

" I want you to know it means a lot to me for you to be wth me tonight" He said.
she looked back at him but said nothing.

" I don't mean to make you uncomfortable by saying these things." He said.

" It is OK. I was just thinking about doctor Bernard and myself. We are both very similar in a lot of ways. And if I get on with you just as much, then it must mean that you are both important to me at the moment, for different reasons. I like the way you and I work together.

It makes me find other things about you to like, and when I do, I like you a bit more. But none of it changes how I feel about him. He is my entire world right now. He may always find a way to forgive all my mistakes and I know he would only do that because he would expect me not to make them again." she said " But in some ways, I admire you too, and I enjoy your company, we share the same point of views and some how manage not to allow our differences affect our work. in terms of ideas, we share so much in common. Perhaps not in the same way I do with Bernard, but I can separate both. considering that you know what's happened so far, I expect you to make this easier for us so we can have a happy life. He is a good man, and I worry that my indecisiveness may lead him astray. I need you to understand what I am trying to say to you Nioclas. I can't be your employee, your star attraction and your lover all at the same time. I am prepared to work with you, but my heart belongs to someone else. she added.

" I know this must be difficult for you, but if you acknlowedge this feeling between us to be so profound, how do you expect me to know how to make it go away?" He said.
she remained silent for a short while after hearing what he'd said. she knew they were both walking on thin ice now, and she didn't want to be the one to take the fall.

" I've never been s comfortable with anyone in my life," He confessed, looking into her eyes. " it is suppose to be the untimate test right? well,atleast for me." He said

" Bernard and I have always been best friends, and I've grown to love him just the way he is. It is difficult to explain how impossible it is for one to share what I feel for him with someone else on equal measures, not to say that there aren't some kind of feeling here between us." she said, feeling disloyal to doctor Bernard when she said it.

" Alright, so it can't be such a bad thing after all. We clearly love each others company, and we spend so much time together just like other business partners do, and it may be more than it should be when spouses are involved, but that my dear is the natural order of things in the corporate world we live in. It is our gift and curse."

They both smiled at that, and she helped herself to more wine.

God knows she needed it to help her find some reasonable way to handle the situation.

They sat and talked for a long time, and at quater to twelve they rounded up for the night. in tha time, he glanced at her once or twice smiling at her intently. she realized it was an odd feeling being with him, although a part of her was beginning to accept that she belonged there, with him. she wanted her aspirations to come to fruition and perhaps, this was just a small price to pay to make that a possibility. It was a strange illusion, and she was quiet for a while as she battled with her mind ad body to bring this night to a halt before matters got anymore complicated than it already was.

she annouced her departure and he walked her to the door. But as she approached the doors to open it and say her goodbye, she turned around to see that he was right behind her, then, he simply pulled her gently into his arms and kissed her. And without hesitation, she pulled back. she looked at him startled by his approach, and it did seem odd at that precise moment because a part of her felt she wanted to kiss him back. Awashed by the complexities of the emotions she felt, she started crying.

" I am so sorry... I don't know what to do anymore Nic... I feel like my whole world has come crashing down and there is nothing I can do to stop it. I am beginning to have a whole new life here and I do not know if this is where I truly belong." she said

" I shouldn't have put you in this position Judith. I

am sorry...." it had felt so right, to him particularly, for an instant, and for her, she knew this was only going to make matters worse. This was leading them into a world that they both knew they had no right to.

" Please forgive me, I do not know what came over me. I think the wine may have gotten to my head a little." He said. it was a lousy excuse, but he was determined to stick to it.

" I am not sure how to respond to any of this any more. I must leave now." she said. There was so much about him that she liked, if they were both in this world absent of doctor Bernard, then none of this would be an issue at all, but considering that he did exist, and they'd planned to be together for the rest of their lives, they both had no righ indulging each other so recklessly.

" it won't happen again." He said, trying to reassure her.

" Good night Judith" He said gently, but she only shook her head. Perhaps now would have been a perfect time to tell him that she was expecting doctor Bernards baby, so atleast this way, he knew that nothing was ever going to come out of this affair if that was the appropriate term for what was brewing between them. Suddenly everything seemed topsy-turvy, and she knew that it was only a matter of time before it became obvious to everyone that she was carrying a child. For the first time, she felt that she was going to loose doctor Bernard and that feeling was as terrifying s it had ever been.

" I'll talk to you in the morning." he said as she walked towards the taxi waiting to take her to the apartment. she was upset by what had happened. It wasn't easy to expalain any of it to herself, let alone doctor Bernard. Nicholas had no one in his life to explain any of this to, so it seemed perfect on his part. Their loneliness may be the source of this fatal attraction, but it was a good enough reason to risk loosing the man she loved more than any other.

They saw each other at the office after the incident but couldn't speak to one another because of what had happened. Without speaking, they were convinced they both needed a breather before they made the same mistakes they'd already made. He needed her to remain in his world and not to push her away. He didn't care what he had to do, or not do, but more than anything, he knew he didn't want to loose her this way. He knew she could be a bit unpredictable so he neede to approach matters with her more sensitively.

"I am sorry, I know how much your relationship with Bernard must be. I do not know what has come over me lately." He said, but he knew, and so did she, and they both knew it had to end very quickly. she was concerned that if this wasn't treated well, a slight infartuation could turn ghastly for the both of them. she hoped that if nothing more was said about it, the moment would pass and never resurface, and they could go back to the positve work relationship that they both set out to accomplish.

"I am prepared to put this behind us if you are sure that it would never repeat it self again." she said. He knew how difficult it was for her, but he didn't trust himself enough to admit that it wouldn't. But for the sake of keeping her around he agreed.

"Yes I am." He replied.

It was a relieft for her to hear him say those words, and this made her miss doctor Bernard Oakfield. Nicholas left her office, and she sat at her desk for the rest of the day thinking about her life as it had come to be. she had made a few mistakes in her life but this was beginning to top the list for her. Enough so to make her questions her feelings for both men. she knew that it was time for her make amends because she couldn't continue living like this for very much longer. she took advantage of Nicholas's offer to take a break from work if she wasn't feeling very strong, and before the end of the day, she booked the next flight to london without letting doctor Bernard know about her arrival.

When she arrived at his flat, she let herself in as she'd been given her own set of keys. And when she walked into the bedroom, steve was there, sound asleep in his bed. she took off her clothes, and slipped silently under the sheets next to him.

Unconciously, her felt the warmth of a body he was very familiar with, and in his sleep, he pulled her close to him and she huged him.

CHAPTER 15

Judith's arrival into london was everything she'd hoped for it to be.

Doctor Oakfield had taken the week off to compensate her efforts. They played in the house like two teenagers home alone knowing their parents weren't going to be back home for the time being. They took long walks and had dinner at their favorite restaurants whenever they wanted. They made love more than they had since they first met each other. This made them open up to talk about their problems.

" Where are we going to begin from?" Judith was the first to ask.

" We certainly can't just abandon everything and elope" He said with a smile.

" Eloping yes, but abandonning things, No. And I hope we wouldn't have to." she said. with Judith with him now, he felt it was ideal for him to re-assure her that things would be resolved in no time. The time they shared was idyllic and they both were beginning to understand the depth of their love for each other.

" If I had my way love, I'll be on the next filght out of here with you." He said.

" Don't tempt me to make you do it." she replied with a smile.

" I will quit everything for you Judith. You are my life, and I must admit, it is awful without you." he said. They had been apart for several months, and with all the plans they were making, their seperation seemed to be the one aspect of their relationship that made them unhappy.

" I know you would, that is why I believe I am makig the right plan and decisions with the perfect person."

she said calmy.

" What if it take another year Judith. Will you still be as patient as you are now?" HE asked.

" Then I'll wait for a year, maybe I might loose my cool alittle bit along the way if it takes that long, but anything worth doing with you is worth been patient for." she replied

" This will not turn out that tragic baby. it is just sad that this is one of those things that you have to wait for to come to you. If you decide to be hasty about it, you might loose it all." He said.

" It makes me wonder how many people have to deal with this sort of thing dialy." she said.

" Millions baby. And it dosen't always end up favourable for them for the struggle to make it out." He said, looking worried. The incident with Nicholas had helped her understand that no one was invulnerable. she could see that it was such seperations that brought about cases of infidelity, and somehow, she was caught up in that very same twist. For Judith, it had been her first experience as such. Alhough the situation presented a real danger for them, she had no intention of saying any of it to him. Not now, not this way, not ever if she could bear to surpress the thought for long enough. she truthfully didn't want to hurt him.

" That only sound to me like a lot of divorce cases." she replied" It certainly would put a lot of pressure on those with loving relationships like ours." she added.

" I know what you mean dear. It isn't easy, but if it has to be done, it has to be done. And we are going to do it." He said.

" It is going to be worth it Bernard. For all of us. I promise." she said.

" I know it would baby." He said, pulling her into his arms, and kissing her." I an few year time, we will look back on all of this and laugh. This is going to be the single most important decision I've made all my life, and I am going to have you to be thankful for it." He said.

They felt deeply connected now, but it also felt as though they were pulled away from each other by their desires. It was as though it was conspiring aganist them, but this didn't matter much now they were in each others arms.

" How ever long it takes, just make sure we make time to see each other as ofen as we can until we are finally settled down under the same roof." she said. From that standpoint, it was clear to see that they were struggling to be together.

" I think we can make that happen. Hey if it takes this seperation to have me wake up to find you in my bed suprisingly, then that has got to be something to always look forward to.

" You really did like that didn't you?" she asked pensively, and he nodded.

 I would'n ask for that to become a pattern either, but if it helps, either one of us just has to make this sacrifice every now and again." He said.

" I'll do it for you baby. it is all I can say, and I am glad to have shown you that it is something I am very capable of doing to let you know how important all of this is to me." she said.

" As it is for me too." He replied. He sounded hopeful more so than he had in a long time. Being together had reallt boosted their spirits and they were beginning to believe more in eachothers love life.

" I believe it is." she said, and with that, they kissed each other. They spent the evening watching TV, without interference from their respective jobs. Doctor Bernard had actually called in sick, and his leave was automatically granted as it was unheard of in his entire time at the hospital. After an entire week of rest and enjoying each others uninterrupted company, she thanked him dearly for been such an angel. she was packing her bag to return to New York and their conversation made them both feel sad. But he encouraged her to look on the bright side as it was only going to be a matter of time for them to be together again.

" I'll see you soon baby OK." He said. What he said to her made her feel reassured that he was going to do his very best to speed things up. They needed to live past this misery that exisited between them eventhough they chose to mask it. she took a deep breath and continued packing her personal effect into her suitcase. He told her he would come out in any event the sale of his flat and re-assignment at work took longer than he envisaged.

They had just made love again, and after an hour he took her to the airport. They looked very much in love as they hugged, kissed and held each other. They had promised to take time off work in exactly three weeks, no matter how busy they both were. They knew now more than ever that this was the only way to keep them actively working towards their plans to be together as a couple. At the airport it seemed as though he had only accompanied her, but he had another agenda in mind. They sat down waiting for her flight to start boarding when Doctor Bernard decided to pop the question. As he dropped to one knee, she wasn't sure what he was about to do until the words came out of his mouth.

" Judith, My one and only true love, will you marry me?" He said, reaching for the ring box inside his jacket as he opened it.
she knew now more than ever that he was hers forever. With tears in her eyes, she returned an answer any man in love would love to hear from his proposed girlfriend.

" Yes I will doctor Bernard Oakfield." she replied as she stuck out her fingers for him to put the ring on it.

" You are full of surprises these days, what else do you plan to do to sweep me off my feet?" she asked feeling euphoric about what he had just done.

" You are going to have to wait and see my love. This my only way of letting you know, that even time can't separate us anymore. You are my world and I want to be the man in your life for the rest of mine." He said. They sat and chatted for a while, and shortly after wards, she could hear the announcement for the departure of her flight. she left him with a last kiss, boarded the plane, and thought about him all the way to New York. His proposal made her feel a lot better than she did before she arrived.

" she arrived at her apartment in just before midnight, and fell asleep dreaming of her fiance. The next day, she couldn't tame her excitement so she was up bright and early to prepare for work. Later that morning, she was at her desk, admiring her engagement ring when her assistant Marcus Billingham walked into her office. she didn't notice him at first, but he stood in her office doorway for a moment before she did.

" Is that what I think it is? He asked as he approached he desk. she looked up and smiled at him.

" It sure is." she replied and stuck her hands out for him to take a closer look. she looked happier than she did the last time he saw her, and he was pleased to see her happy.

" Wow, it is gorgeous. I am going to go blind if I stare into it any longer." He said.

" Tell me about it, it was absolutely unexpected. I didn't think he was ready for this for another few years. Now, I am mesmerized." she replied. she sounded at ease with him and he was relieved to see her in high spirit.

Nicholas was away for the week on official business, so the atmosphere at work was a lot more relaxing. Marcu and Judith settled into an unusal territory for the first time talking about their love lives. she found it easy to talk to him, and now, she spilled everything there was to know about her relationship. They trusted each other to safe guard their intergrity, and as such, they both knew they had found someone they could truly open up to without fear or prejudice.

" I am so happy to see you have finally found the one" Marcus said.

" Oh yes I have. He is the one and then some." she replied sounding elated.

" How is Nicholas dealing with all of this?" He asked, aware of the fact there was more to the pair of them than what met the eye.

" He wouldn't be dealing with things very well especially after he hears about my engagement." Sh replied.

" And Doctor Bernard, How do you intend to convince him that Nicholas isn't steering already troubled waters?" he asked cautiously realizing it was a sensitive subject for them to discuss.

" Well, I wouldn't have to do any of that at all. He may have his doubts and suspisions but I'll let it pass. I am his now, so there isn't much for him to worry about anymore. By the time this news gets out, all m possible suitors would have to go find another girl to hound. I am taken now, and this time, it's for good." she replied.

" Taken by a very lucky man I must add." He said.

" Do you really think so?" she asked unassumingly.

" Yes I do, and I am sure he knows it too." He added.

" I really do hope so. If I had the power to go back in time, there are things I would change to make him realize that he truly is a lucky man. But seeing as these things have happened the way they have, I know our engagement would be my strength to prevent anything that would interfere with our relationship from re-occuring again. Nicholas and I would have to be strict professionals or risk the chance of making anything valuable emerge from this opportunity. It is either that or

I quit. That's it." she said.

" Well, I want you to know I have your best interest at heart 100%, and if there is anything at all you need me to do, I will be more than willing to help." He said.
" So when is he finally moving into the country?" He asked.

" Well, he has to finalize a couple of things, and then there is his work, which seems to have a special way of keeping him busy for weeks on end, I really can't wait for us to begin our lives together. atleast now I knw he is very serious about our future." she said.

" it sems like you two are going to have to make some serious efforts to make this work. But I m pleased to see that he is being reasonable about the entire situation." Marcus said.

" He is so adorable when he is that way with me. He might be stuck there for the next 7-8 weeks but I know we will be thinking of each other every step of the way. He says he will join me in a week or so. I jusst can't wait to see him again. " she replied. It was plain to see that she was in love with her fiance and their conversation made her miss him more.

" I am sure he will come visit you soon. " He said." Just before I forget,I have received confirmation for a few talk show interviews lined up for you, I would like to know which ones you fancy attending so I can get the dates in." He added.

" Sounds good to me. Send over the itenerary and I'll go over the details and give you my responce before the end of the day." she said " on second thought,We do have a lot of work to do" she added

" We do indeed." He replied, and he disappeared to his office to prepare what she had requested for. They worked together through out the day and he could detect only the faintest changes in her attitude towards work. she was indeed happy as any woman would who had just been proposed to by the man she loves, but he was convinced there was more to it. There was a certain glow about her appearane that made his mind wonder, but he chose to over look it. By the end of the day, they completed a lot of work together, and she was happy returning to her apartment. They hugged and waved cheerfully as thy said their goodbyes for the day until they met again the next day.. she had managed to think less of Nicholas through out the day and she couldn't say that she was wrong to do so. Nicholas on the other hand had thought about her every single moment of the day since the last time he kissed her, and now she was all he could continue to think about. He had managed to seize communications with her within the last week, but he knew he had to check in on her soon enough to find out how his business was coming along. this was always a perfect reason to talk to her.

she spent as much time in the office during the day, and at night, she arranged to see more houses in and around the city. she was getting into the swing of things, gradually learning how to apply her self despite her all consuming work schedule. By the end of the week, she was pleased to begin making a few offers for some homes she'd seen, and by now, she had been informed that Nicholas was due back in new York. They hadn't spoken since she left for london, and the thought of his arrival made her remember the fact that they had ventured into dangerous waters for a little while, and she wondered if they were now clear of them. she knew it was the right thing to do not to indulge with him any further recklessly. she had to draw a clear line between their professional and personal life and she was convinced it was better for them this way. They knew they couldn't avoid each other for very long but the reality of it all way that they had grown terribly fund of each other, and they both felt oddly close to each other more than they cared to admit.

FLAWS AND PASSION

CHAPTER 16

Dr.Bernard had been pre-occupied at the trauma unit trainning Maria lopez on the preferred methods of running the hospitals administrative duties. Within two days of her arrival, he was pleased to see that she was catching up way faster than he anticipated. she was coming to grips with what had to be done, and she didn't hesitate to voice her opinion on any issue she felt needed a review.

She was a good listener and Dr.Bernard commended her whenever it was necessary. she took direction well from him and asked all the appropriate questions as they progressed. By the end of the first day, she had gained significant insight into the affairs of the unit, and Nicholas was confident that she would be able to begin full duty after her first week.
By the beginning of the second week, he was pleased to see her in top flight. she reported to him about everything she had done, and also, she filled him in on new ideas she felt could be implemented for the sake of efficiency. What's more, he liked her proactive approach towards her job.
" You are going to be well experienced to run the entire unit all by yourself if you keep up at this pace." He said humourously
" Awww, do you really think so?" she replied. she was astonished to hear this from the man everyone adored and respected in the hospital.
" Yes I do. I fact, I believe, it's a bit of a waste of time even trainning you to begin with. You seem proefficient with everything I've thrown at you so far, I am beginning to wonder if there is anything you can not do." He said.

" Well, I can't perform any major surgical procedures like you doctor. That sort of skill set is something I actually do find fasinating working in a hospital." she replied.

" So you wish to be a surgeon then?" He asked.

" Yes, but that's a far cry from my current ability. I think I'll just stick to the basic stuff for now." she replied smiling faintly.

" Yes, I think you should. The risk factor of been a surgeon superceeds the glamour attached to our profession. Trust me, it isn't easy to do what we do" He replied.

" So do you make time for socializing at all? I hear you practically live in here for the most part of every month." she teased

" I like to have a lot of fun, but that's mostly plausible when I am awake on my days off." He said somewhat sternly. Inspite of her prying into his social life, she'd actually reminded him that that part of his life was non-existent. she was a pretty woman and looked much younger than her actual age. He found it fasinating how she had kept herself flourishing the way she appeared. There was something about her that said she was a great personality to get acquainted with despite her all business like attitude. she was clearly a woman of many facets and he could sense her incredibly gentle way of dealing with other members of staff.

By the end of the second week, he was beginning to feel like he knew her very well. she was relentless at work and was able to keep up with him. His past recruits were the opposite, but she seemed to do it all with ease and vigour. she never seemed anxious to go home, and he immediately noticed that she was a workaholic just like him. From things she said, and when he asked her questions about her private life, he presumed that she was single and without children. But he was shocked to learn that only the former was infact the case.

" So how many children have you got?" He asked.

" Just one. From my last relationship." she replied.

" How do you mean from your last relationship, are you no longer with the father of your child?" He asked.

" Yes I am not with him anymore. He turned out vicious towards me just after my son came into the world. At first he wasn't convinced it was his, but after I ran a paternity test and it was established that he was, I filed a restraining order against him. I am seeing someone else now, but it is nothing exclusive." she said

" Do you find it less of a hassle to maintain a non-exclusive relationship at the moment?" He asked

" Yes I do. I don't want to have to expalin to my partner why I am not home every early night, or in most cases at all for one or two nights at a time. After my last relationship, I could do without the added hassle." she said.

" That seems fair to say. And your child, how is he coping with your prolonged absence while you are working endlessly?" He asked.

" Thanks to my mother, he dosen't feel deprived of love and attention at all. I see him as often as I can, But he is such a strong boy, and he understands mummy has to work to bring home the dollars." she replied. The more she spoke to him about her life, the more intrigued he was about her. There was something reserved about her, perhaps it was a way for her to safe guard her heart, and yet at the same time, he enjoyed listening to her voice her opinion on life.

" It must be tough going through this stage of your life, by the sounds of it, you've done quite a lot to remain sane." He said

" You can say that again." she replied with a tired smile. He could see she had been through so much, and was now cautious about asking her questions concerning her private life. But He was curious about her and there was no way he could find out all the relevant details about her without asking personal questions. He was never afraid to ask questions of any sort, especially when he believes he needs the right answers to help him see things clearly. more than anything, he could see she was guarded about her emotions and considering she had opened up to him about her troubled relationship with the father of her child, he knew she was habouring a lot of resentment towards the opposite sex. she had been hurt, and she wasn't about to let it happen again. He admired the harding working side of her character.

" I hear you are newly engaged and soon to be married, you must be over the moon." she said.
" You heard right. Newly engaged yes, but only God knows when we would get married. My partner and I are currenty bicostal" He said.

" Oh. That must be difficult. How are you two coping with this?" she asked
" It isn't easy at all. It is great when we are together, but it literally feels like someones boring a hole in my heart eachtime we are apart." He replied

" It sounds excruciating" she said.
" It is, especially, when you feel you are deeply in love with each other." He said. They sat in his office discussing about their partners and how complicated their relationships were considering their individual circumstances.

" Relationships do get complicated. Especially when you want it to work out so much for the better, life begins to throw all sorts of challenges your way." she said, referring to his current situation with Judith.

" It sure does. You ar absolutely right. she has an amazing career ahead of her, I happen to be coming to the end of mine, but truthfully, I wasn't prepared for such a huge leap into a marital way of life until we started discussing matters more seriously. It seems like the right thing to do, but the again, it is the most difficult process to conclude. Right now, I am stuck here for another 8weeks and there is no telling if it would be over in that time." He said.

" That dosen't sound pleasant at all" she said, her eyes bore into his, and were full of compassion. she knew he was a decent , charming man at the height of his profession, although perhaps marginally eccentric, but she could sene he was an all round nice guy.

" It isn't" He said " I want her to do well, and I've encouraged her to pursue her aspirations with all she strength, but it seems like it is I who needs the encouragement now." He added

" I understand your predicament. You want her to do well, but you do not want her feeling discouraged about her decisions." she said

" Precisely. A part of me wishes things were different. Like a lot simpler without the pressure of having to make hasty decisions about the future." He said

" Nothing worth having is is ever easy to get. if it was, nobody would ever take important issues seriously. That's why I've decided to keep my relations non-exclusive. This way there is very little expectation from the beginning" she replied

" You do seem like you know what you want after all." he said.

" you can say that, besides, I have come to realize that it works better that way. I don't get to blame him for any shorthcomings and he dosen't get to blame me either. It's a win win situation for us." she replied.

" I see." he replied. By the sounds of it, he knew she was keen on having a stress free relationship. she had won her custody battle against her babies father, and there wasn't much she could ask for now but work to make ends meet. she had given him a different perspective on the matter at hand between him and

Judith and he was beginning to see things differently. He appreciated her honesty. They spoke easily about real life and the world around them. For steve, it was the first time for him to discuss about his personal life with any one. They formed a strange bond between each other and it seemed as though they were on another planet beyond the walls of the hospital.

They returned to work, and after a few days apart, they were back in his office to discuss her performance review. It was a long day for them, and after two major surgeries, Dr Oakfield was starving and he ordered chinese take away for them. They seemed to have gotten considerably close and she was happier now she had been offered full-time employment.

" So when was the last time you saw your non-exclusive boyfriend?" He asked, as they wrestled with the spare ribs, and she laughed at the question.

" A month ago." she said bluntly.

" That's terrible. I thought I was the only one in an estranged relationship." He said casually, and she smiled in response." You are the only one in an estranged relationship with a woman who has relocated to a different country."

" Well. you do have a fair point." He replied.

" When do you plan on seeing each other again?" He asked

" Perhaps this weekend. But that's only if I am up for it. This job does have its own unique way of leaving a person miserably knackered everyday.

" Welcome to my world." He said. He took a sip of his drink and their eyes met. He could see they were lit up with excitement as she was pleased to be in his company.

He was always too busy to date, and with the introduction of Judith into his life, he believed he was prepared for a committed relationship. He wondered if he'd made a hasty decision to engage her. He still thought it was the right decision, and for the first time, he felt nervous about it.

" So what if you got knocked up by this guy this time?" He asked jovially.

" Not a chance. I like him but I do not see him as someone whom I could raise a family with. Plain and simple. I have actually had this particular discussion with him, and I am positive he agrees with me on that point." she replied.

" You don't say." He replied. He was puzzled. He did have a few flings in the past that were strictly physical, but nothing with a single mother. He knew he wanted a stable relationship with the mother of his child, and he couldn't imagine a situation like hers. He imagined what it would be like if he was seperated from Judith after they had one or two children. she would be exactly like Maria, in the company of another man, telling of what a failure their relationship had been. He couldn't bear the thought of such references even if he gave himself the chance.

It was amazing sometimes how relationships got torn apart by one issue or the other. None of it surprised him any more. He had heard too many stories and it all made him even more cautious than he'd been since he was in medical school. He thought about her situation and couldn't help but feel sorry for her. she was on her own raising a child as a single mother. it was a scary thought and under the circumstances, he knew life had to be tough for her. It was such a far cry from his situation with Judith. He was earning a good enough salary to cater for him and two others, but to think that he would have to do it all on his own some day was discomforting. it made him feel more than a little guilty listening to her stories as it only increased his level of emotional interest. His life was far more comfortable than hers, and his understanding of her situation made him want to support her in any way possible. He knew the first step was to make sure she secured this employment which he'd done.

" So what about you, when do you plan to have children of your own with her?" she asked.

" One day soon I guess. We do have this huddle to get past first. I am sure it would happen eventually." He replied.

Despite his lack of knowledge of the fact that Judith was actually pregnant, Maria could sense that he wanted a family of his own sometime soon. It was an honest responce to her question and for the first time since she began her work trainning at the trauma unit, she saw him in a different light. He knew how important a family life would be for them, but he also knew it wasn't going to be easy for them.

Maria and doctor Oakfield worked together day after day, and he grew fonder and fonder of her. The brittle outter shell was only a protective layer, and inside there was an extraordinary sensitive woman. He could see that she was indded an exceptional kind of woman, who if dealt the right set of cards, would turn her life around for good.

By the beginning of her third week on duty they were fast friends, and he had come to rely on her. An emergency surgey had altered his plans to visit Judith, and through Marias efforts, he was able to deal with the work load at the unit. she worked well under pressure just as he did, and he liked that about her. she maintained her dedication to her role, making sure she was at his beck and call whenever he needed her and it made their time pass with ease. Although he outranked her, they worked together like best friends. By the end of that week, he finally traveled to New York to see Judith.

It wasn't easy for them at this point. They were

trying desperately to make their lives mesh with the little time they had to spend together and it seemed to be getting more challenging for them at present. Judith was at the office all day, and In the studio all night for the first two day when he arrived, and when she finally got to return to the apartment, she was irritable from lack of sleep. she hd tried her best not to let the situation ruin their time together, so she planned a night out in town for two. They made the best of their evening, and unavoidably, argued argued over petty irritations over dinner.

They chatted for a few hours, and a few hours later, their conversations were getting a lot better than it had earlier in the day. There was no denyng that the atmosphere between them was a bit unsettling than it had ever been. They hadn't experienced this aspect of their relationship before, and for the most part of the day, they felt like strangers. their earlier arguements made them realize that they had been apart for way too long, and it made them increasingly aware that they now lived in separate worlds. It was no longer as easy falling into step with each other, and they seemed constantly out of sync with each other now at times.

After a few days together, Dr Oakfield flew back to London. When he arrived, Maria called and invited him to have lunch. He had one more day off work, and she did as well. she chose a restaurant at oxford circus and it was one he too had dined at several times. It was the best she could do but he did accept her invitation. it shocked him to realized that she did think of making such a gesture, particularly knowing that she knew he'd been away to see his fiance.

" It's a welcome back invitation." she said to him, but it was more than that and they knew it. But something about her invitation touched him dearly. she was dressed up in style to impress him and he could see she was a totally natural woman, with an incredible body. It was easier been with her as it was on the basis of their free flowing conversation that made him realize the stresses of living thousands of miles away from Judith.

Maria was sympathetic and sorry for him. And as their date progressed, it was clear to see that they both shared a lot in common in terms of their personal interests.

But inspite of that, he was getting used to having her around. They talked late that night, and this made him miss Judith a lot. He remebered how they used to talk to each other about everything and anything. He thought about calling her at that very moment to tell her he was having lunch with a colleague and that he was sorry the weekend didn't turn out the way they'd both expected it to be. On second thought, he passed on the idea of ringing her. He was having a fantastic time with maria and they were both behaving well just as friends would.

When he returned home, he did call her mobile but got no answer, so he left her a message on her machine before he went to sleep. He saw maria the following day and they worked together all day. He decided to take a few of his juniour staff out for pizza, and they all had a great time together. It was a good way for them to get acquainted with maria, and it worked brilliantly. It was easy and relaxing just being with out with his work colleagues and they appreciated him for making such great effort. Maria hadn't found the right time to talk to him in person as the others were asking her several questions about her background, so she used the first moment she found to do so wisely.

" Do you do this with the guys a lot?" she asked.

" Not quite. But I thought it'll be a nice way for you to get a lot more conversant with them." He said.

" You are a good guy, you know," she said

" Well, thanks maria, you are an awesome lady as

well." He replied.

" Your fiance is a fool to leave you on the loose here. If I had a man like you in my life, I'll have him on cuffs 24 hours of the day." she said with a smile. They were having a nice evening and the wine made it all the more relaxing for them to communicate with each other freely.

" My fiance could be a lot of things, but a fool is one thing she isn't. she dosen't have much of a choice for the moment, but I know it's going to be tough for us until we get settled."

" Do you not feel discouraged about the engagement due to the difficulty you face at the moment?" she asked

" I do have moments when I ask myself serious questions about my committment, but I also keep telling myself that things will work out for the better in time." he replied.

" There's got to be a lot to be hopeful for. I do hope there is some light at the end of the tunnel for you two." she said sympathetically.

" I am getting used to the way things are with us, I hoestly do not not want to make her feel any worse about this than she already does." He replied. But his words didn't convince her the slightest. It didn't help that she could see that he was struggling with the entire plan.

" You shouldn't have to get used to being lonely. Dosen't it bother you that she might be up to no good with some other guy?" maria asked thoughtfully. she asked him questions sometimes that probed too deep and made him uncomfortable, but it also alerted him to things he'd tried to avoid thinking about.

" There are certain things I do worry about, but at the same time, I have to give her the benefit of doubt. she hasn't given me reason to doubt her yet." he replied

" That is admirable" she said. she knew how much it meant to him to believe that Judith wouldn't betray his trust for her, moreover, she hadn't given him the impression that she had. Maria hoped for his sake that she hadn't cheated on him, but she knew people were people, and if they got lonely enough, they did foolish things.

Living in two different countries was always going to be the greatest challenge they'd ever face, but it was also suppose to be the end of their past as single individuals and the beginning of a new chapter of life together. It was hard as hell, but it was only temporary, and they knew that. A part of him was prepared to forgive whatever may happen during this troubling times for them, but he didn't want to be the cause of anything damaging that would screw up their chances of a happy future together.
It was getting too stressful to be apart, and seemingly,
        they were both only human. If he could give her the life she dreamed of, he would do so in other for her to remain in England, but it wouldn't be fair to her if he was to go against her wishes. He owed it to her to remain supportive of her aspirations and the last thing he wanted to was break his promises.
        " You are a good man Dr Oakfield . I just hope she deserves you." she said.
        Her remark forced a smile onto his face, and after their group dinner, he found himself thinking about her when he returned to his flat. she was right. He deserved so much better, and so did Judith, but who was to say that they did not deserve each other. When he went to bed that evening he found himself thinking about what maria had said about Judith's possible unfaithfulness. It had become an inescapable thought, and one he most certainly found discomforting.
        The possibility of it was terrifying enough as it was, but now he questioned his loyalty. As he lay awake in his bed, he thought about everything as it had come to

be.

He accepted that their lives were flawed, but he was glad there still was some passion to move things forward.

CHAPTER 17

Nicholas had scheduled for his entire production team to lodge at the MGM Hotel in Las Vegas as part of their pre-production agenda for the movie project. It was scheduled to last for a week and everyone was in high spirits as it was a unique opportunity for Nicholas to observe his teams skill set and performance ability before they launched into full production.

He had put together thirty of his best crew members to attend, and managing the arrangement was like organising a camp trip for a bunch of high school kids. He had arranged for top of the range catering service for the entire crew, along side planned entertainment for every night, and of course, an itinerary for his meetings with all his acquired investors in Las Vegas.

Nicholas was meticulous with his plans for this trip and as such, he compelled Judith to be on top of every thing to ensure that their plan was executed accordingly.

" I do not want to miss out any single detail once we take off." He said, as they went over the final bit of details as scheduled.

The meetings wih his investors were suppose to be a way to allow them gain transparency into their spendings. In truth, it was a way to keep them onboard and excited about the project at hand.

" I'll do my best to keep things in line. But I do hope you remember, I have a more significant role to play in the actual movie production itself." Judith said.

" Just do the best you can to see that your executive roles are satisfied. This much is expected of you as well. I will assign an extra pair of hands to assist you as we go along." He told Judith as he called out for Brian Moore. Nicholas placed Brian in charge of arrangements and with his eye for details, he believed Brian would be off good use to her. He did not want to over work her, because he knew she had to be involved in the actual set up of the shoot.

" For the first time, I wish I did not take on your proposal to be your Managing director. it is clearly going to be very distracting for me to juggle both responsibilities as we move further." she said,

" I trust your sense of Judgement. I am convinced that you are up to the task." Nicholas said.

" Thanks for the vote of confidence Boss." she replied, remaining good humored. she was looking forward to it, and was particularly saddened by the fact that her fiancée wasn't here to support her emotionally. she knew he would have come along if he could, and knew he would have loved it. But the trip had to go on nonetheless. Before they left, Nicholas assigned everyone to their respective rooms and signed over individual cheques for miscellaneous expenses for the entire week. It was the best he could do to ensure that they remained less complaisant during their stay in Vegas.

Before they left for the airport, she called her fiance to let him know she was soon to leave for Vegas. But unfortunately, she could not reach him on his mobile. she tried paging him, but still no response, so she decided to leave him a voice message instead.

" My love, I am leaving for Vegas in a couple hours. I have missed you terribly. I wish you were able to accompany me on this trip, but I know you have casualties to save at the hospital. Do give me a call as soon as you are out of surgery, OK. I love you." she said as she ended the call.

Two hours later, the entire crew congregated at the airport and they were all in good spirit. By the time they'd checked in their individual luggages and boarded the plane, she was exhausted. They were all travelling business class seated next to each other.

" What may I serve you?" The flight attendant asked" Champagne or coffee?" she was an absolute eye candy and was noticed by everyone on board, male and female.

Judith settled for Coffee, but Nicholas requested for Champagne instead. He maintained that it was good for morale, but she had to reduce her intake of alcoholic beverages for obvious reasons. When confronted by Nicholas about her choice to settle for coffee, she maintained that she was all she craved for. Once they took off, she found it uneasy to relax as there was a ton of reading she had to catch up on. Momentarily, she reclined her seat and began to read her manuscript.

" I am impressed to see you've brought your work onboard." Nicholas said.

" I have no choice in the matter. You are not going to recite my lines for me are you?" she said smiling sheepishly.

" I guess not." He replied returning a warm smile.

" Although it is a pre-production shoot, I still need to be at my very best." she said.

" I understand that totally Judith, but you still have to get a little fun out of it. Everyone else will be doing just that on this trip."

" Not too much fun I hope. After all, they can afford to have as much fun as they please. That may prove to be too costly for me if I follow suit." she replied.

" Very costly indeed. But who ever screws this up should be prepared for the sack." He said.

He took some time out to look through the last minute details for the meetings, and the list of his investors request, and the outlines he had drawn up for discussion, and eventually, he found himself reorganizing the itinerary. They were on a direct flight to Vegas, and the flight was just long enough for him to put together every last minute detail. Afterwards, Judith put her papers away and had a short nap. she passed on the aeroplane meal and snack as it wasn't her favourite thing to do while flying. When she woke up, she realized that Nicholas was watching a movie. Halfway through the flight, she found herself looking pensively out the window, and Nicholas couldn't help wondering what she was thinking about.

" What seems to be troubling you?" He asked her gently.

" Nothing much. Just the obvious I guess. a lot seems to have happened in such a short space of time. It all seems a bit overwhelming, it really does." she said.

" I couldn't agree with you more. You've worked hard for all of this, and I am grateful for all the efforts you've made so far to take this company to new heights." He said.
No one had shown this level of dedication to his business besides himself, and he felt she truly needed to be rewarded. she was one of his greatest assets now and he was convinced she would give it everything she had to pull through.

" I hope you'll soon find it rewarding to have come onboard our company. If you never hear this from anyone else, We are truly grateful to have you with us." He said

" I am thankful for all of this. I truly am. I know things would be perfect and back to normal when we finally conclude this project. We would all be deserving of a good holiday somewhere tropical. I am thinking Hawaii." she said.

" Indeed so." He replied.

" So when were you going to tell me.?" He asked.

" Tell you what?" she replied as she noticed he was staring at the ring on her finger.

" OH! That. It may have even skipped my thought for a moment considering all of which we have going on now." she replied.

she looked sad as she said it. It was so hard for her having her fiance apart from her daily life. she was suppose to be enjoying his company and their engagement period.

He seemed so far away now, and for the first time since he proposed, she truly felt estranged from him. she felt they were no longer as close as they used to be before she left London. it seemed OK for her to deal with his busy work schedule when she was there with him, but now she was on the road, she felt he was no longer part of her world. she thought about the child growing inside of her, and found it somewhat comforting to realize that it was the only bond they both had.

" Well, congratulations." He said reluctantly.

" Thank you.I know this might be difficult for you to live with, but there is nothing I can do to change this." she said

" Maybe one day there will be. In the meantime, we just need to focus on getting this project completed." He said. He felt bitter about his knowledge of her engagement. He would have done everything within his power to stop it from happening if he knew any sooner, but it was too late now. He hated the fact that he wasn't the one to make that proposal.

" He caught me unawares. But it was something I've always wished for. I hope you truly are happy for me." she said.

" Why shouldn't I be. He has got to be the luckiest man to have won your hand in marriage." He said philosophically." There sure is very little hope for anybody else now." He added.

" I hope it works out for us just as we've planned." she sounded sincere as she said it. More than anything, he wanted her to be happy, but he knew he wasn't going to be, especially living with the fact that she would never be his wife. He knew how much he needed her personally and he knew that her marriage to dr. Bernard

Oakfield would most certainly hinder his chances to court with her again. They had started as mutual partners in the business, but now there was more that that to it. she had become his confidant and co-conspirator. she now had full knowledge of the inns and outs of his entire business affairs. at times he wished he didn't let her in on so much of his dealings but he trusted her to safe guard his business affairs that were better known to him self and his father.

" You seem so interested in your future plans with this man, have you forgotten how important your career is. I am beginning to think that you are loosing you sense of purpose here Judith" Nicholas said.

" I will have to fend for myself if it came down to it. My life with him is just as important as my career. I understand I need to find a balance but I am not going to be made to choose one over the other. But if it came down to that, I'll choose my life with the man I love." she replied.

Nicholas could see how important this was to her, and he wasn't particularly pleased to hear her say the things she said. He was beginning to realize that she could give up on his business at any point and this could prove to be very costly. He tried to disguise his dissatisfaction as they talked about other things concerning their aganda in Las Vegas. He re-empahsized on how important it was for her to give her best performance on set in Las Vegas as this was what their investors needed to see to remin on board.

" I will try to give it my all" she said as Nicholas looked at her pensively for a long moment, and she was suddenly reminded of how serious he could be.

" I hope you do." He said but she didn't answer him. He could be so serious sometimes that it frightened her. In some ways, Nicholas would have hoped for their relationship to remain untainted by their indulgencies during the tour, and he blamed himself for the lack of ease that had now developed between them.

It was difficult for him to figure out how to dispell what had come between them, and now, his thoughts were suck on what to do.

They were not their usual comfortable selves and this much was obvious. The times when the strength of their personality was like a magnet had passed much sooner than he expected. It was as though they had been destined to meet each other just to face this conflict as it appeared. He now felt like they were two halves of separate entities that would never fit perfectly, and now, he couldn't understand why. It was hard for him to accept that they were coming to a cross road, and eventually, they would both have to go their separate ways.

It felt that way now, and even more so, he did not know what to do about it. He remembered when he once thought that they met because they were destined to be soul mates who shared the same passion for success and the finer things of life.

He knew he was of a higher social status compared to her, but he'd desperately tried to hide his intentions towards her. she had made him a different kind of human being now. He found himself deeply engrossed in her emotionally than he had ever felt for any other woman and he knew this was unhealthy. He knew he had swayed her into his world with his money although his motives seemed to be proffessional.

He knew how much she wanted to be casted as the lead role in this project so it didn't seem unusual for him to give her a taste of what her life as a super star could be like. It was the perfect catch 22, and he knew exactly how it worked and what he was doing. He was convinced that he had played all the right cards to get her to this point, but now she was engaged to a man she loved more than she liked him, he felt inferior, and suddenly less powerful. He had to regain his superiority fast, and infact, how he was going to do so was of great importance to him. he understood the position he was in now. In so many ways he knew things were about to get very difficult for them.

Their flight arrived just on schedule, and she and Nicholas herded their charges off the plane, and also managed to get everyone on the coach to the hotel. she was almost like their tour guide how she gave them directives and issued orders. They used a separate coach for their luggages, and they managed not to loose anybodies luggage. They would spend the rest of the day settling into their respective room and sight seeing the city of sin, but by the break of dawn, the shoot would commence.

They had prepared a separate manuscript to serve as their gide for this short film, so Judith had promised herself to stay up all night studying her lines. The meetings were scheduled to start after the first three days of the shoot. That way, they could make their presentation supported with the right report. They had it all organized and everyone was looking forward to it.

For now, there was nothing left to do but relax and enjoy the night life in Vegas. For those who hadn't been to Vegas before, It was as busy as most of the crew members had imagined and none of them were disappointed.

" I have made dinner reservations for us, I hope you don't mind." He said as they checked into the hotel. He had secured the executive suit for the both of them which was at the very top of the hotel. Although they were going to be in separate rooms, the shared a single terrace which showed the beauty of the city from its vantage point.

" Dinner sounds good. I am fermished." she replied

" Great, then we will get our things in for now, and meet at the main reception area at 11." He said.

" Sure, Sounds good to me. That will give me enough time to soak in the bath and pamper myself alittle bit." she replied.

" Very well then. See you in a few hours." He said, and then carried their suitcases to her room after dismissing the appointed staffs as they attempted to assume their duty. It wasn't Nicholas's first time in the hotel, and as such, he knew his way around. When they stepped out of the elevator at the top floor, she was amazed to embrace the magnificence of their suit. she recognized he had personally reserved it for them, but she was used to him lavishing his wealth.

Anything short would be an absolute let down. It had a white and gold finishing, and such beauty was nothing like she'd ever seen before. It was in grand style and she was in awe when she walked into her own room. Everything was laid out perfectly, and she felt she would ruin it all if she placed any of her belongings carelessly. Nicholas was just behind her and he could asberve that she was mesmerized by all of it.

" This is spectacular Nicholas. You really didn't have to." she said to him as she walked towards the flush doors that seperated her from the spectacular view of the city.

" I thought you wouldn't mind. It is beautiful isn't it?" He said and added." I wanted you to have the best view in the house."

" I would have settled for any view at all. it is Vegas after all." she replied.
it didn't occur to her that this was part of his ploy to seduce her which had been clever of him, but she was way too distracted to notice any of it.

" I'll be next door if you need me. Use the intercom if you need room service. And please have whatever you like." He said as he left her to her own wonderment.

Nicholas went to his own room and left her to settle in. He unpacked his luggages and was indeed delighted to be back in this establishment. It was where he proposed to his late ex-wife, and it did bring back a lot of fun memories. it was nothing short of a nostalgic moment for him as he let his mind run back in time. He had pre-ordered his favourite Dom perignon champagne, so he popped a bottle as he allowed himself relax.

Nicholas was first to arrive at the reception area and he'd ordered Judith some wine. When she arrived he was pleased to see her dressed as impeccable as ever.

" You look irresistable tonight Mrs judtih." He said. she laughed. she knew he was flirting with her but she made no attempt to entertain any of it. Her glass of wine arrived shortly after they met and she reached for a glass and sipped from it.

If I must say, it is only fashionable that I keep up appearances." she said demerely. she sipped from her glass and realized how lovely the wine tasted. It was too strong but he didn't mind. she sipped al little of it again as they walked torward the terrace. They were pleased to see everyone in high spirits as they smiled good naturedly at their crew members. Every one admired her as she walked the floor and this was what Nicholas enjoyed the most about her company. she complemented him in several ways. He always believed that they would have made a handsome couple, but now, he knew there was very little he could do about it.

He remembered they used to be so close to each other. Their intimacy would have easily been spotted by anyone of his workers if they were not already aware that she was in a serious relationship with doctor Bernard. it still was very hard to believe that they'd slept with each other but only the pair of them knew better. Nicholas commented on it as the approached the terrace. They were alone now and he felt the environment was free from prying eyes and ears for him to speak.

" It might be impossible to say forsure, but I can see how they look at us. Do you think they can tell?" He asked vaguely

" Do I think that they can tell what?" she asked inquisitively.

" Do you not see the way they look at us. It is obvious they must be wondering if we are lovers the way they look at us. Their mouths might not speak it, but I can see it in their eyes." he said. It seemed to amuse him but Judit didn't find any of it amusing at all.

" I could care less what they think. In fact, It dosen't bother me at all. So long as you and I Know where to draw the line now, there would be no point for the mindless suspisions." she replied.

" I know how you must feel about it, but it is far from suspisions Judith. You know it and I do too. It confuses me how you choose to devalue what we've shared together." He replied.
" What you think we shared together means nothing to me. it should never have happened. In fact it has no value whatsoever. Thinking it does only complicates matters for me." she replied.

" Why would you say such hurtful things.?"He asked saddened by her response.

" It is true. I am caught up in all of this, but all you seem to be interested in is making matters worse by speaking of things we ought to never speak of." she said.

" I understand how you must see it now, but If you look around you Judith, you'll see that I've made your life a lot more meaningful than it was before you decided to take on this project." He said
" That may be true, but isn't it also true that I have a man to answer to when it is translated to be that I have cheated on my fiance with my boss. Or worse enough, that we are having a prolonged affair. Which one sounds better to you Nicholas, please tell me, because I can see clearly now that I am the only person here who see how damaging this is going to be if ever it gets out." she replied.

" Well then, seeing that you seem to worry so much about your reputation, I suggest you think long and hard before you say your next words concerning this issue, because I can't gurantee anymore that I want this to remain a secrete." He said.

" I wonder what our doctor friend would have to say about all of this." He added

" Nicholas how dare you. After all we have at steak. How cruel can you be to say this to me. The press would slander us and your entire corporation would loose its credibility if the public gets a wift of any of this." she said.

" It may well be the case, but none of it matters as much as not being able to re-connect with you intimately." He replied.

Judith remained silent. she was always beautifully dressed, and everything about her was neat. And tonight, she was in her element. Nicholas guessed correctly that by telling her he could no longer hold their secret, she would be vulnerable to his demands. For a moment, he felt like he owned her. He did. in fact he owned everything he desired, thanks to the likes of Judith who bring him good fortune that fulfilled his desires. she looked impeccable in her flowing red dress, but her mind was unsettled. she understood the intention of his words, and knew exactly where he was heading with all of this, but she couldn't believe any of it was happening now.

" Is something wrong Judith?" He asked, suddenly concerned that he may have said something to offend her, but she only shook her head then finished the last of her drink. He was worried about her as he knew how compelling his current demands were. He wanted this to go his way but he also did not want to hurt her feelings. she made no comment, and walked back into the room. He walked with Judith in such close proximity so as not to loose sight of her. He wanted to speak to her about the way he was feeling but there were too much eyes on the both of them. It would raise their suspicions and then he really would have a great deal of problems.

They circled the room interacting with the others, and although she shown a smile or two, Nicholas could tell that she was troubled.

Their eyes met at several times and he wanted to ask her if she was OK, but the words couldn't come out of his mouth. she was reluctant to acknowledge him most of the time, but she could always feel his eyes boring into her flesh, like he was a hawk and she was his dinner. she found it impossible to concentrate on any thing, so she kept her conversations very short and moderate.

He was worried about her. Shortly afterwards, she walked towards the elevators, and a few minutes later he followed her slowly. He didn't want to intrude on her, but he had an odd sense that now was the perfect time to have her alone to himself. So he didn't hesitate. she had gotten to the elevator before him, so he assumed she was heading back to her room , so he caught the next one. As she got out of the elevator about to let herself into her room, he emerged.

" I know you are upset Judith, I do." But she wasn't convinced.

" I don't think you have the faintest idea." she said. she opened the door and stormed right in.

" Maybe you are right Judith. Maybe I do not have a a clue how up set you are, but have you ever just stopped and questioned yourself or even wondered what may have brought this on us." He said
She was surprised by the things he said. He sounded unhappy but she couldn't understand why. It was like a dark cloud that had suddenly passed in front of the bright sun, and everything around her disappeared into the darkness. she strained her mind to find the right words to convince Nicholas that she already felt

defeated about their situation, but she was so overwhelmed that it brought tears to her eyes.

" I guess you are beginning to loose track of the important things,Nicholas. Your family, you business, and most importantly, your reputation. Listening to you now seems like we've wasted our time all these months." she said.

" I refuse to see it that way. I choose to determine what is important in my life and what isn't. Been with you is important because it is the only thing I can seem to think about lately. how do I know my family will not turn their backs on me some day? Or that my business wouldn't fold some day despite all my efforts? I think I am right so much of the time, that once in a while, I wonder if it would be so wrong to make a mistake now and again." He replied

" I've tried very hard to make sure we don't let this sort of thing ruin our work, but it seems unavoidable now, more so, because you insist on making it difficult for us." she said.

" You know for a long time I have tried to keep this emotion to myself, but it is not going to be possible at all. I have spent so many years avoiding feeling with other girls that I've believed I had no future with. But now with you in the picture, all of that has changed." he said.

" What do you mean, all of that has changed?" she was startled by what he was saying to her. They were serious thoughts to have seeing that they've been working together for this long.

" So what? You mean that I have now become someone you can't live without. I might be in your world now, but you do not have a say at all when it comes to who I choose or choose not to be with." she replied.

" You and I have a lot of time to make this work between us, if you want it to. No one says it has to be so wrong. If it so happens that your relationship doesn't work out with Bernard, then you know it wasn't meant to be." He said.

" Maybe that's the problem. Maybe you are so delusional that you can't stand to see me with anyone but yourself." she said.

" Maybe you are right Judith. So much so that I am prepared to ruin it all if I can't have you." HE replied.

" Maybe it is time to look in a new direction." she said simply. she wasn't prepared to cut through this situation any more than she had already tried to.

" You know what you have to do to make this work out for us Judith. Why make things worse." He aid.

" Well I am glad you can finally admit that it is bad." she said.

" What do you intend to do? Whatever it is, I must let you know that your decision would bring this entire project to an end if it is something that doesn't sit well with me." He said.

" To someone who could care less about who he uses, I am not about to allow myself be trolled around like a piece of rubbish." she said.

" So it is better you do as I say, or face the ultimate penalty." He replied.

she couldn't believe her ears. Now, she was truly overwhelmed about the entire situation. she couldn't afford to loose her role in the project. It was the last thought on her mind, but everything else made her so confused. Living in a separate country for Dr. Bernard had put a tremendous strain on her relationship, and now she was frightened. she felt as though she had thought about the entire thing differently. she felt like she was the one being inconsiderate and less cooperative. she felt as though she was being pulled apart by fate and a host of other forces greater than herself and her love for Dr. Bernard. she had never felt this way before and it was a really terrifying feeling.

" I do not know what you want from me, neither do I know what you want me to do." she said honestly. " You are demanding the impossible from me, I am engaged now Nicholas. I cannot afford to loose my marriage over this. I just cannot loose him, ill be lost without him. I love him more than life, and my life would be a huge dark hole without him." she said, and she felt that way now, as though she would fall into an abyss of self pity haunted by her past if she lost him. she found the thought discomforting. But she knew that if she didn't stop things from going any further with Nicholas, she would never forgive herself. she was now beginning to face the fact that she had no way out of this. After several months of touring and waiting for the right time to commence this project, she is finally confronted with what appears to be one of the most difficult decision she would ever encounter.

" All I want is you Judith." He said. she turned her back on him then. she knew she had betrayed her partner, and nothing could feel any worse. she hated pondering on the thought. she had invested a lot into her relationship to let this matter set her back, but realistically it was too late. Nicholas threatening to tell the doctor that they had slept together would prove to be very damaging to their relationship because he had trusted and believed in her all along. she knew she would never recover form this, even if she ever did, she would always remember how horrific this particular feeling was. she was completely unaware of her effect on him until he touched her shoulders and spoke.

" I hope you find it easier to know that I am beginning to feel like my world cannot exist without yours. I just want to show you how hard and cynical I can be, so you know how serious my feelings are towards you. Right now, having you is all that matters to me, and I want you to want me too." He said.
" But I will never want you in the same way Nicholas. Never. I just want to move on with my life. Nothing you do will make me change my mind. All you are demanding for only makes me wonder what the hell it is

I am doing here." she said.

" But you are still here Judith, doesn't that mean anything to you?" He asked.

" I do not know what you expect me to say. No matter what you choose to do, my heart does and always will belong to Bernard." she said.

For all their talk about what would happen if they carried on recklessly, he knew that she was right. Her heart would never be his. she was very much in love with her partner and she wasn't going to give up on their plans to be together.

" Then so be it Judith, He can have your heart but I will have your body and time whenever I please." He said with a sinister grin.

He then proceeded to kiss her shoulders, but she said and did nothing, but let the tears flow down her face. The cloud that seemed to overshadow her could not dispel, instead, it got darker and darker. It made her feel sad seeing that there was nothing she could do to stop what was happening now. she always seemed to be able to dissipate problems before they occurred, but she couldn't bring her self to tap into that strength. Everyone was unaware of what was happening except for Nicholas and herself. Nicholas himself was very well aware of what he was doing to her, and it seemed like there was no one to stop him from doing so.

" You are truly amazing Judith. Do not think so much about it, it will be over soon." He said. AT this point she disliked everything about him. she had been startled about the entire situation when he started talking about his feeling, but now, his actions were more disturbing. she was so confused and everything was moving too fast, and the wine she had earlier was beginning to have an effect on her. she hadn't had anything to eat, and this made her feel worse. she knew things would never be the same for them after this, but she was clear she would never see him the same way ever again. They stood there quietly, she was uneasy standing there with her back turned, but with him being, he didn't need to say any more to her. He knew he had finally conquered her for the moment, and he would be the only one enjoying the fulfilment of his pursuit. Judith felt powerless in his arms, and she could feel her world falling apart by the second. she tried to stop him the best way she could, but she couldn't. For the sake of the life growing inside her, she wasn't prepared to get into any physical struggle with him. That alone was the source of her lack of strength to fight him off, so she tried to block out the thought of whatever was happening now.

He turned her around, unable to resist the strength of his masculinity, he kissed her forcefully. she felt the tears running down her face uncontrollably now, and the sense of panic was very intense. she wasn't her usual self any more. she wasn't kissing him back and he noticed this. All this did was make him angrier. He knew he should apologize to her like he did the last time, but he couldn't bring himself to do so this time around. He knew it wouldn't make anything better.

" I shouldn't say this to you, but I will give you everything you need so long as you let me have you. Right now, I need you this way, and I promise to do so much more for you as long as you keep this quiet. she couldn't comprehend the force that she felt that was allowing this to go on. For the first time since she she self harmed, she had never felt so weak and vulnerable. It wasn't just desire that raged over Nicholas, it was so much more. it was his passion and flaws mixed with his obsession over her. That was the force she felt so over powering that she couldn't resist. Every inch of him hungered for her, and slowly she submitted. He had her on her back on the bed, hurriedly taking off his clothes and then hers. His hand slid in between her legs and then he slipped off her underwear. This made her feel sick to her guts. Now she was naked in all her glory feeling as worthless as can be, he had a boyish grin on his face.

" Please do not do this to me." she said softly, sounding frightened and unable to scream for help. She had done this before thoughtlessly, but this time it made her feel horrible. It was a feeling so over powering that took over her, and indeed, it made her feel bad.

His hands roamed all over her, and each time he tried to kissed her she turned away. she had never experienced this with anyone before. All she could think of now was the voice of her mother echoing in her head, telling her that she worried for her, and that she hoped she was in good hands. she had believed she was since the beginning, but now all she felt was heartache and misery. she hated the man over her deep inside her heart each time she opened her eyes to see him labouring himself. So she shut it tighter and prayed in her soul that all of it would be over. In that time,she tried to force the thought of her fiancée out of her head.

This was a nightmare she wanted to wake up form very quickly, and shortly afterwards, she felt he was off her and all she did was roll over to the opposite side of the bed with the bed sheet wrapped around her body. He knew he had broken her, and unable to wait around to see her this way, he left her room without saying a word. And when she heard the door shut, she began sobbing uncontrollably.

CHAPTER 18

The time Judith was spending in Vegas was nothing short of a living nightmare.

Neither of them could say a word to each other the next day because they both knew that what had happened would inexorably change their lives. Judith worried for this more because she'd never been through this before. Judith had no idea how to resolve it. There was no question in her mind any more, she had to tell Dr Oakfield . But the question was how? and when. Nicholas had no right to what he took from her, and she had no right to break her fiancées trust in her. she was in a minefield of turmoil and she needed to understand what it meant and how to deal with it.

" What are my going to do about this she asked her self sitting in her room a few night before the pre-production shoot was due to conclude. she had forced herself to take this secret to her grave the first time it happened, but now all she wanted to do was cry out for help. The thought of what had happened tormented her overnight, and she found herself as like now, unable to sleep.

They were working just well together, but the new dimension that has now corrupted their working relationship changed everything. There was exactly four days left before she returned to new york, and between the time she had arrived in Vegas, she had only spoken to her fiancée twice.

What had happened in the very same room she was sitting in now and its impact was significant enough to create a storm of horrific proportions with very dangerous implications. Whatever waited for them beyond the shores was going to be justification for what had happened and she prayed she could handle her fair share of blame. Nicholas had no idea which way Judith was going to turn, and this left him on the edge. she knew the weight of what had happened was drowning her into oblivion.

Either way, she had decided to do something about it or do nothing.

Either was a possibility, but she was drifting slowly towards doing nothing.

A part of her couldn't go through with it. People would blame her in so many ways. who where they to judge her she imagined. How many of them had really been through such terrifying experience. she was perplexed and she knew it. she felt as though she was trapped between two walls. To do something about it meant that she stood the chance of loosing her contract with the Wrights business, her marriage to the man she loves, her place on the project, as well as her source of living. she believed she would lose face before her very own mother. Possibly raise a child on her own as a single mother. To do nothing meant that she remained silent, and allow this virus eat at her insides until her heart can't take it no more. she chose not to make any decision now, at least until she returned to New York. she tried to stay calm and think sensibly. she nodded silently in answer to her own bewilderment as she stood up from the couch she was sitting on.
she listened to her mind speak to her as she slowly walked around the room.

"... I can't... I just can't give up on Bernard... I can't leave him either... He is the reason I am able to pursue this project... Even though we are just engaged doesn't make it OK to explore the advances of the opposite sex... I love him... Oh my God, I am still in love with him. What have I done to bring this on myself...I have to talk to him...I really do... I need to let him know everything that is going on now..."

she forced herself to get some sleep as she was having the first pre-scheduled meeting with Nicholas's associates in the morning. They had to feed them the itinerary before proceeding, and it was a great opportunity for Nicholas to re-establish his worth. In the morning, she got herself prepared. she didn't need to contact Nicholas for anything even though he was just next door. she knew exactly what had to be done and she got on with it.

she was one of three people expected to sit for this meeting who arrived very early the next morning.. she kept up this practice since she was in sixth form, as it allowed her prepare herself before any event. As so she did. she looked through her reports and made sure she hadn't left out any relevant information.

When Nicholas and the others arrived, he couldn't keep his eyes off her, but they were extremely circumspect when they were around other people from the media or in public. she tried to avoid any direct eye or physical contact with him while they were in the room. They presented the plan they had prepared supported by a well detailed report, and Judith had summarized with an excellent speech. It was as perfect as she'd expected it to be, so she was happy to feed back their crew some good news. They were pleased to hear what she said to them over lunch, and as such, it meant that they had to get straight to business in the morning. she encouraged all of them to keep a clear head for the next 3-4 days, and afterwards, there would be good need to celebrate. Nicholas was present at this lunch gathering, but he had barely been able to say a word to her. He let her lead the group. After all, that was her responsibility.

Even the most observant of their colleagues would have been hard put to find anything out of the ordinary between them. But what Judith felt when she was around him now, more than anything, was a kind of unspoken hatred ignited by her passion to make the best out of this project. she was exhausted mentally, but no one was able to detect this much. It was so overwhelming how flawed the basis of their relationship now seemed to her. Her expectations had come crashing down like a pack of dominoes faster than she had ever imagined. And it was so obvious to her that it seemed incredible that no one else could see all the misery she was dealing with.

she was quickly becoming unhappy and she could feel herself becoming very irritable. More so than she deserved, what she had discovered was that her pregnancy was becoming obvious. For the sake of the bump in her stomach, she dressed smartly now to avoid the knowledge of this by others. But she feared she was running out of time, and fast. For the moment, she knew she was on borrowed time, and sooner or later she would have to come clean.

But not yet.

For the moment it was still her playing field. she knew enough to leverage upon so she needed this much time to reveal her next move. she came into this opportunity knowing exactly what to expect. Although she was prepared to make amends, she felt disappointed in herself for letting this become a part of her life's story. she had tried to avoid any speck of uncertainty that may hinder her ambitions, but how it had come to this, and why, to her , was nothing short of another one of life's great illusions. The force that had pulled them all together was more powerful than she could ever imagine, and strangely, it now seemed like the same force was soon to tear them apart.

While they were having lunch, she imagined a life with Nicholas if Dr Oakfield was not in the picture. This particular thought was very hard to dismiss. she wondered if what had happened between them would be normal if she didn't have to answer to any one. Could it be that it would be morally sound to treat both men as just potential suitors despite her current engagement. If she had to pick one that fits her life now, who would it be. she did wish to find the man of her dreams, the perfect fit that made everything a dream come true. she pondered on several other ways of looking at her current situation to ease the frustration and guilt she was currently feeling, but none of it was good enough to make her feel better.

Despite her present train of thought, she wasn't willing to hurt Dr Oakfield . she knew he did not deserve that. in spite of what had happened between her and Nicholas, she couldn't imagine a life without the same that saved her life. He had become such a very relevant part of her life and she owed it to him to remain devoted. He had her mind, body and soul, more than Nicholas could ever acquire. Things were complicated now and it made her increasingly agitated. she had never been unhappy with her fiancée, but she worried now that he may never trust her again. Circumstances had changed her perception on the entire situation and she blamed herself for her recklessness.

They finished their meal with the others and some of the crew members stayed at the lobby area for some late evening entertainment. Nicholas had hired musicians and comedians to entertain his staff, and they were pleased to see the show. Judith passed on socializing with the rest of the crew. she had so much on her mind that she wasn't convinced that anyone could cheer her up. she returned to her room and decided to call Dr Oakfield . she had to hear his voice, and she was startled when the phone rang and she heard him speak. And the moment she heard his voice she became frightened to tell him what was on her mind.

" How are you sweetheart. You almost missed me, I am in surgery in 20mins." He said.

" I am fine, lucky me then." she replied begrudgingly.

" You don't sound too well, is everything OK?" He asked, noticing she wasn't her usual self.

" I am OK. Its been great so far, but all too exhausting that's all." she replied, trying to mask the fact that she was on the edge of a mental break down. she felt like a criminal keeping the truth of the situation away from her future husband, she knew it wasn't the right thing to do, but she was scared.

" I bet you've been working like a dog to make things happen, perhaps you need to relax more after each days work." He said. He was always so thoughtful and caring, but absolutely clueless as to what the reality of the situation really was.

" You know me too well. But I think I may have bitten too much than I can chew this time." she replied. Dr Oakfield laughed at her witty response to his reference to how busy she was, but he could never had imagined she was trying to tell him something more. she thought now would be the best time to get it out once and for all, but she couldn't summon the courage to do so.

They talked for a short time and he told her he needed to run into surgery.

" Call me later on dear OK. Look on the bright side, in a couple more days you'll be back at your apartment. Try and make the best of your trip OK, it might make you feel better." He said

" OK I will try babe." she replied. Everything he said made her feel so bad. she knew how he cared for her, but the only way to describe what she had done to him was betrayal. she took his advice to have a bit of fun. It was the best she could do under the circumstances. she couldn't stuff herself away in the room in a bid to avoid Nicholas, it only made her feel worse by the minute.

As she returned downstairs to join the group, she saw Nicholas, and immediately, he sensed her tension.

" How long do you intend ignoring me for?" He asked softly.

" For as long as it takes." she looked unhappy as she said it, and for an instant, he panicked. He was terrified of what she would do next, and this made him curious.

"Don't tell me you are still hung up over what happened the other night." He said. He knew it was good enough to be a reason why she was avoiding him, but he tried to play it down.

" And what if I was Nicholas? Don't stand there with a smirk acting as though you care about what I am feeling. I am beginning to find it very redundant." she replied

He was still trying to feel his way through the issue between them. He noticed that she felt awful about it all, so he figured they needed some time to adjust. What he did not know was that she was prepared to tell her fiancée before he heard it by way of a third party. They only thing she knew she wanted was to stop the guilty voices in her head giving her countless sleepless nights.

" So how do you propose we get this matter resolved between us then?" He asked.

" If I knew, it would have been done already, and all this would be a thing of the past, but right now, I just want to be left alone." she replied.
" Don't you think it is a little too late for that now?" He asked.

" That for me to decide. After all I have earned my right to a little bit of peace and quiet whenever I so please." she replied.
" Not at my expense." He countered. And there was no hiding from the fact that he was now crossed with her.
" You work for me remember. DO I need to remind you about this fact. So darling when I say jump, what you need to do is ask me how high Mr. Wright?" He said.

" What are you saying to me Nicholas. That I

should be prepared to bend over backwards when ever his lordship pleases. Is that it?" she replied with a furious look. And she wondered if he was determined to make this any more detrimental that it appeared to be.

"Yes I do. And as a matter of fact, I expect you to say thank you sir, every time I've had my way with you." HE said

" I understand." she replied nodding her head. she remained silent for the moment then excused herself. " Well, I will be with the rest of the crew if you need me, sir." she said as she walked into the lobby to join the others.

For the rest of th trip they kept well clear of each other and did what they had come to do, and the pre-production shoot went extremely well from everyone's point of view. And for Judith and Nicholas. They discovered new worlds not being able to communicate with each other. It was excruciating to deal with for the both of them but by the time they left Vegas, Judith was pleased to be out of there. Judith was so angry at Nicholas that in some ways, she wished she had never met him. There was no way for them to escape the inevitable. More than ever, they could no longer be discreet about all that had been going on between them.

Judith arrived at her apartment, and when she got into the house, she spent hours in the bed room. she was troubled by her present predicament. And this was rapidly becoming more than she could cope with. she pondered on how she was going to do this, could she be sensible and give into Nicholas advances until she got what she wanted, or could she do the wise thing and tell her partner what had been going on between them, or carefully remove herself from their lives. Judith had thought about this lot. she had a lot to think about and she knew it. she had told herself from the beginning that she was not going to leave Dr Oakfield . But what that meant, for her particularly was that she was going to do the wise thing and tell him. It was the right thing to do and she knew this much was true. it was only a question of when would be the best time to do so.

she wondered how she would go about it with the least possible damage for everyone involved. For the moment, she was convinced it would be, no matter how much she tried to avoid. Judith knew she had to accept this, although she didn't like it, she knew there was very little she could do now to make it all go away.
she forced herself to sleep and the following morning, she didn't bother going into work.

Mr Billingham her assistant had called her several times to ask why she wasn't at the office, but she ignored his calls. she did however try to reach her fiancée at the hospital, but she was told that he was busy dashing in and out of surgeries. He was running a tight four weeks schedule at the trauma unit, and as such, it meant that he was on a high wire without a balancing pole, riding a unicycle, and juggling oranges.

Dr Oakfield barely had time for himself, and he found   himself sleeping in his office most nights. He missed being able to come home to Judith every night. He didn't want to put undue pressure on her by making her give up on her dreams. But as he thought about their lives as it were now, he knew he was truly ready to get married and start a family. Judith on the other hand was ready to begin a family life with him, but she had a huddle to over come first. As soon as she could get a hold of him, she was prepared to tell him everything that had happened between her and Nicholas.

she called Dr Oakfield back that evening, and told him that something terrible had happened at work, and she needed to speak to him urgently. The moment she hung up as he said he would call her right back, she felt a rush of guilt flow through her veins, and He understood that she didn't sound too happy, so he took some time out and returned to his office to have a chat with her. she had found herself being a certain way that she had never been with him. she didn't want to keep things from him, neither did she want to begin lying to him.

And it also occurred to her that she was becoming in this relationship the exact same person she hated other people for, now, she hated her self for it. she had slept with her boss voluntarily once, perhaps it was one big mistake she had made and would never forgive herself for, but now, it had turned into physical, emotional and mental abuse. It wasn't a pretty picture and she knew her fiancée would be devastated. Dr. Oakfield walked into his office and he called her back.
" You sound distressed dear, what's the matter?" He asked with a distinct tone of concern.

" it's all gone pear shaped Bernard, and I can't live with myself any more." she replied.

" What is wrong Judith you are beginning to scare me." HE said.

" I don't know how to say this to you Bernard. But I want you to know I love you very much." she said.

" What is wrong Judith, tell me, what has happened at work?" He asked emphatically.

" I want you to know I hate myself already as it is, and maybe it would destroy me to know that you may never forgive me, but I have to tell this to you regardless." she said.

" Whatever it is, you can talk to me Judith, tell me, what is wrong?" He asked.
Judith was silent for a while, and by that time, he knew that something terrible had happened, but he wasn't sure what.

" Judith, come on, talk to me, it doesn't help matters if you choose to remain silent." He said. He could hear that she was sobbing, so he encouraged her to take a deep breath and talk slowly.

" Take a deep breath Judith. OK, now tell me. What

do you need to say to me?" He asked
" I had sex with Nicholas Wright." she said. It felt like
everything around him had turned dark when he heard
the words she'd just said resonate through the phone.
He couldn't believe what his ear heard, and so he
remains silent for her to continue speaking.
" It was a terrible, terrible mistake Bernard. I feel so
ashamed of myself. It first happened while we were on
the road." she said,
" What do you mean it first happened, you mean it has
been more than once? You mean to tell me that you two
have been screwing each other all along? " He asked
furiously.
       " Bernard, No, it's not like that. It's not like that at
all. It only happened once, before you proposed. I was
in such a bad way, and one thing led to another. It was
impossible for me to see things clearly at the time but
now I do." he said.
       " Well, congratulations Judith. You certainly get to
win a big award for this. This would most certainly go
down in the books as one of your greatest acts."He said
       " I am so so sorry Bernard. It does take so much
for me to tell you this. Especially this way." she said
       " How dare you Judith. You wait until after I
propose for your hand in marriage to tell me of such
despicable act between you and that son of a bitch." He
replied.
       " I know you are angry at me Bernard, I know you
must hate me now, but please, find it in your heart to
forgive me because I cannot forgive myself." she
replied.
       " It is too late for forgiving now Judith. You have
ruined everything. And to think I trusted you. I can't
believe you would do this to me." He said.
       " I can't believe I have done this to us either. You
mean the world to me, that is why I couldn't keep this
from you. If I never told you and you had to find out
through a third party, then perhaps I'll be less deserving

of your forgiveness, but please, please find it in your heart to pardon my reckless behaviour. I wish I could have explained to you what I've been dealing with mentally prior to this happening, maybe it would have never happened." she said.

" Oh please don't. Just don't do that. I gave you every opportunity to communicate with me. It was your choice not to tell me what was going on. And it was your choice to allow yourself fall into bed with your boss. I hope it was worth it Judith, I hope it really was." He said, sounding angrier after every statement he made.

" It wasn't worth it at all. Not one single bit, in fact, quite the opposite." she replied.

" What in Gods name do you mean. Isn't it a bed of roses for the two of you now. I hope you are both happy and live happily ever after." He said.

" It is far from that Bernard. There is more." she said.

" What?!" He exclaimed.

" I quit my job with the Wright's. It was doomed from the very beginning, I just was too blind to see it." she said.

" What do you mean you quit your job. Is this official." He asked.

" No it isn't. In fact you are the first person I am saying this to. I wanted you to hear it first." she said

" Oh Judith, what had you done?" He asked

" Worse than I can say for sure now, but I am so sad Bernard, I do not want to live any more." she said.

The moment those words came out of her mouth, he knew immediate that he was dealing with potential suicidal victim. He knew her medical history, and it was circumstances like this that she had been warned to avoid.

" Now calm down Judith. We can talk about this. where are you now?" He asked

" I am at the apartment." she replied

" Are you there alone?" He asked

" Yes I am." she replied.

" Now whatever you do, I want you to remain calm and seated" He said,

" I am seated, but I can't say I am calm at all." she replied.

" OK that is fine. So when you say you quit, you mean you have made up your mind to do so, but you haven't told Him yet?" He said

" yes, precisely. But I intend to do so as soon as possible." she said.

" And this is so because you have had sexual relations with him, or you just do not want to pursue the project any more?" He asked.

" It is both. I do not want to be anywhere around him any more, because not only did it happen once, he now chooses to force himself on me whenever he wants to if I don't give him what he needs." she replied.

" Are you telling me he has been physical with you?" He asked

" Yes, Just a few days ago, I had told him that I accept that I may have made the greatest mistake of my life allowing it to happen in the first place, but I wouldn't do so a second time around. But he persisted and forced himself on me, threatening to tell you of how disloyal I had been if I didn't let him have his way with me." she said.

" Why is it so you never told me any of this until now Judith, why?" she asked.

" I was afraid Bernard, I was afraid I would loose you for ever if I did, and now, I am prepared to end my own life if it mean that I loose mine with you." she replied.

" Now hang on a minute Judith, Do not do anything stupid now OK. It is clear to see that you've bottled up all of this for so long. That must be so awful, but it is not enough for you to begin contemplating suicide." He said.

" It is so hard not having you here with me Bernard. I have been afraid that I might start using again, but somehow, Nicholas had managed to keep me busy with the project." she said.

" I always knew you two together was going to create something epic, who would have thought it would turn out to be a scandalous affair." He said

" It sounds bad I know, But I do not know what else to do." she replied.

" So he threatens to expose your ordeal if you didn't get into bed with him when he wanted, and he has forced himself on you once already. Has he suggested terminating your contract also?" He asked.

" Yes he has, in so many words. I've had to fulfil my pre-production shoot requirements, but now, I do not have the will to go ahead with any of it." she replied.

" It is a shame it has come to this Judith. It really is. I am not sure what you expect me to say or do about this situation." He said. It was obvious that despite whatever foibles existed between them now, he genuinely cared for her.

" This is why I've contacted you. I want you to know that I have confronted him about this situation, telling him how much I do not want any more of it, but he seems to overlook the fact that I am now engaged and soon to be married. Moreover, I have told him of how dangerous this would be to our working relationship, but he doesn't seem to be bothered about any of it." she said.

Dr Oakfield could tell that she was bitter about what had happened. They both talked about things a bit longer, and in that time, he advised her to tell Nicholas that he was now aware of the situation, and that it would be in his best interest if he kept his distance from her.

" OK, I will do just that. But I would need you out here as soon as possible. I am afraid of what may happen if and when this takes a nasty turn." she replied.

" OK, I'll on the next available flight. But this doesn't mean I have accepted any of this Judith. I am utterly disappointed in you. And to think that we were making plans for the future, now you have brought this upon us to ruin the beauty of it all." He said.

" I think I know what I have to do to fix this. But please I need you here as soon as possible. I am terrified being here all by myself Bernard." she said.

" I had a very busy schedule at the unit this week, do you know how difficult it would be for me to get away." He said

" How ever difficult it would be, please make it happen, I am afraid my life may depend on it." she replied.

" Look, Judith. I don't care about any of this any more, I feel deeply wounded by all this. You should have thought about the repercussion of your actions before you decided to go dancing with the devil." He said.

" I would live to regret it, Bernard but please for the love of God, I need you here as soon as possible." she said. she was sobbing uncontrollably and he could tell that she was deeply upset about all that had happened. And as this was the case, he owed it to her to be there for her to prevent the worse from happening. He was really irritated with her, but he knew this was something he had to do for all the right reasons.

" I will be out there within the next couple of days,if not, it'll be at least another week. But I can't guarantee you anything. I don't know the depths of what you have gotten yourself into with this man, but it is your responsibility to clean up the mess you have created. And I must tell you now that a part of me never wants to see you any more." He sounded very angry and Judith admitted to herself that she would feel the same exact way if she was in his shoes.

" I know you hate the bones of me right now, but I

am sorry." she was frightened by the thoughts of loosing him, and she sounded apologetic as she said it.   she was feeling desperately guilty, but a lot more determined to confront Nicholas again.

No matter how bad things seemed now, she knew her fiancée loved her very much. He only said the things he did to let her know he was very upset. she couldn't expect him to accept this and give her a pat on the back for a job well done.

" I will let you know when I've booked the next flight out to New York." He said." I will see you when I see you Judith. I have to get back to work now." He added. He almost hung up on her, and she laid in bed crying all night, thinking about her life. But she didn't say anything to Nicholas until the following morning.

Nicolas had just concluded a meeting with his legal team and they'd informed him that his project had now gained the financial edge it needed to trade publicly. They were enthusiastic about the returns it would yield, and Nicholas was pleased to hear their thoughts on the matter. when he was told that he had a call waiting from her, he asked his assistant to forward the call to his office.

As it turned out, he noticed she had been absent from work again, so he needed to hear from her. He walked into the office, and shut the door behind him while he took a sit behind his desk. He knew things were not good between them , but he was thrilled to take a call from her.

" I see you've decided to take a couple more days off work since we returned from Vegas," He said, showing superiority as he spoke.

" I certainly have you to thank for the time off" she said.

" Well, then don't form a habit of it. We have serious work to do. We are opening trade of the projects stock in six weeks." He said

" Lucky you then. As for me, I think I have come to end of the road on this journey." she said.

" What in the world are you talking about." He asked besides himself.

" I quit Nicholas. I want out, and I happen to have the courtesy to let you know I've made up my mind."

" You can't be serious Judith. You have signed the dotted line. That means that I own you legally for the next five years." He said.

" Yes, you are right, I was expecting you to remind me of that. But may I say to you first of all that I have told Bernard about us. Again, I must let you know that I have kept records of all your illegal business transactions with faceless associates. Records I would be prepared to take public, as I am sure, the world would like to know all about the tale of the infamous mogul, who finds him self facing a lengthy law suit of, Money laundering, racketeering, sponsoring underage sex trafficking in Asia, and may I add sexual assault on a member of your work force, among other things that I may decide to add to the long list if I chose to." she said.

" You don't seize to amaze me Judith. Are you making threats now? You are in no position to make threats Judith." He said.

" You don't say. Well I wouldn't think of it as threats just yet. You say I have signed the dotted lines which means you own me for another five years right? I want you to see it this way Nicholas. Think of it as my insurance policy within that five years. In which time, I own you, and keep you obliged to fulfil all the requirements of that contract." she said.

" Ha Ha Ha Ha. You are truly sensational. Who would have thought that little miss Judith could raise a fierce head over the one person who believed in her dreams." He said.

" Well you should have thought about that when

you decided to play god over my life. You do not own me Nicholas, You never did, and you never will. I am prepared to accept what ever comes my way by standing by this conviction." she said.

" Well then, you leave me no choice. Your life depends on me whether you choose to see it that way or not. and I will begin by telling you that I have, as we speak, cancelled all your credit cards and I have withdrawn any other incentives that you have been granted by this organisation. And please may I remind you that, you did sign to agree to have you replaced as lead character on this project in any event some unforeseen circumstance occurred." He said smiling.

" You bastard. How dare you Nicholas. How dare you." she said, yelling at the top of her lungs. Nicholas laughed in response to her outburst.

" I am sickened by the lives of you and your pathetic fiancée. How could you so much as think of telling him you had been unfaithful, and then He what, intends to forgive you and forget all about it. Truly pathetic." He said.

" That is why I choose him over you Nicholas. He is ten time everything you will never be." she said in defence to her fiancée.

" And you know that how? because of some lousy escapade between you and I? Please darling, I see girls like you a dime a dozen come and go every time. And they always end up the same way, poor, miserable and alone. Is that how you want your life to become Judith?" He asked.

" It would never be that way. You may have claimed and ruined the lives of many other, but I will not allow you ruin mine." she replied.

" My terms remains that I complete the time on my contract and walk in peace or I am going straight to the press with all I have on you." she said.

" I would be very careful what I say next if I were

you. I have entertained just about every sentimental crap you could come up with, but now you are just pushing your luck. You can keep your pathetic excuse for a relationship with who ever you please. I have given you a taste of a better life but you insist on making a mockery of my good will." He said.

" It is you who chooses to make a mockery of me. I expected you to understand my position and leave it at that, but you decided to force my hands." she replied.

" You have forced mine too. It is out of my hands now what ever happens from this point on. Good luck." He said, and he hung up on her.

Judith said in for the rest of the day. she wasn't up for anything. she did not want to see or speak to any one. she opened a bottle of wine and poured herself a large drink. For the first time since her last self harm episode, she really did feel like ending her life now. she felt there was nothing more to live for. But it wasn't about her any more. she had to think for herself and and her child, and her dear mother who she knew categorically, would not be able to withstand the trauma. she drank herself into oblivion, and after six hours of none stop drinking, she was sprawled across the living room sofa.
Nicholas had made a few calls, but there was one that was more important than the others. It was a call to Diego Costella his God father. Diego Costella was the head of all of the Wright's associates. He was a billionaire by virtue of a tough up bringing, and he had gotten to know a lot of very powerful people over the years, Some of whom still worked for him until this present day.

Nicholas had asked to see and speak to him about very pressing matters and he had obliged. Diego Costella told Nicholas where to meet him, and as always, so long as it was in public, it was always some place remote, and away from the prying eye of the public.

Nicholas arrived at the location, and he was pleased to see the man that had gotten him through thick and thin in the corporate world. Diego Costella was responsible for his success in America and England combined. Nicholas respected everything Diego told him, and most times, even when his advice wasn't favourable to Nicholas, he would take it nonetheless, believing that it was for a greater purpose. They hugged each other and Nicholas sat down to tell of what troubled him.

" I understand you've ran your self into some difficulty." Diego Costella said then smiled at him. It wasn't the first time they'd met to talk about one issue or the other that Nicholas was struggling to deal with.

" It does appear so. But I thank you for making some time to meet with me," Nicholas said revealing his mark of respect for the man sat across from him.

" I hear you are trading publicly. on this particular project, in less than eight weeks. That's brilliant young lad." He said Jovially.

Nicholas smiled at him, remembering that they had strategic several times in the past on a few of Diego's past deals. He knew it was a big deal to the likes of Diego Costella, and he was proud to be a product of one of Americas most successful business men.

" Well, I have you to thank on that note. Let's say I took good lessons from the master of all things corporate America." He said.

" Ha Ha Ha, Don't be ridiculous. I happen to think I don't get the same kick from any of it any more like I used to In the eighties. Hmmm. But any ways, enough about me, what brings you to us today?" Diego asked.

" I happen to have a bad egg in the bunch. it is an issue that I fear may run out of hand without due caution." He said.

" Spoken very wisely. But for you to sound this compelled, what exactly are we dealing with?" Diego asked.

" An Eminent threat of the Exposure of some of our trusted associates in the other lines of the families foreign and domestic affairs."

" And this, bad seed, or bad egg as you rightly put it, are they public or civilian?" HE asked.

" Civilian." He replied and they both remained mute for several moments.

" What level of risk are you afraid you may be exposed to?" Diego asked.

" We stand the risk of having stone cold facts revealed to the public if due caution isn't applied. I am talking, Financial records with very detailed transactions, coupled with a list of affiliates on their government name basis." Nicholas said

" Too many of our people would be pulled down without..." Nicholas was stopped short by Diego who already got the memo.

" Spare me the details Nicholas. My question is why has it taken you this long to clean up this mess?" Diego asked.

" I would be making excuses if I had a direct answer to your question," Nicoll's replied bluntly.

" And the subject of this eminent threat, who are they?" Diego asked.

" Judith Meridian. My lead cast in the proposed Project." Nicholas replied.

" Interesting. Now the all most important question is was she worth it?" He asked. Diego knew Nicholas dared not to give him any form of a response to his last question. By the sounds of his report, it seemed as though Nicholas had let his guards down and allowed his emotions get the better of him.

" I'll tell you what. This doesn't sound like good news at all, and you know I have never been the bearer of bad news. What I suggest you do is retrieve all and every relevant document that may have slipped through your grip and destroy it. By any means necessary." He said.

Nicholas understood what he meant, and by Diego's last words, he understood exactly what had to be done. And this made him feel very uncomfortable.

" By the next time I see you, I expect to hear that this has been taken care of." Diego Costella said.

" Indeed so." Nicholas replied.

" I will be talking to your father about this personally very soon." He said as he stood up to leave. But before he was out of sight, he turned around and said,

" When you get yourself entangled with a sweet ass, like I assume lady Meridian. is, you always loose something you may never get back in a life time."

Diego had long since promised Nicholas that he would never let anything bad happen to him, but he always feared that they may some day be that one thing that he might not be able to stop, in attempts to save him. In that sense, he knew it was not always about the money.

Nicholas didn't reply as he watched his god father disappear into thin air. It was going to be a long day for Nicholas and he could already feel the anxiety wash over him as he walked towards his car. He had handled several other assignments that posed the same level of threat all by himself, but none of them had made him feel this bad. The ultimate penalty for anyone who opposed him to the point of making threats of a public lawsuit in attempts to humiliate him was death. But

This was not what he wished for Judith. When he arrived at his private lodge, he was glad to be alone.

The kids had arrived to spend time with him for three days before they travelled to Paris, so he knew they would be a noisy bunch if he returned home for the night. He called the baby sitter he had appointed and told her to break the news to them, that he would see them by noon the latest the next day. And afterwards, he sat down and allowed himself ponder on his next point of action. It wasn't going to be an easy call for him to make, but it was one he had to, and fast.

CHAPTER 19

Judith did not want to be seen in public.

she had spent four days in her apartment, and she still did not fancy leaving the house. she knew what day it was, and what she needed to do now. she planned on leaving New york to California to get away from Nicholas.   Her fiancée hadn't confirmed his flight yet, and she was running out of patience. Dr Oakfield had already told her that it may take a week before he could come out to see her, but she hoped it would be sooner. she couldn't wait yet another day as she feared what might happen if she was alone for any much longer. For the most part, they had cancelled too many weekend plans together, and it was worrying her that they seemed to be in such a challenging place and that this could be a good enough reason for him to call the entire marriage plan off and decide not to see her any more. she wouldn't blame him either if he decided to do so. It worried her even more that the life she had planned to live here in America was nothing short of a fantasy. And now, the reality of it was that her life was in absolute ruins.

she tried to force herself to eat, but she had lost her appetite. A few hours ago, she had spoken to Marcus Billingham for the first time since she returned from Las Vegas. she thought he was the only one she could confide in now. she remembered when he told her that she needed to be careful with Nicholas, so perhaps there was need for them to meet and talk. Thankfully no one at work had spotted anything unusual between Nicholas and herself. All they'd noticed is her absence from work. As Marcus Billingham didn't seem to have any suspicions either, whatever she had to say to him

later on in the day would come to him as a total
surprise.

Marcus Billingham seemed to assume that they
had kept things strictly professional, and by so doing,
would be the only reason they'd secured all their
entitlements to spear head this project. Marcus and
Judith had been friends even before he started working
for her, so she knew he would understand better what
she was going through. Sooner or later, someone was
bound to find out, so what harm could she possibly be
creating by being the first to tell those who needed to
know. she wanted Marcus to know because he had
worked for the Wright's family for a few year in the past,
and it made her wonder how much he truly knew about
what she had discovered. It would have been normal for
her to assume that the world would accept that she is a
victim in all this, but she wasn't seeking for public pity.
He was concerned that it would be too late before the
public caught on to all of which she had found out about
the wrights family business.

" OK meet me at my favourite coffee shop on the
corner of 55th and Broadway, you do remember where I
am on about right?" Marcus asked. He had called her
again to make sure she was actually still attending.

" That's fine, ill see you in an hour." she replied.

" OK an hour is fine, see you soon." He said.

It sounded good to both of them, and Judith forced
herself to get out of bed and make herself presentable.
Judith had tried not to think of what she was going to
say to him, but she was convinced that it was all going
to come out one way or another. she seemed to be
thinking less and less about the project, and this made
her realize that she had exhausted too much of her time
and energy on actualization process of her role. Her
refusal to no longer want to be on the project would only
be a loss to her than it would be to Nicholas and his
company, but it was a loss she was willing to bear. she
had been leaving a fantasy that felt like everything to

live for, but now, she felt as though her life was at steak. No matter how she decided to approach the situation, she knew she would have to face it heads on. What she had experienced with Nicholas was too bitter for her to fold her arms and do nothing. she knew it was selfish of her to have entangled with Nicholas to begin with, but by her actions now, it was the only way she believed she could let him know that she was sorry for making such a terrible mistake.

she took her bath and dolled herself up. And as quickly as she could get out of the apartment, she did. she hailed a taxi, and within minutes, she was at the coffee shop waiting to meet Marcus Billingham. He arrived a few minutes after her, and for the next three hours, they engaged each others minds with all the saucy details about everything and anything that had to do with her, Nicholas, his business and her relationship with Dr Oakfield . What Marcus had to say in return was in a lot of ways fair and unbiased. He took a neutral stand in view of the entire situation and this made Judith not regret asking for him to meet her. After their long conversation that afternoon, Judith returned to the apartment Nicholas had given to her to use for as long as she wanted. she was increasingly becoming unsettled living there, and she felt it was no longer safe for her.

She let herself into the apartment, and as she walked in, she was stunned to see Dr Oakfield sitting in the living room. she felt her heart almost jump out of her chest. The last thing she expected was to see him there.

" How did you get in here?" she asked as though he was an intruder, and he smiled at her as he got up and walked towards her.

" Have you forgotten so soon. You gave me a spare key remember?" He said looking at her with an odd expression.

" Of course I did. I totally forgot about that." she said

" That's understandable, judging by the way you sounded over the phone, I can imagine would been mentally exhausted." He said.

" I have." she replied, forcing her mind back to when she handed him a set of keys the last time he visited her.

" I have hoped for you to be here, but I just did not expect to see you today, or at all if I may add." she said

" I can't say I wanted to surprise you. You did however sound distressed, how am I suppose to live with myself not being able to attend to your needs when you find yourself in a fix." He said. He wanted to reach out to her and hug her, but he thought that would have been an easy way to let her know he was going to forgive her. He knew they had a lot to talk about, and she prayed that he was not going to turn animalistic if he got angry. Truthfully she was frightened of how he would react because she had never seen him upset before. she was desperately afraid that the things she had said or was going to say would spark a reaction that would make him loose his temper. It had been obvious from her expression that she was in fear of a lot of thing, so he tread carefully.

" Why don't we have a sit down. I am sure there are a lot of things you want to say to me." He said as he put his arm around her and led her to the sofa.

" What a mess you've gotten yourself into!" He said valiantly, and then allowed her to open up to him.

" I figured it was time I told you the truth Bernard. I haven't been able to live with myself since this whole thing started. I thought I could handle it, and make it all go away but it has gotten out of control." she replied. she wanted him to know that it meant a lot to her to come clean, and he admired her for it. As long as he had gone to the trouble to come out to see her, he felt it was only fair to give her a listening ear.

" So now you have come clean, have you told him that I know?" He asked.

" Yes, as a matter of fact I have." she replied.

" And then what did he have to say about it?" He pressed on.

" He made a lot of threatening remarks, and tried to make a mockery of our engagement. labelling you as a weakling who would still accept to be with an infidel. I must tell you, I was furious at him for saying those things to me about us." she said.

" Anything less from him would be a let down. And your contract with him, what is his take on that?" He asked.

" He aims to have me replaced. The contract allows for the management to do so in the case of unforeseen circumstances." she replied.

" Brilliant. IT sounds to me like you have been this man's play toy since the very beginning. SO basically, now you have decided not to dance to his music, he wants to revoke all privileges. Am I correct?" He asked.

" Exactly. But it doesn't end there." she replied.

" OK. What else is there?" He asked.

" Well, Since I started work at the office, I happen to have dug into some records that he did not expect me to have access to." she said,

" What kind of records are we talking about here?" He asked.

" Business transaction records." she replied.

" And so what?! He is a business man, he is bound to keep all kinds of records." He said.

" Well, yes, but these are not your conventional day to day business transaction records. I am talking about records of his underworld dealings, drugs and arms dealings, sex trafficking and money laundering just to say the least." she said.

Dr Oakfield could not believe his ears. It all sounded surreal to him.

" So you mean to tell me that this guy has that much skeleton in his closet and his still loves to push people around like his slaves." He said.

" Precisely so. I told him I have collated all the relevant aspect of my findings and I would not hesitate to reveal all to the media, if he did not allow me complete my contract in peace." she said.

" WHOA WHOA WHOA WHOA. You mean to tell me that you've told him that already?"

" Well, yes, I did not know what else to do." she replied frantically." That's why I need you here. What do you want me to do, what can I do? I am so confused." she said breaking into tears.
He could see she was distraught. He was thinking of taking her out to dinner or a movie, but he wasn't sure how either would help the situation.

" OK. Look, You are going to have to pull yourself together alright. You wanted me here, so here I am. We can stay here for the night, but by the end of tomorrow, I want you out of here. We could check you into a hotel somewhere in the city, or leave the state. It's your call. I do not think it is safe for you here any more." He said

" I agree" she said nodding her head while she was sobbing. she felt completely disoriented, and for some odd reason, she felt as though she had destroyed her bond with the man she loves. Having slept with Nicholas, she felt as though she had committed the most unforgivable sin in the whole world, and her life was out of balance now and would never be the same.

" Now pull yourself together. You look like you haven't eaten in weeks." He said. And he was right. she had not eaten in over six days and the thought of it had completely skipped her mind.

" How do I find the appetite to do so when it feels like my whole life is hanging by the balance." she replied.

" OK, we will work this out, but for now, you need to go have yourself a wash, and I'll see what I can make out of whatever you have in that kitchen." He said.

" You are so kind, I do not deserve your kindness right now." she said, patting her eyes with a tissue.

" Well, I am not here to pass any form of judgement. I want to help, and for me to do so, I need you to think properly, and for you to do so, you need to eat and rest sufficiently, so one thing at time OK." He said.

" OK." she said amiably. " But you must be exhausted. Why don't you let me do the cooking." she added.

" Not in the state that you are in now, I don't think so." HE said. He looked surprisingly refreshed, despite the long shifts he'd been putting in at the hospital,but she looked the total opposite.

" I can mange." she said.

" No, I insist." He said" Now run along." He said There was no denying it, she had missed the bones of him. They hadn't seen each other in several weeks, and it seemed as though it was over a year. Feeling flustered and awkward, she moved toward the bedroom and thanked him for coming. As he watched her walk away he couldn't help but feel sorry for her. He could see that she was broken, and that Mr,Wright had shattered her dreams, and that it would take nothing short of a miracle to reinstate her.

she disappeared into the bedroom to undress and take a shower. she let the water run down her body as she stood in it motionless. Moments later, she started crying. she was in there for over half an hour, and Dr Oakfield became concerned so he went into her bedroom.

" I'm making some mash and steak, I hope you still like them." He said, speaking through the bathroom door.

" It is fine." she replied. He could hear the strain in her voice, and immediately he could tell she'd been crying.

" I Think you really need to pull yourself together Judith. Sobbing all day is not going to fix any thing right now. You need to eat, so hurry up and join me at the dinning table." He said.

" OK. I'll be out in a minute." she said quickly. Shorty after she'd finished having her bath, she dressed up and joined him in the living room. They sat and chatted lightly, and minutes later, he served their meal. she could see the man she fell in love with, he was kind, patient, self-less and perfect in every sense imaginable. she couldn't believe she'd almost destroyed all of this for absolutely nothing. she felt she would never forgive herself for lying to him all along. She remembered when he'd asked her about the nature of her and Nicholas's relationship and she'd covered the truth and said to him that it was strictly professional. That had quickly come back to haunt her in ways she never thought it would. Now the reality of her deceitful ways was staring her dead in the face. The only man she needed forgiveness from now was the man right before her, her saviour,her fiancée, and soon to be father of her child.

" It is alright Judith, I understand exactly what you are going through. The guilt hurts more than the deed itself, always remember that. I will put off any discussion about our future for now, at least until everything is resolved." He said modestly.

" Please do not give up on us Bernard. I may have to be paying for my wrong doing for the rest of my life, but I'll rather that than loose you, I can't imagine what my life would be like without you." she said.

" Just eat you meal Judith. I think You need that more than my forgiveness right now." He said as he dug into his plate. There was an air of mystery about him that was unusual. she couldn't understand how he was so calm and collected about everything that was happening.

" I want you to know I love you very much Bernard. You are my world and my foundation." she said." You are a very good man, and I am sorry for hurting you the way I have. I would never forgive myself." she said. she realized that he was more than she deserved. she felt guilty and it hurt her so deeply that it was driving her crazy.

" I love you too." He said with a boyish grin. Outwardly he was indeed calm and reserved, but he was deeply unsettled. He was disappointed in her, and hated what they'd done. He hated the existence of Nicholas, but he Loved her, and this much was true. While they ate, he thought endlessly about what to do. He needed to protect her and get her as far away from Nicholas as possible. But then again, he didn't need to go into hiding over this. He didn't see Nicholas as a threat at all, he just worried so much for the woman sat across the table from him.

" Tonight you begin packing you things. By this time tomorrow, we are getting out of this apartment." He said.

" OK. I think it is the right thing to do." she replied.

" For now, we just have to be patient. Things appear to be going down hill fast. Not too long ago, it seemed like we were making some progress." He said.

" I know. I am so sorry. I Feel like it is all my fault." she said,

" I wouldn't beat myself up too much if I were you. You have just been misguided." He replied.

" It is clearly taking too big a toll on us." she said

" It would be that way for a while, so we need to act fast." He said.

" I will settle for what whatever plan you drum up, I was too selfish to make you want to give up your career to be here with me. Now I know that all I want is just to be with you. Nothing more" she replied.

He nodded and said nothing in answer. He left the

table, and she took the dishes away. He sat around the living room for a while and made several phone calls. It was difficult for her to make out who he was talking to, so she left him to it. she was upset that she'd put him through this much stress to begin with. she returned to her bedroom and gradually began to pack her belongings into her suit cases.

Dr Oakfield left the apartment about an hour later but didn't tell her where he was going to. For the first time since they met each other she felt just how lonely she would be if their relationship was to come to an end.

she cried uncontrollably and couldn't think of any body else to speak to but her mother. she called her, and the moment she heard her voice, she began crying again. she spoke to her mother at length, and some how she was able to find some strength to pull herself back together after they spoke for about an hour. she remained in the apartment for several hours and wondered where her fiancée was and how long it would be until he returned. He did not have a mobile phone so it wasn't possible to ring him either. While she waited, she returned to packing her things. Momentarily, she heard the front door open but didn't hear him call out for her. she suddenly had an odd feeling. she sensed, more than saw anyone for at the time. Then she called out for him.

" Bernard, is that you?" she said, but heard nothing in answer. There was just an eerie feeling as she walked out the bedroom slowly. And as she did, approaching the living room, she was attacked. There were four huge men inside the house dressed in all back with ski masks over their heads. One of them grabbed her from behind and placed his hand over her mouth, telling her not to make a sound. Judith was terrified. she did not put up a fight or try to struggle. she simply did as she was told. They took her into the living room and sat her down.

" You have upset a lot of people Ms Judith. And those you have upset make my life a living hell when they get upset. so I have to tell you this. It is not going to be very pleasant for you if I do not get what I need." One of the men spoke in a deep tone of voice.

" What do you want, and how are you so sure I have what it is you are after?" Judith asked

" oh, I am very sure you know what it is I need, and I am equally sure you know exactly how important it is for me to get what I need." He said

" Are you too cowardly to show your face?" she asked.

" What I look like should be of no interest to you. Besides, where I am about to send you to, you will not need to remember what I look like." He said.

" Who sent you here?" she asked.

" I'll do the questioning from here on Ms Judith. Now,Where are they?" He asked

" I do not know what you are talking about." she replied.

He pulled out his gun and shot her in the arm. Judith screamed in agony. The masked man's gun had a silencer which muffled the sound.

" I've got a lot more from where that came from Ms. Judith. Now I am going to ask you one more time. Where are those documents?"

" What makes you think I'll give them to you. I'll rather die than hand them over." she said.

He shot her in the leg, and then grabbed her hair. Judith was in tears now and she was bleeding profusely.

" I see You are ready to die. Well, I have been sent to kill you. With or without the documents." He said.

" Get on with it then. I am not afraid of you or who ever sent you to do this. They are obviously just as cowardly as you that they couldn't come to do it themselves." she said.

The man let go of her hair and began laughing. His

laughter was loud, long and sinister. When he stopped, he held out his gun and aimed it towards her head. Then he lowered it to her body.

" Mr Wright sends his regards." He said, then he let off one shot to her chest area. The men left the apartment hurriedly, and she was left laying in a pool of blood.

Dr Oakfield returned to the apartment, and to his greatest bewilderment, he found Judith gasping for air and spluttering blood through her mouth and nostrils. He dashed towards her and dropped to his knees. Instinctively he jumped into action. He had save hundreds of lives under similar circumstances over the years, and now, he had in his arms the bleeding body of his fiancée. He could not believe his eyes as he ripped open her clothes to observe where she was bleeding from. Judith had been shot several times and was at the brink of death. He did not have his surgical tools or the equipments to do what he was brilliant at, but he wasn't deterred by this. He did everything he could under the sun to stop the bleeding, and as he battled to keep her alive, he spoke to her. He was devastated as he pleaded for her to fight to stay alive.

" Just keep breathing Judith. Breathe.. You are not going to die on me, not today, not ever. Do not give up on me Judith. Gaddamit Judith, keep breathing. DO NOT close your eyes Judith. I am here. Keep looking at me" He said as he managed to get her off the floor after tying up some vital parts of her body and applying pressure where necessary.

He knew he had to get her to the nearest hospital, and fast. Luckily for her, he'd seen that none of the body shots where close to the centre of her chest.

He lifted her off the floor and stormed out of the apartment. He had hired a private car with a chauffeur on his way back who was waiting for him outside. Seeing that he had emerged from the house with a body in a critical state, the driver hurried to assist him.

" Quickly, get us to the nearest hospital immediately." Dr Oakfield said.

The driver opened the back door, and quickly, he returned behind the wheel then sped off. Within a short few minutes, they arrived at the trauma resuscitation unit.

" I need help, somebody Get me a surgeon immediately." Dr Oakfield said as he stormed into the trauma unit carrying Judith who was quickly turning pale from loosing so much blood. Within seconds of their arrival, a few highly trained rapid response medics rushed towards him, and together they placed Judith on a trolley.

" You need to get her into surgery immediately. she is conscious but not alert. she has suffered multiple gunshot wounds to the chest area, arm and leg. Her breathing is deteriorating fast so she's going to need IV immediately. Hurry, she is fast getting into hypoglycaemic shock.

" Who are you?" One of the Medics asked as they took over control.

" I am her fiancée, I am a trauma surgeon. I believe she has been suffering for the last 10-15mins. More or less. I found her in her apartment." He said. He could barely get his final words out as they took her into the operating theatre and out of his sight.

What a remarkable twist of fate he thought as he stood there and watched them push her into surgery. It was usually on his operating table that patients who had suffered similar traumas ended up. Now, he was treated as just the victims partner. He was covered in her blood, and unable to stand the sight of it, he motioned to storm into the operating room and take over the surgery, but he was stopped by the units staffs.

" I am a surgeon, let me go, that is my fiancée been rolled in there." He said, as he tried to muscle his way through five member of staff who found it difficult to contain the largely built man.

After what appeared to be a chaotic attempt to restrain   him, he was brought under control. He was absolutely frantic but he brought himself to think rationally. He insisted on speaking directly to the over all head of the unit. A few minutes later, following very technical and expert communications approach , he was granted access into the operating room where Judith was. Without question, they allowed him take part in the surgery.

The surgery went on for six hours and the entire team was pleased to have saved her life. Dr. David Newman the head of the department in emergency medicine at Mount Sinai Hospital in New York city had spent most of his career treating all manners of gun shot wounds and for 14 years, he'd never seen anything like that which had happened with this particular patient. He was convinced he had lost her after the first ten minutes when she was put in his operating bed. He called Dr Oakfield into his office to have a post operation review with him and he obliged.

" You were brilliant in there Doc. How she has survived this remains nothing short of a mystery to me." Dr. Newman said.

" I happen to believe there is something truly special about her. Earlier in the year, she was pulled into my operating theatre at the point of death, and some how, just some how she managed to pull through." Dr Oakfield said.

" What was the diagnosis then?" Dr. Newman asked.

" Self-Inflicted Trauma." Dr Oakfield replied

" And how has she been shot three times? I know gun crimes are at an all time high in the city presently, but who in the world would do such a thing to her. Doesn't it seem odd to you?" Dr. Newman asked

" It beats me how this has come about. There is a lot I'll like to know from her as soon as she comes back around."Dr Oakfield replied sounding perplexed.

" Like how she must feel learning that she did not loose her child. she must be over the moon particularly about that I presume. So must you" Dr. Newman said.

" Absolutely." Dr. Oakfield replied with a grin. He was mortified to have learnt about her pregnancy during the operation when the X-ray and CAT scans came to his attention. He tried desperately to hide his surprise then. And now, this was the one thing on his mind. He could not believe that she had kept such information from him. Her pregnancy made the surgery a lot more complicated, but he was glad it was over.

" Well, I understand you are both engaged. So I'll treat you as her next of Kin. Now, you do know there are legal formalities to be followed when casualties of gun violence are drawn in right?" Dr. Newman said.

" Yes absolutely. Now about that." Dr Oakfield said, but he was interrupted by his fellow surgeon who'd observed that he was clearly distressed about the entire situation.

" I can see how distressing this might be for you. Your mind seems a million miles away. I'll tell you this much. I am happy she is in stable condition. We have you to be thankful for the steps you took to control her bleeding before she arrived here. I will hold up on contacting the police on this particular matter. After all, it wasn't the emergency services that brought her in." Dr. Newman said.

" I appreciate your utmost discretion at this point. I know how all of this may seem, but I assure you, when she is fully recovered, you will be hearing from her directly on how she chooses to deal with the situation. Hows that?" Dr Oakfield asked.

" That's fine by me. I'll get one of the guys to give you the clearance you need to check in on her periodically. it seems like she responds to you more than she does to anybody else." Dr. Newman said, forcing a faint smile onto both their faces.

" Thanks doctor. I appreciate your assistance. I truly do." Dr Oakfield said.

" Do not mention it." Dr. Newman replied." I'll be here if you need me." He added.

" Very well then." Dr Oakfield replied. He shook his hand and left his office. Dr Oakfield was in a quandary. He had pondered hard and long on how to exact the same amount of pain on Nicholas. He couldn't believe how he'd taken matters so far. As he walked the corridor of the hospital, he felt Judith was carrying a child, and there was no degree of certainty whose child it was. For the most part, she was laying in the post operation ward unable to be spoken to for at least another 48 hours at best. That was too long for him to wait to get the answers he needed. Besides, he was in a rage. He had spent all his career saving lives, but for the first time in his entire life he hungered to take one himself. Nicholas would have to answer to him now. He wouldn't have it any other way.

CHAPTER 20

Nicholas had been expecting to be informed by his agents that his troubles had been taken care of. But when the news finally came, it didn't make him feel better. This was not how he expected it to be.

This was not how he anticipated it to end between Judith and himself.

Many times, he had dealt with people who he did not have any emotional ties to, and it made what ever decision he had to make towards them easy to reach.

His whole world seemed dark now. He did not want to speak to or see anybody. He did not go to his office for an entire week since he ordered the hit on Judith.

Although he had kept an unusually low profile staying at one of his private resorts in Long Island, he had created himself an alibi, people who could testify to his whereabouts at the time Judith was attacked. And now, he decided to return to his home in New Jersey. He was pleased to do so, as he knew it would be void of any disturbance from family and friends. His children had returned to England, and he had put the entire project on hold until further notice. He needed time to himself as he felt he needed to begin a fresh new start.

Nicholas arrived at his home unaware that he wasn't alone. As soon as he walked into the house and shut the door behind him, he was knocked out.

A few minutes later as he regained his consciousness, his eyes opened to a face he'd know very well. Dr Oakfield had tied him down to a chair. Dr Oakfield remained silent giving Nicholas a few moments for his brain to process what he was confronted with. And when he did, Nicholas struggled to get himself loose.

" It's of no use trying to set yourself free Nicholas. You know, we never got to really know each other. So I am going to tell you something about me that you certainly do not know. You see, I was a trained boyscout. Through out high school I used to lead group of kids and take them camping wherever they choose. That's when I got very good with ropes. So right now my friend, Not even a tornado could untie you from that chair." He said.

Dr Oakfield stepped closer to Nicholas and looked into his eyes. He could see his fears and Nicholas knew then that the face in front on him was going to be the last face he would ever see.

" You know, I had my doubts about you from the very beginning, but I overlooked it because I thought you would turn out to be one of those exceptional guys. But boy was I right. You have lived up to my expectations. So now, I hope you do appreciate the high horse you are sitting on." He said, circling Nicholl's as he spoke.

Nicholas knew he was toying with him now. He couldn't believe that Dr Oakfield had got him in this position. He was speechless the entire time, and he had never felt so helpless in his entire life. His pride and ego wouldn't let him scream for help. Although the house was empty, one would have thought it useful to do so, hoping that someone would hear them calling for help. But Nicholas didn't want to do so. He struggled some more but the rope tied around him was too tight.

" Go on boy. I know you wish you could set yourself free so could fight me," He said, laughing.

" Now you know how it feels to be vulnerable. How many time have you mentally strapped people to the point they feel as helpless as you do now?" Dr. Oakfield said.

" You love to prey on the weak don't you Nicholas.?" Dr Oakfield asked speaking in ways to break him down into tears, and for a moment, Nicholas almost did. But he fought it. He tried to fight of the idea of this been his final moments in Life. He wasn't sure what the doctors intentions were, but Nicholas could see that he was troubled.

" she is very beautiful isn't she,my Judith?" Doctor Oakfield said with a smile standing beside Nicholas and saying the words into his ear.

" she wasn't yours to have, but you couldn't help yourself could you? You misled her, ruined her life, and then tried to get her killed." HE said.
Nicholas's eyes were wide now after he heard the words spoken by Dr Oakfield. For the first time since the attack on Judith, He'd just heard that she wasn't dead.

" Oh, I guess you've been thinking she was dead right?" Dr,Oakfield said laughing out Loud. " Your plan may have worked out for a moment, but I brought her back to life. she wasn't yours to kill either Nicols." He added.

" It wasn't supposed to be this way. she had managed to lay her hands on information that she wasn't privy to. That's a violation even I have to answer to" Nicols said, his words trembled as he spoke.

" So answer this, do you think she deserved to die?" Dr Oakfield asked.

" We all die some day doc, you of all people must have some confusion about this basic fact of life. Look Whatever happens to me now, I can I assure you it would not end here." Nicholas said.

" Well then, as I am convinced you have embraced this basic fact of life, I'll leave you with a bit of last minute detail." Dr Oakfield said as he looked into the eyes of Nicholas again. The words that followed as spoken by Dr Oakfield left Nicholas paralysed in the chair he was sitting on.

" she was pregnant Nicholas. How could you do such a thing to her?" Dr Oakfield said. Nicholas was lost for words now, and he knew he had subjected Judith to a terrible fate. In so many ways he felt responsible for the things that had happened. But there was no turning back now. He fate was sealed too, and his destined now fully rested in hands of the man in front of him.

" I bet it now makes you wonder who the father is. Well, I'll let you think about that for a minute while I prepare a special cocktail for you.

He prepared a high dose of calcium gluconate with the intention of initiating a lethal electrolytic imbalance that would disrupt the normal level of sodium, potassium and chloride in Nicholas's body's cells. These electrolyte imbalances would interfere with and slow his heart to a dangerously low levels, eventually creating a heart attack.

Nicholas was sweating profusely while he watched Dr Oakfield draw the dose into a syringe.

He walked towards Nicholas and stuck the syringe into his neck. He injected the dose slowly into his body, and after a couple of minutes, Nicholas' skin began to turn red.

He was sweating bucket loads now, and he was beginning to feel a bit of nausea, a tingling sensation and an irregular and slow heartbeat.

He returned to the table where he prepared his doses and then, he prepared a second injection- Potassium Phosphate.

By doing so, the calcium and phosphate in these solutions will interact and form an insoluble bond that would create what's known as an aggregate anaphylaxis—severe hypertension and right ventricular heart failure.

He approached Nicholas again, and injected him with the second dose.

When calcium gluconate and potassium phosphate solutions are mixed together, they form an insoluble precipitant. Therefore, they must be injected separately to prevent precipitate formation. So the time in between his first injection was just enough time for the second one to allow both solutions to have it's desired effect in Nicholas' bloodstream.

Dr Oakfield stepped away from his subject's body and looked at him.

After about 5 minutes, Nicholas started vomiting.

Within a short few minutes afterwards, he was dead.

Dr Oakfield cleaned up after himself. He untied him and cleaned up Nicholas' vomit. He took off his clothes and shoes, he changed his clothes, and put every item he took off his body into a bag. Along with the syringe and solution bottles. He was careful not to leave his finger prints around the room, but he swept through it with a clean cloth and disposed of it neatly.

He laid Nicholas down on his bed wearing his night gown and boxer shorts. And after a quick glance around the room to make sure he'd cleaned up any and every trace of the likelihood of somebody ever been inside that room besides Nicholas, he walked out of the house undetected, and disappeared into the night.

CHAPTER 21

Dr Oakfield returned to the hospital to check in on Judith. He was pleased to hear that she was responding well to treatment. It would be atleat two more day before she regained full consciousness. He was prepared to wait for however long it took until he could speak to her again.

He returned to the apartment after a few hours and cleaned up the blood Judith spilled on the day she was attacked.

On the third day, he put a few of her essentials into a bag, and some clean clothes then took it to the hospital. When he arrived, he went straight to her room and he was pleased to see that she was awake. Her mother was also in the room with Adriana they were both distraught.

she did not believe she would ever see her only daughter again, and as it was, the doctor assigned to her recovery had told them that she was carrying a healthy baby.

Despite her distress over the trauma Judith had suffered, her mother was pleased to see that she was recovering well and she was soon to become a grand-mother.

Mrs Meridian. spotted Dr Oakfield outside the room, and invited him to join them. she had heard that he was one of the surgeons who'd operated on Judith, and she was thankful. If there was any face in the world she was delighted to see, it was his. He walked into the room, and after they exchanged pleasantries, and a few hugs, she gave them some privacy.

" So how are you feeling?" He asked Judith as he sat beside her bed. He had kept the private driver he hired to drive him around town whenever he needed.

Thanks to Michael Garner, he was able to get around town easily without any trouble. He told her that he had Michael ready to take them out of the hospital to anywhere she wanted as soon as she was fit enough..

" I feel like I've been hit by a train." she replied, pleased to know that she could leave anytime she felt fit enough to do so. she hated hospitals and Dr Bernard knew this much was true.

" It might take a while before you are feeding normally again, but there is enough supplement running through you drip to keep you going for a few days." He said looking at her blankly. she looked tired and drawn and as usual, her mind was still unsettled about the situation concerning her and Nicholas.

" I think food can wait. I have a bad feeling knowing that Nicholas is still out there walking freely. I don't know what's happening, but I'll say all hell is about to break loose." she replied

" You need to focus on getting better dear." Nicholas said.

" How is that possible, when I have a mountain of problems over my head." she replied.

" Well, I like to think that a problem shared is a problem half solved. And for the other half, let just say we have our future back in our hands." He said, and it made her cry.

" you mean the world to me Bernard. You always have and you always will." she said. she looked and sounded exhausted. He looked sorry for her, and wondered if he had made the right decision to kill Nicholas.

" What do you think is happening out there?" He asked. And she was intrigued by the way he responded to her.

" Honestly, I do not know. Nicholas been his usual self is always up to one mischief or the next. I can't believe he has done this to me." she said. " Hey, what do I know. Maybe I brought all of this on myself." she added, feeling a bit of self pity.

There was a question on the tip of Judith's tongue, but she was afraid to ask him. she felt like she had caused too many problems to be asking for favours. she loved him too much to want to hurt him. But he could see that she had some real worries about how to go about making her troubles disappear.

If he knew much sooner about things between Nicholas and herself, he would have thought of a more subtle way to handle the situation, but it was too late by the time he found out.

Nicholas was out of the picture was the only sound option for him. His manner of killing Nicholas would puzzle the finest murder investigators for centuries.

It was his only option he thought, but now, he wanted her to know he was determined to do anything to protect her.

" Is there something you'd like to say to me?" He asked.

" It is probably nothing to worry about." she replied. she knew him too well, she sensed that he had done a lot for her already, but if not, she believed that he was going to do so. He was perfect to her in that sense. He was very bright, but coy in most cases. It was the one thing about him that she was more intrigued about.

" Maybe You should rest this one out." He said, getting up to readjust her bed.

" I should not have kept this from you as long as I did. It is your baby Bernard. Our baby. Having to deal with him at the time knowing I was pregnant with you child was why I hesitated to tell you I was having problems at work with Nicholas." she added.

" It might have been a good reason at the time doesn't make it OK Judith. I trusted you way more than that." He said.

" And I may have broken that trust by my actions, but I never did in my heart where it mattered the most. I honestly believed I could handle it all on my own." she said.

" Judith?" he looked amused. " That is you all over again. always trying to save everybody in the world but herself". He said. Maybe she's freaked out about it, and feels guilty. "I may find it in myself to forget that you cheated on me with him, but not to have told me you were pregnant the moment you knew is unkind." He said.

" I'll let you know now that I am prepared to spend the rest of my life with you regaining your trust." she said.

"I can accept that our time apart may have turned you frigid and neurotic, but I wouldn't want you feeling like you are indebted to me in anyway." He said.

" I'll recommend therapy for as long as you need it, because all you been through isn't just going to vanish into thin air. We'll have to get you some help to manage the post traumatic cycles." He said.

" What ever you recommend is fine with me. After all you are the doc." she said trying to win his affection.

" No one said it was going to be easy." He replied

" Thank you, doctor, for saving my life yet again. I am not quite sure that's a pattern I want to keep up with." she said, appealing to his witty side.

" I can't say I want to be your husband, babies father, and psychiatrist all in one. So you are going to have all the time you need to decide what sort of patterns you'd like to keep up with after we get you out of here within the next few of days." He replied. He looked grim as he sat back down and watched over her.

" You are right on the score. I do not deserve all the beautiful sides of your true self that you can share with me. But If I have to choose now, I will accept you just ask the father of our baby. That would mean the world to me." she said, and then she cried. In some ways he understood her point of view on the matter. By her choice, they would always be together, and she hoped that by this choice, he could find other ways to love her again.

They spent the day together with her mother, and by the next day, she was feeling much stronger to be discharged. Dr Oakfield recommended one more day, and by the end of that final day, she was pleased to be heading some place far away from the walls of the hospital.

After the second day, she was granted conditional discharge. The hospital officials believed that under Dr Oakfield's supervision, Judith would be in good hands.

He agreed to bring her back in if there were any further complications he couldn't handle himself. He had booked them into a five star hotel, where she could receive the best room service. They stayed together all day, and he helped her get comfortable. The next day he went out to pick up a few things Judith had requested for.

He had taken six weeks off work, and considering he was now approaching the end of his second week, he felt like it was a race against time each time he came to visit Judith. He had made up his mind to return with her to England, but he needed to approach the matter delicately.

After a few hours, Dr Oakfield returned with all the items she requested for, and to brighten up the atmosphere, he brought her fresh flowers.

" You always are the perfect gentleman, Bernard," she said, looking at him with so much admiration.

" Some times I feel like I do not deserve a man like you." she added, she had a lot of pride and a lot of heart, but all of it seemed to be suppressed by her love for him. she knew she was lucky to have him in her life, but she hoped now that things were a little bit different.

" I don't mean to make you feel uncomfortable. It's just that I've just been getting a lot of mixed feelings lately. It isn't so much about our love for each other, but simply about my expectations of us. I wanted it to be perfect, Bernard, I really did, but now I can't help but feel I may have ruined all of it." she said, as she watched him set the flowers down next to her bedside.

" You know I don't disregard your feelings Judith. if anything, I think I should cultivate the habit of listening closely from now on. Perhaps you are always trying to tell me something important, or give of some warning sign about the eventuality of something to come that I need to prepare for when you get like this." He said. She considered what he'd said to be an honest way to let her know that he wasn't prepared to abandon her. And she appreciated him even more for this.

" But whatever must be troubling you, I suggest that you focus on getting your bed rest to regain your strength, or you can choose to stress yourself out and the baby about your what, if, and maybes." He said.

" I know you understand that my worries are legitimate. I'll only be a child throwing her toys out of the pram if this was just my way of seeking for attention. But it is more than that Bernard. If I did not have you in my life, I'll be dead and forgotten by the world, whom I try to let know that I exist. Isn't it ironic that those I have relied on to make this a reality may in a lot of ways now become the hindrance to my success." she said.

" Okay I see your point." He replied. " Your concerns are legitimate." He added with a faint smile. He knew how meticulous she could be about organising things, and he had come to understand that she was prone to missing out on some of the more important details that may not seems as such initially.

" Do you mind if I order us some room service?" he asked.

" You certainly could. After all, it's been paid for." she was smiling at him, and she knew he had forgiven her in some ways.

That night, he stayed close to her, making sure she

was well looked after.

There were time she cried feeling the pain from the bullet wounds on her body, but he was there to comfort her. He made sure she was fully assisted, dressing her wounds and changing her clothes. The opportunity to be this close to her made him realize how much he had missed her.

She looked pretty and soft each time he looked at her and touch her her body. He had admired the beauty of her woman form many at times, but this time, her saw her in a totally different light. Her hair was down most of the time, and he got her the most comfortable slippers he could find.

But in spite of their differences, they loved each other very much and this much was in evidence. she was finally regaining her appetite, so he was pleased to see that she was beginning to feed regularly.

" You wouldn't mind feeding me would you? I seem to be useless with this arm." she said motioning to her arm that was still in a sling.

" Of course I would." Dr Oakfield replied." That's why I am here isn't it?" He replied.

she knew she could take advantage of this situation, but either way, she was pleased to be taken care of by the man she loves. He was always nice to her but she was sorry for all the things she had done to hurt him. she wondered about Nicholas sometimes, what he maybe up to now if he got wind of the fact that she was still alive. she had the feeling t times that Nicholas may have been obsessed about her all along. Dr Oakfield fed her a piece of cheese cake, and she was increasingly getting used to the special treatment she was receiving. A few hours later he called for the items they had ordered to be removed, and by the time the hotel staff were through, Judith was very relaxed and felt like falling asleep.

" what else would you like for me to do for you?" Dr

Oakfield asked.

" You have done so much already, thank you so much." he said, reaching for his arm as he sat on the bed next to her.

" Don't thank me, everything I do now I my duty to you. I would not loose sight of that just because you took a detour with our life plans." He said. she was bitter by the fact that she had managed to give him reason to doubt her, which was absolutely normal, but she accepted he was hurting.

" The roses are beautiful. I can smell them from over here." she said. she remember he always brought her flowers, and as she admired them, he reached for one and handed it to her. As she pulled it closer to her nose to inhale, tear drops came running down her face. He leaned in the hug her, and he planted a kiss on her forehead. He sat next to her and she was pleased to have a shoulder to cry on. she admitted she had missed him and more so, her family.

" I miss my family, my father and brother most especially. I miss a lot of times we spent together camped around the fire place and watching TV. It was all the movies we used to watch then the ignited my passion for becoming an actress." she said. she still wanted to pursue the project, but she knew that would be wishful thinking. she felt perhaps her dreams were such a tall order as she seemed to find herself constantly in the trauma unit. " Maybe someday, I'll have such moments again. And if any one of our children decide to want to become actors or actresses, I'll have the safety manual for them to study." she said as she set the rose down on the table.

" You are a brave girl. You can have whatever you set your mind to. And if it's a career as an actress that you still wish to pursue, you are bound to land yourself several other roles." He said.

" Now that you've mentioned, I am convinced that

this is what I want." she said.

" Then you go for it." He replied.

" But with the likes of Nicholas controlling any project worth pursuing, I don't feel veru optimistic." she replied.

" Well, won't you be pleased to know that you wouldn't have to worry about him anymore." He said.

" And how do you mean?" she asked with curiousity.

" Let's just say that he would never bother you again. Infact, You may never have to set eyes on him ever again." He said.

" Are you telling me what I think you are saying?" she asked, still seeking for a direct answer.

" Yes. I think believe you know exactly what I am saying. I paid him a little visit and helped him understand who is who and what is what. Now, I am sure he has learnt a very valuable lesson" He replied

" Then I guess I could still pursue the project. With Nicholas out of the picture, there would be no one to contest the contract. Legally, I can still serve my term on the contract. Besides I know all the facts and details like the back of my palm." she said. she always insisted that she didn't care about the material things been on the project afforded her. But she was particular about playing her role perfectly. she had been able to mirror herself into the role of the lead character better than she thought anyone else could, and to some etent she was right. Despite others who had been screened, she was the only one selected, and she believed that she earned it. Sometimes she had to remind herself about this, and truthfully, there was better time to do so than now.

" You are so damn politically correct, sometimes I do not know how you do it." He said, with a grin. He felt relaxed with her, and very happy. He also knew she had a valid argument, and some how, he knew she was going to go after her rights.

"I may have been spoiled a little bit along the way, but I did read my terms and conditions before I signed the dotted lines." she replied. He was beginning to think that maybe it hadn't been quite as awful as he first thought it was. So now the discussion was in the open, they talked about her options.

" You might need to fine a very good lawyer. God knows you will need one." He said.

" I certainly would have to get one outside of their family's influences" she replied.

" Then you need to remain mute about been shot. As a   matter of fact it never happened." He added. " Have you told anybody about it besides your mother?" He asked.

" No I haven't." she replied.

" Then It stays that way. If there are no clauses that terminates the project in the eventuality of the death of Nicholas, then you are still contracted to them, which means that the company owes you legal obligations they are bound to fulfil by law." He said.

" Exactly." she exclaimed. " Tha sounds very appealing," she added, feeling her first real sense of happiness since she arrived in America.

" Do not get your hopes high. These things have a way of backfiring if one isn't careful" He said. she enjoyed being with him as she saw how quick witted he was. And he helped her gain clarity.

" I've always liked the odds. On occassions like this, I think its only going to even out the score if you ask me." she said.

" Haven't you learnt any lesson following all of this? Do you want to loose your life over all of this?" He asked.

" The odds have been stacked aganist me ever since, it I bound to even out beard. This might be my only chance to get back all I deserve. My life, my dignity, and peace of mind knowing that I do not owe anyone anything." she said.

" That's sensible," Dr Oakfield said matter-of-factly. " I have considered it all too, but all I am worried about is your safety. I can't imgine what I would do if anything was to happen to you again."

" You are truly awesome. It is impressive how you happen to be the one to help me put the pieces together." she said.

" That wouldn't happen if you weren't being honest with me." He said.

" Well, at least you can see that I am being honest." And there was something sad in her eyes as she said it. He didn't doubt her, he just understood that there were forces greater than her that would always somehow influence her decision making over time. And he worried that she would get too distracted to see any of it coming before it was too late. He owed it to her to support her in any way, so he felt it necessary to vent his concerns to her.

" I know you love your work a lot, but you have to be extremely careful out ther Judith. I would not lways be around to save you, or give you advice on every decision you need to make." He said. she knew there was a lot of sound reasoning in what he had said, and feeling his intensity and honestly coming through, she listened deeper.

" I love you, and as such, that means I support you all the way through no questions asked. Sometimes, it will feel like we are not a couple because of the distance between us, or just friends because of the way we communicate with each other, but once you always remember how important it is for you to keep your dreams alive, you would be compelled to do only the right things." He said.

" It is a lousy feeling to feel like you were in the world alone," she said

" It must be, but it doesn't make it OK for us to always use that as an excuse to make misguided decisions." He said

Judith had her own theories about it, but she didn't want to appear too demanding. For her next attempts to have its desired impact, she needed him by her side voluntarily. But she knew the man she loved. He loved her just as much. she had also begun to think that he might just be prepared to give her the approval she needed to make her next move. beyond this, she wished it would work out for the better, so she could live with him and her child in America. It just wasn't happening she thought. she imagined what it would take to convince him a second time around. But she didn't say that to him either. Besides, she loved England, and she couldn't see her self never returning home.

" Isn't it funny how people drift apart, but then they find themselves constantly been reminded of the committent they made to each other. I have always wanted to have my first child with someone I love who loves me just as much, and I found him. I have also wanted to star as the lead character of my film, and I am on the path of accomplishing that. The setbacks have been very profound, but it is not going to stop me. I have four of the most important people in my life right now, and they are always going to be the strength I need to stay alive. Being with you is all I can think of. If I have to live apart from you, one day, I fear we may see each other again as total strangers. I do not want to ever feel like I've been living a fantasy far from my reality." she admitted and he smiled at her.

" I can accept that you are determined to re-define what this experience means to you. You wouldn't need to convince me at all.

" That is the issue, I want you to be who you've always been in my life, and leave the rest to me." she replied. He suspected that it would come to this so he asked the all most important question.

" Will you at least return to englad with me first, and then you could return to finish your project with the promise of retuning home straight afterwards.?" He asked. And without hesitation she replied.
" Yes I will."
They sat and talked for a long time, and at mid-night she yawned, and he looked at his watch.
" I should return to my room." He said, but she hated to be alone, especially at this time, and he was very good company.
" You don't need to go, we have just enough room in here for two." she said.
" He wanted to avoid sleeping with her at the moment, but his heart felt different. The best part of him wanted to cuddle up with her, and make passionate love to her, but he restrained his emotions.
" OK, I'll sleep on the sofa." He said softly. They were both lonely in a city full of people, but being together now in the same room made that less important. He reached for a pillow, and almost instinctively he kissed her cheek, and was surprised by himself. she was extraordinarily appealing despite her messy state. she blushed after he kissed her, which surprised him. It made him realize she wanted him too, just as much as he did, but they both knew it wasn't the right moment.
It was hard for either of them to ignore the fact that they both fancied the pants off each other, right at this very instant, but they played it down. He wanted this to happen naturally for them. He took a pillow to the sofa, and picked a blanket as well. It was all so different than it had been for them over the past months since they met. How could something so sweet, and pure, and simple, become so complicated. They were both longing for the passion between them to be reignited. she had no illusions about him, and expected nothing but his true love. she knew they would always find a way to warm back into each others arms. He said

goodnight to her and turned off the single light next to the sofa. she left hers on for a few minutes so she could get her bearing.

There were no words between them, but there were long silent thoughts. They were completely overwhelmed with passion to make things work out for the better, but they were flawed by the challenges between them.

Being with her was like jumping of a cliff constantly with a parachute. And for her, she just felt safe being with him. she smiled faintly realizing that she was still alive, and very much in love with the man of her dreams. And they were going to be parents. It was the happiest thought she had had in a very long time, longer than she could remember. And as she let her mind settle, she turned off the single light next to her bed and fell asleep.

CHAPTER 22

Two weeks had passed and Dr Oakfield had been dedicated to taking care of Judith each day of the week.

Her time recovering had presented a unique opportunity for them to iron out their differences. At times, she sensed that her engagement was on the brink of breaking down so it made her increasingly agitated. she hoped for things to return to how it was when they first met, and now, she felt she had to reveal how she was truly feeling. As soon as he saw her face that day, she knew that something was brewing. He wasn't sure what was on her mind, so he sat down quietly on the couch next to her bed.

" Should I ask what may be troubling you?" He asked quietly. He knew a lot had happened to her in such a short space of time, and it was enough for all of it to leave her feeling disorientated. Her concern was that she could see in his eye that something was different, and she needed clarity.

" It is just becoming increasingly difficult for me to see us the way we are. I wanted the best for us Bernard, I still do." she said, watching him, trying to read his face, but he looked guarded. Having an affair with Nicholas was the worse mistake of her life, and although she knew she had to stop it, she felt as though the damage was irrepairable. He didn't want to pry into the details, it would only make him furious, but although he wanted to fix things with her, he knew things were not going to be the same.

" It isn't particularly easy for me either. I have to live with the thought of what had happened for the rest of my life, and I have to deal with the misery of it all each time it crosses my mind.

" I am sorry for whatever heart ache this may

cause you, but I am deeply sorry, You have been kind to me. I cannot take that for granted, I just can't." she said. More than anything, despite how damaging he knew the situation was, he didn't want to say anything that would hurt her.

" What fate awaits us is not for me to say," he said calmly. He was stalling for time, in order to maintain his composure.

" I mean it. What I need to do is make sure there is a roof over your head and the babies, and I am prepared to play my full role as a parent. I do not want to contribute to however much difficult this must already be for you.

" Do you not want to Love me any more?" she asked in spite of herself.

" I would always love you Judith. But we will just have to deal with the reality of this situation for now. You mean so much more to me now you are carrying our child, but how I feel about what has happened between you and him bears heavy on my heart." He said.

" It should never have happened Bernard, and I know I should never have pressed you about moving out here. I felt so alone on many nights, and all I could think about is having you become a part of my life permanently. But I lost my guard Bernard, I truthfully did" she replied.

He knew that if he left her, the damage to Judith would be greater. And he wanted to save her any form of discomfort while she was recovering.

" It has happened Judith, and that is what makes it so bad. I do not want to leave you, but a part of us had been corrupted by what you have done." He said.

" I do not want to fuck up you life any more than I have by my actions. I deeply ask for your forgiveness. I have been living a fantasy with him. There was never anything real emotions involved, I want you to understand that this much is true." she said.

" I do not know what you want me to do Judith. The situation is very lousy now, and I've got to go out there and try and put things back together." He said.
" We could do it together Bernard. I know we can." she replied.

" This is the worse time of your life, and we've either got to set it right, or give it up. What happens from here on, only time will tell." He said

" I do not want us to give it up. We can not let this destroy us Bernard. And I'll need your strength to fight this battle." she said.

" You have to assume that I am going to play the role of a father first Judith. I can't make any promises about the other aspect of my life. Not now anyway." He said it softly but firmly, and for an instant, she felt the words like a dagger piercing through her heart.

" That is so painful Bernard, it is not going to be easy for me." she said as tears filled her eyes."
He had fallen in love with her too, so it wasn't difficult for him to understand how she was feeling now. she was the best girl he'd ever had, but loving her came with a set of complications that worried him. A part of him was beginning to feel like he deserved so much more than just Judith could give him. But he couldn't bring himself to leave her, not now, not ever. she needed a husband, a father, a brother and a good friend, and he knew he could sign up for the job, he already made up his mind before now, but his mind was in a quandary.

" I don't know what to say to you Judith," He said, choking on his own words. I do not want to cause you any kind of pain. I love you very much, and I want us to be together. If things were different, we would be having that moment right now. I want to marry you Judith. But I have to let this situation dawn on us first, and then, if your still very sure this is what you want, then we would head straight to the alter." He said hoarsely.
His words sounded harsh to her ears. she was beginning to feel hopeless, but this was not his intention

towards her. He knew it wouldn't be fair to crush her hope of finding happiness with him, but with luck, he believed things would work out for them. And if it didn't God only knew he'd tried his very best.

" I am going to work hard at this relationship, and begin to do thing differently. I do not want to fail at my first attempts of having a family life. I wasn't raised that way. I do not mind if you choose to return here to complete your project, but I will return to England and remain there until I am convinced it is safe to come back here." HE said,

" I understand what you mean by saying that. I feel I am so lucky to have you, but It is times like this that make me question if I deserve you at all. We can return to London and we can have our baby there. Nothing in the world would be more fulfilling than raising our kids in Britain." she said, convincing herself s much as him.

" You should feel lucky, you've survived two fatal incidents within a year, and here you are, still hoping for a happy future. I must say, it is truly inspirational. You just seem to be able to pick up your feet, and carry on with life like nothing had ever happened." He knew she understood what he was talking about, probably more than he could. But he actually did feel a lot of compassion towards her. He did not want to see his union with her fail, and he certainly did not want to loose her over this. It was time for him to really take a bold step with her, instead of just trying to exempt himself in other ways.

" You are not just any man to me Bernard, You are my fiancée, the love of my life, my saviour and soon to become the father of our child. I do not want anything more from you but your love and another kids one day." she reminded him.

" And I am grateful for the chance to meet a girl like you. Someone who I can marry and take care of with all my heart. But I have been in a quandary for months, not to now realize I wasn't being paranoid. It hurts me that you allowed yourself to be lured into this by a person like Nicholas Wright. They are out there, a dime a dozen.

They present themselves as helpers, but some how end up denying you true happiness when you need it the most. I have done for you something that doesn't only go against my professional ethics, but contradicts the principles I have stood for since I became a qualified surgeon. But I wouldn't use any of this against you Judith. I don't have the right to do that to you. So I am putting it in your hands to show me how you want this to work. I want you to gain absolute control of your life. I am giving that back to you now. You can have your freedom, and I will give you all the support I can afford."

" If that I what it would take for me to prove to you that I want this more than anything else in this world, then I'll take it." she said sadly. " You will love me all over again Bernard. I promise." she said slowly getting angry at herself for being a part of my things have become this way between them. What right did she have to indulge so recklessly, especially in a way that affected her so deeply? she loved him more than she had any man, and she had known the repercussions for breaking the ground rules. she just hadn't expected to fall in love with him to the extent she had, and so quickly, that she was now carrying his child.

" And I will accept loving you all over again Judith. I promise. But for now, we have a mountain of issues to deal with, and that responsibility takes away all the excitement of what may or may not be between us from here on. But I will be here for you, just like I've always been." He said bluntly.

" I love you so much more because of the efforts you have made. I have always felt free to do what I wanted, but I have come to learn that there comes a point when you invest that freedom in wanting to be closer to the one you truly love. I know when I fell in love with you, and looking at things now, I can say that none of that feeling has changed. I am deeply sorry if I have let you down, but I promise it will never happen again." she said remorsefully.

Her words were sincere, and he knew it instantly. He knew what the deal was from the beginning. There was no use staying angry at her. He just didn't think he was ever going to have to deal with this with her. He now realized that it was something he was either going to have to live with, or loose her forever. It made him realize just how desperate he was to make this work. He once believed it was worth it, so he re-visited that feeling. It felt good, and what made it feel better was that she was still here with him.

" Is there anything else you want to say to me?" He asked, standing up.

" Not really. Just that I love you, Bernard. I want us to always be happy together. Most of all I want you to never give up on our love for each other. I mean absolutely nothing without you."

" I understand you perfectly well. I will not forget that in a hurry. I want you to be happy too, always remember that. I never wanted anything like this to come between us. But it is here now, and we have to deal with it."

" You mean so much more to me than this thing between us. I want you to know I really love you." she said, as the tears swam in her eyes.

" I know that too Judith. That's why I am willing to go the distance with you. but I need some time for this to resolve itself.

" So why does it feel like you are about to leave me?" she asked

" I am not. I just need some time to myself." He replied and walked slowly to the door, and opened it. He wanted to hold her, and kiss her and make love to her again, but he had to compose himself, watching her in tears was always too much for him to bear, but he needed this time to serve as a lasting memory if she was true to herself about never allowing such a thing happen again. it would be tough not being intimate with her for a couple months, but at least he could see that it would be worth it.

He turned around to look at her as he held open the door, and with a last look at her crying, without saying another word to her, he closed it. He stood on the other side of the door for a long moment, torn by the fact that perhaps he was being too hard on her. He could hear her crying softly through inside, but he couldn't bring himself to go back into the room. He just stood there. He held the door knob to let himself back in, but momentarily, he walked towards the elevators.

He went downstairs and drank himself to a stupor. He spent hours talking to the bar tender, telling him how disappointed he was in love. The bartender had seen a lot of men in his position, so he understood. HE told Dr Oakfield that he was pleased to be his companion for as long as he needed, but he also advised him to make peace with the lady in question if he wanted to get married to her.

" It sounds to me like you truly love this bird." James Wilson said, as he poured him another double Jack Daniel neat.

" Why wouldn't I? she means the world to me, but it seems like the worlds trying to take her away from me." He replied.

" Then that is all that should matter." He said." It's not advisable to loose someone you love over a difference of opinion or some of the basic challenges of life. I get the feeling she wants this just as much as you do." He added.

" she actually does." Dr Oakfield replied. James was right, he thought. He wanted a fresh start and he was convinced she wanted the same, so he had to let her have it if that is what they both wanted. He considered that she had already lost a father and brother, he didn't want her feeling like life was always going to be so cruel to her if he left. It wasn't a pretty picture to imagine, but neither was his distaste towards what had happened between her and Nicholas, and he knew that.

" I guess I can see how this may make a person turn selfish minded." He said to James, motioning him to keep the rounds of cognac coming. He had had a couple of long rough days and nights, with no sleep thinking about this particular situation, and now, perhaps it was time to let it go. He believed it was the right thing to do.

" There you have it. You just can't afford to have this become the base of a union. It's a hell of an important decision to make if you want to remain together, but I am sure you'll make the right decision." James said.

" I hope so too. I'll hate to loose her. I don't think my unborn child will ever forgive me." He replied.

" That's right. It is no longer about the both of you. It is everything to do with the life of your unborn child. That I all that matters now. He or she would need to feel the love of both their parents equally. if not, in a few years time, you will have a lot more to worry about than you think you do now." He said.

" I am sorry for being such a burden right now." Dr Oakfield said.

" It's OK. I do not think of this as such at all. At one point or another, we all need someone to confide in, with the promise of getting good advise." James said.

" Unless you love it, you must get bored listening to people lament about their private lives when they get on your bar." Dr Oakfield said.

" I can't say it happens all the time, but I am always pleased to listen. I take away a few things to apply in my own private life as well." James replied.

" That's got to be recommendable." He said pensively. " I'll be sure to point my patients in your direction whenever they start to show symptoms of hardship over their relationships." He replied

" Unless you get bored doing the fantastic work I am sure you do at the trauma unit in London. Only then will I accept your recommendation." James said.

" I am flattered that you would think so. It does get heavy at work I must confess. For weeks on end, I find my self getting burnt out." He replied.

" I bet you do a remarkable job nonetheless." James replied.

" I do my very best." He wanted to cry as he said it. James initiated a few clinical jokes that made him laugh as he had his drink. They both spoke easily, and Dr Oakfield wondered if he should call Judith to join them, but after serious consideration of his current state, he didn't.

For the next couple of weeks, he returned to his duty attending to her needs, alternating days to be by her side than he made available for himself. By the end of the second week, they had everything packed up and ready to be transported to London. she had accumulated five times more than the amount of belongings she had initially arrived with. Judith enjoyed her remaining time in the hotel, and on their last day at the hotel, the management gave them a fair well party.

It brought a new surge of bond between them. No one could imagine what the were going through but they were pleased to be smiling and getting into the party spirit.

It was a good way for them to spend their last day in New York. As they boarded the plane, he realized that he was truly grateful for having her in his life. Now, all he could think about was having their first child together. He had missed her terribly the past few months, but he knew he had done the right thing to bring her back home, however temporary it was going to be for.

If he had not done so, it would have been worse for them in the end, and he knew that it was time to introduce new rules to strengthen their bond with each other. They deserved to be happy again, he thought, and as their plane soared into the sky, and New York disappeared behind them, he was pleased to be returning home.

CHAPTER 23

Judith and Dr Oakfield arrived at Heathrow airport on schedule.

Judith was pleased to spend this very moment with him. There was a greater intensity than there had ever been between them before, but Judith was not going to let this influence her in any way.

They arrived at his apartment just about 7pm, and the first thing she did was put the kettle on. They had a brew, and chatted for a few hours then decided to call it a night.

By the second day, they took long walks, held hands, and shared a few kisses. Being able to share this moment with each other eased the intensity between them.

Their late night talks led them to make love to each other and it was all to live for, nothing short of what Judith had expected from her man. There was no talk about the future for them, but even that was fine with Judith. she enjoyed the very moment with all her heart, and he could see that she was inclined to give him all of her.

Dr Oakfield was due back in the hospital the next day, so the night before he left, they stayed in his apartment all day. she had planned on renting her own place now she was expecting a child, but he encouraged her to get used to living in his apartment with him.

" I want you to know I want this to work out for us Bernard, I really do" she said. " I'll be lying if I said otherwise."

" I want you to come back to me every night for as long as it takes." she added.

" I would like the same too." He replied.

The truth of it was, he could no longer see a life without her. The most soothing part of it for them was that they were soon to get married, and she would no longer have to be devoted to any other man but her husband. she understood better now that the relationship she and Nicholas had shared was a fantasy, a delusion, a time warp. she was in love with the man she was with now, and had no room in her heart to accommodate for any other man. Her commitment was to her fiancée, and him alone. she was happy that he came to take her away from her misery in America. she was angry to have allowed herself fall for Nicholas's antiques, but she took a portion of the blame too. she knew it was too late now for her to turn back the hands of time even if she could do it. she had to see things through with her fiancée, and the only way to do so would be by moving forward.

They had come so far together, and she couldn't give all of it up without knowing what would have happened. Although there was some certainty what was going to be, she needed re-assurance more often now that her efforts would not be taken for granted, or wasted in the process of trying to win back his love and affection.

" I can not throw away what we have over a meaningless encounter. I choose to keep that behind me and seek other ways to give this relationship all it truly needs to stand the test of time." she said.
He knew she was right, but in a way he was still upset about what had happened. But her sense of fair play was one thing he had always liked about her.

" It is going to be hard work Judith. And you know that.." He said bitterly.

" It wouldn't be if I was dedicated to making sure we found our happiness again." she replied
He found some peace of mind facing the fact that she would never have to see Nicholas again. Even if he had

to settle for her returning to America to fight for her rights to be on the movie project, at least, Nicholas would be no where close to her, he felt at ease now knowing that their affair was over. He was having a difficult time processing the emotion of his broken heart, but he was too masculine to show it. And what's more, he was pleased that she summoned the courage to tell him what was going on eventually, because truthfully, he would have only had his suspicions without any concrete proof.

" We have enough to keep us going. Once the baby   comes, I am sure it would be so much about how to always be together for the child as opposed to what may have happened in the past." He said.

" I can assure you right now that there is no one I'll rather be with but you. what had happened between Nicholas and I was blind luck, and you know it. I am determined to turn all of that around for the better. We have always been on separate career paths, and there are certain hazards that come with the territory. I walked right into this mess because I was blind folded, and now, I know such mistakes do not happen twice." she said.

" It is easy for you to say so. After all theses things happen more to even the more cautious people." He said.

" I am not even sure I understand what you mean by that, but you are just going to have to trust me. As much as I may have failed you just this once, I do not plan for it to happen again, not ever." she said.

" You've wasted yourself on him. All for what? Super-stardom and a few bullet wounds to show for it. I hardly think it was worth it if you ask me." He said pensively.

It was a plea from him to help her realize how much it would mean to him if she never went down that road again, but he knew it was the best he could do. He was furious about the reality of what had happened, but

rather than reject her for it, he felt it was finally time to let go of the misery he felt. It hurt so much, and he couldn't carry on his days feeling this way.
she realized he was hurt and this made her cry for hours that night.

He kissed her on the forehead and consoled her. He was slowly coming to realize that it would take more than what had happened to make him love her any less than he did right now. After about three hours of sobbing uncontrollably, she looked deathly pale, sick, and both her eyes were swollen. she regretted her entanglement with Nicholas with a passion, and she was deeply disappointed in herself. As for Dr Oakfield , he believed this would strengthen their bond if they managed to see this through.

" This would be a perfect time for you to focus on picking up the pieces. There can be no loose ends because there are going to be a lot of questions asked, and a majority of them would be aimed at you." He said. Judith remained silent as she understood what he meant. she would have to give her version of account following Nicholas's death, as everyone knew they were close colleagues. Although she hadn't officially reported the incident of being shot, it was entirely her decision to make whether or not she wanted to make it public knowledge.

" The public prying into this is not going to make it any easier to bear." she said.

" But this is mostly expected. You'll have to prepare for any and everything. it's only a matter of time before you hear that knock on the door." He said.

" I am not sure I can deal with any more of this." she said.

" Well, you do not have much of a choice in the matter. As long as you keep your story straight and simple, there would be nothing to worry about." He said." You can't afford to screw this up, our lives depend on it, any slip up would complicate everything." He added.

" Safe guarding your interest is as important as safe guarding mine. You have shown me the depths of your love, so I think it is my turn to do the same." she said. Her nerves were stretched beyond the breaking point. she was prepared to face what ever inquisition may follow, but she knew it wasn't going to be easy.

" So long as those words are true, we will be fine. I am returning to work in the morning, and may as always, experience the difficulty of returning home every night for the next two weeks, but if it so happens that I get too busy, and you do not feel great, or you need a helping hand, do not hesitate to let me know." He said.

" That's nice to know now." she said." I'm sure I can manage when you are gone." she added, looking tired. Judith felt as though there was chaos around her, so he felt he needed to give her some time to herself. He left his flat momentarily, and she checked her e-mails to see that she had been sent dozens of e-mails by

Marcus Billingham. It was the only way he could communicate with her now, and she preferred it this way. Marcus was beginning to ask questions that she feared she did not have the answers to.

By the end of the day, she was a wreck, and she looked it. she appeared less impeccable than usual, her nerves were frayed, and she felt as though her situation with Nicholas may have spread like wild fire across the office and beyond. she had tried not to think about what the mood could be like, but she forced her mind to think. she knew Nicholas was dead, even though Dr Oakfield hadn't spelt it out right, she knew this much was true.

This was knowledge she was prepared to take to her grave. she was certain she had to protect her family, and everything happening now was more than just about her. In her head, she calculated every step, weighed in on all her options, determined her strengths and weaknesses, and most of all, she promised herself not to be victimized again. In the process she aimed to re-invent herself and for the world to acknowledge her as the woman of steel.

In her mind it was a perfect plot, one most deserving after all she'd been through. From this point on, she was prepared for everything she did and touched to be handle expeditiously.

Predictably, her move to claim her rights on the project, despite Nicholas's death, would make her richer than her wildest imagination.

All she had been through wouldn't matter then, but suddenly she thought about Nicholas's children. she felt concerned for them. she imagined how this situation would affect their lives. she forces her mind to think less of this now. It is business after all, families would suffer for the implications of any wrong business transaction, and her deal with Nicholas happens to be one of such bad business. she would manage until she initiated her plan. It was not the way she wished to start off her career, so she took her revenge plot as an undertaking, one never to be broken. she was already depressed at the prospect of taking on this responsibility, but she knew it had to be done.

She would reveal her intentions to her fiancée in due time, but for now, she prayed to recover fast. There was no way she could explain to anybody how she was feeling, so she trained her mind to deal with the pain and anguish she was feeling. Her tension got worse each passing day her baby grew inside her. Everything she planned to do now, was for her child, who did not deserved to be traumatized as well in the process. As it turned out, she still had records of the information Nicholas wanted to kill her for. it was a massive leverage, so she planned to use it as a last resort. she was about 3 months away from having her child, as she had so much time, she spent every day doing her home work.

For the next few days, things were quiet and normal in the flat. she hated it when she was alone, and when her fiancée came back, she was pleased to enjoy his presence even though he returned exhausted and too depressed to interact with her. The new bed he had bought for their child had not arrived, but there was a certain feel of anxiety that Dr Oakfield felt in anticipation of the arrival of his unborn child. His nerves were stretched and his patience was wearing thinner and thinner. This brought up a peculiar mode of discussion between them.

" Come on babe, don't let it work your nerves. We have so much time to find and decide on the most suitable court for our baby even if the one you've picked never gets here" she said

"It's not the way I wanted to begin this journey. I expect everything to be in place already. I am not sure I would be able to handle the last minute pressure." He said.

" It can be stressful, but we certainly need one of us sane for long enough, and I'll rather it was you. I don't think I have an Idea what the first thing to do would be if the baby came right now." she said.
He finally thought of what most of his night would be like, a child crying in the middle of the night, and it was his turn to check on the baby. He had a particularly vague idea what to expect, but now, to avoid the stress he believed it would be, he suggested for her to consider having a full time nanny.

" We would need to hire a baby-sitter or a nanny whatever they are calling them these day," He said, sound timid at thought of his own words.

" And we would be sending out what message exactly? That we do not have what it takes to raise one small baby together without help?" she said.

" I didn't say that." He replied.

" Oh, OK, you are just suggesting this then?" she said, inquisitively.

" Well Perhaps, Yes. You certainly would need one, when you get ready to leave for America to take care of your unfinished business." He said.

" I hope it doesn't piss you off that this would be our fate in about 6-8 months. It just feels like we are going to start hating each other when the time draws near." she said

" That's not going to be by my making." He said,

" It is written all over your face that it would." she said

The truth was she needed his strength. she knew that the adjustment to living with him and a new born baby was going to be a new experience, and it was going to be harder than she'd ever imagined it could be. An entire life time of living alone was going to be tested by the next few months, when she would learn better about hers and his endearing nature. she knew her life was about to change forever, and in all honesty, she knew she wasn't the same person she had been when she left London on her first trip to America. And now everything about their life together seemed more intense than it had ever been.

" I can't say it is going to be smooth sailing. So I guess we would have to prepare for what is to come." He said.

" The question is, are you happy I am carrying you child Bernard?" she asked.

" There used to be a lot of things I felt terrified about growing up, and raising a child as a young man, was one of them. But now, it is going to become my reality. The only difference is, I am no longer a yuppy. I can be patient for this. I know I can." He said. It was true, and she could tell that he meant it with every iota of passion in his heart.

" I am sorry Bernard. I am sorry for ruining your life

style. The thought of you cleaning a babies back side for a few years doesn't quite match your sophisticated lifestyle." she said, attempting to humour him.

" I do not mind getting my hands dirty. You more than anybody else should know this better." He replied.

" On second thoughts, you might just end up being superb at this than I ever would." she said.

" I'll try not to embarrass you in the process." He replied with a smile. He was beginning to warm up to her, and for a slight moment, she didn't feel like he was going to close the door on her forever. she had hoped they would remain good friends, the way they had been in the beginning. But more than all, she hoped he would love her again, this time, more than he had ever loved her.

There was too much, hope, and love, and loss and disappointment, and she had blamed her self for all the mixed emotions. For him, disappointment had turned to a new source of strength, and he had spent his entire life waiting for the moment when he would give up on all his high morals just to be with the woman he loves. at times he didn't understand any of what he was feeling,but he hung on to them each time they surfaced, promising himself that it will get better. It was a relief for her to see him smile at her. she seemed to enjoy it.

They had both always shared the camaraderie, and compassion, and genuine friendship for each other. hey had come to realize how important it would be to make their relationship work. They'd both wanted the same things all along, and although it seemed as though they'd lost themselves recently, neither of them was prepared for it to happen again.

When their unborn child's furniture finally arrived, after three weeks of delay, it was pleasant for him to build the babies cradle. And set up every other thing necessary to welcome their baby into the world. He felt like a relic of a lost world trying to assemble everything, and none of it seemed to fit the right way initially. And after a few errors, he finally assemble it just as it was described in the manual kit.

By the end of the seventh month of her pregnancy, she was beginning to find it difficult to do things for herself. Dr Oakfield had taken a long leave of absence for the hospital, and they had told him to take as long as he needed.

" I love you so much Bernard." she said quietly while he was still shuffling things around the room. They had decided that they did not want to know the sex of the baby until it arrived. SO instead of choosing a blue colour for a boy as it was most preferred like pink is for girls, they decided to go for everything in the room to be white.

" I love you too. I hope the baby likes it and feels comfortable in here." He said.

" What is there not to like? If I wasn't carrying a pound of flesh in my stomach, I'll get into the cradle myself and I am sure I'll have a sound sleep."

" You wouldn't dare would you? It's only going to take another six weeks for a new set to arrive if you ruin this one. I can't say I want to be doing this chore at least for another three years." He replied.

He was very quick witted and this was what she liked the most about him. He was pleased to be doing these things around the house. It made her love him even more. she refused to let time sweep them away into a raging river and they both had to part ways for all eternity.

" I wouldn't dare put you through this again, at least for a while as you've put it." she said with a smile.

" I trust you wouldn't." He said gently.

" However, I do hope you never have to return to that trauma unit. You would serve me a great deal around here, than you would there." she said forcing a smile to his face.

" Now you are just taking liberties Madam. As long

as I know you need this pampering, I still have a career I'll like to sustain if you plan on having more babies." He said.

" You are right. About having more babies, I'll have to think about that a lot more closely. My back is killing me right now. I am afraid I may never be able to walk straight any more after I give birth to this one. This is certainly not a feeling I want to re-live any time soon." she said, placing both hands on her waist as walked awkwardly across the room.

" Now come on, I think it is time for you to have a sit down in front of the telly." He said, walking towards her and supporting her into the living room. Judith took his hand, and allowed him guide her gently. It was a very delicate situation for him to deal with, but if anything, she was happy he was always there for her. It was a relief for her to finally see that he was going to be a father, regardless of how much she despised of it in the past.

He placed her down gently on the sofa, and placed the remote in her hands. He knew she loved to watch her drama series, so he left her to it and vanished into the bedroom. As she sat there flicking through the television stations, she felt happy, comfortable and safe.

CHAPTER 24

Dr Oakfield stayed home from work for several weeks, and when he finally went back he found himself pondering a lot about taking Nicholas's life.

His personal life had been compromised mostly about what concerned Judith.

As the shock of Nicholas death was soon to raise public enquiry, he wondered if his conscience would get the better of him.

He tried to adjust to work, but each time he tried, he found it difficult to concentrate. Judith had called him several times to make sure he was all right, and he said he was doing just fine, just so she did not worry about him. But as troubling as he mind was, he knew he was capable of dealing with anything that arises following his actions.

Although he had told Judith otherwise, he was seriously thinking of quitting his job at the hospital. He had enough money saved up to begin a new life somewhere in the mid-lands, where he could raise his family in peace. He had considered setting up a small private examination practice just to keep his medical profession alive. But he had decided to wait until the baby arrived before he made a firm decision.

He was still angry with her for what had happened between her and Nicholas, but some how he was beginning to let go. He realized he was slowly backing off and getting distant from her, but now he thought he was being unreasonable with her. The passion and love they had once shared seemed to be returning, as well as the friendship.

He was anxious to spend more time with her, so he arranged dinner nights in the city so she could get out more. Their dinner nights went well, and she was beginning to find it more and more relaxing to be with him. she had a very visible bump now, so her wardrobe style of clothing had changed immeasurably.

Although she was pregnant, she was beginning to feel like her old self, not the one who'd been cavalier in the luxuries of an exotic lifestyle, but the person she'd been even before she'd met Dr Oakfield . And he seemed to notice the change in her demeanour. she appeared more settled, and less apprehensive.

" Why didn't you tell me Judith?" HE asked

" Tell you what dear?" she replied

" Tell me that you were pregnant when you first found out?" He said

" I thought we already talked about this." she replied

" yes we have, but I want you to think of this less critically. Think of it as me just wanting to understand how it must be for a woman as it was in your case." He said

" I felt I would be complicating our relationship if I did tell you at the time I found out. I was a right mess. I couldn't function properly for several weeks. Besides, I wasn't sure I was ready to be a mother. But after the first month, it grew on me. I promise, I wanted to tell you, but I was too busy waiting for the right time." she said.

" I had told you I wanted this with you, although you didn't seem sure, I did not want to press you on the matter. That would have been the easiest thing to do. I even think you should have told him straight away. Perhaps things would have turned out differently."

" You are right. I realized that I wanted more from life with you a while after I found out. A life fulfilled with all the love in the world. A real life with a man who wanted to make a commitment, but in reality, I had so much on my plate than it all seemed too much to ask for. I knew I had put a lot of pressure on you with the relocating plans, so I didn't want to increase the burden. It wasn't intentional Bernard, it wasn't at all." she said.

" I was prepared to do everything to keep us together. And I cannot say I was not hurt by what had happened. I've been so mad at myself that I did not stop it when I first had my suspicions. I was afraid it would ruin the chances of your project turning out successful. Maybe it was easier to turn a blind eye. No matter how much I loved you, I knew I had to let you make your own decisions." He said
she nodded. she couldn't deny that.

" And I am grateful for your kindness and compassion. I believe things can be different. I see things differently now, and I am prepared to take it one day at a time. You said so yourself." she said gently, without challenging what he'd said. How he spoke to her now brought tears to her eyes, and she couldn't hold back.

He was very respectful of her at dinner that night. He knew how to take care of her and this made it feel very pleasant for her to be there with him. she wore a new dress that made her look beautiful.
After dinner, he drove her back to their apartment.

" How are you finding your visits to the clinic." He asked politely as they walked through the door into living room.

" The women seem friendly. Although, they could talk you into a coma if they all conspire to do so. The poor things. Some of them had been there for so long that it almost seems like that was all the life they knew." she said.

" Very much so. Health care practices don't get it easy you know. We dedicate our entire lives trying to save lives, and after a while, it becomes impossible to have a life of your own. That's just the way it is I'm afraid." He said

" Are you still enjoying your time at the unit?" she

asked him as she sensed there was some depth to his response that warranted clarity.

" The commute has been smooth sailing, but it's the idea of always having to fix somebody up after a ghastly incident that seems to bother me more. I mean I know what I am doing so well that most times when I'm in surgery I ask myself, why do these things happen in the first place?" He said.

she understood him very well. she was pleased to hear him express himself the way he did. He hated to live a lie, so he constantly found himself seeking for the truth. There were a lot of new things he had to get used to now Judith was carrying his child. It was all very simple in the beginning. Now, he has two lives to be responsible for, and a third himself, if he wanted to live long enough to see them grow.

" Can I make you cuppa dear?" He asked, as they settled into the warmth of the house. Judith liked it here, it always brought back fun memories, like the first time she saw him when he got out of the shower sowing off him man perks. And the first time they kissed. she smiled at the thought ot it besides herself.

" I kind of wish we didn't have to loose this apartment of yours someday." she said as Dr Oakfield was preparing her cup of tea.

" That's weird. Only about a month ago we had our last bid. If I had sold it sooner, it would be some body else's have by now."

" I wonder if we can keep it just in case the new place we find doesn't live up to our expectation." she said.

" Why does it sound to me like you've fallen in love with my flat." He said, as he walked back into the living room with her brew.

" Maybe I have fallen in love with your flat. I'm just trying to remember when exactly it happened." she said, forcing a smile onto his face.

" You would have to share all the saucy details

when you do remember. For me, I think I'll settle for something new and different. I've lived here for so long, I don't even remember moving in." He said.

" How is that possible Bernard?" she asked, sensing that he may have exaggerated what he said a little.

" It is when you've lived in here as long as I have." He said.

" Very well then." she said " But I still think we should keep it. We can keep this one and have another to raise the kids, so that way, you and I can re-live some of our magic moments when we need to get away." she said.

" I can't say I don't like the thought of that." He said with a smile.

" I thought you would." she replied.

" I've always know you loved it here, but I didn't think it was enough to keep it." HE said.

" Well now you know. I can't believe I was so selfish to encourage you to sell it in the first place." she said.

" Well, good thing I haven't then. That has certainly worked out to my advantage." He said with a broad smile.

" Don't worry, I'll give you plenty of notice when I think it's time for Us to come back here each time." she said.
" I know you would. I'll be waiting for the time you fix a date to it. But I must say Judith, you are making remarkable recovery, and if you keep this up, you'll be up and flying in no time." He said
she smiled at him warmly, and the depths of her adoration for him was overwhelming. He could see her tears rolling down her angelic face, and it was then he understood that she was going to find herself again.

she had endured so much within a short space of time, and he believed she deserved everything in the world to keep her happy. He comforted her, leaving her no room to feel like she was alone.

" You are here, and so am I. So as long as it stays this way, we will always be together." Dr Bernard said giving her a warm embrace.

He held onto her for the rest of the night, and for the first time since she returned home, she was now convinced that he was in her life to stay, and she was indeed, beginning to feel safer.

CHAPTER 25

2 Months Later...

Dr Oakfield had worked every day for the last two months, and after his last shift the night before, he was pleased to be taking his leave off work for the next 3weeks. The baby was expected any day now, and he had planned to be with her just in case she suddenly went into labour.

He woke up this faithful morning to find that Judith wasn't in bed. But again, he could smell eggs, bacon and sausages. He went into the kitchen area where he found his heavily pregnant partner laying out the dishes to serve his meal.

" Good morning my sunshine." He said

" Morning dear. I was just about to come wake you up" she replied with a smile.

" Wow, you do know how to please your man. What have I done to deserve this treat?" He asked.

"I love you, why can't you see that?" Judith said to her fiancée.

They had felt like they were on the edge of breaking up a few months ago. Even with the baby on the way, these two love birds have had to fight to put aside their differences. It could have been because they were young. Or maybe they weren't compatible. Or maybe the impact of her infidelity was way too damaging. Whatever the case may be, they had come to accept that they either get their act together, or else, they stand the chance of losing their relationship.

"You Loving me is good enough!" Dr Oakfield replied. "Its just all I need to make me live everyday of my life a happy man...."

Judith held onto her stomach. "I think the baby is

coming," she sounded hysterical.

" wow baby, are you sure?!" Mark couldn't be in doubt, he knew the baby was due any day now.

" Yes I am sure." she replied. Then, it came. A gush of water came out of her body, causing Judith , and her fiancée, to shriek.

." Do you believe me now?" she added

"Come on Let's go," He said

"Wahhabi!" Judith barely could stand the pain. The couple arrived to the hospital in time. They were lucky; The only available room was the one they'd reserved ahead of time. Room 101. No one has used the room since it was reserved. It was sterile, clean and it was just for Judith.

Laying in the bed, the pain was clear on her face. she screamed every five seconds, hoping the baby would shoot out easily. Though, that wasn't the case. Judith tried breathing in a controlled manner just like the midwife had suggested, still, the contractions continued to wear her down.

"It's time," the doctor said. "Judith, I'm going to need you to be very very strong for me and push." And she listened… she pushed and pushed long and hard. An hour past before they made progress. The head finally showed. To Judith, the pain resembled a watermelon being pushed through a hole the size of a lemon. Good thing she wasn't having twins.

This isn't good," Doctor Issac said. He widened his eyes. "It looks like something isn't right with the baby. It's the umbilical cord… it's wrapped around the babies neck."

"Shit!" Doctor Oakfield grabbed his chest and started heaving.

"What does that mean?!" Judith yelled through her pushing and pain.

"If we don't get the baby out now, she is going to die." Doctor Issac said

"Do a C-section," Doctor Oakfield said.

"It's too late. By the time I get ready to that the baby will be dead. I'm sorry, but we're going to have to rely on faith alone for this." Doctor Issac replied

A doctor, someone who studied science and only believed in the facts, had to now rely on what he could not predict, on something that science alone could not solve. This indeed was the world Doctor Oakfield had suddenly found himself in since he met Judith. But now, he could appreciate that he wasn't the only one who had to defy the laws of science. His learned friend shared the same belief with him now, and together, they hoped for divine intervention.

"I got to throw up," Judith said. Her body was hot, heavy and in pain. she felt like this nightmare would never end.

It was as if she had gone to hell and back, though the fire continued to burn. Yes, this moment was supposed to be sweet and memorable, except it wasn't. Judith wanted all the agonizing sensation to end. Right here. Right now, but her nightmare had only just started.

Everyone hovered around her like wild animals. she needed space. she needed air. "Get this thing out of me!" she shouted, squeezing her fiancées hand tightly. If the baby didn't leave her body soon, she might faint because she'd seen too much blood.

"Do you need water," Dr Oakfield chanted.

" No", she yelled in response as she pushed some more as hard as she could.
"Is the position comfy enough for you?" the midwife asked for the hundredth time.

" It isn't, but I cannot imagine being in any other position besides this." she replied to the devastated woman who wanted Judith to have a safe delivery.
"w ell then, you can remain in this position, a lot of women find it more suitable this way." Doctor Issac said.

"Keep pushing, you're almost there," the doctor reminded her.

Everyone was asking her one question after the other. All Judith really wanted was for them to…. "Shut up!!" she screamed, still heaving and pushing steadily. Then, entering the room was Judith's mother. she went by the bed and held up one of her daughter's hand to help.

"Mother" Judith said, relieved. If anyone could brighten her day it would be her mother."

"It's fine, all you need to do is keep breathing my love, you can do it."Adriana said.

"They said he has a—"
Judith's mother shushed her. "I already know," she said. "Just keep pushing. Don't quit now or all of this was for nothing. Absolutely nothing my dear, do you understand?!"

Judith went on like this for a while. Breathing, chanting, and pushing. It was a repeated CYCLE. she was feeling drowsy and was beginning to pass out. Who knew how long she had left to continue on like this. she had only imagined the birth of a child until now. Truthfully, she imagined nothing like she experienced it to be now. This was absolute torture. she was exhausted from pushing and before her next attempt, she retired to a more unconventional mode of communication. After all, she had carried her child for 9months. she had sang to it, slept, and done pretty much everything a mother would do with her child to build a special bond between them. So now, she was convinced that she could talk to her child in a way only a mother could.

"Please come out baby girl, Judith thought to herself, I held you with love in me long enough. It's time to come out and see the world for yourself. I have prepared a place filled with love, and I promise you would always be surrounded by those who truely love you."

"I am sorry If I have put you through so such trauma, I wished for better, I promise. This is all my fault. Not only is your birth complicated, it hurt me my love. You have a cord choking you and I feel like it is all my fault.. If you don't make it, I vow to end my own life. I don't deserve to live without you."

The baby didn't seem like she wanted to come out, anyway. Doctor Issac saw it's head pop out and back into her mother's body so quickly. Because of the blood being slippery, the doctor couldn't get a good grip on the head. It wasn't until the next long push that got the job done. Half the baby exited Judith's body and the doctor was able to pull out the rest of the body. Immediately after the doctor cut the cord from around her neck, the crying baby girl was put on Judith''s chest. Doctor Oakfield and Adriana stood close, smiling.

"I love you," Judith said, looking deep into the baby's eyes. And with that, the baby went silent. No more crying, just silent. This forced tears out of her eyes. she was carrying her first born child and the feeling was truly overwhelming.

A minute passed by and the mid-wife took the baby to clean her up and do a few tests. Meanwhile, Judith and Dr Oakfield rekindled their relationship as Judith's mother took a video recording of the moment on her mobile phone.

By the time Judith tried breastfeeding the baby in the recovery room, Dr Oakfield had proposed to her. He had a new ring. It was a symbol of a new beginning, a fresh start for the both of them. He had chosen his words very carefully, and this time he promised to stay true to it. This, in effect, was the next part of their destiny together. One which they were both certain would change their lives forever.

Judith and her daughter were like one. They had a perfect bond, something that was indeed natural between a mother and her new born child. Dr Oakfield was over the moon, but this much was expected of him.

The introduction of their baby that would change their world and allow the Oakfield race to continue living.

The baby resembled everything Judith had imagined her to be. Her Lavender coloured skin, large green eyes, golden hair with black streaks, and a SILVER tongue… literally was all very tender. This baby was considered beautiful by any standard.

"You are going to be an iconic earthling. Everyone will want to know you, and everything you do will bring you great fortune. I guess it doesn't matter really; because by your parents alone, you will have everything you ever desire." Judith said, and her words captivated her partner and mother.

Judith," the doctor said, coming in with a huge grin. "What have you three decided to name the future queen of England?"

Maya sat up in her bed and nodded, saying, " Bernard and I have decided on the name Peggy which means the bind that brings me and my husband together, because two of us will need her to restore our love and eternal purpose in this world. I believe we need her for balance."

" I Agreed. I couldn't think of any name more suitable as her first name. Though I imagine we would name her a few other names in time." He said.

Judith's mother spoke up. " In that case I'll have a name for her too, I can't imagine not being allowed to do so."

"Mother, don't be silly," Maya began.

"Adriana , I would like you to do the honours. Most certainly." Dr Oakfield said.

" In that case, I'll take my time."Adriana replied Judith and her mother had tears coming out of their eyes. It was the most amazing feeling in the world to them, and she understood what Judith was feeling because she too had been in this exact position several times.

"Oh, there's another thing I must inform you about. Feeding, the baby and providing her up keep must be done in a very practical way. This is Your is the first, so I presume you need some pointers to prepare you for the others to come."

" Tah!" Judith shrugged. " We would have to wait years for another if ever. Especially after what I've been through in here today. I feel like my lady part is going to need a life time to recover." Judith said forcing a roar of laughter across the room.

" You are so adorable" Judith's mother yelled trying to catch her breath. "You won't forget this moment in a hurry; but your recovery is almost guaranteed".Adriana said.

Judith Kissed her daughters cheek.. Their lives had only begun. What more could this beautiful child bring them…

she thought of her as the chosen one who possess infinite powers to make the world a better place. Moreover, despite how much well wishes she felt to shower upon her new born child, she wondered how she was going to obtain it all.

INNOCENT NLEWEDIM

ACKNOWLEDGEMENTS

The author would like to thank his parents: Chief and Chief Mrs Henry and Comfort Nlewedim for the relentless love and support they have given to me since I was brought into this world.

Also, to my siblings, Pascal, Juliet, Chinasa, Florence and Princess for being the best Sisters and brother any family can ask for.

The amazing team at LR Price publications for the life changing opportunity granted to me. Russell Spencer for his clever, intuitive guidance and Matt Vidler for his firm belief in my ability and dedication since day one.

The lot of my friends and everyone I have met along the way who encouraged me to remain focused when all hope seemed lost, and those who scorned me due to their weak belief and poor vision. You have all generously provided me with the information and determination I needed to complete this book.

Also, thanks to my beloved partner Peggy Henshaw to whom this book is dedicated. Your Love has been my motivation throughout the entire writing process of this book.

Beyond all, thanks to the Almighty God for his infinite mercy upon my life, for protecting me from the claws of the wicked, keeping me alive to realize my dreams and for giving me the talent of which I share with the world through my works.

ABOUT THE AUTHOR

Innocent Nlewedim is a Nigerian born author and artist who was raised and educated in England.

He credits his parents as being his main motivation and inspiration in writing.

As well as being a successful author Innocent is also a musical artist under the stage name St Innocent.

ABOUT THE PUBLISHER

L.R. Price Publications is dedicated to publishing books by unknown authors.

We use a mixture of both traditional and modern publishing options to bring our authors' words to the wider world.

We print, publish, distribute and market books in a variety of formats including paper and hard back, electronic books e-books, digital audio books and online.

If you are, an author interested in getting your book published; or a book retailer interested in selling our books, please contact us.

www.lrpricepublications.com

L.R. Price Publications Ltd,

27 Old Gloucester Street,

London, WC1N 3AX.

(0208) 1449188

publishing@lrprice.com